The Diamond Daughter

By

Janet MacLeod Trotter

The Raj Hotel Series: Book 3

Other Titles by Janet MacLeod Trotter:

The Raj Hotel Series
The Emerald Affair – Book 1
The Sapphire Child – Book 2

The India Tea Series
The Tea Planter's Daughter – Book 1
The Tea Planter's Bride – Book 2
The Girl from the Tea Garden – Book 3
The Secrets of the Tea Garden – Book 4

HISTORICAL
In the Far Pashmina Mountains

The Jarrow Trilogy
The Jarrow Lass
Child of Jarrow
Return to Jarrow

The Durham Trilogy
The Hungry Hills
The Darkening Skies
Never Stand Alone

The Tyneside Sagas
A Handful of Stars
Chasing the Dream
For Love & Glory

The Rebellious Woman Sagas

The Suffragette
A Crimson Dawn

Scottish Historical Romance

The Flower of Scotland (formerly The Jacobite Lass)
The Beltane Fires
Highlander in Muscovy

MYSTERY/CRIME

The Vanishing of Ruth
The Haunting of Kulah

TEENAGE

Love Games

NON-FICTION

Beatles & Chiefs

This is a work of fiction. Names, characters, organizations, places, events, and incidents are either products of the author's imagination or are used fictitiously. Any resemblance to actual persons, living or dead, or actual events is purely coincidental.

Text copyright © 2021 by Janet MacLeod Trotter
All rights reserved.

No part of this book may be reproduced, or stored in a retrieval system, or transmitted in any form or by any means, electronic, mechanical, photocopying, recording, or otherwise, without express written permission of the publisher.

Published by MacLeod Trotter Books Ltd

www.janetmacleodtrotter.com.

Cover design by Michael Star

ISBN-978-1-908359-61-2

*To Flora, our beautiful and engaging granddaughter –
with your lovely smiles and calm strength, you make the
world a happier place.*

Praise for The Raj Hotel Series:

"Richly detailed, satisfyingly long, superb historical fiction."—*Portybelle Book Blogger*

"A compelling read set against a most atmospheric backdrop…another splendid read."—*Swirl and Thread*

"Kept me on the edge of my seat, wanting to know what was going to happen, so that I ended up staying up way too late because I was completely caught up in this story, never have I gotten lost in a book and then realized that it was almost one in the morning, and then hating to have to put the book down, knowing that I really should go to bed and get some sleep."—*Sky's Book Blog*

"Trotter's new book is an intoxicating blend of the last days of the Raj and World War II"—*Netgalley Reviewer*

"Janet Macleod Trotter is an amazing author and I will never forget these two books. Th emotion she brings to the page is outstanding. The audio narration brought the books alive and I could see India in my mind's eye through her wonderful descriptions. I also learnt a lot about the war in India and am keen to learn more ... I would highly recommend you either read or listen to this series. They were truly amazing!"—*Audiobook Reviewer*

More about *The Raj Hotel Series*

In post-World War I India, the Raj Hotel is a charming and vibrant backdrop to the hopes and dreams of those seeking a fresh start. But in the heat and intensity of a country undergoing great change, the residents of the Raj Hotel will be swept up in the turbulence of these dangerous and momentous times. Love, loyalty and friendship will be tested to their utmost. Lives will be transformed – but there will be heartache and betrayal too. Amid the faded grandeur of the hotel, with the world changing irreversibly around them, will friends and lovers find their dreams dashed or fulfilled?

Prologue

The Raj Hotel, Rawalpindi, India, July 1939

Jeanie twisted her wedding ring, her hands clammy. An overhead fan stirred the humid air in the dim foyer which was deserted apart from a portly man snoring in a cane chair. Perspiring, she pushed her wavy dark hair away from her hot plump cheeks.

She longed for a cool drink but Mungo had ordered afternoon tea. Her husband looked composed in his summer suit; his handsome face expressionless. Yet there were tiny beads of sweat at his greying hairline and he kept consulting his pocket watch; the only hint that he too might be feeling agitated.

She stretched out a hand to touch his arm. 'How long till the train?'

'Two hours.' He snapped the cover closed and pocketed the watch. 'You look a bit hot and bothered. I'll ask the manager if you can freshen up in one of their bathrooms, shall I?'

'Not much point,' she sighed, thinking how she'd be drenched in sweat again as soon as they stepped outside but she was touched at his concern. She couldn't believe how different the climate was here compared to their home in the hills just a two-hour drive away.

'Thank you again for coming with me to Bombay–'

'I can hardly have my pretty young wife travelling all that way by train on her own, can I?' He gave her one of his admonishing looks, the kind he used on his pupils.

Jeanie's resolve faltered. Perhaps she shouldn't be embarking on this long journey back to Scotland at such a time. Talk of war in Europe was growing and what sort of

1

wife was she to be abandoning her husband for months on end after only one year of marriage? She knew Mungo didn't want her to go.

'I won't be gone long, I promise. Just enough time to help Mother–'

'Let's not go over that again,' Mungo said, holding up a hand. 'We've both agreed that you must go and see your father. I would never forgive myself if he died before you could see him just because I put my need of you first.'

Jeanie felt palpitations in her chest; his answer only increased her anxiety.

The smiling, bald-headed manager reappeared, followed by a waiter bearing a tray.

'Mr Munro, your tea! I've taken the liberty of adding a jug of lemonade.'

'How kind' Jeanie smiled, watching the waiter carefully unload the tray. She reached for the jug.

'Let him do that, my dear,' said Mungo.

Jeanie hesitated, then sat back. The manager gave her a reassuring smile. 'Is there anything else we can do for you?'

'No, nothing,' Mungo answered, reaching for his pocket watch again.

'Thank you though,' Jeanie added.

The man gave a respectful bow and withdrew to the reception desk. Jeanie gratefully gulped down her lemonade.

'It's more thirst-quenching to drink tea,' her husband said, sipping at his hot drink.

'So you always tell me.' She smiled.

'And you never listen.'

She prodded him playfully. 'I always listen – I just don't always agree.'

He smiled, his brown eyes assessing. 'How did I end up with such a rebellious wife?'

'Because you fell madly in love with me,' she quipped. 'And I with you.' She reached for his hand. 'I'm going to miss you so much, Mungo.'

He glanced at the manager and withdrew his hand. 'Not in public, Jean.'

To her, his bashfulness was part of his charm – the occasional boyishness – that made her forget for a moment how much older he was than her. She hated the thought of leaving him over the brief summer school holidays.

'I'll be fine,' he said, as if reading her thoughts. 'I've got the camp at Ghora Gali to organise and my friend Easterhouse has invited me to Mussoorie to go fishing. You would have been kicking your heels in Murree without me. Best to go home and see the colonel while you can.'

'Yes,' Jeanie agreed, her anxiety returning. Her mother would never have wired her to come home if her father hadn't been seriously unwell. They thought he'd had a stroke and he was now bedbound. The second telegram had sounded more urgent: '*He is asking for you.*' Her eyes welled with tears.

'Be a brave girl.' Mungo thrust a starched white handkerchief at her.

She pressed it to her face. It smelt of his cologne which made her feel even more weepy.

'My goodness!' Mungo exclaimed and stood up. 'Look who it is.'

Jeanie wiped her eyes and turned to look. Her brother, in uniform and dusty boots, came striding towards them.

'John!' she squealed and, leaping to her feet, rushed forward. They hugged in greeting. 'How wonderful of you to come.'

'I got your message, Jeanie,' he grinned. 'And I couldn't pass up this chance of seeing my favourite sister.'

'Your only sister,' Mungo said pedantically, reaching out to shake his brother-in-law by the hand. 'We have less than two hours till the train, I'm afraid.'

'Time for a chat and a cup of tea,' said Jeanie, linking her arm through John's. 'Come and tell us what you've been doing. Have you been fighting Pathans on the Frontier?'

'Just keeping an eye on them,' said John, squeezing her arm. 'I've been doing piquet duty in the Khyber Pass.'

'That sounds romantic but dangerous.'

'Neither, really.'

'You're too modest – I bet it's terribly unsafe. What's Peshawar like?' she asked, and then turned to Mungo to include him in the conversation. 'I was born there in the military hospital.'

'It's a dusty, dirty town,' Mungo said, 'from my memory of my one trip there.'

'The cantonment is pleasant enough,' John replied.

As they settled into chairs, the friendly manager bustled over. 'What can I get you, sir?'

'More tea,' Mungo ordered.

'This is my brother, Second-Lieutenant Grant,' Jeanie said proudly. 'He's with the Borderers in Peshawar.'

The manager beamed and bowed. 'It is a very great honour to meet you, Lieutenant.'

'Thank you.' John smiled, removing his topee and smoothing down his auburn hair.

'And will you be in our illustrious town of Rawalpindi for long, sir?'

'Sadly not. It's a very brief visit to see my big sister.'

The manager nodded. 'Then allow me to furnish you with chota pegs – on the house – to toast your family reunion.'

'Just tea,' Mungo said testily. Jeanie caught his look of disapproval.

John quickly agreed. 'Tea will be fine, thank you.'

4

Her brother began to engage Mungo in conversation about Nicholson School and the success of the cricket team. Jeanie admired the way John could put anyone at their ease and soon Mungo was inviting him to come and stay in Murree if he got local leave.

'You can keep me company while my Jean is away,' he suggested. 'I know you like to fish and there's excellent brown trout to be had.'

'I'd like that very much, thank you, sir.'

Jeanie listened as Mungo continued to talk about their life in the hill station – mostly about the school – while John nodded and sipped tea. Although she was older than her brother by five years, she admired his poise and the way he wasn't overawed by the older man. At twenty-one, John had the social graces and confidence that she still hadn't mastered, despite being the wife of the deputy headmaster of a prestigious private school. No one mistook them for brother and sister: he was slim and auburn-haired while she was full-figured with a mass of wavy dark hair. But they had always been close and one of the reasons she had seized the chance to return to India as a married woman was because her beloved brother was recently stationed there. Now precious time with him was running out.

When Mungo paused to drink tea, Jeanie seized the moment to ask, 'Have you any messages for me to take home?'

John nodded and pulled out an envelope from the pocket of his khaki shorts. 'I pressed some flowers for Mother. Just wild ones I found at springtime. And there's a letter for Father.'

She saw his eyes glinting with tears. Taking the package, she squeezed his hand. 'How thoughtful of you.'

'You'll let me know how he is as soon as you get home?' he asked.

'Of course, I will,' she promised. 'And I'll be able to tell him I've seen you very recently, looking so well and happy. You are happy, aren't you?'

'Yes,' he smiled. 'I love life in the army – and in India. I can see why Father was keen for me to follow in his footsteps.'

'He's very proud of you, John,' she said, keeping a grip of his hand. 'And so am I.'

'Thank you, Jeanie,' he said, his voice husky.

Mungo shifted restlessly. 'Put the envelope away safely, dear.'

After that, she kept the conversation light, asking John about his social life in the military cantonment. 'I bet the young memsahibs are vying for your attention at dances and tennis matches.'

'It's too hot for any of that now,' he answered in amusement, 'and most of the women have fled to the hill stations – I'm sure Murree must be full of them.'

'I suppose they are,' she said. 'We don't really socialise outside of the school, do we Mungo?'

'There's plenty to keep us occupied there,' Mungo countered.

'That's true,' said Jeanie. 'I got involved with the school play this term – helped with painting the scenery.'

'You'd be good at that,' said John.

'I really enjoyed it. Made me want to take up painting again – maybe watercolours or sketching at least–'

'Jean, dear,' Mungo interrupted. 'If you want to avail yourself of a bathroom before the journey you better do so now. We'll have to leave for the station very soon.'

Jeanie felt her stomach cramp with nervousness. She'd hardly had time for more than exchanging pleasantries with her brother and already it was almost time to say goodbye.

6

'I'd rather spend the last minutes talking to John,' she replied.

Mungo frowned. John swiftly intervened. 'Go and freshen up and then I'll come and see you off at the station.'

***

Milling around the grand station concourse were hawkers with tea trays and porters balancing luggage on their heads. They followed one such porter carrying Jeanie's trunk who threaded through the throng of travellers on the platform to the southbound train. Mungo went ahead issuing orders and checking the manifest on the carriage door. Jeanie felt sudden dread at going. Already India had become to feel like home and she was happy being a teacher's wife in the charming hill station of Murree. But now she was going thousands of miles away from her beloved brother – the person she was closest to in all the world. She braced herself to say goodbye.

'Promise me you'll come and see me as soon as I'm back in Murree,' she urged. 'Or I could meet you here in Pindi if that's easier.'

'I promise,' he said, taking her hands. 'Safe journey, Jeanie. Send Father my love and kiss Mother for me.'

'Of course.' They hugged and kissed each other on the cheek.

As they stepped apart, John added, 'Oh, I forgot to say; I was introduced to a retired nurse in Peshawar – she was asking to be remembered to Mother. Do tell her. A Miss Armitage – friendly old soul.'

'I'll tell her,' Jeanie said, 'though you know how she doesn't like to talk about those days. Frankly, she hates talking about India at all.'

7

'Well, Miss Armitage seemed quite insistent, as if she expected Mother to remember her.' He looked reflective. 'I've been wondering if …'

'Come on Jean!' Mungo called out. 'Time to get aboard.' Her husband elbowed his way back and quickly shook John by the hand. 'Best not to draw these things out.'

'What were you wondering, John?' Jeanie asked.

He shrugged. 'Nothing important.'

Moments later, Mungo was steering Jeanie onto the train. She craned round for one last look at her brother, wondering what it was he had been about to say to her concerning the old lady in Peshawar. She'd write and ask him. Their long letters to each other were better than the snatched conversations they had when Mungo monopolised the conversation.

Trying to stem her tears, Jeanie waved from the window as the train began to pull out of the station. She was sure she saw John with topee raised in farewell – and then Mungo was reaching across to pull down the blind against the searing sun – and she finally lost sight of her brother.

Obituary – The Berwickshire Recorder, Saturday 11th January, 1941

Colonel Colin Grant of Rowan House, Greentoun, died peacefully at home on Friday 3rd January, after a long illness. Colonel Grant of the Borderers Regiment served his country in the Boer War in South Africa, on the North West Frontier in India and in Mesopotamia during the Great War. Retiring from the army in 1928 he became a stalwart of the Greentoun Masonic Lodge and President of Ebbsmouth Golf Club. He is survived by his sorrowing widow, Mrs Clara Grant; his son, Lieutenant John Grant (currently serving with The Borderers, Second Battalion in India) and daughter, Mrs Jean Munro.

***

Obituary – The Berwickshire Recorder, Saturday 25th March, 1944

It is with great sadness that we report the death of Captain John Grant of The Second Battalion, the Borderers; son of the late Colonel Colin Grant of Rowan House, Greentoun who was well-known to many of us. Captain Grant was killed on active service in Burma at the end of February. He leaves behind a grieving mother, Mrs Clara Grant and a sister, Mrs Jean Munro who is currently serving with the A.T.S (in 94th Searchlight Regiment of 39th Anti-Aircraft Brigade).

Chapter 1

Rowan House, Greentoun, Scotland, New Year's Eve, December 1945

The only sound in the sitting-room was the ticking of the grandfather clock in the shadows. Jeanie glanced at her watch yet again but there was still fifty minutes to go until midnight.

'I'm going to top up my sherry, Mother?' she said. 'How about you?'

Clara sat rigid in the high-backed chair by the fire – Jean's father's favourite chair – and shook her head. She'd hardly touched a drop of her drink in the past hour. The firelight softened her pinched and haggard features.

Restless, Jeanie got up and crossed the room to the drinks' trolley that she'd wheeled in from the unused dining-room. She'd tried to make the chilly sitting-room festive for the holidays with sprigs of holly and tinsel lining the mantelpiece, while old paper lanterns and streamers – she'd dug them out of a box in the attic – were looped across the high ceiling. Her brother John had always got excited about putting up the Christmas decorations. Her eyes stung at the memory. In the spring, he would have been dead for two years, yet she still couldn't quite believe that he was gone. He had died so far away and a small part of her hoped that he would suddenly appear through the door grinning and shouting hello, filling their desolate home with renewed life.

'Would you like me to switch on the wireless?' Jeanie asked as she refilled her glass. Clara shook her head. 'What about listening to some music? I could put on a record or play the piano for you?'

Her mother shrugged which Jeanie took as acquiescence. She placed her drink on top of the upright piano, opened the lid and, tucking her loose wavy hair behind her ears, began to play some of the jaunty tunes she had learned during the recent war.

'This next one was a favourite in the mess – *The Lambeth Walk*. Irene used to dance on the table to this!' As she played, Jeanie kept glancing at her mother to see if she registered any emotion. But she continued to sit stone-still, hands clasped in her lap and staring into the fire.

Jeanie changed tempo and played a lilting Scottish tune, *Ye Banks and Braes*, which John – had he been there – would have sung along to in his melodious tenor voice. She played a couple more traditional songs and was in the middle of *My Love is Like a Red, Red Rose*, when her mother spoke.

'Please stop!'

Jeanie closed the piano lid and went swiftly to her mother's side. Clara's cheeks were damp with tears.

'It's good to cry,' Jeanie said, kneeling in front and clasping Clara's hands.

But her mother snatched her hands away. 'It's weak to cry! I don't know why you want to play those songs. I can't bear it.'

'It makes me feel closer to John – and to Father – remembering the happy times.'

'Well, it doesn't for me! It just brings home how they will never be with us again.'

'I'm sorry; I was just trying to cheer you up–'

'You can't,' Clara said, shuddering with pent-up emotion. 'I don't want to celebrate the New Year – there's nothing to look forward to – not without my dear husband and my beloved son.'

Jeanie looked on in distress. 'I know how difficult this is for you, Mother, but–'

'No, you don't! You have a husband and a future.'

Jeanie bit back a retort that she hadn't seen Mungo in six-and-a-half years because she had stayed to comfort and support her widowed mother until it was too late and unsafe to make the return voyage to India. Sometimes she found it hard to even conjure up her husband's face. She kept their wedding photograph by her bedside to remind her of the handsome, energetic man she had married before the war. She couldn't wait for the day when he would return to Scotland and be with her. If all went to plan, he would be starting a new job as a schoolmaster in nearby Ebbsmouth by Easter.

But when her mother was in one of her dark moods, Jeanie knew she could say nothing right. She got to her feet and went to retrieve her sherry.

'If it's celebration you want, you should have gone to the Lomax party,' Clara said with an edge of bitterness. 'You could still go.'

'I'm not going to leave you on your own,' Jeanie said.

'I'll be perfectly fine.'

'I'd rather be with you, Mother. They only invited me to make up the numbers. Though I would be interested to meet the Lomaxes while they're over from India – especially John's fellow officer, Andrew.'

'Why do you keep mentioning him?'

'Surely you'd like to meet him too? He wrote such a kind letter of condolence, remember? Perhaps we could invite the Lomaxes over for afternoon tea sometime?'

Her mother stood up. Her beige utility dress hung loosely on her diminished body. 'I'm sorry, I'm tired. I really don't want to stay up till midnight. I'd rather go to bed.'

'Shall I bring you up a hot drink?' Jeanie asked.

'No, thank you. I'll see you in the morning.'

Jeanie watched Clara leave and close the door quietly behind her. She downed her sherry in one. She thought of the succession of New Years she had brought in with her comrades in the Anti-Aircraft Brigade, huddled in draughty Nissan huts in remote postings, downing rum and gingers and singing raucously. Was she bad for feeling nostalgic for wartime? She'd felt at such a loose end since she'd been demobbed a month ago.

She went back to the piano and distractedly fingered a snatch of tune. Why was her mother so resistant to meeting the Lomaxes? They were army people just like them and – although from different regiments – Captain Tom Lomax had served in India at the same time as Jeanie's father had. Above all, the captain's son, Andrew, had served alongside her brother – they had been close friends, according to letters from John. She longed to meet Andrew and talk about her dead brother; he was the last person to have seen him alive. Was it possible that her mother was so resentful that she couldn't bear the thought of meeting this young man who had survived the battle in Burma when John had not?

Jeanie pushed the thought away and put both hands to the piano keys. Without thinking, she found herself playing the popular sentimental song, *The Very Thought of You*. Mungo had won her heart dancing to it during their whirlwind courtship when he'd been home from India on furlough in the winter of '37. Within six months they'd been married and she'd sailed to India to start a new life as a schoolmaster's wife in Murree.

As she played, she thought of the last time she had been with Mungo, taking tea at The Raj Hotel – owned by the Lomaxes – and feeling guilty at leaving him on what turned out to be the eve of war. Abruptly, it was John's smiling face that came to mind. It was the last time she had seen him too. Suddenly a sob rose up in her chest and she began to weep.

13

How she missed him! Missed both her brother and her genial father too; their deaths had left a deep void inside her.

She went to sit in her father's chair by the fire and stared into the flames as her mother had done. Just before midnight, she poured herself a whisky – it's what her father and John would have drunk – and raised her glass in readiness.

As the clock struck twelve, Jeanie said aloud: 'Happy New Year, dearest Mungo!' She took a sip, winced at the strength of the liquor and added, 'and good luck to all my old comrades. I hope you're dancing on the tables tonight, Irene, wherever you are!'

Softly she whispered, 'and here's to absent friends.'

Jeanie put down the whisky and wiped the tears from her face. This was the start of a new year and a fresh beginning for a war-weary world. She must redouble her efforts to lift her mother out of her deep pit of grieving. In the morning she would persuade her to invite the Lomaxes – or at least Andrew and his young wife – to visit Rowan House.

Chapter 2

January 1946

Two days later, Jeanie still could not cajole her mother into entertaining the Lomax family. At breakfast time, she found Clara balanced on a chair-arm, dismantling the festive decorations.

'Mother! We don't have to do that till the Fifth.'

'I want them put away. There's no one to see them, anyway.'

'What about the Lomaxes?'

'You know I don't want them here.'

'Why not? You haven't given me a good reason. Did something happen in India?'

Her mother gave her a sharp look. 'What do you mean?'

'Between Captain Tom and Daddy. Was there a falling-out or something?'

Clara's expression was tight. 'Lomax and those officers in the Peshawar Rifles always thought they were better than the Borderers. They were a law unto themselves and looked down their noses at the Scottish regiments.'

'That all seems a bit petty,' said Jeanie, still baffled. 'And a long time ago.'

'The Lomaxes aren't quite respectable,' Clara said with a sniff. 'That Tom Lomax is onto his third wife. And his son has married a *half-half*.'

'That's not a nice expression, Mother,' Jeanie chided, wincing at the derogatory term for those in India of mixed race. 'What does it matter that Stella Lomax is Anglo-Indian? I'd still like to meet her. And they have a young daughter. Wouldn't it be fun to have a child in the house? We could dig out some of my old toys.'

'They say the girl isn't even Andrew's,' Clara said in disapproval. 'She was already two-years-old when they married and no word of who the real father was.'

Jeanie rolled her eyes. 'For someone who doesn't want anything to do with the Lomaxes, you seem to know an awful lot of gossip about them.'

'I can't help what I hear at church,' Clara said defensively. 'The goings-on at The Anchorage always did get tongues wagging. That Tibby Lomax is the oddest of them all.'

'Just because she never married?' Jeanie retorted. 'And gives a home to struggling artists? I think Andrew's aunt sounds admirable.'

Her mother tugged hard on a paper streamer, causing it to rip. 'It's scandalous what goes on in that place. Miss Lomax has been living openly with an Indian native for years. *And* he's half her age.'

Jeanie bit back the comment that that made her all the more interesting. She'd heard about Tibby's Indian lover – everyone had – and that he was a moderately famous artist who hadn't lived in India for years. 'Let me do that; you're tearing it. I can reach higher and I don't want you falling off the chair.'

'Stop fussing! I can manage perfectly well.'

Jeanie hid her frustration and held out a hand. 'Let's have breakfast, Mother. Then we can tackle the job together.'

Clara hesitated and then her shoulders sagged. She climbed down without Jeanie's help. 'I won't change my mind about the Lomaxes,' she said with a defiant look.

Jeanie stifled a sigh. Her hope that she would become closer to her mother because of their shared bereavement seemed more remote than ever. She had always known that John was the favourite child but had never resented it. Everyone had loved her brother. Yet, far from bringing her mother comfort, everything she did or said appeared to irritate her.

Perhaps when Mungo returned, her mother's coldness towards her might thaw? Clara had been accepting of Mungo as a son-in-law, probably because Jeanie's father had welcomed him so enthusiastically. *'Well, if you can't marry an army man, a schoolmaster is the next best thing!'*

She was sure that her father wouldn't have snubbed the Lomaxes in the way her mother was doing. Even if the officers of the Peshawar Rifles were a bit snooty, his attitude would have been that they were part of the army fraternity and what they did in their private lives was their business.

***

The following Wednesday, a further invitation came from Tibby Lomax at The Anchorage.

'They're inviting us to go beagling and then have tea,' Jeanie announced. 'This Saturday.'

'I've never liked hunting with dogs,' Clara said.

'It would do us good to get out in the fresh air,' Jeanie encouraged. 'Daddy always enjoyed it. You might see some old friends.'

Her mother looked momentarily uncertain and then shook her head. 'You go. I don't want to stop you enjoying yourself.'

'Then I will,' Jeanie replied, wondering how her mother managed to make her feel guilty for wanting to go, even though Clara didn't want her to stay at home either.

Chapter 3

The Anchorage, Ebbsmouth

The road across to Ebbsmouth was slippery with ice, so Jeanie decided to park her car in the main street and walk up to The Anchorage. When she saw the pot-holed track up to Tibby Lomax's house, she was glad of her decision. It was a cold, frosty day and the bare trees and dead grass glinted in the winter sunshine. She gasped at the sight of the imposing building before her; it was more castle than country house, with turrets and serrated battlements and a huge metal-studded front door that was ajar.

A battered green bus was parked to the side and as she approached, it suddenly juddered into life, belching black smoke from its exhaust. Jeanie coughed in the fumes. A dark-haired man in shirt-sleeves jumped down from the cab, closed the bonnet and re-emerged, wielding a large spanner and grinning.

'That's got the old thing going! It's a matter of knowing where to hit the engine. Sorry about the exhaust.'

There were black smuts on his tawny skin and his eyes under dark brows were a deep brown. He may have lived in Scotland for years but she still detected a trace of his accent. The Indian. He quickly proffered his right hand.

'You must be Mrs Munro?'

Jeanie smiled and nodded, taking his hand. 'And you must be the famous artist.' He gave her a quizzical look. 'Er … Mr Lal?' Jeanie faltered.

Something flickered across his face – was it annoyance? – and then he gave a wry smile as he dropped her hold. 'Ah, no. I'm not the talented Dawan Lal, I'm afraid. Just a lowly mechanic. Rick Dixon.'

Jeanie reddened. 'I'm so sorry. I don't know why I thought …'

'Don't apologise,' he said. 'No offence taken. Far from it.'

As she struggled to think of what to say, an apparition in tartan appeared on the castle steps.

'Ah, Mrs Munro!' the tall woman in feathered bonnet and voluminous tartan cape greeted her. 'Welcome to The Anchorage. And well done, Mr Dixon for getting Hamish going again. Wonderful! We'll have a bowl of punch before we set off – warm us up. Now where is Tommy? He's in charge of drinkies.'

Jeanie knew at once that this Amazonian figure was the notorious Tibby.

'It's so kind of you to invite me, Miss Lomax. My mother sends her apologies – she doesn't venture out much these days – but I'm very happy to be included, thank you.'

'Delighted, dear girl,' Tibby beamed. 'Have you been properly introduced to Stella's cousin, Mr Dixon? He's from Rawalpindi. Isn't that where you were living before the war?'

'Not far away,' said Jeanie. 'In the hill station, Murree.'

'Marvellous! Then you'll have lots to talk about.'

Jeanie glanced at the mechanic and gave an awkward smile. So he was from the Anglo-Indian community too. He winked and then reached for his tweed jacket which was slung over the wheel arch. Just then, voices and a clatter of feet made her turn in time to see a family group emerging through the creaking front door. A small rosy-faced girl trussed up in a green velvet coat and hat skipped out ahead of a pretty fair-haired woman and a dark-haired man with an eye patch, who towered over them both. Despite the woman's fair complexion, Jean surmised that this must be Stella, Andrew and their daughter. Behind them came an

19

equally tall man – older and gaunter – arm-in-arm with a slim middle-aged woman in a fur hat. Tom and his third wife, Esmie? She was struck immediately by the warmth between them as they laughed at something the little girl said. A happy family.

Catching sight of Jeanie, the younger man leapt down the steps and rushed up to her. He grasped her hand in a firm grip.

'I'm Andrew. I'm very glad to meet you. I counted your brother among my greatest of friends. I can't tell you how much I miss him.'

Jeanie struggled with a sudden lump in her throat. 'Thank you,' she said, her voice shaky. 'So do I.'

'And he spoke so fondly of you,' said Andrew with a smile of compassion. 'He obviously adored his big sister. I'm very, very sorry.'

Jeanie's vision blurred behind tears. How she had longed to hear an acknowledgement that she – and not just her mother – grieved for John. Her mother had never once mentioned such a likelihood and yet within seconds of meeting Andrew for the first time, this kind stranger was trying to comfort her.

'Are you crying?' the little girl asked. She was staring up at Jeanie, frowning.

'Just a little bit,' Jeanie said, with a tearful smile.

'Would you like my hanky?' She pulled a crumpled handkerchief out of her pocket and held it up. 'It's nearly clean.'

Jeanie took it. 'Thank you.'

'This is our daughter, Belle,' Andrew introduced her.

'And I'm nearly four,' said Belle with pride. 'You can keep my hanky. I don't really want it now you've blown your nose on it. Might be snotty.'

20

'Belle!' her mother stepped forward and put a warning hand on the girl's head. 'I'm Stella,' she smiled. 'I met your brother too. Andy and I spent a few days with him in the hills around Mussoorie before … Well, just to say, he was a very fine man.'

'Thank you,' Jeanie said. 'I'd like to hear more about that sometime.'

Then the older couple, Tom and Esmie, were introducing themselves while Tibby relieved her brother of the large silver punch bowl he was carrying. Jeanie studied the captain. Despite craggy features and faded blue eyes that indicated years of exposure to harsh sunlight, he was still a handsome man. His greeting was polite yet more reserved than Andrew's. His look was almost wary as he studied her and she wondered why. Perhaps her suspicion of a falling-out between Tom Lomax and her father had been true.

With Esmie, she felt instantly at ease. There was kindness in her grey eyes and a warmth in her handshake. 'Goodness, you have cold hands! You must borrow my gloves.' Esmie began fishing a pair out of her pocket.

'I'm fine, honestly,' Jeanie said. 'I don't feel the cold. I've spent the last few winters in freezing postings around our coast – today's weather is lovely in comparison.'

'Ah yes,' said Esmie, 'Andy told us you were in the Anti-Aircraft Brigade. I'm full of admiration, Mrs Munro.'

'It was nothing compared to what Andrew and John did,' Jeanie said. 'And please, you must all call me Jeanie.'

Esmie squeezed her arm. 'Well, I think you're too modest, Jeanie.'

'And you're a true Scot not feeling the cold,' Andrew added. 'Not like poor Dixon here. He can't get used to it.'

Jeanie glanced at Stella's cousin who gave a rueful smile and admitted, 'This is the first place where I've had to put on more clothes to go to bed than I wear during the day.'

21

This caused general laughter and an order from Tibby. 'Pass the punch bowl to my driver before he faints with cold. Then we must get going.'

***

Belle asked to sit beside Jeanie and chattered away as the bus rattled along the icy roads, inland. Rick drove a little too quickly for Jeanie's liking but he seemed assured at the wheel of the ancient vehicle. She felt a warm contentedness inside that she partly attributed to Tibby's strong whisky punch but also to being swept into this friendly family.

'This is an old converted ambulance from the Great War,' Andrew told her as they were bounced around on the hard seats. 'My Auntie Tibby picked it up for a song but hardly uses it – with petrol still being rationed this is a rare treat.'

She wondered where the artist Lal was. Perhaps he didn't approve of dog hunting. She cringed to think of her assumption that Rick was Indian. From what she knew about Anglo-Indians – mainly what Mungo had told her – they thought themselves more British than the British. *'Most have a chip on their shoulder about it – hate to be labelled as Indian.'*

Half an hour later, they were piling out and joining a throng of well-booted people dressed in tweeds or hunting jackets. Beagles ran around excitedly, barking, their breath billowing in the sharp air.

Jeanie had a pang of nostalgia. 'My father used to bring John and I along to follow the hunt,' she told Andrew as they waited for the dogs to be released. 'John would run after the beagles like a mad thing – loved it – until they actually caught a hare. He couldn't bear seeing the animal thrown to the dogs.'

'I can imagine that,' said Andrew. 'He could be brave as a lion but deep down he was also a very gentle man.'

As the hunt got underway and they streamed after the dogs and huntsmen, Jeanie and Andrew kept in step and talked about her brother. She delighted in the anecdotes – some of which she'd known from John's letters – but other trivial moments and funny comments told her what good friends these young men had been. How she wished her mother could be there to hear them too and be comforted by them. John came alive again in Andrew's affectionate telling. If only Clara could see what a fine man Andrew was too – warm-hearted and friendly – and that he bore the scars of war as well.

She plucked up the courage to ask him about his patched eye. 'Your eye injury – was that from the battle when John died? I heard you were injured too.'

He fixed her with a look from his one good eye – a startling blue – and nodded.

'The battle for the Arakan had gone on for weeks – relief was on its way. We were just unlucky. A stray mortar on our trench. I tried to push John out of the way but I think he'd already been hit. That's the last I remember …'

He looked suddenly harrowed, his face rigid, and Jeanie felt sorry for asking. She put a hand on his arm.

'It brings me comfort to know that you were with him at the end.'

The tension in his face eased. He smiled sadly. 'Thank you for saying that. I've felt so guilty not being able to save him.'

'You mustn't,' she insisted. 'John wouldn't want you to and neither do I. You did everything you could, Andrew.'

'Thank you.'

After the intensity of their conversation, they continued in silence across a field and Jeanie wasn't surprised when

Andrew stopped at the gate and said, 'I better drop back and help Stella with Belle. We'll catch you up. Why don't you walk on with Rick?'

Jeanie turned to see Stella's cousin approaching. She nodded in agreement and as Andrew retreated, she went through the gate with Rick. He was muffled in a scarf with only his eyes showing – dark attractive eyes – but she couldn't read his expression. As they walked, she felt she should say something but didn't know what. What was he doing in Ebbsmouth? Was he being employed by Tibby? Why had he left India? She didn't want to appear like a nosy memsahib asking impertinent questions.

Rick broke the awkward silence first. He pulled down his scarf and said, 'Shall we start again, Mrs Munro? I'm Rick Dixon from Rawalpindi, Stella's first cousin. Our mothers are sisters and we grew up together.' He smiled. 'I was always round at The Raj scrounging food and drink from my Dubois relations – Stella's family – and they threw the best parties there.'

'The Raj in Pindi?' Jeanie asked. 'I thought that belonged to the Lomaxes?'

'It does,' he said, 'but Uncle Charlie – Stella's father – was their manager. Wonderful bloke. He died during the war so now my cousin Jimmy runs it.'

'I remember the manager!' Jeanie exclaimed. 'A bald man with a moustache – very well dressed with a purple cravat.'

'That sounds like Uncle Charlie.'

'He was so friendly and obliging. Tried to give us free drinks when my brother John turned up to see me off to Scotland.'

Rick grinned. 'Definitely my uncle. Did you resist?'

'Yes.' Jeanie gave a snort of amusement. 'Mungo, my husband, was a bit scandalised at the thought of chota pegs with afternoon tea.'

'He doesn't sound very Scottish,' Rick said with a wry look. 'The Lomaxes serve out drams with tea at the drop of a hat.'

'Mungo isn't a great drinker at any time. At least he wasn't before the war. I don't know if that's changed …'

Rick scrutinised her. 'Do you mean, you haven't seen your husband for all this time?'

Jeanie shook her head. 'Not since '39 when I came home to be with my sick father.'

Rick whistled. 'My God, that's awful. You must be longing to see each other again. Are you returning to Murree soon?'

'No, I'm not going back to India. Mungo is coming here – starts a new teaching job in Ebbsmouth soon.'

Rick sighed. 'I suppose he thinks things are too uncertain in India now.'

'What do you mean?'

'Well, with the new elections. Some sort of Home Rule will be coming.'

'Really?' Jeanie was surprised. 'I haven't been following what's happening, I'm afraid.'

'Indians will be pushing for independence,' said Rick. 'Some of my family are worried about it. But then who knows? Nothing might happen for years.'

'I hadn't really thought about it,' Jeanie admitted. 'And it's not the reason Mungo is leaving. He's doing it so that I don't have to leave my mother on her own. She's not coping well with widowhood and losing John.'

He reached out and touched her shoulder. 'That's understandable. And very thoughtful of your husband.'

Jeanie was startled by the sudden gesture. She swallowed hard, not wanting to get emotional again.

'So is the move towards Home Rule the reason you've left India?' she asked, keen to turn the conversation to him.

'Oh, I'm only here for a short visit,' he replied. 'To see my fiancée.'

Jeanie was astonished. 'Your fiancée? Here in Ebbsmouth?'

'No, Pamela's in Yorkshire. But her whole family has come down with influenza so I've been banished to stay with Stella till they give the all clear.' He gave that rueful smile again that made his eyes crinkle. 'Then I'll be whisking her off to India to get married.'

'To Pindi?'

'No, Pammy wants to live in Calcutta. It's where we met. Her father was in jute – ran a factory there – but has just retired back to Yorkshire. Pammy came home to help them settle in. It's where we Dixons came from originally too – so I've always wanted to see Yorkshire.'

'And do you like what you've seen so far?' Jeanie asked.

He gave an amused huff. 'Bit grey and soggy, to be honest.'

Jeanie laughed. 'You should have waited till summer to visit.'

'Just want to get on with married life,' he said. 'War brings that home to you, doesn't it? How precious life is. You must feel the same – wanting to have your husband with you to start some bloody living again!'

Jeanie was taken aback by his sudden outburst. She envied him his passion for his fiancée and being optimistic about the future. It struck her how she was just treading water, trying to keep her mother happy while all the time feeling underlying anxiety about seeing Mungo again.

Of course, she longed to be with him – he was her husband and she loved him – but what would he be like after all these years apart? She knew she wasn't the same person who had left India as a fairly immature young woman who readily deferred to others and was socially gauche. Three years with the ack-acks being drilled as a soldier had made her tougher – she was more outspoken – and would have defended her female crew with her life. Would Mungo even like this new Jeanie?

Rick misread her silence. 'Sorry, it was bad manners to swear like that. And to make assumptions ...'

'Don't apologise,' she said quickly. 'You're quite right – we should all thank our lucky stars we've come through the war and have another chance.'

'That's exactly it,' Rick agreed. 'We owe it to brave men like your brother to live life to the full, don't we?'

Jeanie's eyes smarted. 'That's a good way of putting it. Thank you.'

He smiled at her. He really did have the most attractive eyes; not the deep brown she had first thought but with lighter flecks of hazel and amber too.

She looked away. 'So, what were you doing in Calcutta? Are you in the jute trade too?'

This seemed to amuse him. 'No, I was stationed there. Met Pammy at a dance in The Grand.'

'You were in the Forces, then?'

'Indian Air Force,' he replied.

'That sounds very dashing,' she smiled.

'The uniform helped in getting dancing partners,' he admitted, 'but I was in the unglamorous transport division.' He put a gloved finger to his lips. 'But shush, don't tell!'

Somehow, with his easy conversation, Jeanie found herself recounting stories from her service with the Anti-Aircraft Brigade.

27

'… And the latrines were medieval – buckets with a plank over them – and we had to wash in a couple of inches of cold water – also out of a bucket. But I probably had the most fun with those girls than at any other time in my life. We'd go to the village dances together and share each other's letters and rations from home – we knew more about our Searchlight mates than our own families. I suppose we *were* a family.'

She glanced at him, embarrassed by how much had come pouring out.

'Is it very terrible of me to admit that I miss all that?' she asked. 'Not the war itself – seeing aircraft shot down was hellish – but the friendship and the awful jokes and just living each day as it came?'

They had stopped by a stone wall. Ahead they could hear barking as the dogs pursued their quarry, while behind them, Belle's high-pitched voice rang through the clear air as she and her parents waded through dead bracken.

Rick held her look, his expression contemplative. Finally, he said quietly, 'Not terrible at all. I feel the same too. As the saying goes, they were the best and worst of times. I never felt so alive – and so afraid – as when on a mission.'

They swapped knowing smiles. Then something about what he said struck her. 'Flying missions? I thought mechanics were part of ground crew?'

Just then, they were interrupted by Belle shouting. 'Hello lady! Wait for me!' Jeanie turned and squinted into the low sun as the girl and her parents caught them up. Belle beamed up at her, cheeks ruddy with the cold. She thrust out a half-eaten stick of liquorice.

'I've got lickle-ish for you!'

Stella laughed. 'Sweetie, I think Mrs Munro should be allowed a fresh stick, don't you?'

Belle ignored this suggestion so Jeanie took the proffered liquorice. 'This bit looks delicious, thank you.'

Belle looked pleased and plucked a fresh piece from her pocket. 'Uncle Rick, this is for you.'

Rick grinned. 'Yum, my favourite!'

As they sucked on their sweets, Andrew carried Belle on his shoulders and they walked on together until they caught up with Tibby and the older Lomaxes in a clearing in the woods.

Tibby laughed. 'We appear to have lost sight and sound of the dogs. Perhaps we should beat a retreat and go home for an early tea?'

The wintry sun was already fading into dusk although it was barely three o'clock. Everyone agreed.

***

Back at The Anchorage, Tibby insisted Jeanie stay for refreshment. She readily accepted, reluctant to return early to Rowan House and curious to see inside the old castle.

Tea was served in a cosy library around a blazing fire. There was a mismatch of shabby sofas and chairs and the carpet was threadbare but electric lamps threw cheery light onto book-lined walls and artwork. While Tibby and Rick embarked on a noisy game of cards with Belle and her parents, Jeanie went to study a portrait hanging by the door.

'All the paintings are Dawan's,' Tom said, noticing her interest. 'Tea and shortbread should entice him out of his studio, so you can ask him about them.'

'It's very …' Jeanie paused as she assessed the bold and garish depiction of a woman carrying a baby. 'Arresting.'

Tom chuckled. 'It is, isn't it? I've always been envious of his ability to paint people.'

'Do you paint?' she asked.

'I dabble.'

Esmie joined them. 'He does much more than dabble. Tom paints the most beautiful landscapes.'

Tom gave an embarrassed shrug. 'My wife is touchingly biased. What about you, Jeanie? Do you paint?'

'Not since before the war. I know it's the acceptable thing for young memsahibs to busy themselves with watercolours,' she said wryly, 'but the only painting I did in Murree was the stage set for the school production. Which I have to say, I greatly enjoyed.'

'Good for you,' Tom said. 'A worthy profession.'

His reserve towards her seemed to be thawing, and as the hubbub from around the fire masked their conversation, Jeanie decided to broach the topic of her parents.

'I was wondering if you remember my parents from India? My father was a colonel with the Borderers – Colin Grant.'

Tom frowned. 'I remember the name. We were stationed in the same garrison as the Borderers before the Great War, so might well have come across each other.'

'Yes, Peshawar, wasn't it?' She saw him tense and exchange glances with Esmie. 'Daddy would only have been a junior officer then.'

'I'm sorry, I don't recall your father – but it was a long time ago.'

Jeanie was disappointed. 'Yes, I suppose so. Though my mother seems to remember you.'

'Really?'

'Yes. I got the impression that both she and Daddy knew you. But I must be wrong. I was born there, though I have no memory of the place.'

Tom looked flustered.

Esmie said gently, 'Perhaps your mother knew Tom's first wife, Mary?' When he said nothing, she went on. 'Mary might have been friendly with your mother as they would both have known the Ebbsmouth area and had something in common.'

Jeanie was surprised. Her mother had never mentioned a Mary Lomax and she could see how the subject was making Tom suddenly agitated. His former affability was gone.

Curtly, he said, 'please excuse me. I think I should go and see what's delaying Dawan.' With that, he hurried from the room.

Jeanie turned to Esmie and asked in a quiet voice. 'Have I upset Captain Lomax?'

Esmie gave a sorrowful look. 'He doesn't like to talk about Peshawar. It was a painful time for him. His wife Mary died there.'

Jeanie felt terrible. 'I'm so sorry!'

'Don't be. You weren't to know. It happened over thirty years ago but Tom's only just been able to acknowledge his loss very recently. At times it's still rather raw. They'd been married such a short while, you see.'

Jeanie swallowed, thinking how awful it would be if Mungo had been taken from her after their brief time together. 'How did she die?'

'In childbirth,' Esmie said. 'Both mother and baby died.'

Jeanie was stunned. Had her mother known about this? If so, why had she never mentioned such a thing? Had she been forewarned, Jeanie would never have intruded into Tom's private grief and stirred up anguished memories. She went hot with shame.

'How – how dreadful,' Jeanie stammered. 'I'm very sorry.'

Esmie steered her back to the fireside and no more was said about it.

Chapter 4

Jeanie drove home in the dark, still shaken by her conversation with Tom and Esmie, and angry at her mother's unkind words about Captain Tom. How could she resent him when he had suffered cruel bereavement too?

By the time she reached Greentoun it had started to snow and she clattered in through the front door of Rowan House, shaking fresh flakes from her hat and coat.

'I'm back!' she called.

Clara was sitting in her usual place by the fire. The warmth did not spread beyond the hearth.

'Don't let the cold in!' her mother scolded, pulling her woollen shawl tighter.

Holding her patience, Jeanie quickly shut the door and made for the fire, kneeling on the rug and holding her hands to the flames. 'It's started snowing.'

'I know. I was worried about you driving. I expected you back sooner.'

'Miss Lomax insisted on me staying for tea and then Belle wanted to play dominoes.'

'Who's Belle?'

'Andrew and Stella's wee girl. She's delightful – they all are,' she added pointedly.

'So, it's Andrew and Stella now, is it?' Clara snorted. 'You hardly know them.'

'They made me feel very welcome,' said Jeanie, trying to stay calm. 'Stella must be about my age – and I suppose Andrew's a bit younger but he seems very mature. Did you know he'd lost an eye in the Battle of Admin Box?'

'No, how could I?'

'He talked a lot about John. I wish you'd been there – it was so comforting to–'

'I don't want to hear!' Clara interrupted. 'It's too upsetting.'

Jeanie felt herself losing patience. 'Won't you even try to be nice to them while they're here? John would have wanted that.'

Her mother's expression tightened. Abruptly, she picked up a letter that was lying on the side table by her chair. She flapped it at her daughter.

'This came for you today. It's Mungo's writing.'

'Mungo!' Jeanie's spirits lifted as she scrambled to her feet. 'Let me see.'

She took the airmail letter and sank into the chair opposite. 'I wonder if he's booked his passage yet? I hope so.'

Eagerly, she opened it up and began to read.

'My dear Jean,

Happy New Year, my darling! At last, the year when we'll be man and wife again. It's been far too long. I hope you've continued to miss me as much as a wife should! I can't wait for us to be reunited.

There has been a big development over here. Old Bishop has suddenly announced he's retiring as headmaster and he's recommended me for the position. Today, the trustees confirmed my appointment. Isn't that wonderful news? It's what I've always wanted but thought Bishop would hang on until he was carried out in a box. It seems his wife is keen to leave India as there's talk of unrest. I think it's a fuss over very little. We British could be here for years to come in some form or other. There will certainly be a need for good British schools whatever happens.

I know the plan was for me to take the teaching job at Ebbsmouth but I'm sure you'll agree it would be wrong of me to turn down this opportunity. I see it as my duty to do the very best for the boys of Nicholson's – and it's a far better

33

life here than being a mathematics master and us having to live under your mother's roof. Of course, she is welcome to come and live with us in Murree – I hope you will urge her to travel with you – but it's quite a different matter having my mother-in-law under my roof than vice versa, don't you think?

I hope you are as excited about the prospect of being the wife of the headmaster of Nicholson School, as I am of being the Head. You'll have a far bigger house to run but there are plenty of servants – and lots of room for the arrival of little Munros in the near future!

Now that I've made my decision, you must book on a boat as soon as you can. There's no reason to delay. Speak to your mother and try and persuade her to come. I know she's not a fan of India but she doesn't know Murree well and how beautiful it can be. I'll introduce her to some of the other old memsahibs who live in the station and she can be a help to you once we start a family.

I can't wait to embrace you again, my dearest.

Your loving husband, Mungo x

p.s Thank you for the photo of you in uniform before you were demobbed. I'm glad to see you haven't lost your figure. I keep it on my desk – soon to be moved into the headmaster's study!'

'Well, what does he say?' Clara asked impatiently. 'Why are you frowning? It isn't bad news, is it?'

'No ... well not exactly.' Jeanie gulped. 'It's just a bit of a shock.'

'What is? You're making me anxious.'

'Mungo's been appointed head of Nicholson's. He's not taking the Ebbsmouth job after all. He seems really pleased.'

'Oh!'

34

Her mother looked lost for words. Jeanie felt a mix of emotions herself. Shock at the unexpected news, happiness for Mungo, a kick of excitement at the thought of going to India again and a tug of resentment that he had taken the decision without consulting her.

'Mr Bishop's taken sudden retirement. I suppose it all happened so quickly during the winter break,' Jeanie reasoned, 'that Mungo had to make up his mind at once. He's always hankered after a headship and thought he would make a better leader than Bishop.'

She couldn't read her mother's expression as to whether she was glad at the news or not. Once again, she was overwhelmed with anxiety at leaving her mother on her own.

'But he's very keen for you to come out to India, Mother. He's quite insistent.'

Clara gave a huff of disbelief. 'I'm sure he's just being polite.'

'No, he means it,' Jeanie replied, keeping to herself his main motivation to have his mother-in-law there to help with domestic family duties. 'Besides, I'd like you to come too. I'd hate the thought of leaving you here on your own.'

'I've been on my own since your father died,' Clara pointed out bitterly. 'I'm quite used to it.'

'But you're not alone now,' Jeanie pointed out. 'You've got me – and you'll have Mungo too. And hopefully, in time, you'll have grandchildren.'

A flicker of anguish crossed her mother's face. 'You know I can't face India again. I'm too old and I've never liked the place. It was only bearable when I was with your father.'

'But Murree is different. It's a hill station with a climate more like here. It's not the hot plains or the barren mountains around Peshawar.'

Clara stiffened. Jeanie wondered if it was the mention of the garrison town that upset her. But why was the birthplace of her two children not a place that held any happiness for her?

'Please come!' Jeanie urged. 'Or at least think about it. You could travel out with me and stay for a visit – see how you liked it. You'd be there for the spring and summer when the town is looking its best and there are lots of army families on leave.'

'I wouldn't want to mix with them,' Clara said with a note of panic.

'Well, you wouldn't have to,' Jeanie said swiftly. 'There would be enough going on at the school to keep you occupied. You could take up Bridge again. You could teach me.'

'You'll be far too busy being the headmaster's wife.' Clara was dismissive. 'I'll only be a burden.'

'You won't be!'

'You're just saying that.' Her mother's voice was querulous. 'Why would you want me there when you'll have your husband?'

'Because you're my mother! Of course I want you with me. We're the only family that each other has.'

For a moment, Clara's eyes glinted as if she was on the point of tears and then she glanced away.

'Your duty and loyalty are to Mungo,' she said. 'He is your family now.' Her mother stood up. 'I'm going to bed. Will you bank up the fire when you're finished in here?'

'It's not even seven o'clock,' Jeanie said in dismay. 'Stay up a little longer and we can talk about all this.'

'I won't change my mind,' Clara said as she crossed the room. 'I don't want to leave Greentoun. Goodnight, Jeanie.'

'Sleep on it, at least,' Jeanie called after her. But Clara didn't answer as she closed the door, and then was gone.

Chapter 5

The Anchorage, mid-January

'Uncle Rick!' Belle came clattering into the study. 'You're in charge of party games and hide and seek, and a tressy hunt–'

'Treasure hunt,' Stella corrected, walking in behind her.

'With sweeties,' Belle continued. 'Come on, Uncle Rick!'

Rick looked up from his card game with Esmie and grinned. 'We're having a party? Great! Is it your birthday, Belle?'

'No,' she giggled. 'Mummy's friend is having a birthday.' She turned to Stella. 'What's the lady's name again?'

'Mrs Munro.'

Rick felt a kick of surprise. He hadn't expected to see the Munro woman a second time.

'I just rang her this morning,' Stella explained, 'and she wasn't doing anything, so I thought we could spoil her a little.'

'Mummy says you do the best parties, Uncle Rick,' chattered Belle, 'and this is going to be the bestest party for Mrs Mun-ow.'

Rick stood up. 'Well, your granny was beating me hands-down, so you've saved me from further embarrassment.'

Esmie swept up the cards. 'So, Jeanie has agreed to come, that's lovely. And Mrs Grant too?'

Stella shook her head. 'No, just Jeanie. I really don't know why her mother is avoiding us. Andrew won't say anything but he's rather hurt by it. He and John were such close friends.'

Rick saw a thoughtful look cross Esmie's face. 'Grief affects people in different ways. But perhaps it's something else that keeps her away ...'

'Such as?' asked Stella.

'Maybe she disapproves of Tom and I. There's still such a lot of gossip about Tom's time in the army – and about our marrying ...'

Rick knew there had been some scandal about Tom leaving the army after the Great War – something about a court-martial – and people said he had deserted his second wife for Esmie. But Stella's view was that the couple were wrongly maligned. Tom had been a war hero and Esmie a brave nurse who had had nothing to do with the collapse of Tom's second marriage to Andrew's mother – a spoilt and selfish woman, according to Stella. Rick didn't care either way; he took people as he found them and wasn't influenced by gossip. To him, Tom and Esmie were kind people and good company.

'Come on, Belle,' Rick said, diverting the conversation. 'Let's go and wrap some sweeties for the treasure hunt.'

'Have you got some?' Belle squealed in delight.

'No, but I know where Great-Aunt Tibby keeps her secret supply of toffees.' He winked.

'Once they're wrapped, you must let Uncle Rick go off and hide them,' said Stella, 'so you can search for them with Mrs Munro.'

Belle shook her head. 'No, I'm going to hide them too. Then I can show Mrs Mun-ow where to find them.'

Her mother laughed. 'Belle, a treasure trail is supposed to be secret.'

Belle's face fell. Rick said quickly, 'I think Belle's version of a treasure hunt is the best. We want all of the toffees to be found, don't we, Belle?'

'Yes!' She beamed.

Rick found the diversion was just what he needed. He spent a happy hour helping Belle plant the toffees around the garden, wrapping up a prize for pass-the-parcel and hunting out an old gramophone so they could play musical statues and other games. He hated sitting around with nothing to do.

The Lomaxes all seemed content to spend hours in front of a fire endlessly reading, whereas he needed to be doing something practical. He'd spent a week tinkering with Tibby's old bus, fixing up the seats as well as overhauling the engine. He thought fondly of his father who had taught him from an early age how to mend bicycles and then cars. Dixon's Garage was known as one of the most reliable in Rawalpindi and he had always imagined he would go into the family business alongside his father and his younger brother Sigmund.

Yet the war had widened his ambition. The Indian Air Force had been like a close-knit family and he missed it more than he had imagined. Rick recalled that Jeanie Munro had said something similar about her life in the Anti-Aircraft Brigade. He shook off the thought. He must look to the future.

He had dreams of working in civil aviation and it was something his pretty, blonde fiancée was encouraging. *'You should train as a pilot for one of the big new airlines. It's the travel of the future and much better paid than working in a garage, darling.'* He liked it that Pamela was ambitious for him too.

That was why kicking his heels around Ebbsmouth was so frustrating. The last note he'd had from his fiancée – they couldn't speak on the telephone because her parents hadn't installed one yet – was to say that her mother was still poorly and he wasn't to travel. *'Pa is being very protective of Ma and doesn't want any new infections brought into the home. But I'm feeling a lot better and looking forward to seeing you, darling. Just be patient – I'll work on Daddy.'*

Rick sighed. She made him sound like he was some sort of disease.

'Here she comes!' Belle's excited cry curtailed his brooding. As he and Stella followed the girl onto the castle steps, he saw their visitor approaching.

It was typical of his cousin Stella to have found out that it was Jeanie Munro's birthday and then to have acted on it. 'She puts on a brave face,' said Stella, slipping an arm through his. 'But she strikes me as rather lonely. Her mother sounds a cold fish and Jeanie must be missing her husband terribly. I just want her to have a bit of fun.'

'Leave it to us.' Rick smiled. 'We're in charge of fun, aren't we, Belle?'

'Fun, fun, fun!' Belle chanted and hopped around in the wintry sunshine.

Rick watched Jeanie walking briskly towards them down the drive, wearing a tweed jacket and boots but otherwise without hat, scarf or gloves to protect her from the raw air. Her dark wavy hair lifted in the breeze and her full face was pink with cold.

'Welcome!' Stella called out.

As Jeanie reached the steps, she gave a wide smile – her full lips enhanced by red lipstick – and her dark blue eyes lit up. Sexy eyes.

'This is so kind!' she said, breathlessly.

'Reception committee at the ready,' Rick grinned. 'Happy Birthday, Mrs Munro.'

'Hello Mr Dixon. I didn't expect you still to be here but what a nice surprise.'

Rick felt ridiculously pleased at the remark. 'I didn't expect to be either but I'm glad not to miss a party.' He smiled back.

Stella greeted Jeanie with a kiss on the cheek and Belle grabbed her hand.

'Uncle Rick and me have done a tressy hunt and I'm going to show you where all the toffees are!'

Jeanie laughed. 'Toffees are my favourite; how did you know?'

'They're Great-Aunt Tibby's,' said Belle. 'She's out with Granddad and doesn't know but Mummy says it's okay and we can buy some more for her. Don't go inside yet, Mrs Mun-ow. All the toffees are outside.'

'Well, let's get started then,' said Jeanie, holding onto Belle's hand. 'And you can call me Auntie Jeanie if you like.'

'Yes, please.' Belle nodded. 'Let's go everybody!'

Esmie and Andrew joined them as they set about hunting for toffees. Rick had to keep prompting Belle about where they were hidden and Stella took charge of the haul of sweets so that the girl didn't eat too many.

'One now,' Stella allowed. 'Then we'll share the rest out at teatime.'

Rick was impressed by Belle's acceptance of this without protest.

'I don't remember you holding back on eating sweets at our family parties,' he said, nudging his cousin.

'That was to stop you and my brother Jimmy scoffing the lot,' she teased back.

'We had a Sunday tin,' Jeanie remarked. 'Any sweets John and I were given would go in the tin and my mother would let us have three after lunch on a Sunday.'

'Only on a Sunday?' Stella exclaimed.

'That's why you have such perfect teeth,' said Andrew.

41

Rick saw Jeanie's cheeks dimple and glow an even deeper pink at the compliment. She gave a bashful laugh.

'Now it's time for games,' Belle declared. 'Come on, Auntie Jeanie.'

'I hope you don't mind being commandeered like this,' Stella said with a roll of her eyes.

'I love it,' Jeanie smiled, allowing herself to be led by the hand back to the house.

In the library, Rick put himself in charge of the gramophone music for a series of games: musical statues, musical bumps and pass-the-parcel, while Belle and the other adults joined in. When he stopped the music, he shouted out judgements about who was out and who was still in the game. He admired the way Jeanie joined in wholeheartedly, pulling funny poses and throwing herself onto the floor as enthusiastically as Belle did. He couldn't imagine Pamela doing so. She was far too poised and careful over her appearance.

Tibby and Tom returned from visiting a sick friend and Dawan emerged from his studio as afternoon tea was brought in by Elsie, the housekeeper. They sat around the table in the window and tucked into scones with homemade jam, while Jeanie had an animated conversation with Dawan about art and got Tibby and Tom talking about their ancestral home.

'This food is delicious,' Jeanie enthused, sitting back and licking her fingers. 'I feel so guilty you must have used up all your precious rations on this!'

'What better way to use Auntie Tibby's sugar?' said Andrew cheerfully.

'And toffees!' cried Belle, pointing at the bowlful.

'My toffees?' Tibby roared with laughter. 'Come with me, Belle, we have a job to do.'

A few minutes later, they returned, bearing a cake on a tray between them. Everyone broke into a chorus of happy birthday as they placed it in front of Jeanie.

'Couldn't find any candles, I'm afraid,' said Tibby. 'But you can make a wish as you cut the cake.'

Rick saw Jeanie's eyes gleam with emotion. 'How kind!'

As she cut pieces and handed them round, Tom said, 'We have a present for you too.' He handed over a brown-paper package.

Jeanie unwrapped it to find a set of watercolour brushes and paints.

'To inspire you to paint again,' Tom said, smiling.

Jeanie appeared overwhelmed. Her chin trembled. She swallowed. 'Thank you,' she rasped. A tear spilled down her cheek.

'Auntie Jeanie, you're crying. Don't you like them?'

Jeanie cleared her throat. 'I love them. So kind and thoughtful.'

'Once your husband is back teaching in Ebbsmouth,' said Dawan, 'you are welcome to come here and paint in my studio on wet days.'

Rick saw her expression change. 'Oh, that's very generous, Mr Lal, but I have news to tell you all. I'm going back to India. My husband has been appointed headmaster of Nicholson's.'

'Headmaster?' repeated Tom. 'Finally got rid of old Bishop? Well, well.'

'You knew him?' Jeanie asked in surprise.

Looks were exchanged around the table. Andrew answered. 'I was at Nicholson's for a few years. I wasn't his favourite pupil, I'm afraid.'

'But that's wonderful news!' cried Stella, dispelling any awkwardness at the mention of Bishop. 'If you're in Murree, we'll be able to see each other.'

'You must visit us in Kashmir,' Andrew insisted. 'Or we can all meet up in Pindi.'

'I'd love that,' Jeanie said, smiling tearfully.

She glanced at Rick as she said it and he felt a jolt inside. It was just coincidence that she'd caught his look. He wasn't even going to be in Pindi in the future; he and Pamela would be living in far off Calcutta. A twist of regret tugged at his stomach. He was growing very fond of the Lomax family.

Stella was making enthusiastic plans. 'When are you returning? Have you booked your passage yet? We're sailing in late March. Wouldn't it be wonderful if you could book on the same boat!'

'Can Auntie Jeanie come and live with us, Mummy?' Belle asked.

'Not with us, sweetie,' said Stella, 'but we'll be living not far away so she can visit whenever she wants.'

'That's good,' Belle said, grinning.

'I'd like that too,' Jeanie replied, reaching across to squeeze the girl's hand. 'And I haven't booked a ship yet – I'm still trying to persuade my mother to come out to India with me.'

'I'll give you our details before you go home and see if we can travel together.'

After tea, they settled around the fire and Rick organised a raucous card game of 'snap' and then Tibby taught them 'old maid'. Belle sat in Jeanie's lap and together they shared their cards. There was much hilarity when Rick ended up as the old maid.

'Even old maids can be very good air force mechanics,' Jeanie teased.

'Mechanic? Is that what he told you he was?' Andrew said in amusement. 'Rick might be a mechanic in civilian life but he flew planes in the war.'

Jeanie gaped at Rick. 'You were a pilot?'

44

Rick gave a wry smile and nodded.

'Goodness!' Her eyes widened. He could see her reassessing him which made him uncomfortable.

'It was chaps like Rick who kept us troops supplied in Burma. We couldn't have won without them. They were the real unsung heroes.'

Rick was embarrassed to see Jeanie looking emotional again. 'Did you fly over the Arakan?' she asked.

'Yes,' he answered, knowing she must be thinking of her brother. 'We dropped food and medical supplies. Not as brave as the men on the ground.'

'You were damn brave!' Andrew said with vehemence. 'Flying your Dakotas so low you were brushing the treetops – and being fired on from both the ground and the air.'

'That must have taken a lot of courage,' Jeanie said, admiringly.

Rick shrugged. Stella ruffled his hair playfully.

'Don't be so modest, cousin,' she said. 'We're all very proud of you – and Auntie Rose is so pleased you're going to be flying commercial aeroplanes – even if Uncle Toby thinks you should be running the family garage.'

Rick gave a grunt of amusement. 'Mother's not so happy I'm going to be living in Calcutta.'

'None of us are,' said Stella.

Rick was aware of Jeanie's appraising blue eyes and wondered whether she disapproved of his decision to cut loose from his family.

Andrew slipped an arm around his wife. 'He's keeping his beloved fiancée happy. Isn't that a good enough reason?'

'I suppose so,' she conceded, laughing.

Soon afterwards, Jeanie got up. 'I mustn't leave Mother on her own any longer. I've had the most wonderful birthday party – thank you all so much for organising it. And for the presents.'

45

Stella wrote down the details of their return ship while Andrew helped Jeanie into her jacket. 'It's dark outside,' said Andrew. 'Where is your car?'

'I parked near the lodge house,' she admitted.

'Don't blame you,' laughed Tibby. 'The potholes in the drive are the size of craters.'

Impulsively, Rick said, 'Let me walk you to your car. I'm an expert now on where the potholes are.'

Jeanie looked surprised but smiled in acceptance. 'Thank you.'

After cheerful goodbyes and promises to see one another again soon, Jeanie stepped into the dark with Rick at her side. Rick felt a sense of excitement that he couldn't explain. Jeanie wasn't conventionally pretty but there was something very attractive about her; a warmth of personality and a lack of sophistication that he liked. She drew people to her in the way that Stella did; spontaneously and without guile. Being with her had made the afternoon pass quickly and pleasantly.

The uneven track was turning icy with the dropping temperature and Jeanie took his proffered arm as they negotiated the first large pothole.

'Still waiting to go to Yorkshire?' she asked. 'I hope that doesn't mean that your fiancée and her family are still unwell.'

He felt a twinge of guilt at the sudden mention of Pamela. 'Pammy is better but not her mother so I've been told to stay away a bit longer.'

'I'm sorry,' Jeanie murmured. 'How frustrating.'

'And how do you feel about going back to India?' Rick deflected her questioning.

She paused before answering. 'Shocked at first. I had no idea Mungo was thinking of staying on at Nicholson's. But the more I've got used to the idea the more excited I am. I loved Murree before the war.' She hesitated. 'Of course, it

46

may be very different now – and things in India are a bit uncertain, aren't they? I remember you saying so, the last time we met. Mother is using that as an excuse not to go with me, though Mungo says it's all a fuss about nothing.' She turned to look at him. 'What do you think?'

'About you going back?' Rick asked in surprise.

'No, not about me.' She sounded amused. 'About the situation in India? I've been reading up about it and from what I can gather, things seem to be hardening between Congress and the Muslim League over the future.'

'Sounds like you are more informed about Indian politics than me,' he admitted ruefully. 'It's probably just politicians jockeying for position. In the Indian Air Force, we all got along fine, whatever our background. I can't see why it won't be like that post-war too.'

'Good,' she said. 'I like a fellow optimist.'

Soon they were at the end of the drive and Jeanie was disengaging her arm and searching her pocket for the car key.

He held open the driver's door. 'Ah, a Hillman Minx. Lovely condition.'

Jeanie smiled. 'That's because it hardly gets used and Mother doesn't drive. I like to polish it once a week and think of family expeditions before the war.' She put out her hand to shake his. 'Thanks for walking me here, Mr Dixon.'

He pulled off his glove and took her hand. 'Pleasure Mrs Munro. Good luck with persuading your mother to go with you.'

Abruptly, she said, 'I miss John so very much. Going back to India gives me comfort that I'll feel closer to him there. I don't feel any sense of him here. If Mother came, we could try and visit his grave in the Arakan …'

Rick squeezed her arm. 'Tell her how you feel. And if she won't go to Burma with you then Andrew probably would. So do it anyway.'

He saw her eyes glitter in the light from inside the car. He let go her arm and she quickly climbed into the driver's seat. 'I hope you are reunited with Pamela soon. Goodbye, Rick.'

He waved her away and walked briskly back down the drive, pondering the sudden intensity of their final conversation and her use of his first name. Had she spoken so frankly with anyone else about this deepest of reasons for returning to India; the desire to pay her final respects to her brother at his resting place? It struck him that Stella was right about Jeanie being lonely here. This was the sort of thing she must want to discuss with Mungo.

He found Stella waiting for him at the entrance. Rick said, 'Mrs Munro is safely dispatched.'

He knew that look in his cousin's eyes. 'She's a married woman, Rick,' she said pointedly. 'I hope you weren't flirting with her.'

Rick gave an embarrassed snort. 'No flirting, I promise. I'm soon to be happily married too, remember?'

'Quite!' she said, patting him on the cheek.

They returned inside arm in arm. Rick felt rightly rebuked. He hadn't said or done anything remotely improper but he had spent far too much time that afternoon engaging with Jeanie and enjoying her company. The sooner he got on with his new life the better. He would write to Pamela at once and insist that he was coming to Yorkshire whether her father wanted it or not.

Chapter 6

Rowan House, February

Not only had Jeanie failed to persuade her mother to return to India but she had lost a further battle – the method of travel.

'Why delay your reunion with Mungo by going by ship?' Clara had questioned. 'I'll pay for you to fly and then you'll be there in a matter of days.'

'But the expense …?'

'I can afford it – especially as I won't be paying for my own passage. Surely you want to be back at Nicholson's with your husband as soon as possible and in time for the start of the new term?'

'Of course, but–'

'Well then, that's settled.' Clara was firm. 'I'd be much happier to think of you flying than going by sea. They say there are so many unexploded mines through the Mediterranean that it's much safer by air.'

Jeanie hadn't been able to argue with that. She suspected that her mother's real reason for buying her an air ticket was to prevent any plan for her to travel with the Lomaxes on a three-week voyage. She couldn't get to the bottom of why her mother was so against the Lomax family – it just seemed like petty jealousy – but it was easier just to go along with what Clara had decided.

As the date of departure grew closer, Jeanie couldn't voice her nervousness at returning to India. Part of her yearned to be with Mungo as soon as she could but she was also apprehensive at the thought. They had been apart for so long and neither of them would be the same people who had kissed goodbye on the Bombay dockside.

Jeanie hadn't lain with another man since leaving India, but had her husband remained faithful to her? She remembered their energetic lovemaking with pleasure – Mungo was a man of routine and liked to engage in it twice weekly – so how had he managed for nearly seven years without her? Could she blame him if he had sought comfort elsewhere? After all, she was the one who had caused them to live apart for so long.

Jeanie tried to dismiss such thoughts. She would never ask him about anything so intimate. As her friend Irene would say when embarking on another casual liaison after some local dance: '*What happens in the war, stays in the war, duckie!*'

In five days' time, Jeanie would be setting off on her eastward journey; a train to London and then flights to Rome, Cairo, Karachi and finally Lahore, where Mungo would be waiting for her. Her stomach somersaulted every time she thought of it. She had sent word to Stella that she would not be travelling with them and hadn't arranged to see them again. She wanted to spend her last days in Scotland with her mother and not antagonise her by going off to see the Lomaxes.

Only to herself could Jeanie admit that she was wary about visiting the Anchorage in case Rick was still there. Seeing him on her birthday, she had felt an instant connection as if they had always been friends. He was so easy-going and amusing – a lady's man she was sure – but there was an underlying modesty and kindness about him too. He was lovely with Belle who obviously doted on her Uncle Rick.

To discover he had been a pilot and veteran of the Burma campaigns, had been startling. To think that he had probably flown over the Arakan and dropped vital supplies to her brother battling below, had made her feel closer to Rick. Had

John looked up into those same skies – the last he would ever see – and been encouraged by the sight of help arriving? Useless to speculate on such things and nothing had prevented John's death.

Yet talking to Rick about her brother and her desire to see where he was buried had eased her loss a fraction. Rick had understood. So why had she unburdened herself to a man she hardly knew when she couldn't even talk about it with her own mother? Jeanie didn't like to dwell on her motives. Best that she forgot the handsome pilot and trained her thoughts on the future – on Mungo and India.

One thing that had improved since her acceptance to fly east was her fraught relationship with her mother. Clara had been less censorious and more open to taking walks in the frosty February air. Jeanie sometimes coaxed a smile from her with chatter about her ack-ack friends. They even talked occasionally about her father and John – or rather Clara didn't object when Jeanie reminisced about them.

Many times, when on leave and since John's death, Jeanie had sought comfort in his old bedroom. She would sit at his neat desk surrounded by orderly shelves of nature books and his map-covered walls. Their mother had kept everything as it was.

With two days to go before departure, Jeanie slipped into John's room. She picked up a large pinkish stone that he'd used as a paperweight and remembered how she'd found it on the beach at Ebbsmouth and given it to him to add to his collection of stones and fossils.

'What are you doing in here?' She spun round at the sound of her mother's accusatory tone.

Jeanie stood her ground. 'I often come in here. I'm saying goodbye.'

For a moment, Clara's face was taut with disapproval. Then abruptly, her expression softened. She nodded and

51

came further into the room. 'I sometimes come in here too,' she admitted.

Jeanie watched her smooth down the counterpane on the bed. It was such a tender gesture that her heart went out to her unhappy mother. When Clara sat down on the bed, Jeanie joined her.

'John always kept his room so tidy compared to mine, didn't he?' Jeanie said with a wry smile.

'Yes,' Clara agreed.

'Remember when he used to ask Dad to do mock inspections,' Jeanie continued, 'and he'd lay out his clothes and polish his shoes like a real soldier?'

Clara allowed herself a smile. 'Your father was so proud when he joined the Borderers.'

'There was never any doubt that he would, surely?' Jeanie queried.

Her mother sighed. 'I hoped he might pursue his love of the outdoors – botany and geology – perhaps go into teaching.'

Jeanie was astonished. 'But I thought you were just as keen for him to follow Dad into the Army?'

Clara shook her head. 'Not really. I was proud too, of course, but I didn't want the same for John. Too much danger – and ...'

'And what?' Jeanie prompted.

With an effort her mother added, 'Too hard on a wife.'

Jeanie scrutinised her. Clara had never complained about her marriage before; all her criticism had always been directed at India.

'But you never regretted marrying Dad, did you?'

Clara didn't answer directly. 'I wish he hadn't been in the army.'

Jeanie was shocked by her mother's admission, but sensing she wanted to say more, Jeanie kept silent.

Quietly, Clara said, 'It took its toll on me. The babies I lost.'

Jeanie's heart thudded. 'Babies?'

'Before you were born. I lost three baby boys. They came before their time.'

Jeanie saw tears welling in her mother's eyes and quickly squeezed her hand. 'Mother, I had no idea. How very terrible for you.'

Clara struggled to control her emotions. 'That's why losing John has been so – so – devastating. The last of my boys.'

'Of course,' Jeanie said, a lump forming in her throat. 'I quite understand.'

'No,' Clara whispered, 'you can't understand. You haven't carried life inside you that you've lost, time and time again.'

Jeanie winced. 'No, I didn't mean–'

'I worry for you, Jeanie. In case you've left it too late to have children. You should have gone back to Mungo sooner.' Clara withdrew her hand.

'I'm only thirty-three!' Jeanie tried to make light of it. 'Still time to make you a grandmother.'

Clara met her gaze and her look softened. 'I hope so. You will make a good mother, Jeanie.'

Jeanie felt her chest constrict. 'Thank you.'

'A better one than I have.'

'Don't say that. You've always cared for us–'

'No Jeanie, I haven't always been kind to you and for that I'm sorry.'

As they sat side by side, Jeanie didn't know what to say, not wanting to break the spell of intimacy between them and yet unable to deny what her mother had said. She was sure that Clara cared for her but knew that her mother could never love her as much as she had John. Perhaps the bond between

53

mother and son was especially strong? Or was it because her mother had seen in John a precious glimpse of what might have been had her other sons lived? Impossible to know.

'Will you promise me something, Mother?'

Clara gave her a wary look.

'If I give you a grandchild, will you come out to India to see us?'

Her mother smiled. 'I think I could promise that.'

'Good.' Jeanie leaned over and kissed her cheek before she could move out of the way.

Her mother stood up and smoothed down her skirt. Just then, Jeanie remembered something.

'That nurse in Peshawar; was she anything to do with the babies who died?'

Clara looked at her in alarm. 'Nurse? What nurse?'

'The one John met. He mentioned her to me in Rawalpindi. Said she wanted to be remembered to you.'

Clara put her hand to her throat in a flustered gesture. 'He said nothing to me.'

Jeanie tried to recall. 'Some name like Armistead … or Armitage.'

Her mother tensed and her expression was once again guarded. 'No, that means nothing to me.'

'Never mind.' Jeanie let the matter drop. She didn't want to pry too much. It was enough that her mother had taken her into her confidence about her marriage and past losses. They had never had such a frank conversation.

As she followed her mother out of the bedroom, Jeanie felt closer to Clara than she had done in years. How sad that it took their imminent parting to bring them together again. Yet it gave her hope for the future. Her mother had all but promised to come and visit her in India. Maybe then, she could persuade her to stay and they could strengthen these tentative bonds of love.

54

***

Two days later, Jeanie and Clara stood on the station platform in Ebbsmouth as flurries of snow fell from a leaden sky and an icy wind blew in from the sea. Jeanie was travelling with one suitcase and a large travel bag, while a trunkful of clothes had been dispatched by sea.

Clara's thin face was pinched and almost blue under her black felt hat.

'Shall we go in the waiting-room, Mother?' Jeanie asked in concern.

Her mother shook her head. 'Don't want to miss the train, do you?'

They both stamped their feet to keep the blood circulating.

'It's hard to remember what the heat of India is like when it's so cold here. I bet I'll be longing for Scottish weather when I'm baking hot again.'

'You won't be too hot in the hills,' said Clara. 'Probably still be snowing when you get to Murree.'

'That's true.'

'Or it could be heavy rain. I hope you've packed enough warm clothes.'

Jeanie exclaimed, 'Listen to the pair of us! We're about to be parted for goodness knows how long and all we can talk about is the weather.'

Her mother huffed in semi-amusement. 'We've said all that needs to be said.'

Jeanie felt that they hadn't. Since her mother had confided in her about the lost babies, she had avoided any intimate conversation. Jeanie had tried to ask her more about her years in India as an army wife, but Clara had put her off.

55

'I don't see why you're so interested. It's all in the past. It was mostly hot and tedious – not an interesting life at all.'

The train arriving, prevented Jeanie from asking any last-minute questions.

There was sudden activity on the station platform, with people alighting from the train and others clambering on with luggage. The porter that Clara had paid to carry on Jeanie's heavy case appeared. As he took charge of her luggage, Jeanie turned to her mother and grabbed her in a hug, kissing her cold cheek.

'I'll miss you, Mother,' she said tearfully.

Clara's eyes brimmed with tears but Jeanie couldn't tell if it was just from the cold.

'God keep you safe, Jeanie,' she said. For a brief moment, she raised her gloved hands and cupped them around her daughter's face in a gesture of tenderness. Then she was gently pushing her away. 'On you go, lassie.'

Jeanie's throat was so tight with emotion that she couldn't even manage a goodbye. She nodded and hurried towards the open carriage door. Moments later, there was a slamming of doors and whistles blowing. The train shunted forward.

Jeanie rubbed at the steamed-up window for a final glimpse of her mother. She expected that Clara would already be walking away but through the billowing engine smoke, she saw her mother waving. Jeanie let go a sob as she waved back. She had a sense of foreboding that she would never see her mother again. However difficult their relationship had been over the years; Jeanie still loved her mother. Clara had always provided a safe haven for her to return to during the war and cared for her in a practical way. Surely that showed that she was loved in return?

As Jeanie wiped her tears away, she clung on to the hope that her mother would one day come out to India – and prove that she did indeed love her daughter.

Chapter 7

Punjab, India, late February

Jeanie's heart was palpitating as she alighted from the plane at the Walton airstrip, outside Lahore. The midday air was springlike – almost hot – and she was already sweating, even though she'd changed into a summer dress in Karachi for the final flight of the four-day journey. Strong sunlight momentarily blinded her.

She had a sudden panic that she wouldn't recognise Mungo. She'd travelled with the old photograph she had of him in her handbag and gazed at it often, re-committing every feature to memory. But what if he had gone bald or put on weight? Or perhaps he'd grown much thinner and sunken-cheeked? He hadn't been one to send her photos of himself. He'd been forty-five when she'd left him; at the beginning of March he'd be turning fifty-two. Then she chided herself for such thoughts. In a few minutes she would be reunited with her beloved husband – the moment she had longed for these past difficult years – and it didn't matter what he looked like.

In the terminal, as her eyes adapted to the gloom, she saw a tall man in blazer and pale trousers striding towards her. His brown fedora cast a shadow over his face but she knew at once from the vigorous walk that it was Mungo. She felt a wave of relief and raised her hand in greeting. For a moment he hesitated, then he waved back. Seconds later, he was standing before her, smiling.

'Jean!'

'Mungo!' Heart pounding, she attempted a hug but the handbag and jacket that were slung over her arms, got in the way.

He gave her a peck on the cheek.

'You've grown a moustache!' she cried.

He pulled at its edges. 'Goodness, I've had this for ages.'

'Really? You never said …'

He offered her his arm. 'Come on, Mrs Munro. Humza has tiffin prepared. We'll stop and eat it on the way.'

Jeanie linked arms happily, glad that Mungo didn't want to delay in getting her home. From the first snatched impression – apart from the rather military moustache – he appeared much the same. He rattled out questions.

'Are you hungry? How was your journey? All the flights on time?'

'Yes, no real holdups. And yours?' she asked.

He grunted. 'Hardly comparable.'

'No, but I was wondering about the roads … whether there's still snow in the hills …'

'Yes, there is. Little bit tricky. But I managed fine.'

'Good.' After a pause, she asked, 'how long will it take us to drive up to Murree?'

He shot her a look. 'Don't you remember?'

'I've never driven there,' she reminded him. 'Before the war, we went by train to Pindi, then Mr Bishop sent a car for us.'

His answer was brisk. 'Well, it'll take a few hours but if we hurry, we'll be there by nightfall.'

Spotting his bearer, Mungo disengaged his arm and set about supervising the retrieval and transfer of Jeanie's case to the car. Jeanie greeted Humza and received a dignified bow from the thin, sparse-haired servant. A man of few words, he treated her to one of his rare smiles when she asked after his family.

'They are very well, thank you, Memsahib.'

Within minutes, they were on the road; she sitting up front while Mungo drove and Humza sat in the back nursing the tiffin baskets. Jean slid a look at her husband, his large hands firmly gripping the steering wheel, his hat now discarded on the back seat. In profile, she could see that the lines around his eyes and mouth had deepened and the skin sagged a little at the jawline. Yet it was a noble profile – the nose straight and cheekbone pronounced – and his hair was still thick, though it had gone completely grey. She wasn't sure about the moustache. It made him look older, like a retired major.

As they headed onto the Grand Trunk Road going north, Jeanie answered his questions about her mother and home, cringing at their stilted conversation. It was as if they were two acquaintances forced into a long car journey together and struggling to find things to say. But, of course, it would be like this to begin with while they got to know each other again.

As the questions dried up, she took to staring out at the passing scenery of trees already in blossom, and the sight of men on bicycles weaving around other cars and bullock-drawn carts. She wound down the window to allow air into the stuffy car.

'It's all so green here,' she said, peering out and shading her eyes from the glare. 'And the light – it's dazzling, isn't it?'

'Make the most of the warmth now,' said Mungo. 'It's still hardly above freezing in Murree.'

'Then I'll capture it in my mind's eye and paint it later.'

'Paint it?' he queried.

'Yes, I've taken up dabbling in watercolours again. Some friends gave me paints for my birthday – the people I told you about who own The Raj Hotels in Pindi and Kashmir.'

'The Lomaxes?'

'Yes. They're such a nice family–'

'I've made enquiries about them and they're not exactly *top drawer*.' She heard the disapproval in his voice. 'Tom

59

Lomax is a failed soldier turned hotelier who goes through wives like Henry the Eighth.'

'Mungo, that's just gossip!' she laughed. 'I found him charming. And his son, Andrew, too.'

'Did you know,' his voice hardened, 'that Lomax Junior was expelled from Nicholson's for nearly killing a boy?'

'Goodness, no!' Jeanie was shocked. 'I can't believe that.'

He shot her a look. 'Well, it's true. Captain Rae, our games master, told me.'

'Perhaps he was exaggerating?'

'I doubt it,' Mungo retorted. 'He was the one pulled young Lomax off the other boy and stopped an even worse beating, so he ought to know. It was before my time, of course, but from what I've heard, Andrew Lomax was a little savage.'

Jeanie was about to protest that Andrew was a war hero who had been a close friend of John's, but something made her hold back. She recalled the awkward looks that had passed between the Lomaxes at the mention of Nicholson's and how Andrew had swiftly changed the conversation. Perhaps there was some truth to Mungo's story. She was uncomfortable that her husband had been checking up on the Lomaxes but even more dismayed at the story of Andrew's violence. But Captain Rae might well have been exaggerating; she remembered him as someone prone to gossip. Besides, the last thing she wanted was to disagree with Mungo within the first couple of hours of their being reunited – nor did she want to argue in front of Humza. Abruptly, Jeanie dropped the subject.

'Tell me about Nicholson's and the new job,' she urged. 'I'm so proud of you. I want to hear everything.'

He smiled at that. 'There's a lot to be done. Bishop let things slide during the war. It was difficult to keep things going, what with younger members of staff leaving to join up and some of the boys stuck in Britain at the start. But numbers soon went up again when boys were evacuated from Britain and we had to bring teachers out of retirement. Parents were glad of the stability and moral leadership we were providing their sons amid all the horror. It'll be a challenge now that the war's over. Some of the buildings are quite dilapidated – it's been make-do-and-mend for quite a while. Bishop has lost the stomach for it – or at least his wife has. They're still in the town but are packing up to leave before the monsoon. I've spent most of the long winter holiday getting the place patched up and ready. Boys are back now; we've been up and running for a week.'

'So, you're not worried about the uncertainty?' Jeanie queried.

He frowned. 'Meaning?'

'With all this talk of India going independent.'

He was dismissive. 'I can see you've been filling your head full of alarmist nonsense from the British press and the Atlee government.'

'Is it nonsense? The national elections here showed a real appetite for the parties demanding independence.'

'That's a long way off.' He was dismissive. 'A bit of Home Rule perhaps. But it won't change things in hill stations like Murree or schools like Nicholson's. The rich rajas and nawabs want a British education for their sons as much as our colonial administrators do.'

'That's good.' she smiled.

He put a hand out and patted her knee. 'So, you're not to worry about such things, my dear. I've got ambitious plans for Nicholson's – and you're going to be at my side for all of it. Isn't that exciting? You'll adore living in the headmaster's house – twice the size of our old home and with a wonderful big garden.'

61

'Yes,' said Jeanie, 'I remember the lovely garden.'

'Perfect for a family.' Mungo smiled and gave her knee another pat.

Jeanie felt a jolt of excitement at his alluding to them having children. It seemed he was as eager as she was for them to be intimate again.

'And,' he went on, 'you can decorate the drawing-room and dining-room to your taste – within budget, of course. The dining table's enormous – seats up to fourteen, so you'll be able to entertain more than we used to. You'll like that, won't you?'

'Yes, I will,' Jeanie agreed, a little surprised. Mungo had never been keen on dinner parties or socialising in large numbers. Perhaps he saw it as part of his new duties as a headmaster. She let the thought pass. She was going to throw herself into her new role as headmaster's wife with enthusiasm. For too long she had been out of the school environment – out of Mungo's life – and she wanted to belong there once again.

'Perhaps I could chat with Mrs Bishop before they go,' she suggested. 'She might have wise words on what I should expect – and what will be expected of me.'

Mungo nodded in approval. 'That might be a good idea. She can tell you all the foibles of the servants and how to handle them – that sort of thing.'

'That's not exactly what I meant,' Jeanie said. 'More what my role will be within the school – pastoral care of the boys – that sort of thing.'

He flicked her a look and laughed. 'Jean, dear; I do all of that, so there's no need for you to concern yourself. If you're unsure about how a headmaster's wife should behave, then there's no need. I'll be the one to guide you on such matters.'

She felt a stab of disappointment at his words; she wanted to be involved in looking after the pupils, especially those who might be feeling homesick or suffering bereavement from the recent war. She thought she could be helpful with that. Jeanie knew that men like Mungo had been schooled in believing that to show emotion was weak – it was somehow letting the side down – but she had never held to that view. She'd seen in her own mother how bottling up feelings had just led to deeper distress. She should have tried harder to get Clara to unburden her grief over John, sooner. It pained her to think it might be years until she saw her mother again.

The conversation in the car petered out. Mungo seemed happy just to drive and Jeanie dozed, succumbing to a wave of tiredness. She woke when they stopped for tiffin by the roadside. Shooing away a gaggle of children who were staring with amused curiosity at the new arrivals, Humza spread out a rug, dispensed sweet milky tea from a flask and handed out soggy egg and tomato sandwiches, and stale scones with gingery-tasting jam. Jeanie chewed, silently comparing them to the soft and fluffy scones she'd had on her birthday at The Anchorage. Obviously, the cook at the headmaster's house was not as skilled as the one they'd had in the staff quarters before the war.

She gulped at the tea which was surprisingly refreshing, though she normally drank it black.

'This reminds me of the tea Irene used to brew in the army,' she said. 'Tinned milk – and as much sugar as she could scrounge.'

'Irene?' Mungo queried.

'Yes, my best friend in the ack-acks,' Jeanie reminded. 'I told you about her in my letters.'

'Ah, yes, you did. The one from Wales?'

'London,' she corrected. 'The Welsh one was Phyllis. She was lance corporal – our Number One – a spotter for enemy planes. Irene was Number Seven – one of the radar crew

63

pinpointing enemy planes. I was Number Nine, in charge of the generator. But you know all about that.'

Mungo nodded but didn't ask any more. He wolfed down three sandwiches and two scones. Wiping a fleck of egg from his moustache with a napkin, he said, 'I don't want to rush you, my dear, but I'd rather we didn't linger. I need to be back for evening prayers in chapel and a meeting with my prefects.'

Jeanie was happy of the excuse to abandon her half-eaten scone, though she was disappointed that Mungo would have duties to attend to on their first evening together. As she got back into the car, she had a sudden craving for a cigarette. It must have been thinking about Irene and the old army days, as that was the only period in her life that she had smoked. *It's very unladylike to smoke, don't do you think?'* She remembered Mungo saying so when he was courting her, and in those days she had agreed.

'Would you like me to drive?' she offered. He gave her sceptical look. 'I got quite good at it during the war,' she insisted.

'Not on Indian roads,' he said. 'You're not familiar with the route or the car, so I think it's safer if I drive, don't you?' She must have shown her disappointment because he quickly added, 'But thank you; maybe another time, my dear.'

As they drove on across a rather monotonous dun-coloured plain, Jeanie wound up the window against the dust and grew drowsy. Soon, with the gentle rocking and bumping of the speeding car, she succumbed to sleep.

She was jolted awake by the car suddenly breaking and spinning. It lurched across the road, clipping a low wall. As it came to an abrupt standstill, Jeanie grabbed at the dashboard to stop herself pitching forward but one of the tiffin baskets came hurtling from behind and struck the back of her head. She cried out.

'My God!' Mungo shouted. 'Are you alright?'

Jeanie clutched her head. Mungo turned in fury. 'You blithering idiot, Humza!'

'Sorry, Memsahib!' Humza sprang out of the car and opened Jeanie's door, leaning in to retrieve the basket. 'Sorry, sorry.'

'I'm okay,' Jeanie said, shaken.

Mungo was out of the car now too, barging the servant out of the way to reach in and help Jeanie. She stepped shakily from the passenger seat.

'Are you sure you're alright?'

'Yes, really. It was just the shock.' She turned to the bearer. 'Are you okay, Humza?'

He nodded, his face a picture of concern.

'Don't worry about him,' said Mungo. 'He's tough as old boots. Aren't you, Humza?' He nodded again in agreement.

'What happened?' Jeanie asked, still feeling dizzy.

Mungo surveyed the car. 'Looks like a burst tyre. And dammit all; the front left headlamp is smashed.'

'Well, everyone is fine,' said Jeanie, 'and that's what matters.'

Mungo gave a huff of impatience. 'It's not all that matters. I can't drive in the dark without headlights.'

'But won't we be back in Murree before dark?'

'Maybe not now.' He kicked the flat tyre in frustration.

Ignoring the growing throbbing in her head, she asked, 'Where's the jack? I can help you change the wheel.'

Mungo looked aghast. 'Certainly not. You've had a bad shock. We men will do it. Come on, Humza; help me get this off.'

Jeanie stood and watched as they wrestled with the jack and freeing the damaged wheel. To her, it looked like the tyre was badly worn and that it wouldn't have taken much for it to be punctured. She itched to help them – they were taking an age to get the spare tyre in place – but thought that Mungo would just be annoyed. He was swearing away under his breath and blaming Humza for the amount of time it was taking. A bullock cart trundled by with a cheery cry from the driver and a couple of bicyclists stopped and offered to help but Mungo waved them all away.

By the time the car was roadworthy again, the sun had already lost its strength.

'How far away from home are we?' Jeanie asked.

'Still about three hours,' Mungo said with a sigh. 'We must be about half an hour from Rawalpindi. We could drive in the dark if the lamp wasn't smashed – but at this rate we'll have no option but to stay the night somewhere.'

Jeanie's heart sank at the possibility of their getting to Murree being delayed. She was dreaming of sinking into their marital bed together and falling asleep in her husband's arms. Then she had a sudden thought. 'Dixon's Garage! In Pindi. It has a very good reputation. Perhaps they could do a quick repair.'

'How on earth do you know about garages in Pindi?' Mungo looked incredulous.

'It's run by cousins of Stella's – Stella Lomax. In fact, one of her cousins was staying at The Anchorage when I visited.'

'Well, that's hardly a recommendation and I've never heard of them.'

'It might be worth a try,' Jeanie encouraged. 'If it means we get home tonight.'

'I suppose so.' He still looked undecided.

Humza spoke up. 'Dixon's Garage is good, Sahib. Pukka reputation.'

For all he had spent the past hour lambasting his bearer, Mungo seemed to take note of the man's opinion on such matters.

'Very well,' he agreed. 'We'll head for Pindi and track down these Dixons.'

Chapter 8

Rawalpindi

As they crossed a churning brown river over a cantilever bridge, Jeanie saw the town emerge out of the plain, its distant temple roofs and domes catching the glow of early evening light. They drove through a wooded area and then the outskirts gave way to tree-lined streets as they entered a vast army cantonment. The roads were busy with traffic – army trucks, cars, tongas and bicycles – and Jeanie saw Mungo grip the steering wheel as he narrowly avoided a milk cart.

'Where is this Dixon's Garage?' he asked.

'I've no idea,' said Jeanie.

'Humza, I'm asking you!'

Jeanie turned to see the servant shrug. 'In the cantonment, Sahib; not the old city.'

'That's not very helpful,' Mungo muttered.

'Why don't we stop and ask the way?' Jeanie suggested.

'I'll find it,' Mungo said.

They drove around aimlessly, Mungo growing increasingly irate and blaring his horn at pedestrians stepping out in front of the car. Jeanie resisted the urge to jump out and ask for directions and stared out of the window, curious to see something of the garrison town as they trundled past endless rows of brick barracks – some made pretty by neat flowerbeds – and imposing churches and municipal buildings. Eventually, she recognised where they were.

'Look, there's the Mall! We must be very near the Raj Hotel.'

'Is it near Dixon's?' asked Mungo.

'Possibly. After all, they are close family to the Duboises who run the hotel. We could go to the Raj and ask.'

Mungo gave a sigh of impatience and abruptly stopped the car.

'Humza, get out and ask a local for directions,' he ordered.

The bearer scrambled out of the car and hailed an Indian youth on a bicycle. As they conversed, Mungo drummed his fingers on the steering wheel and Jeanie silently prayed that Humza would be quick.

'I should just have pressed on for Murree,' Mungo fretted. 'We'd be half-way up the mountain by now if I hadn't listened to you.'

Jeanie flushed. 'Better to be safe, don't you think?'

His reply was cut short by Humza's return. 'He will show us the way, Sahib. We must follow.'

'How kind,' Jeanie said, with a wave of relief.

The boy turned around his bicycle and waited for Mungo to do the same with the car, then they doubled back the way they had come into the army cantonment. They passed many of the streets that they had driven around before but gradually the roads became narrower and even busier, lined with more densely packed housing and shops, and where the population looked more Indian.

At the end of a street, the cyclist stopped and pointed to a large building with a pillared front and a metal sign above the open entrance proclaiming, 'Dixon's Garage'. Mungo pulled in alongside.

'Give the boy something,' Jeanie prompted. But the youth was waving goodbye and disappearing back down the street before Mungo was out of the car.

'Stay here, while I find a mechanic,' he said, closing the driver's door behind him.

Jeanie peered out in frustration. Very soon, a young man emerged out of the gloom of the garage and greeted Mungo with a smile. Jeanie's insides fluttered; his smile was just like Rick's. But the similarity was fleeting. This man had curly hair and a thinner face – slimmer altogether – yet she was sure this must be the brother. He came over to look at the smashed headlamp and prodded the tyres. Jeanie smiled out of the window and he nodded politely. Returning to Mungo, the man gave a regretful shrug and as he talked, she could see her husband growing agitated.

Swiftly, Jeanie climbed out of the car and went to join the men.

Mungo said in annoyance, 'He says he won't be able to fix it till tomorrow.'

'I'm sorry,' the mechanic said, 'we have several jobs still to do. But I can get to work on it early tomorrow.'

'We need to get back to Murree tonight!' Mungo said sharply. 'Don't you have others who can help? I came to you by recommendation and I don't expect to be let down.'

'I could lend you a car.'

'That doesn't solve anything. I'd have to drive back down and waste a further day.'

Jeanie stepped forward. 'You must be Sigmund Dixon?'

His brown eyes widened. 'Yes, I am.'

She held out her hand. 'I'm Mrs Munro. I'm friends with your cousin Stella.'

'You know Stella?' He beamed, shaking her hand warmly.

'Yes, and I've also met your brother Rick when he was staying with the Lomaxes in Scotland.'

'Rick! How is he?'

'He was very well when I last saw him. By now he'll be back in Yorkshire with his fiancée.'

'Ah, the beautiful Pammy,' Sigmund said with a grin. 'My brother always lands on his feet.'

Jeanie could sense Mungo's impatience, so she swiftly said, 'The thing is, Mr Dixon, I've just spent four days flying back from Britain and then we've had this long car journey and I'm longing to get back home to Murree.' She put a hand on Mungo's arm. 'This is the first day we've been together for over six years. Is there any way you could manage to do the repair so we could get home tonight?'

Sigmund gaped. 'Goodness! When you put it like that, of course you must take priority. And I'd do anything for a friend of Stella's.'

'Thank you,' said Jeanie gratefully, 'that would be most kind.'

'Yes, thank you,' Mungo added, a little stiffly. 'Have you a waiting room we can use while you get on with it?'

'We can do better than that,' Sigmund answered. 'You must come upstairs. Mother will give you tea – and my sister Ada is visiting – she'll want to hear all about how the Lomaxes are and what our brother is up to.'

'We couldn't possibly impose,' said Mungo.

'I insist,' said Sigmund.

'Well, if you're sure,' Jeanie replied, 'then we'd be very grateful.'

He nodded. 'Of course! I'd be in the dog-house with Ma if I didn't bring you upstairs for a bit of Dixon hospitality. Sir; if you give me the key, I'll bring the car inside and give your servant some chai in the back. Come, come; follow me.'

Sigmund led them round the side of the building and mounted a flight of outside steps, leading up to a balconied upper floor. Flowerpots lined the staircase and the front door was painted a cheerful sky-blue. Sigmund barged in, shouting their arrival and was soon introducing them enthusiastically to his mother, a stout woman with neatly coiffured grey hair and his sister, Ada, an attractive dark-haired woman about Jeanie's age. A pretty, dark-eyed girl of about three or four, clung to her mother's stylish dress and was introduced as June but was too shy to say hello.

'Mr and Mrs Munro are friends of Stella and Rick's. They've had an accident on their way up to Murree, so I'm fixing the car–'

'An accident?' Mrs Dixon cried in horror. 'Are you alright?'

'Perfectly,' Mungo said, smiling. 'Nothing to worry about. There's really no need for any fuss.'

'Of course there must be a fuss! Please come and sit down. Make yourselves comfortable. Or would you like to freshen up? Ada; show our guests the bathroom. I'll tell Noor to make tea.'

Jeanie followed Ada, curious to see more of Rick's former home. The flat was deceptively spacious with high ceilings and white-washed walls hung with gilded mirrors and paintings of British landscapes. Back in the sitting-room, she noticed a large framed photograph of Rick in uniform that stood in pride of place on a table crammed with family photos. She gave her husband a cautious glance, wondering if he'd ever been into an Anglo-Indian home before – she certainly hadn't – and hoping he wouldn't show any of his disdain for them.

To her surprise, Mungo was chatting easily with Ada and had managed to entice the bashful June from hiding behind her mother. He was showing the girl his pocket watch.

'Press that to open it. See? You try.' He held it out.

June touched it tentatively. Mungo helped her open the case. She stared at the watch and then up at the visitor. He held it to her ear.

'Do you hear that? Tick-tock. Can you tell the time?'

'I'm afraid she hasn't the first idea about that,' Ada laughed and June quickly scuttled back to her mother and buried her face in her lap.

'Plenty of time for learning later,' Mungo smiled. 'Tell me more about your husband's work, Mrs Gibson. Does he enjoy working in the Posts and Telegraphs Department?'

'Very much,' said Ada, 'though he's worried about this threatened general strike.'

'What general strike?' Jeanie asked, sitting down beside Mungo.

'Oh, just a handful of agitators trying to stir up trouble,' Mungo said dismissively. 'Communist babus in Calcutta mostly.'

'And a sailors' mutiny in Bombay,' Ada added, putting a protective hand on her daughter's head. 'They're not all hotheads.'

'What's it all about?' Jeanie asked.

'Putting those men on trial,' Ada replied. 'The ones from the Indian National Army.'

'Traitors, more like!' Mungo protested. 'They fought for the Japs against their own country. We have to make an example of them if we don't want lawlessness to spread.'

'I quite agree,' said Ada. 'But it doesn't stop me worrying. And Clive, my husband, says there is more popular support for the men on trial than we hear about in the newspapers.'

'You really mustn't worry about it, Mrs Gibson,' Mungo reassured her. 'British justice will prevail.'

Rose Dixon bustled back in. 'Quite right, Mr Munro. We mustn't worry.' She shot Ada a warning look. 'Or talk about such things with our guests. Gloomy-doomy. What will they think of us Dixons? Now, tea is on its way. I wish my husband was here to meet you but he's had to drive a car up to the brewery at Ghora Gali. I hope he'll be back before you go.'

'I'm sorry to miss him too,' said Mungo, 'but you really mustn't go to any trouble to give us tea.'

'No trouble at all,' cried Rose. 'It is our pleasure.'

Moments later, their bearer appeared with a large tray stacked with cups, saucers, plates, tea knives, a silver tea set and finger bowls. Following behind, was another servant carrying a tiered cake stand laden with samosas, sandwiches, slices of fruit cake and fairy cakes with butter icing. They set the table and Rose invited her guests to sit around it.

'Noor, please hand round the plates,' said Rose, 'and I'll pour the tea.'

'This is a feast, not tea!' Mungo exclaimed. 'You really shouldn't have.'

'How kind of you, Mrs Dixon,' Jeanie smiled, her mouth watering at the delicious-looking spread. 'I hadn't realised how hungry I was.'

As Jeanie tucked in enthusiastically, both Rose and Ada bombarded her with questions about Scottish weather and Ebbsmouth, about the Lomaxes and whether Rick was enjoying his first trip to the home-country. Between mouthfuls, Jeanie tried to convey that all seemed well.

'And how is Belle enjoying her first trip home?' asked Rose.

'She seemed very happy and she's a delight,' said Jeanie. 'Belle and Rick laid on a treasure hunt and party games for my birthday.'

'Has Stella managed to avoid Andrew's mother? A dragon by all accounts,' asked Ada.

'Now, now,' Rose reproved, 'I'm sure she can't be as bad as you make out.'

'She was simply horrid to Stella when she stayed with her before the war,' Ada retorted. 'And she led poor Captain Lomax a merry dance when she was married to him.'

Rose held up her hand. 'Enough gossip! Tell me, Mrs Munro; how was my son? We miss him so much.'

Jeanie tried not to blush as she thought of Rick's engaging smile and the way he'd made her feel attractive by his attention. 'He was very well. Finding Scotland a bit cold, I think. But being helpful to his hostess, Miss Lomax, by fixing her old bus and that sort of thing.'

'What did the glamorous, Pamela Dacre make of that?' asked Ada, with a smirk.

'She wasn't there,' said Jeanie. 'Her family in Yorkshire had come down with the flu and told Rick to stay away so he didn't catch it.'

'So, his fiancée didn't go to Ebbsmouth with him?' Rose queried.

'No, I think she might have been ill too. I'm not sure. But he was keen to get down to Yorkshire to see her.'

'I bet he was,' Ada said. 'Fancy going all that way to meet his prospective in-laws and being banished to Scotland. He only had three or so months of furlough. He's due to start his training—'

'Ada!' Rose gave a wave of her hand. 'I'm sure the Munros aren't interested in the ins and outs of Rick's plans. Let me top up your tea, Mr Munro. So, you're on your way to Murree?'

Mungo held out his cup. 'Yes, Nicholson's School. I'm the new headmaster there.'

'Oh, how wonderful!' Rose exclaimed. 'Such a good reputation. I would like Rick to have gone there – he had the brains for it – but well, in those days we couldn't have afforded it.'

'Rick's done very well without going to a pukka school,' Ada defended. 'He was a pilot during the war and saw action over Burma.'

'Is that him in the photograph over there?' Mungo asked.

75

'Yes, that's our dear Rick,' said Rose, her look softening with pride.

'A veritable war hero,' Mungo said with a nod of approval. 'Nicholson's would have been proud to have him. Perhaps, in time, your son and his wife-to-be will have strong sons of their own that they'll send to our school.'

Rose put her hands to her cheeks and simpered, 'What an honour that would be.'

'But not very likely,' said Ada, 'seeing as they are going to be living in Calcutta.'

Rose's face fell but Mungo quickly countered. 'We have boys from all over India who attend Nicholson's. Distance is no barrier if the boys show vigour on the playing fields and aptitude in the classroom.'

Rose preened. 'I do wish my husband was here to talk to you and not just us women, Mr Munro. He'll be tickled pink to think that the headmaster of Nicholson's has been sitting in this very room. Please, have more cake.'

Mungo held up his hands. 'I've had plenty, thank you. Perhaps I'll just go and see how Sigmund is getting on.'

'Oh, you mustn't worry,' Rose said, flapping her hands at him to stay sitting. 'Sigmund will let you know as soon as it's ready. Please help yourself to more food.'

It grew dark and Noor came in to shutter the windows and turn on lamps around the room, which bathed the pretty chintz furniture in a warm golden glow. Rose ushered her guests to the sofa. Jeanie, aware at Mungo's growing impatience, tried to engage June in conversation.

'Do you like playing cards? Your cousin Belle loves 'snap'. Would you like to play it while we wait?'

But June shook her head and started whining.

'It's time I took her home,' said Ada, getting up.

Mungo sprang up too. 'I'll come down with you and see how much longer your brother's going to be.'

'It's been lovely meeting you, Mrs Munro,' said Ada. 'I hope you'll call again when you're in Pindi.'

'I'd love to. And please, call me Jeanie.' They smiled at each other.

Rose fussed over her daughter and granddaughter, bidding Noor to parcel up some leftover food for them to take home and waving them off. When she returned, she said, 'you and I will have a little drop of sherry while we wait for our men to return and you can tell me what you really think is going on between Rick and Princess Pamela, as Ada calls her!'

'I'm not the person to ask,' Jeanie said with a laugh of embarrassment. 'Perhaps Stella will know more. Rick didn't confide in me. Why should he?'

'Because you strike me as a sensible married woman who would be full of good advice,' replied Rose. 'I don't like to think of that girl leading my son a merry dance.'

'I don't think you need worry about that,' Jeanie said hastily. 'Rick can't wait for them to start married life in Calcutta – and it sounded like Pamela was just as keen as him.'

'Well, that's good.' She raised her sherry glass. 'Here's to a rosy future for us all!'

After a short while, Jeanie heard the sound of footsteps and men's voices on the outside stairs. She turned to see a dapper middle-aged man with a thin grey moustache leading Mungo back into the flat.

'Toby!' cried Rose. 'You're back at last. I was beginning to worry. I'm glad you've met Mr Munro – he's the headmaster of Nicholson's, don't you know? And this is his charming wife, Mrs Munro. She's a friend of Stella's and met Rick in Scotland. Isn't that wonderful?'

Jeanie stood to shake hands. 'How nice to meet you, Mr Dixon.'

When Toby smiled at her, she was struck by the likeness to Rick. Their eyes crinkled in a similar way and they had the same strong dimpled chin. This is what Rick would look like as an older man.

'Pleased to meet you too, Mrs Munro,' he said, shaking her hand warmly. 'And I'm glad I've caught you before you attempt to set off. I was just telling your husband that there's been a landslide on the Murree road – melting snow – it's nearly impassable. I was lucky to get back down the mountain.'

Jeanie glanced at Mungo in dismay. 'Oh, dear, what shall we do?'

Mungo looked resolute. 'If the road isn't completely closed, I think we should press on.'

'Do you think that's sensible?' she asked.

Rose said in consternation, 'Oh, you mustn't risk it, Mr Munro! Tell him, Toby. You can stay here with us tonight and try in daylight.'

'Certainly not!' Mungo retorted, and then modified his tone. 'I mean, that's terribly kind of you, dear lady, but we wouldn't dream of imposing.'

'No imposition at all,' Toby declared. 'We have a spare bedroom–'

'Rick's bedroom,' Rose interjected. 'I'll have the servants make up the bed right away.'

'No, please, you mustn't,' said Mungo firmly. Jeanie could tell he was dismayed at the idea and she also felt alarmed at the thought of sleeping in Rick's bed. This would be their first night together after all this time apart and she longed for them to be alone. She didn't want to be thinking of Rick at all.

'Why don't we book into the Raj Hotel, darling?' Jeanie suggested. 'Then you can ring the school and tell them what's happened.'

Mungo seized on the idea. 'Yes, we'll do that. Of course, if it was just me, I'd plough ahead tonight, but with you it's different. It's too hazardous with a lady on board.'

'I quite agree,' said Toby. 'Let us make the arrangements. Rose's sister and family run the hotel and will be happy to accommodate you.'

'There's really no need,' said Mungo. 'We'll drive straight over.'

Ignoring this, Rose told her husband, 'Go and ring Myrtle at once – and make sure she gives the Munros the best room in the hotel. They've been apart for so long; it'll be like a second honeymoon!'

Jeanie blushed deeply. 'Any room will do,' she said with a bashful laugh. Even Mungo was turning red-faced. Toby hurried below.

'Sit down, Mr Munro,' Rose insisted, 'and have a sherry while you wait. The telephone is in the garage but Toby won't be long.'

Mungo toyed with his sherry glass, taking the merest sip, while Jeanie accepted a refill. She felt a mounting nervousness, tinged with excitement, at the thought of them spending the first night of their reunion in a hotel. Maybe it really would be like a second honeymoon and this disruption to their journey was a blessing in disguise.

She thought back to the night of their wedding spent in a hotel in the Scottish Borders, and which she still remembered as blissful. Mungo had been attentive and his lovemaking gentle, and she'd wished they could have stayed there longer. But after two days, they'd gone back to her parents' house in Greentoun in which they'd both felt inhibited in bed, and then a fortnight later they had sailed for India.

Ten minutes later, Toby returned. 'It's all arranged. And my nephew Jimmy has rung the school to alert them to your delay. He thought you'd want them to know as soon as possible.'

Mungo struggled to hide his annoyance at this. 'I really don't think that was necessary. I'd rather have done so myself. Who did he speak to?'

'Miss Lavelle, the school matron,' said Toby.

'The matron?' Mungo said crossly.

'She's a cousin of Ada's husband so Jimmy rang her straight away.' Toby's look faltered. 'I hope that's all right? She's very reliable and Jimmy rang me straight back to say she'd pass on the message to the deputy headmaster.'

Jeanie saw the tension in Mungo's face and knew he was struggling not to lose his temper. It seemed that this family had connections everywhere.

'That's very kind of Jimmy,' she said quickly and stood up to go. 'And we can't thank you enough for all you've done for us. Isn't that right, Mungo?'

'Of course,' he said, forcing a smile. 'You've been most hospitable and Sigmund has done a good job on the car. So, thank you. Now my dear,' he nodded at Jeanie, 'it's time we left the Dixons in peace.'

They all shook hands and Toby insisted on accompanying them downstairs.

'Do come again, won't you?' Rose called after them. 'Call anytime you're in Pindi. Toodle-oo!'

Jeanie turned and waved. 'Thank you, we will!'

Sigmund, who was still working in the garage, came to see them off. 'Would you like me to guide you round to the Raj?' he offered.

'No, I'll find my way, thank you,' Mungo replied.

Toby began giving directions to Mungo as he distractedly hurried Jeanie and Humza into the car. Minutes later, they were driving off. The streets looked more romantic in the dark with the lights from open-fronted shops spilling across the road and a large moon rising above the rooftops.

'What a nice family,' Jeanie mused.

Mungo huffed. 'I thought we'd never be allowed to leave.'

Jeanie said in amusement, 'Mrs Dixon certainly seemed keen for us to stay.'

'What a nightmare that would have been,' grunted Mungo. 'Does that woman ever stop talking?'

'I thought she was lovely,' Jeanie countered, 'and so kind of her to give us that enormous tea. I won't need supper tonight.'

'I hope the hotel serves good plain food,' he said. 'My mouth's still on fire from those spicy pancakes.'

He turned the car left at the end of the road.

'Mr Dixon said to go right here,' Jeanie reminded.

Mungo ignored her and drove on. They drove around for quarter of an hour and then found themselves back in the street where the Dixons lived. This time Mungo took the turning that Jeanie had suggested and within a few minutes they were driving down the Mall, passing familiar landmarks and drawing up in front of the hotel.

Chapter 9

The Raj Hotel was more down-at-heel than Jeanie had
remembered. The blue paint of the wooden verandas was
flaking and the sign proclaiming Tom Lomax as proprietor
had faded to the colour of old parchment. But there were
cheery electric lights strung in the palms by the entrance and
the porch was well swept.

'Greetings! Do come in.' A portly young man with
Brylcreemed hair and dressed in an old-fashioned coat and
tails, beckoned them into a lobby that was festooned with
potted ferns and cluttered with cane furniture. It was just as
Jeanie had remembered it. The clink of cutlery and murmur
of conversation came from a room beyond.

'Jimmy Dubois at your service,' he continued, leading
them towards the reception desk. 'My cousin explained
everything. How very unfortunate to be so delayed on your
journey, Mr Munro. But every cloud has a silver lining – and
you are ours.' He chuckled. 'We are honoured to have you
as our guests: the headmaster of prestigious Nicholson's and
his lady wife.' He bowed at Jeanie. 'A heroine in your own
right, Mrs Munro.'

Jeanie laughed. 'Hardly.'

'That is what my sister, Stella, says. Her last letter was
full of your bravery in the recent war.'

'Stella is being too kind,' Jeanie said. 'I so enjoyed
meeting her.'

'And she, you.' Jimmy smiled.

'I'm looking forward to seeing more of her once she's
back in India. We won't be living that far apart.'

Mungo, having quickly signed the register, cleared his
throat. 'If we could be shown to our room, Mr Dubois.'

'Ah, of course.' Jimmy beamed as he produced a key from a rack behind the reception desk. 'The owner's suite. I'll have your luggage taken up. Dinner is being served in the dining-room as we speak. I'm sure the regulars would feel it a great privilege if you joined them.'

Mungo and Jeanie exchanged looks. To her relief, he said, 'My wife is very tired from her long journey. Perhaps you could send up some supper to our room?'

Jimmy nodded vigorously. 'It would be a pleasure. You must make yourselves completely and utterly at home.'

He insisted on showing them the way and chattered as he led them upstairs and along to the end of a dimly lit corridor. 'The Lomaxes use this suite when they stay, though that is seldom, as they reside for most of the year at their other hotel, The Raj-in-the-Hills in Kashmir. Have you been there?'

'No,' Jeanie replied, 'but I'd love to.'

'Stella says it is heaven on earth,' Jimmy said in amusement. 'But I'm a city boy and Pindi is the place for me. Here, I have my family around me, all the facilities of an army town and friends with whom to play cricket and share a chota peg or two. What more does a man need?'

'Quite,' said Mungo.

'Here we are.' Jimmy threw open the door with a flourish.

A servant followed them in, lugging Jeanie's suitcase, and Jimmy handed over the key. 'If there's anything else you desire ...?'

'No, thank you.' Mungo cut him short.

'Don't you want to ring the school?' Jeanie prompted.

Flicking a look of irritation at Jimmy, he muttered, 'They've already got the message.'

'Just supper on a tray, thank you,' Jeanie said, smiling at the manager.

'We'll require an early breakfast,' Mungo instructed. 'Seven o'clock, if that's possible.'

'Absolutely possible, sir,' Jimmy replied enthusiastically. He bowed again and left, closing the door behind him.

'Good heavens, that man can talk,' Mungo said, loosening his tie as he surveyed the sitting-room with a critical eye. 'This furniture looks like it came from a Victorian bordello.'

Jeanie discarded her hat on the gaudy chintz-covered sofa and gave an amused laugh. 'I think it's rather cheerful and probably very comfortable.'

They regarded each other. Jeanie felt her nervousness at being alone with him return. She didn't know what to say next. He looked away first, crossed to a small inlaid table and poured himself a whisky. She hadn't remembered him as a whisky drinker but perhaps he was as nervous as she was.

'Can I have one too, please, Mungo?'

He gave her a sharp look but then nodded and poured out a smaller amount into the second tumbler.

Taking the glass, she smiled. 'To us and our reunion!'

'To getting my wife back,' he said wryly as they clinked glasses.

The liquor burnt its way down her throat and made her instantly heady. She watched Mungo as he crossed the room to open the door to the veranda. Sounds of evening invaded: a squawking of birds and someone singing as they clattered pans in a nearby kitchen. Joining him, Jeanie leant on the railing, so close that their arms touched. It set her pulse thumping and she realised how much she'd been longing for him physically.

'What a gorgeous sunset,' she murmured, watching the final orange glow blazing over the rooftops of the neighbouring bazaar. The jacaranda in the courtyard below

84

was alive with twittering green parakeets. An aroma of oily cooking and acrid smoke tickled her nose. She'd forgotten India's assault on the senses.

Mungo's strong profile was lit by the dying rays. How handsome he was! She took another gulp of her drink.

'I'm so glad to be back,' she said. 'I can't tell you how much I've missed you.'

He turned to scrutinise her, his pale brown eyes showing surprise.

'Thank you.' He smiled and then added, 'And I've missed you, of course. You know I never wanted you to go.'

'If I'd known how long we'd be apart, I'd never have gone,' Jeanie admitted. 'And if I'd stayed, I would have seen John again before …' She swallowed down her emotion.

'Yes,' Mungo agreed. 'I'm very sorry about John. He was a fine young man.'

She felt a wave of gratitude towards him for saying so. Her own mother had been incapable of acknowledging that Jeanie was also suffering over John's death.

'Tell me about the last time you saw him, Mungo.'

He looked away. 'Best not to dwell on these things.'

'Please,' she urged.

Mungo sighed. 'It was early in the war – not long after you left, I suppose – when he was still stationed on the North-West Frontier. He came for a couple of days local leave. But he must have written to you about it and I'm sure I did.'

'I just want to hear you reminiscing about him,' Jeanie encouraged.

'We went fishing. Did an early morning shikar too. Shot a blackbuck, if I remember correctly. Don't really recall much else.'

'And did you play chess in the evenings? He was passionate about chess.'

Mungo shrugged. 'I'm not sure we did. I would have had evening duties – going the rounds of the house with my head prefect – so I probably left him to entertain himself, I'm afraid.'

'But he was in good heart when he saw him?' Jeanie persisted. 'Happy?'

'Young John was always in good spirits,' he said. 'No doubt that's what made him a good officer.'

Jeanie's eyes pricked with tears. 'That's what Andrew Lomax said too. John was the best officer he ever served with.'

Mungo's eyes narrowed. 'How much time did you spend with the Lomaxes?'

'Not very much but they were so hospitable and kind. It gave me comfort to talk to Andrew about John. I wish Mother hadn't shunned them because it might have helped her too. She absolutely refused to see them. I think there must have been bad blood between Captain Tom and my father in their Peshawar days, but Mother refused to say what it was.'

'Well, I can't blame her,' Mungo said dismissively. 'As I told you, Tom Lomax was a shirker and a womaniser who left the army under a cloud.'

Jeanie let the matter drop, not wanting anything to spoil the growing ardour that the dramatic sunset and the whisky had ignited inside her – and that she hoped Mungo was feeling too.

She touched his arm and said softly, 'Let's forget about the Lomaxes, skip supper and go to bed.'

With delight, she saw him flush and give a bashful smile. 'Good suggestion, Mrs Munro.'

***

86

When Jeanie awoke the next morning, cracks of light were showing around the shuttered window. She stretched out to touch Mungo but the space in the bed beside her was empty and the sheets cold. She felt a stab of disappointment that he hadn't woken her with kisses and more pleasurable lovemaking. Last night, he had been tender and careful, making sure that after all these years of abstinence he didn't hurt her.

For her, it had been a blessed release of her pent-up longing, as well as relief that they were still compatible. She'd shed tears.

'My dearest,' Mungo had said in alarm. 'You're upset.'

'N-no,' she'd reassured him. 'I'm just so h-happy.'

He'd kissed the top of her head. 'You're a funny old girl.'

She'd snuggled into his encircling arm and had soon fallen into a deep sleep.

Now she could hear him talking to a servant beyond the bedroom, issuing orders and then a door closing. Jeanie climbed out of bed and slipped on her dressing-gown. Entering the sitting-room, she saw that the gateleg table by the window had been set for breakfast with a pot of tea, metal tureens of hot food and a rack of triangles of toast.

'Ah, sleepy head,' said Mungo, 'I was just coming to wake you. It's quarter past seven and I'd like us to be on the road by eight.'

He was already shaved and dressed. Humza must have found him a clean shirt as it looked freshly laundered.

'I'll go and dress then,' she said.

'No, eat breakfast first, while it's hot,' he encouraged.

They sat down opposite each other and he tucked his linen napkin into his collar to cover his white shirt – another habit of his that she'd forgotten – and held her gaze.

She smiled back. 'Last night was lovely.'

'Yes.' He nodded at her. She waited for him to say more and then realised his nod was her cue to start serving out the food. She lifted the lids to reveal steaming containers of scrambled eggs, bacon, kidneys and rather watery tinned tomatoes. The aromas made her stomach rumble and she realised she hadn't eaten since tea at the Dixons' the previous afternoon.

'Gosh, I'm hungry,' she said. 'Sex does give you an appetite, doesn't it?'

Mungo gaped in surprise and reddened. He began tucking into the large plateful that Jeanie doled out. 'Glad to see there's not a spice to be seen,' he said. 'Can never be too sure with these Eurasians.'

'Anglo-Indians,' Jeanie automatically corrected.

He shot her a look. 'Same thing.'

'You know it's not. Eurasian has a negative connotation these days.'

Mungo gave a huff of amusement. 'You've been back in India five minutes and suddenly you're an expert. I've been here twenty years, so I'm not going to take lessons from my much younger wife.'

Jeanie let it pass. She was ravenously hungry and devoured as much as Mungo did.

With a satisfied sigh, she sat back and asked, 'What time did you get up this morning?'

'I'm always up by six,' he said, carefully dabbing at his mouth and moustache with his napkin. 'But you woke me at five. Did you know that you snore?'

'Do I? The ack-ack girls never told me I did.'

'Perhaps it was the whisky then.' Mungo pulled off his napkin and stood up. 'I'll leave you to get dressed and go and settle the bill.'

As he passed, he brushed the top of her head with a kiss. 'Meet you downstairs in twenty minutes.'

Dressed in a fresh cotton frock, Jeanie descended the stairs to see Mungo in the lobby, surrounded by a group of chattering elderly residents. Mungo caught sight of her.

'Ah, here's my lady wife!' She saw the relief on his face.

As Jeanie joined him, the jovial group turned their attention on her. A tall, skeletal man with a stick, stuck out a bony hand and gave her a vigorous handshake.

'Name's Ansom. Pleased to meet you. What a journey you've had. Meet my fellow koi hais. This is Fritwell – and old Bahardur.'

Jeanie shook hands with a portly man with a choleric face and then with a slim, dapper Nepalese.

'Call me Fritters,' said Fritwell, 'all my friends do. I was in the army like your father and brother.'

'We hear that you served in the army too, Mrs Munro,' said Bahardur. 'You're one of us.'

'We hope you slept well after your epic travels,' said Ansom.

'I hope she didn't sleep at all,' laughed a thin, white-haired woman in an old-fashioned beaded dress. 'First night back with her beloved husband after years apart!'

Jeanie burst out laughing.

'May I introduce you to the jewel in our crown,' said Ansom. 'Baroness Cussack.'

Heavily made-up and wreaking of perfume, the elderly woman clasped Jeanie with a bejewelled hand. 'So wonderful to meet you, darling.'

'And you too, Baroness.' Jeanie smiled, entranced by the warmth of their welcome and the baroness's forthright greeting.

'Call me Hester,' she insisted. 'Stella's last letter was full of admiration for you. Come and tell me all about your time in Scotland. We can chat about it over breakfast. Have you eaten chota hazri here before? Chef does the most mouth-melting puris, absolutely drenched in syrup.'

She linked her arm through Jeanie's but Mungo stepped in and took his wife by the elbow.

'I'm sorry, Mrs Cussack, but we've already had breakfast in our room. We really must be off.'

'But surely you've time for an extra cup of tea while I talk to your pretty wife?'

'Sadly not.' Mungo was firm. 'I have a school to run and can't delay our departure any further. We should have returned last night.'

'Well, that's too bad,' said the baroness, looking disappointed.

Jeanie gave a smile of regret. 'I wish we had more time but I'm sure we'll be back. And when Stella returns, perhaps we could all get together?'

'What a good idea,' Hester agreed. 'If not here, then up in Kashmir. I always spend the hot season on a houseboat at Srinagar. You must come and visit me there, darling. You and your handsome husband. It's the most perfect place to unwind after a busy term. Do say you'll come!'

'That sounds idyllic,' said Jeanie, touched by the offer. 'Doesn't it, Mungo?'

He gave a distracted nod; she could tell by the way he gripped her arm that he was growing agitated at the delay.

'Well, thank you,' Jeanie answered for them both. 'I'm sure we'd love to visit. The school has a short summer break in August.'

'Wonderful, darling. I'll drop you a line with all the details. You simply must come.'

'Goodbye, then.' Jeanie said as Mungo steered her towards the door.

They met Jimmy on the path outside. The manager beamed at them. 'Your luggage is safely stowed in the car, Mrs Munro – and your servant awaits you, sir. I've taken the liberty of providing refreshments for your onward journey.'

'How kind, thank you,' said Jeanie.

'I hope everything has been to your satisfaction at the hotel?' he asked.

'Everything was fine,' Mungo said.

'I hope you will grace us with your presence again,' Jimmy said, 'and mention us to any of your colleagues who might need to stay in Pindi. All will be welcome.'

Mungo gave the briefest of nods, so Jeanie said, 'Of course we will. You've made us feel very at home – and thank you for letting us use the Lomaxes' rooms – we were very comfortable.'

Jimmy grinned with pleasure and bowed. 'Thank you, and have a safe journey home.'

Minutes later, they were back in the car and Mungo was driving them speedily down the Mall and onto the Murree road. He didn't seem interested in her chatter about their stay at the Raj, except to comment on the manager's impertinence in touting for the school's business, so she soon gave up. His mind was obviously racing ahead to his duties at the school.

Her stomach twisted in sudden excitement at the thought she would soon be back in Murree. She was eager to see Nicholson's again and once more be part of the community there. Would much have changed? She felt another nervous flutter. The biggest change would be that she was returning – not as a schoolmaster's wife – but as the wife of the all-important headmaster.

Chapter 10

Murree

Half-way up the mountain road, the temperature plummeted and Jeanie regretted wearing the light frock that had been perfect for Rawalpindi's mild air. She had to ask Mungo to stop while she unpacked a jumper and coat from her case.

'Shall we have some of the tea from the hotel thermos?' she suggested, shivering. She felt slightly queasy on the twisting, rising road and wished she was behind the driver's wheel. She had never felt car sick when driving during the war.

'We haven't time for that,' said Mungo. 'You can have proper refreshments when we arrive. It won't be long, my dear.'

After that, Jeanie concentrated on looking out of the window at the increasing grandeur of the scenery; tall pine trees dripping in the recent thaw and the glimpse of mountain slopes. Twice, Mungo had to slow down and inch past narrow bends where the road had been partially washed away. Coolies were already making repairs, carrying baskets of stones on their heads and backs.

She was thankful Mungo hadn't attempted the forty-mile journey in the dark the previous evening. Besides, the burst tyre had meant that she'd got to meet Rick's hospitable family and had a pleasurable reunion with Mungo at the Raj Hotel, where everyone had been so friendly and kind. She might not dare say so to Mungo, but she'd enjoyed the delay and the time spent in Rawalpindi.

Finally, they were reaching the outskirts of Murree and Jeanie sat forward, clutching the dashboard in excitement. Emerging from the trees around Pindi Point, she saw the hill station unfolding along the saddle-shaped ridge, its densely packed wooden buildings, clustering around the Mall and the stone-built garrison church, the town's most prestigious edifice. Wreaths of smoke from chimneys sat like an extra layer of mist above the rooftops, the veranda-ed shops and muddy pathways looking drab in the grey light. Jeanie wound down the window and breathed in the aromatic woodsmoke.

'Ah, this is what I remember of Murree,' she mused. 'So much nicer than the smell of coal fumes at home.'

Mungo tooted and waved at a couple emerging from the post office.

'The Golightlys,' he explained. 'Did you ever meet them? Used to run the mission school in the Thirties. He came out of retirement to help us teach Latin and Greek during the war – still does. Don't know how we would have managed without all the retired teachers coming back to the school.'

'Golightly?' Jeanie queried. 'No, I don't think so. But wasn't she your school matron for a while?'

'Yes; well remembered. She stood in for two terms until Miss Lavelle arrived. Boys found her a bit of a dragon. Think she was always shouting because Godfrey Golightly is pretty deaf. She's not a bad sort.'

'So the boys prefer Miss Lavelle?' Jeanie asked, amused.

'I think they do. I've never heard her lose her temper with any of them.'

'That's good. I like the sound of her. And the Dixons obviously think she's very trustworthy and reliable. Is she Anglo-Indian too?'

Frowning, Mungo avoided her question. 'I'd rather they hadn't interfered and rung the school on my behalf. Lavelle is good at her job but that doesn't include being my secretary. Her place is firmly on the boys' side of the green baize door.'

Jeanie kept to herself the suspicion that the real reason Mungo was annoyed at the matron using her initiative and liaising with the deputy head was that she was Anglo-Indian and had acted above her station.

'Well, it'll be nice for me to have another woman in the household,' she said, touching his arm, 'and not be completely surrounded by men and boys.'

'Lavelle is a very private person,' Mungo warned, 'so don't go bothering her or try to get too pally. Consult her on issues about the house, by all means, but if it's friends you want, there are far more suitable wives of staff members or army-wallahs in the town.'

'I thought most of the staff were bachelors?' she queried.

'Not these days. There's Golightly and the chaplain, Reverend Ord. And Robert Dane has just returned from naval service with a young wife.'

'The Viking?' Jeanie said with pleasure. 'I remember him as good fun.'

'There you are then.' Mungo nodded. 'No need to go fraternising with the school matron.'

Jeanie kept quiet, but his dismissiveness towards the matron made her all the more intrigued to meet her. He warmed to his theme.

'I think all future housemasters should be married. So much better to have a wife in charge of the household rather than a bearer who can fiddle the books. I've just appointed Dane as housemaster of Trafalgar House this term. Golightly was covering the post and was pressing me to find a replacement.

And by the way, don't use the nickname, "Viking", in public. It's not really suitable. He's a naval veteran and a married man – not a wild bachelor anymore.'

They drove on towards Kashmir Point, the promontory that marked the far end of the hill station and beneath which lay Nicholson's, fenced off and gated. It looked incongruous, its red-roofed brick buildings and terraced playing fields pressing up against the Himalayan forest, as if a giant hand had plucked it from a corner of Britain and dropped it by mistake in this alpine jungle.

To her amazement, as the gates were opened, a school brass band struck up a jaunty tune and several boys in army cadet uniform, stood to attention saluting the passing car. Jeanie gasped. 'Mungo, is this just for us?'

'Just for you, my dear.' Mungo smiled.

'How lovely!' she exclaimed, waving out of the window as they passed. 'I hope they haven't been standing there too long. Some of them look purple with cold,' she said, noticing how snow still covered the tennis courts and clung to the bushes that lined the steep drive.

'They're used to it,' said Mungo. 'Captain Rae has them out running every day no matter what the weather.'

As the strains of music grew fainter, Jeanie said, 'That was a very kind gesture. Did you organise it, Mungo?'

'Yes, I rang the school early this morning to arrange it. This should have happened last night, with a drinks reception for you to meet all the staff. That's why I was so annoyed at our delay. But you'll see them in the dining-hall at lunchtime instead.'

Mungo drove through the quadrangle and brought the car to a halt in front of the rather austere School House (also the headmaster's house), devoid of any flowering creepers to soften its brick frontage. Jeanie leapt out of the car and breathed in the sweet, sharp air.

'Careful, Jean,' Mungo warned. 'It'll be slippy underfoot.'

As she slithered in her court shoes across the icy ground, she was aware of servants lining up at the entrance ready to greet them. At once, Mungo was at her side, providing a strong arm for her to cling to as they approached the house staff. Ranked either side of the large front door were a dozen male servants wearing cummerbunds and turbans of Nicholson's navy blue with their white tunics. Standing apart from them was a slight bespectacled woman in a grey uniform with a nurse's starched apron and headdress. Dinah Lavelle?

Humza was soon issuing orders for Jeanie's luggage to be brought inside, while Mungo introduced her to a stocky, bearded man with a Sikh-styled turban.

'This is Dalip Singh, our khansama, who will help you run the household.' Dalip bowed as Jeanie greeted him. 'He can tell you all you need to know about the other servants,' said Mungo, with a sweeping gesture at the others. 'And this is Matron Lavelle.'

Jeanie shook hands with the diminutive woman. She was light-skinned and didn't look Anglo-Indian. It was hard to gauge her age – perhaps in her forties – as her severe white headdress hid her hair and the wire spectacles gave her brown eyes a severe look.

'Pleased to meet you, Matron,' said Jeanie. 'I met your cousin's wife, Ada Gibson, yesterday, while her brother fixed our car. Delightful people.'

The matron frowned and Jeanie faltered. 'They – er – spoke highly of you ...'

'I don't know the Dixons that well,' she answered quietly. 'I seldom get down to Pindi.'

'But you have family still there?' Jeanie asked.

She hesitated. 'My parents have passed away and my brother is in Poona. So just my Gibson cousins.'

Jeanie felt bad for making the woman uncomfortable. 'I'm sorry about your parents.'

'Come, my dear,' said Mungo, 'and stop grilling poor Lavelle.'

'I didn't mean to,' said Jeanie with an apologetic look. 'I'm just pleased there'll be another woman in the house.'

The matron gave a tight smile. Jeanie followed her husband inside. Perhaps he was right in suggesting she found female friendship elsewhere. She didn't like to judge people on first impressions but she hadn't warmed to Dinah Lavelle.

Jeanie had vague memories of the headmaster's house from the occasional social gatherings when the Bishops had been in charge. To the left of the large gloomy hallway, she glimpsed the high-ceilinged sitting-room furnished with an array of solid armchairs. Off to the right, a dining-room still appeared to be stuffed full of dark teak furniture. Fires blazed in both reception rooms.

She had never been upstairs before and, stepping into their bedroom, she had to hide her dismay. The curtains and bedspread were a dowdy brown and the bare floorboards were polished only around the edge of the room. The Bishops must have taken their carpet with them and Mungo hadn't bothered to replace it. The walls were devoid of pictures and no photos or mementos stood on the chest of drawers. He must have sensed her disappointment.

'It's a bit spartan but I wanted to give you free reign on how it's decorated.'

She crossed quickly to the large casement window and her spirits lifted as she caught sight of the view across the back garden to mountains shrouded in cloud.

She gasped. 'Is that Kashmir I can see from here?'

'Yes,' Mungo confirmed, joining her at the window. 'We get a good view of the sunrise over the Himalayas on a clear day.'

'How delightful!'

It had the feel of a neglected bachelor's room but she could soon change all that; what gave this room its charm was the breathtaking view.

'Oh, Mungo,' Jeanie said, leaning up to kiss his cheek, 'I'm so happy to be here.'

'Good,' he replied. He checked his watch. 'I'll give you an hour to unpack and settle in – Humza will help you – then I'll take you across to the dining-hall for lunch. Wear something a bit more sensible on your feet,' he added with a wry smile.

Then he was striding out of the room.

***

The vaulted, high-windowed dining-hall was just as Jeanie remembered it, with its rows of trestle tables and benches, shields and honours lists displayed on the wood-panelled walls and the overpowering smell of cooked cabbage. The room echoed to the sound of boys chattering.

The instant Major Lucker, the deputy headmaster, saw them, he clapped his hands and bellowed at the boys to be quiet and stand to attention. A hush descended on the room.

Jeanie knew that very few of the boys she had known seven years ago would still be at the school, and those that were would now be sixth formers. She smiled self-consciously as dozens of pairs of eyes followed her progress across the hall. Mungo ushered her up the steps onto the dais where the staff were standing around a long table, and nodded at the chaplain to say grace. Once this was done, Lucker turned to Jeanie and said, 'Please sit, Mrs Munro.'

Her sitting down appeared to be a signal for the boys to start lunch. There was a hurried scramble onto benches, the chatter resumed as tray loads of sausages and vegetables were doled out by the prefects at the head of each table.

To her relief, she found herself seated next to Robert Dane. He still looked like a Viking with his full red beard, though his hair was now rapidly receding.

'I'm so glad to see someone I recognise,' said Jeanie, smiling. 'I feel like Rumpelstiltskin coming back after all these years.'

He gave a familiar bellow of laughter that had other members of staff glancing over.

'I know what you mean,' said Robert. 'Six years of war feels more like a dozen in some ways, doesn't it?'

'Exactly,' Jeanie agreed. 'I hear you were in the Navy. Were you serving out East?'

'No, I went home. Ended up on the Arctic convoys.'

'Out of Loch Ewe?'

'Yes.' He looked surprised. 'Do you know it?'

'My ack-ack detachment was stationed up there for a while.'

'Well, I never! How marvellous.' He grinned. 'One of our guardian angels.'

'I was so admiring of you sailors going through those terrible seas,' Jeanie said, 'and facing such dangers, again and again.'

For a moment, he looked reflective, then shrugged. 'We all faced danger, sailor or civilian. I'm just glad it's all over and I'm back on dry land for good.' He gave another of his booming laughs.

They talked about the war and of how he'd found romance at a dance when on leave.

'Mary's people are from Yorkshire. They weren't at all sure about her marrying a sailor-turned-schoolmaster and then being whisked off to live in India – not happy at all. But luckily for me, she agreed to come. She's a plucky sort.'

Fleetingly, Jeanie was reminded of Rick and Pamela – another wartime romance – and of Pamela's family who came from Yorkshire. Was Rick still in Yorkshire or were the couple on their way to Calcutta and the start of married life? She felt a strange sensation – was it envy? – at the thought of these couples just embarking on a lifetime together. She and Mungo's marriage had been ruptured by war – something she felt was her fault – so it was up to her to recapture the loving intimacy they had once shared.

'I look forward to meeting her,' Jeanie said, forcing her mind back to the conversation.

'You'll get on like a house of fire,' he assured her.

The lunch passed more swiftly than Jeanie imagined it would, as they chatted about books they'd read and films they'd managed to see while in Britain.

'We should set up a supper club for the staff,' Jeanie suggested, 'where we can talk about books – and maybe arrange to go to the cinema together.'

'Excellent!' Robert agreed. 'Mary would love that.'

'Please tell her to call round any time she likes,' Jeanie encouraged.

***

That evening, Jeanie huddled close to the fire in the large sitting-room and talked excitedly to Mungo about her plans for a supper club.

'Who else do you think might like to join?' she asked. 'I imagine Reverend Ord must like reading and talking about books. What is his wife like?'

Mungo looked up from a report he was reading and gave an indulgent smile. 'Perhaps you should wait until you get to know the staff a bit better, my dear, before issuing invitations. You haven't even put round your calling cards yet.'

Jeanie laughed. 'They don't still do that here, do they?'

'Why not? It's the polite way to introduce oneself – we don't want you foisting yourself on people without them wanting it.'

'Mungo, you do sound like a Victorian at times!'

'Nothing wrong with the Victorians,' he retorted.

'Well, you better help me draw up a list of households where I can drop off visiting cards. Then I can go ahead with planning my supper club.' Jeanie pressed him. 'You do agree with a supper club, don't you?'

He hesitated. 'In principle. Or at least a meeting to discuss literature.'

'Good. That's agreed.' Jeanie glanced around the room. 'If we brought a table in here, this could be a cosier room to dine in than that gloomy room across the hall.'

'There's nothing wrong with the dining-room,' Mungo said.

'At supper, our voices echoed like we were in a cave,' she teased. 'Let's bring a table in here, darling, and we can have intimate dinners for two. You said I could arrange the rooms how I wanted.'

'I'll think about it,' he half-relented. 'We do have to adhere to certain standards in the house.' He shuffled his papers back into a file and stood up.

'Where are you going?'

'To my study to drop this off,' he said. 'Then I have to do my circuit of the house.'

'Can I come?' She stood up too.

'Certainly not. This is house business not a jolly. My head boy, Tasker, accompanies me. I may have boys to discipline.'

Jeanie swallowed disappointment. 'When will you be finished?'

'Ten o'clock. Maybe half-past.' He stuck the file under his arm and leaned over to kiss her forehead. 'I imagine you're feeling whacked after today. Get an early night. If you're asleep when I come to bed, I won't disturb you.'

'I'm happy to be disturbed,' she said, kissing him back on the lips.

He gave an embarrassed laugh as he turned away and marched from the room.

Chapter 11

The next morning, Jeanie was woken by Mungo sitting down on the bed beside her. He was fully dressed.

She asked groggily, 'What time is it?'

'Quarter to eight,' he said.

'Goodness, I've slept in!' She sat up, squinting in the light from the uncurtained window. 'Give me ten minutes and I'll join you for breakfast.'

'I've already had it. And I must go over to the dining-hall to put in an appearance before chapel.'

Jeanie protested. 'You should have woken me. I want to do all these things with you.'

He gave an indulgent smile. 'There's no need. I've ordered you breakfast in bed. Take your time getting up.' He stood.

'That's very thoughtful of you.' Jeanie grabbed his hand and kissed it.

'I'll see you for tiffin,' he said.

'Good. I enjoyed meeting some of the staff yesterday.'

He answered, 'I thought we could have a quiet lunch together rather than making you sit up there on the dais in front of all the boys.'

'I don't mind that,' Jeanie said in amusement.

'Well, I'd prefer to have my wife to myself,' Mungo said with a smile. 'Unless you'd rather not?'

'Of course I'd prefer lunch just with you,' Jeanie said hastily. 'I'll look forward to it.'

Jeanie didn't linger over her breakfast, finding it lonely perched in bed in the drab brown room with a tray load of eggs, pilchards, toast and tea, but no one with whom to share it. Eager to get on with her new role as headmaster's wife, she abandoned the half-eaten meal and got up. Her starting point would be to explore the house. Anticipating her needs, Humza knocked and asked if she'd like him to run her a hot bath.

'That's kind of you but I can manage,' she told him. He looked non-plussed and she felt she had said the wrong thing. She'd forgotten how much the British in India relied on servants to do everything for them. Quickly, she added, 'But could you arrange for Dalip to come to the sitting-room in an hour for a chat?'

'Yes, Memsahib.'

***

By the time Mungo returned for lunch, Jeanie had got Dalip to show her the kitchen and storerooms, introduce her to the servants and gardeners, hand over the housekeeping books and discuss the week's menus.

'And I've asked him about decorating and refurnishing,' Jeanie told Mungo with enthusiasm. 'He's going to guide me as to what workmen to use in the town, where to buy materials, that sort of thing.'

Mungo's eyes widened. 'You have been a busy bee this morning.'

'I'm not one for lying around in bed,' she admitted. 'I need to be doing something and I want to be a help to you in any way I can.'

He nodded in approval but warned, 'Just don't go running up an account before you've cleared any expenses with me and my bursar. And any firms that Dalip suggests will have to be approved by our clerk-of-works first.'

That afternoon, Jeanie waited until Mungo was closeted in his study with Major Lucker, and then set off into the boys' side of the house. Beyond the downstairs green baize door, a long stone-flagged corridor stretched ahead with doors on one side and high windows through which she could just glimpse the central quadrangle. All was quiet as the pupils were in lessons in the classrooms on the other side of the quad.

She passed a large room lined with books and set out with tables and benches; this must be the prep' hall where they did their evening schoolwork. There were two smaller rooms which smelt of jam and fusty armchairs; studies for the prefects? On the next corridor she glimpsed a row of baths in a changing-room which smelt of muddy rugby kit and gumption cleaner. Beyond it was a drying room with wooden racks covered in steaming linen.

Jeanie nodded at two dhobis who were folding dry clothes into laundry baskets and hurried on to a stone staircase that took her up to the floor above. Here were the boys' dormitories. At least these floors were of polished wood and a bit warmer, though she noticed that the dormitory windows were thrown wide open to the chilly wind and the narrow iron beds appeared to have only one blanket per boy.

She felt she was intruding and was about to retreat downstairs when she heard a chesty cough from further down the corridor. Exploring further, Jeanie found an open door leading into a warm room lined with shelves that were stacked with boys' clothes. A woman was poised over a ledger, reading out boys' names, while a servant lifted laundry from a basket and put them on the shelves.

'Matron?' Jeanie said.

The woman looked round, startled. 'Mrs Munro. I didn't hear you …'

'Sorry, Miss Lavelle, I don't want to disturb you if you're working. I just wanted to pop along and say hello.'

The matron pushed her spectacles firmly onto her nose and regained her poise. 'Not disturbing at all.'

They stood for a moment, assessing each other. Jeanie said, 'I'm trying to find my way around the house. I feel a bit like the new girl.'

Dinah Lavelle gave a cautious smile but said nothing.

'Do you have accommodation on this floor?' Jeanie asked.

'Yes.'

Jeanie wondered if the matron would offer to show her but she didn't.

'Well, I'll leave you to it,' Jeanie said. Turning in the doorway, she added, 'Are there any afternoons during the week that you're off duty?'

'Thursdays,' Dinah said.

'Why don't you join me this Thursday for a cup of tea? Then you can tell me all about the boys' welfare.'

Dinah hesitated. 'Thank you, Mrs Munro, but I'm already busy this Thursday.'

'Next week then, if that's more convenient,' Jeanie suggested. 'If the weather warms up, we could take tea in the garden.'

The matron nodded and glanced at her watch. Jeanie took the hint, said goodbye and retreated.

***

At supper, Jeanie was going to tell Mungo about her foray into the boys' side of the house but abruptly he got called away by Tasker to deal with some misdemeanour in the prep' hall.

'Carry on eating, my dear,' he said, throwing down his napkin, 'I'll be back soon.'

Jeanie finished her soup, watched attentively by Dalip and a young skinny servant called Nitin who pounced on her soup bowl the moment it was empty and carried it away. The only sound in the dimly lit dining-room was the deep ticking of a grandfather clock and the spitting of the fire as rain came down the chimney.

When Mungo didn't return, Jeanie ploughed on with the fish course and then tackled a tough cutlet that might have been lamb. Dalip ordered Nitin to take the Burra-sahib's meal back to the kitchen to keep it warm.

Jeanie gave up on her main course. She stared down the long table at Mungo's empty chair and thought how ridiculous it was that they dined in this vast room alone. It should be filled with guests and echo to the sound of clinking cutlery and merry conversation. She'd plan a dinner party for Mungo's fifty-second birthday, which was in two weeks' time.

'Dalip.' She beckoned to the khansama. 'Can you find me a small table which could be put in the sitting-room, where I can take meals with Mr Munro? I really don't see the point of heating up this huge room just for the two of us – or just for me as it turns out.'

'Certainly, Memsahib.' Dalip smiled.

'And I won't bother with pudding, thank you.' Jeanie stood up. 'But if you could bring through some tea to the sitting-room, that would be perfect.'

***

It was late into the evening before she saw Mungo again. A boy had been accused of stealing a fountain pen and her husband had ended up interviewing a score of pupils.

'I threatened to punish the lot if the culprit didn't own up,' he told Jeanie as they readied for bed. 'No going into town for a month.'

'And did you find the thief?' Jeanie asked, pausing to look at him in the mirror as she removed her make-up.

107

'Yes. A vicar's son, would you believe? Gave him six of the best and fifty lines saying, "thou shalt not steal".'

'Why did he do it?'

Mungo shrugged. 'It doesn't matter. It's the deed that counts.'

'Perhaps he's homesick or had bad news,' Jeanie pondered.

'I'm not going to let my boys hide behind spurious psychoanalysis,' he retorted.

Jeanie bridled. 'Not spurious. These children must have had to bear a lot of anxiety and unhappiness during the war – separated from their parents and worrying about whether they'd see them again. Especially those with fathers on active service.'

'We at Nicholson's have been their surrogate fathers,' Mungo said, his tone sharp. 'It's not just the men in the forces who have played their part – though they get all the limelight. We have been responsible for the physical and moral wellbeing of our next generation – and we've done it with minimal help or resources. So I'll not be lectured on how to deal with wayward boys by someone who has no experience in the matter.'

Jeanie looked at him aghast. 'Mungo, I never meant to criticise–'

'Well, let us say no more on the matter,' he interrupted. 'We'll each keep to our own domain in School House.'

Jeanie bit back a rejoinder that they should be working in partnership. Now was not the time to tell him about her earlier roaming around the boarding house. They climbed into bed in silence and Mungo switched off his bedside lamp. A saying of her father's came back to her: *don't let the sun go down on your wrath.* She snuggled up to her husband and kissed his cheek.

108

'Sorry,' she said. 'Am I forgiven for my Freudian musings?'

He gave a huff of amusement. 'Yes,' he conceded. 'Now turn off your lamp, Jean.'

She lay in the dark waiting for him to kiss her but he turned away and was soon asleep. It was disappointing; she longed for the intimacy of two nights ago but she would have to be patient. First and foremost, Mungo was dedicated to his job as headmaster which took up all hours of the day and left him tired out by nightfall. She would have to find ways to carve out some time for them together – and support him as much as she could. She had six years of making up to him for her absence. Although he had never put it that bluntly, she felt an undercurrent of resentment that she had not only gone away but stayed away for the whole of the war – and chosen to live an army life.

Chapter 12

Life at Nicholson's soon settled into a regular pattern. Jeanie would take breakfast in bed, then spend the morning dealing with domestic duties; agreeing menus and ordering supplies with Dalip and liaising with the head mali over cut flowers for the house.

Mungo acquiesced in taking lunch and supper together in the more intimate surroundings of the sitting-room and she instigated coffee there for the staff in-between morning lessons. At first this was just on a Wednesday but proved so popular that it was extended to every weekday. It amused her how the all-male staff delighted in gathering to gossip about people in the school or town.

Captain Rae, the games teacher, was the worst. He'd taken her aside and whispered, 'Have you heard about the chaplain's wife? Hasn't been seen in chapel for a fortnight. Reverend Ord says her sciatica is playing up but I've seen her out walking. If you ask me, she's having a crisis of faith – or maybe's she's about to run off with a younger vicar!' He'd chuckled at his own joke.

Jeanie's attempts to get closer to Dinah Lavelle proved more of a challenge. She soon discovered that the matron did her own ordering and running of the school sanatorium and dealt directly with the bursar without deferring to the headmaster or to Jeanie. Dinah also evaded her attempts to take afternoon tea together, always seeming to have some other commitment.

'I don't think she likes me,' Jeanie told Mungo one evening. 'Though I haven't a clue as to why she should take against me.'

'Matrons can be very territorial,' he said. 'I'm sure it won't be personal.'

'Do you think she was the same with Mrs Bishop before me?'

'Umm?' He was only half-listening as he read through some papers. 'I wouldn't worry about it. She's a good matron and that's all that matters.'

Most afternoons, Jeanie would take a walk along the ridge to the Mall and browse in the shops, or post a weekly letter to her mother. It heartened her to receive regular airmail letters back – far chattier than Clara had ever been in person – and it gave her hope that in time her mother could be encouraged to visit.

Her heart lifted at the sight of spring coming to the hill station; blossom on the trees and a warmth in the air. Most of all, the view from their garden towards the snow-capped Himalayas took her breath away. Some days, the peaks were so clear that they looked near enough to touch. It made Jeanie think of the Lomaxes and wonder if they were already on their way back to Kashmir. At this time of year, they might well travel via the southern route and Sialkot, rather than through Murree. Even so, she hoped to hear from them soon.

She had to admit that, despite her coffee mornings and superficial conversation with the teaching staff, she missed the closeness of female friendship that she'd experienced in her Searchlight regiment. Mungo had never got around to drawing up a list of acquaintances in the town for her to visit and she didn't like to badger him. It struck her that her husband was happy with colleagues and didn't need friends outside of school.

Mary Dane, the English master's new wife, was the nearest person she could call a friend in Murree. They had met for afternoon tea twice; once at School House and once at Trafalgar House. But Mary was busy setting up home for her and Robert and grappling with being a housemaster's wife for the first time, so Jeanie didn't like to keep asking to meet up.

Mary was sweet-natured but not very curious about her wider surroundings and was largely ignorant about things Indian. She didn't give an opinion on anything without reference to her husband. When Jeanie asked anything topical, such as what Mary thought of talk of a British delegation coming to India to discuss more Home Rule for Indians, Mary seemed baffled. 'Oh, I leave all that to Robert – he knows more about that than me – you should ask him.'

To Jeanie, it was like seeing the person that she used to be before the war; eager, naïve and lacking in self-assurance, and whose world revolved around her husband. It made Jeanie feel uncomfortable and galvanised her into action in an aspect of her married life that appeared to be drifting.

Jeanie craved intimacy with Mungo but for three weeks there had been abstinence. She had had their bedroom redecorated in butter yellow, with flowered curtains to match a bright floral counterpane and durries on the floor (Mungo had said a full carpet was too much extravagance). But at least it felt less like the cell of a monk. Eventually, she'd been blunt.

'I thought we were trying for a family,' she confronted him. 'Isn't that what you want?'

He blustered. 'Well – er – yes – I er – of course it is.'

'Well, we're never going to have a baby unless we do something about it, Mungo.'

That very night, after they'd turned off the lamps, Mungo had reached for her. The lovemaking had not lasted long but Jeanie felt a wave of relief that intimacy had been restored. Since then, they had established a routine of making love on Mondays, Wednesdays and Saturdays. For Jeanie, almost better than the act itself, was falling asleep in his arms afterwards, content and suffused with tenderness towards him.

To her frustration, he would always be up and gone by the time she awoke. She slept so deeply that she was never aware of what time he rose in the morning. One night, though, a scrabbling at the window woke her early. It was still dark but reaching out for Mungo, she found his side of the bed empty. Jeanie got up and went to peer beyond the new curtains. Something swayed on a nearby branch. It must have been a monkey. Now fully awake, and seeing that the bedside clock showed it was half past three, she wondered where her husband could be. Surely not working at this unearthly hour?

Pulling on a cardigan, she padded into the adjoining bathroom and switched on the light. He wasn't there. A door opposite led to his dressing-room. Hesitating only a moment, Jeanie opened the door. From the flood of light behind her, she could see him sleeping on a camp-bed. As soon as she stood over him, he came awake.

'What's wrong?' he sat up at once.

'Nothing, but what are you doing through here?'

He sighed and rubbed his eyes vigorously with the heels of his palms. 'I sleep better. I'm not used to sharing a big bed anymore. You grind your teeth and babble in your sleep.'

'Oh, darling!' Jeanie sat down on the canvas bed. The old wooden frame creaked under her. 'I'm sorry. I feel terrible.'

'Don't. I'm fine in here. And it means that I don't disturb you when I get up at six to start work. I just nip quietly down the backstairs.' He nodded at a far door. 'I know you're not an early morning person like me.'

Dispirited, Jeanie returned to bed alone. She couldn't blame him. He'd had to get used to sleeping without her for years and he was a man who lived by routine. She would just have to be content that he spent the first half of the night with her and perhaps, given time, he would get used to sleeping as a couple again.

Chapter 13

York Railway Station, England, late March

Rick paced to and fro in the draughty cavernous entrance to the station, his coat collar turned up against a cutting east wind. He checked his watch and then scoured the road outside, his view obscured by crowds of passengers disgorging from various trains. Some were still in uniform, some in demob suits. He wished he still had his Air Force uniform and hoped his rather dated double-breasted pre-war suit wouldn't embarrass Pamela.

His pulse was racing with nervous anticipation at seeing her again. It had been nearly three months since they'd been together at her parents' house in the outlying village of Haxton. When she'd written in early February to put him off again – and to say her father wouldn't countenance her going on her own to Scotland to stay with him – he'd decided to seek temporary work. With Tibby's help he'd secured a job at a garage in Greentoun run by a cheerful man called Lorimer. Rick thought how his own father would have got on well with his new boss; they both had a passion for cricket and vintage cars.

Travelling every day to Greentoun, he'd soon discovered which was Rowan House where Jeanie's reclusive mother lived. He'd seen her once or twice, walking through the village and had raised his hat to her when she'd passed by. He'd slackened his pace to introduce himself but got nothing more than a wary nod as she hurried on.

Lorimer had talked about the Grants with a shake of his head. 'Colonel Colin was the life and soul of Greentoun but Mrs Grant has always kept to herself. Nice children – and bonny too. A good family. But she's not got over losing her son, poor woman. Daughter's gone off back to India – your neck of the woods. Friendly, like her father, is Jeanie. We miss her in the village.'

Rick had admitted that he knew Jeanie. It made him wonder how she was getting on in Murree and whether she was finding it easy to adapt again to married life in India. Perhaps their paths would cross some day in Pindi ... But he tried not to think about her too much.

Rick glanced at his watch anxiously. He'd hoped to be able to stay a few nights at Haxton on his way to London and the boat to India, but Pamela's father had vetoed the suggestion.

Mr Dacre could no longer use the excuse of Mrs Dacre's influenza to keep him away but apparently having guests to stay would put too much of a strain on her health which was still delicate. When Rick had finally been able to speak to Pamela on her parents' newly-installed telephone, she had made excuses for them.

'Mummy's really not coping very well with running a house over here. She gets in such a tizzy about the slightest thing. Daddy wants complete calm to help her adjust. The trouble is they had such high standards in India and the domestic help here isn't up to scratch.'

Rick had muttered, 'Perhaps your dad should spend some of his vast jute wealth on paying them more.'

'Ricky, that's not very kind!'

'Only teasing,' he'd relented quickly. 'I'm just going mad not seeing you. That's the reason I came over here, so we could help your parents settle in and I'd get to know your family. But I've hardly met them.'

'That's a blessing for you,' Pamela had laughed. 'The Yorkshire Dacres are all pretty dull.'

He'd been firm. 'I'm not going back to India without seeing you, Pammy. Even if it means coming to Haxton and climbing up a drainpipe into your bedroom; we have to meet.'

'You're such a romantic!'

'Pammy: you do still want us to marry, don't you? Because if you're getting cold feet …'

'Of course, I do, darling! Don't be so silly.'

They'd compromised. She would pick him up from York station and take him home for afternoon tea together. He had three hours between trains. The kind Lomaxes had gone ahead with his luggage, but he felt deeply resentful of the Dacre parents for making him so unwelcome. Not only had his savings been wiped out making the trip, but his parents were now helping him meet the cost of the return voyage – money Rick insisted he would pay back when he began earning as a pilot again.

His thoughts were interrupted by a hooting car horn. In relief, he saw Pamela waving out of the back window of her father's Wolseley, and hurried over. He clambered in the back of the car and kissed her eagerly on the lips.

'You look divine,' he said and was rewarded with a heart-melting smile. She'd had a new permanent wave put in her blonde hair which perfectly framed her slim fair face and large blue eyes, and she wore a pink coat and jaunty pillbox hat that matched her lipstick. His pulse raced. She looked even prettier than ever.

'You look fairly scrumptious, yourself,' she giggled. She tapped the driver's seat. 'Off we go, Braithwaite!'

The chauffeur eased the car into the traffic. Rick shifted closer to Pamela and took her hand in his as they drove out of the city and headed down country lanes. The landscape still looked flat and a dreary brown under a leaden grey sky but he didn't care. Pamela was chatting happily beside him as if they'd never been apart and allowed a few chaste kisses on the cheek.

'And I don't want Pamela living anywhere squalid or dangerous,' said Geoffrey Dacre. 'It must be somewhere respectable like Tollyganj. If you can't afford it then I'll arrange a loan until you can pay me back.'

'Thank you, but we'll manage,' Rick replied, trying to keep calm.

'I'll continue to pay Pamela's personal allowance, of course. I can't have her stuck in Calcutta without money or means.'

Rick tried to laugh it off. 'You can rest assured that I won't be holding your daughter captive against her will, sir. Pammy will do as she pleases.'

He reached for Pamela's hand at the tea table and squeezed it. She blushed prettily.

Her father frowned. 'We can't let her travel until it's all sorted out, Dixon. Job, house, wedding. Then we'll bring her out.'

'Oh, Daddy,' Pamela protested, 'stop being so Victorian. I'm twenty-five and perfectly capable of travelling out on my own. You can follow on for the wedding.'

'Certainly not!'

'More tea, Mr Dixon?' Margaret Dacre asked, her expression strained. Her once pretty face was scored with lines from years in a tropical climate.

Rick hesitated, neither wanting more nor wishing to offend. The tea was weak and the cake indigestible. 'Thank you,' he said, offering up his cup.

'Do help yourself to more cake,' she said with a tight smile.

Rick was finding the whole visit to the Dacres' large ugly villa excruciating. He'd been brought straight into the dining-room for afternoon tea and a grilling by Geoffrey Dacre. Why had he taken a job fixing cars in Scotland? Had he no private means? Who were these Lomaxes? What exactly was his family connection to Yorkshire and how far back in time? Margaret Dacre had barely said a word and had the distracted look of someone heavily medicated. Who could blame her, thought Rick, having to live with her censorious and pompous husband who no longer went out to work all day? All Rick wanted was to be left alone with Pamela for these precious couple of hours. Outside, it had started to rain so he couldn't even suggest a walk around the bare dismal garden.

After another twenty minutes of stilted conversation and two more cups of tea, Rick asked to use their bathroom.

Pamela stood up quickly too. 'I'll show you.'

'Mr Dixon knows where the cloakroom is, Pamela,' Geoffrey said tersely.

'He hasn't been here for months,' she said with spirit, 'so he might have forgotten.'

Rick hid his amusement as they left the room. As soon as they were across the hall and in the cloakroom, they reached for each other and began a frantic kissing.

'God, I've missed this,' Rick said, when they pulled back.

'Me too.' She grinned at him.

'Your father's not going to give us any time alone.'

'He's just being protective.'

Rick felt his frustration return. 'It's obvious he doesn't want us to marry, Pammy. We have to stand up to him or it's never going to happen.'

'Of course, it'll happen. Once you've got everything sorted out in Calcutta, he'll be much happier.'

Rick doubted that was true but saw no point in arguing over it. He had to believe that Pamela would return to India – that their relationship was strong enough to withstand her

119

father's disapproval – and that their post-war life could begin.

After an hour sitting in the drawing-room by a coal fire, while he and Pamela played cards and her parents looked on, it was time to return to the station. The chauffeur drove Rick and Pamela into York.

On the platform, they hugged each other goodbye.

'You'll come to Calcutta as soon as you can, won't you?' Rick urged.

'Yes, of course, silly. Just as soon as you get everything organised.'

The passionate kiss that she gave him, not caring that there were dozens of people close by, made Rick's hopes leap. She still loved him. It was just a matter of time before they would be together again. Pamela was strong enough to stand up to her father and his prejudices.

It was only later, on the train as it rattled south, did doubts set in once more. Why did she have to wait until he had secured a marital home? She had friends still in Calcutta she could stay with – friends of the Dacres – who would give her a temporary home until they were married. Instead, Pamela was meekly going along with her father's wishes.

Yet, she had been just as friendly and affectionate towards him as he'd remembered. He had every reason to be optimistic. They were right for each other and a fun married life in Calcutta beckoned for them both.

Chapter 14

Murree, mid-April

From her favourite bench in the garden – the one with the uninterrupted view of the Kashmir hills – Jeanie saw the chaprassy arrive with the afternoon mail. She lingered; it would largely be office dak for Mungo and she'd had a letter from her mother two days ago. It was pleasant to sit in the temperate sunshine after several days of seesawing temperatures, cloudy skies and sudden thunderstorms.

The air was full of the scent of flowers and Jeanie thought how her mother would love it. Strange how she thought about Clara so much these days. Her poor mother who, for years, had bottled up her grief over losing three babies. Jeanie wished she had known about the tragedies sooner and asked her more about her time as a young wife in India. If only Clara had come to Murree with her then she would have been able to share her new secret.

Jeanie hugged herself, finding it hard to keep the smile from her face. Each day she was more certain. She hadn't had a monthly bleed since leaving Scotland in late February. That was about seven weeks ago. Should she go to a doctor to make sure before she gave Mungo the good news? And if so, should it be the school doctor or one in the town? Could they even confirm this early on that she was with child? What about confiding in Dinah Lavelle? The elusive matron had finally agreed to take tea with her the coming Thursday. But then what would a woman who had worked all her life with schoolboys know about pregnancy?

No; Mungo must be the first to be told. Her husband would be as thrilled as she was. Then in time, she could tell her new friend, Mary Dane, and write to her mother. She would ask advice from Mrs Ord, the chaplain's wife, who had brought up three children in Murree, although they were all now in boarding school in Darjeeling. Would they have a girl or a boy? She thought of Belle Lomax and rather wished for a daughter. She liked the name Fiona – or maybe they should call her Clara to please her mother? Mungo would probably want a boy. If so, could she persuade him to call their son, John, after her beloved brother?

As if he could read her thoughts, Mungo suddenly appeared on the steps of the house and made his way towards her across the immaculate green lawn.

'You've got post,' he called and waved a brown envelope in the air. 'It's a telegram, so I thought I better bring it straight out to you.'

Jeanie felt a spasm of anxiety. Telegrams in the war had always brought bad news. Jeanie rose. 'Not mother?'

'No, don't worry.' Mungo handed it over. 'It's from Pindi. Got me intrigued. Sit down, dear. You look all wobbly.'

Jeanie flopped down and tore open the envelope. Relief flooded over her. 'Oh, it's from Stella! How lovely. They're at the Raj. Travelling through Murree in two days' time.'

'Travelling through?'

'Yes, on Wednesday. Wouldn't it be lovely if they could stay for a night? Pay them back for their hospitality to me in Ebbsmouth. We could have a dinner party for them and invite some friends. We haven't had a big one since your birthday.'

Mungo gave a dubious look. 'What friends could we possibly invite who would want to see the Lomaxes?'

'Other members of staff?' she suggested.

'Like Bishop?' he said with derision. 'The man who expelled Andrew Lomax. Or maybe Captain Rae, who stopped him beating up Major Gotley's son? I really don't think the Lomaxes would thank you.'

Jeanie flushed. 'I didn't think of that. Well, we don't have to invite anybody. It would be lovely just having Stella and her family to stay.'

'I know you've taken to this Stella Lomax, darling, but Wednesday really isn't convenient. There are the house matches in the afternoon and the school concert in the evening. You said you wanted to go.'

'I'd forgotten,' Jeanie admitted. These last few days, she'd been able to think of little apart from being pregnant.

Mungo brushed her cheek with a finger. 'Don't look so sad. Why don't you ask them for lunch instead? You could make it an early one – a picnic in the garden – so that they could still reach Kashmir in the day.'

Jeanie brightened. 'That's a lovely idea! Thank you, darling. I'll ring the hotel and suggest it to Stella.'

'Good.' He patted her knee and stood up. 'Now, duty calls.'

Jeanie took a deep breath and caught his hand before he could step away. 'Mungo, there's something I must tell you.'

He frowned. 'Oh? Can it wait?'

'It's good news.' She gave him a trembling smile. Suddenly, she thought she might burst into tears. 'Mungo … I'm … we're going to be parents. At least I think so …'

She saw his serious expression turn to incredulity and then triumph. He sat down heavily on the bench beside her. 'You're – in the family way?' he whispered.

She nodded. 'I haven't had … well, you know … nothing since I've been here and that's nearly two months.'

Mungo gripped her hand. 'That's marvellous news!' He kissed her forehead. 'You clever girl!'

Jeanie laughed. 'I rather think you deserve some of the credit too.'

Mungo chuckled. 'Yes, that's true. Either way, it's wonderful. So, when will he be born?'

'By my reckoning, he – or *she*,' Jeanie said with a teasing look, 'will be due in November.'

Mungo nodded. 'Marvellous; it'll coincide with the start of the long school holidays. Plenty of time to organise an ayah and sort out the nursery.'

'I'm not so sure about an ayah,' Jeanie said. 'I'd really like Mother to come out and help to begin with.'

'Of course, she must come,' he agreed. 'But you'll need an ayah too. Everyone in India has one. You can't expect to be a full-time mother as well as the headmaster's wife, now, can you?'

'I suppose not.'

'I'll have a quiet word with Golightly and see if he can recommend a Christian girl from the mission who might fit the bill.'

Jeanie felt dizzy at the speed of his planning. His enthusiasm made her joyful.

He kissed her once again and sprang to his feet. 'We'll talk about this over supper, dearest. You make me so proud.'

She said, 'I suppose we better not say anything until I've been checked over by a doctor?'

He nodded. 'I don't want you examined by the school doctor – wouldn't seem proper, somehow. There's a good chap over at Pindi Point – ex-army. I'll sound him out.'

As he walked away, he began to whistle. It was years since she'd heard him do so. Excitement gripped her. Talking about it out loud with Mungo made it all real. She was delighted to make him so happy. This is what they needed to consolidate their marriage and put behind them the years of separation. It wasn't that she felt particularly lonely in Murree – she was still finding her feet in the role of headmaster's wife – but a baby would give her a new purpose and joy.

Deep down, Jeanie knew that having a child would also go a long way towards filling up the hollow she had felt inside ever since her brother had died. Her hope was that a new life might help ease her mother's grief a little, too.

Chapter 15

An hour later, Jeanie was in the cloakroom on the house telephone, putting through a call to the Raj Hotel which was answered promptly by Jimmy Dubois.

'Many felicitations to you, Mrs Munro! I hope you and Mr Munro are in the best of good health?'

'We're both very well, thank you, Mr Dubois. And you?'

'Tip-top form! It's most kind of you to ask. We are all so happy to have the Lomaxes here. My son Charles is racing around with my niece, Belle; they're like a pair of puppies. You can probably hear them! But you don't want to hear my chit-chat, I'm sure. Would you like to speak to Stella?'

'Yes, please. If this is a convenient time?'

'Most convenient. She has just returned from a visit to our cousin Ada. Let me summon her to the telephone.'

Jeanie smiled to herself as she heard chatter in the background and the squeal of children. Stella was so lucky to be at the centre of a large extended family who all seemed to get on with each other.

'Jeanie?' Stella sounded breathless on the other end. 'How lovely of you to call! You got my telegram?'

'Yes. I wanted to invite you all to lunch on Wednesday on your way through to Kashmir. We could make it an early one. It would just be so wonderful to see you all again. I'm dying to hear about the rest of your stay in Scotland and the voyage back. Everything went safely, I hope?'

'Yes, we're all fine. Rick sailed with us too so it was fun having his company for longer.'

Jeanie felt a jolt. 'Is Rick in Pindi with you as well?'

'No, he left us in Bombay and took a train to Calcutta. But I'll tell you all about that when I see you.'

126

'Yes, of course.' Jeanie was glad Stella couldn't see her flushed cheeks. There was no mention of Pamela and she wondered if that meant that Rick's engagement was in doubt. She wanted to ask but knew she would have to wait for all of Stella's news. 'It'll be so good to see you again. I've been looking forward to you and Andrew getting back to India and being near neighbours – well near in terms of the size of India!'

'So have I,' Stella agreed. 'Being at Tibby's was fun but I've been homesick for Pindi and Gulmarg – and I've missed the family. It's lovely to be home. But more importantly, how are you settling in?'

'Well, there's a lot to learn,' Jeanie admitted. 'But things are becoming more familiar.'

'And you're happy?' Stella queried.

'Yes, very.' Jeanie felt a thrill as she thought of her pregnancy. It was on the tip of her tongue to blurt out her news to Stella but it was not something that should be relayed over the phone.

'That's the main thing,' said Stella. 'Well, I'd better dash. We're having afternoon tea with the residents. I haven't stopped eating since we got to Pindi – I'm still full from Auntie Rose's huge tiffin.'

'She was the same with us, kind lady,' Jeanie said in amusement.

'Oh, I almost forgot,' said Stella. 'Hester Cussack will be travelling with us to Kashmir – she always spends the hot months on a houseboat on Dal Lake. Would you be able to give her lunch too?'

'Of course,' Jeanie said at once. 'Love to. I'll look forward to seeing you all on Wednesday. Come anytime it suits; I'll be waiting.'

'Thank you. Wednesday it is, then.'

Stella rang off. Jeanie stood holding the receiver as the sudden silence washed around her again. How good it had been to hear Stella's cheerful voice and the background hubbub of the hotel. She wished she could have stepped into that world for the afternoon and joined in the conversation and laughter. She shook off the feeling of anti-climax. The day after tomorrow, she would see them all and, in the meantime, she would go and find Dalip and plan an al fresco lunch for her guests.

***

Come Wednesday morning, Jeanie was up early, unable to sleep. Excitement curdled in her stomach. She hardly touched her breakfast. She chose a pretty yellow dress with a sweetheart neckline that Mungo used to like her in, but that had languished in her wardrobe in India since before the war. She was surprised to see that she had to draw in the belt a couple of notches; she had trimmed down over the years.

She didn't see Mungo until mid-morning, when he trooped in with other staff members for coffee and biscuits.

'You're looking delightful and springlike in that frock, Mrs Munro,' said the chaplain.

'Thank you, Reverend. I've friends coming for lunch and we're hoping to eat in the garden.'

'Hill station friends?' Captain Rae asked, hovering close by.

'No, they're passing through,' she answered. 'They live in Gulmarg.'

'Really?' queried the games master. 'I didn't think anyone lived full-time in Gulmarg – it's snowbound half the cold season.'

Jeanie hesitated before saying, 'They divide their time between there and Pindi where they have business interests.'

128

'Box-wallahs are they?' Rae said with a disparaging look. 'What's their name?'

Jeanie reddened. 'Lomax.'

She saw his eyes glint with interest. 'Not *the* Lomaxes? The hotel-wallahs?'

'Captain Lomax and his family run the Raj Hotels very successfully, if that's what you mean.'

She saw the men exchange meaningful glances and felt annoyance.

'Bit awkward for the headmaster having to entertain them, isn't it?' said Rae. 'He must have told you about the scandal–'

'That was a lifetime ago.' Jeanie cut him off. 'Stella Lomax is my friend and I don't care to hear her husband's family gossiped about, Captain Rae.'

She wished that Mungo was nearby to defend her but he was across the room, absorbed in conversation with Major Lucker. It was a relief when coffee was over and the masters began dispersing to their lessons. Rae goaded her with a parting remark. 'I hope to see you with the headmaster this afternoon, Mrs Munro, supporting the boys in their tennis matches. Guests allowing, of course.'

Mungo gave her an enquiring look after the others left.

'Odious man,' she muttered. 'Trying to stir things up about the Lomaxes. Well, he's not going to spoil my enjoyment at seeing them again.'

'Don't let him upset you,' said Mungo with an affectionate peck on the cheek. 'I'm sure your lunch party will go well.'

'Our lunch party,' Jeanie corrected.

Mungo gave a regretful look. 'I won't be able to join you till after twelve-thirty at the earliest,' he said. 'You carry on without me.'

'Oh darling, please try and get away sooner,' she said in disappointment. 'I so want you to meet them and see how nice they really are. I want them to become your friends too.'

'I'll do my best,' he said, 'but duty comes first.'

Ten minutes after Mungo left, a car, heavily laden with roof luggage, drove into the quad, tooting loudly. As Jeanie rushed outside, the Lomaxes began clambering out of the cramped interior.

'Is it all right to park it here?' Tom asked, stretching his long limbs.

'Of course,' said Jeanie. 'Goodness! How did you all manage to squeeze into that?' She laughed and held out her arms to Stella. The women hugged.

'With Belle on my knee,' said Stella, 'and poor Meemee squashed between me and Andrew.'

'I'm fine,' said Esmie, emerging looking cool and composed, with hardly a crease in her dress and kissed Jeanie's cheek.

Andrew helped Hester Cussack from the front passenger seat.

'Welcome, Baroness.' Jeanie smiled.

'Darling! It's wonderful to be here. So kind of you to invite me.' She took both of Jeanie's hands and clasped them in hers. 'Where is that handsome husband of yours?'

'He's working but will join us for lunch as soon as he can.'

Hester gave a laugh of delight. 'I'm glad to hear it. You're looking well. Blooming, I'd say. Obviously married life in the hills is suiting you.'

Jeanie blushed. 'It is. Now you'll want to freshen up, so follow me.'

She led them inside, directing the men to the cloakroom, while offering her bathroom to the women. Afterwards, she took them outside around the house to the garden. As they passed Mungo's study, Jeanie could see him sitting at his desk, head bent over his books. He didn't look up.

Andrew gave a wry look. 'I saw the inside of that room more often than I care to remember. That's where I was expelled by Bishop.'

'Not expelled,' said Tom gruffly. 'We took you away. The school was in the wrong, not you.'

'Water under the bridge, Andy,' said Esmie quietly.

Jeanie saw their looks of discomfort and wondered how awkward this was for the family, returning to the place of Andrew's disgrace. Perhaps she should have arranged to meet them for lunch in the town? Too late now.

'Nobody cares about any of that these days,' said Stella. 'The school is run by Mr Munro not the awful Bishop.' She linked her arm through Jeanie's. 'And I'm sure he wouldn't discriminate against a boy for having a father in the hotel business, would he?'

'Of course not,' Jeanie assured her quickly. 'Lots of the boys here have fathers in trade. It's not just for army officers' sons anymore. Not since the war.'

'Just look at this delightful garden!' Esmie cried.

'I can't take any credit for it – Mrs Bishop apparently had a way with plants.' The words were out of her mouth before she could stop them.

Tom said caustically, 'Well the view is wonderful and the Bishops had nothing to do with that.'

Belle, who was looking pale and being uncharacteristically silent, clung to Andrew's hand. 'She's feeling a little car-sick,' he explained.

'Would you like to go and look inside the summerhouse?' Jeanie asked the girl. 'There are some bats and balls; I thought you might like to play with them.'

The girl looked away shyly.

'Don't you remember Auntie Jeanie?' Andrew asked. To Jeanie's disappointment, Belle shook her head.

'You gave me a wonderful birthday party at Auntie Tibby's house,' Jeanie reminded her. 'And we had a treasure hunt for toffees.'

A flicker of a smile crossed the girl's face and she gave a slight nod. 'With Uncle Rick,' Belle whispered.

Jeanie felt a pang. 'Yes, that's right. It was the best birthday party I can remember.'

'Ha-ha!' Hester cried. 'If you want a party to go with a swing then ask Rick Dixon to organise it. Isn't that right, Stella?'

'Absolutely.' Stella grinned.

'How is Rick?' Jeanie asked as casually as she could.

'Full of plans,' said Stella. 'He's training as a civilian pilot – it's what he and Pammy want. He's gone ahead to Calcutta to sort out a place for them to live.'

'So, Pamela's not with him yet?'

Stella shook her head. 'She's still helping her parents settle back home. I think her father is a bit of a worrier – doesn't want his only daughter setting off for India until Rick's got everything in order – job and house.'

'But they're madly in love,' said Hester, 'and that's all that matters. No problem is unsurmountable. Love conquers all. Just like it did for you, Stella, and darling Andrew.'

Stella and Andrew exchanged amused looks. 'Very true, Baroness,' said Andrew.

Belle tugged at his hand. 'Come on, Daddy. Let's play.'

He took her off to the summerhouse while the others stretched their legs around the garden. Tom chain-smoked; he seemed ill at ease. Jeanie had a sudden craving for a cigarette. Perhaps that was what pregnancy did. She'd heard of expectant mothers getting yearnings for the strangest things, such as eating coal or ice.

'How was the boat trip back to India?' she asked Stella.

'Surprisingly quiet,' said Stella. 'Those that were on it were full of talk about the Cabinet Mission and whether it will mean independence for India. Have you heard much about how it's going? Jimmy says the British officials have been having meetings with Indian leaders.'

Jeanie shrugged. 'We don't really hear much in Murree. I think a conference is going to be held in Simla next month.'

'I've heard that they're training militias to fight in the Punjab if they don't get their Pakistan,' said Hester. 'They're even teaching women how to handle guns.'

Tom grunted. 'I bet that's Fritters spreading alarm at The Raj. You know how he likes to dramatize things.'

'Not just Fritters, but Bahadur too. They say that demobbed soldiers have been contacted.'

Jeanie hid her disquiet. She'd heard similar tales at the staff coffee meetings. 'I think there's great reason for optimism,' she said swiftly. 'The Attlee government have come in good faith to hand over power to Indians and make sure the transition is peaceful.'

'But just look at the way there's already unrest in the cities between the two sides,' Hester continued. 'I think it's too soon to be handing over power. They're just not ready.'

'Of course they're ready,' said Esmie, joining in. 'They've just helped us win the war. Brave men like Rick; they're the future of this country.'

'I don't think dear Rick would think of himself as Indian,' retorted Hester.

'Anglo-Indians have every right to be part of the new India,' Esmie insisted.

'They do, but that doesn't mean the Indians will welcome them with open arms. Quite the contrary. Fritters says they won't have special treatment like they have under the British.'

'What special treatment?' Tom said in disbelief.

'Given preference in certain jobs like on the railways,' Hester pointed out.

'And barred from holding senior positions in most branches of the civil service,' Esmie countered.

'Well, they're given jobs where they've demonstrated certain talents.' Hester waved her hands and set her bracelets jangling.

Jeanie glanced at Stella, who had fallen silent. She felt uncomfortable at the turn of the conversation.

'Shall we have lunch?' she interjected.

Stella nodded. 'I'll go and fetch Andy and Belle.'

***

As food was brought out to the guests, the fractious nature of the previous exchange seemed to infect the atmosphere. Belle burst into tears at being made to sit at the table.

'I want to play!' she howled.

'Let the little darling, if she wants to,' said Hester.

'She needs to eat something,' Stella said firmly.

Hester rolled her eyes. 'She'll probably just be sick in the car if she does.'

'Belle; sit up nicely,' Stella ordered.

'No!'

Andrew picked her up. 'You can sit on my knee.'

But the girl struggled and screamed. Her parents grew cross.

'Where are your manners?'

'You can go and sit in the car if you won't behave.'

'Too much spoiling at Auntie Tibby's,' said Tom, looking agitated.

'It's all the journeying,' Esmie reasoned.

Jeanie went and crouched beside her. 'Would you like a special picnic on your own rug? You could have it with your dolly.' Belle's crying subsided a fraction. 'And we could get my teddy bear too.'

The girl stared at Jeanie through puffy red eyelids. 'Y-you h-have a teddy b-bear?'

Jeanie nodded. She held out a hand. 'Come with me and see if we can find Big Ted.'

Belle slid a look at Andrew, who sighed and let her go.

'Please start eating,' Jeanie told them. 'We'll be back very soon.'

As she crossed the lawn, hand in hand with Belle, she heard muttered accusations between the adults. Jeanie wondered if it was the strain of having to return to Nicholson's that had put everyone on edge, or whether it was underlying worry about talk of India's future. Perhaps it was a bit of both. It left her feeling leaden and a little anxious.

***

Returning with a happier Belle, clutching the teddy, Jeanie saw that Mungo had joined them. Her heart leapt. The baroness was flirting with him, her peals of laughter ringing out.

'Ah, isn't that a charming sight?' Hester said, as Jeanie approached them with the child. 'Your wife is a natural mother, Mr Munro. She calmed dear Belle out of her tantrum and peace has been restored.'

Mungo stood up to greet her and pulled out a chair next to his. Before sitting, Jeanie spread out a rug next to the table and Belle sat down on it with a triumphant look at her parents. Mungo kissed the top of Jeanie's head as she took her place at the table.

'How delicious to see a couple so in love,' said Hester. 'It won't be long till there are the patter of tiny feet in this house, I bet.'

Jeanie was delighted to hear Mungo give a bashful laugh. 'Nothing would make me happier,' he said.

Jeanie's previous anxiety eased. Her husband couldn't have been more affectionate since he'd heard about her pregnancy and she felt closer to him than ever before. The lunch progressed. Jeanie was baffled by how subdued the adults appeared. This wasn't how she remembered them. But perhaps her memories had been coloured by the vivacious presence of Rick and their long, lively conversations.

Guiltily, she banished such thoughts and concentrated on what Mungo was saying. He was holding forth about his plans for the school and how he wished to attract bright students from all over India.

'My predecessor was a bit stuffy about such things,' he said. 'But I want to make Nicholson's a beacon of academic and sporting brilliance.'

'Bravo!' cried Hester. 'I'm glad you're not being put off by all the gloom and doom about India going to pieces if the British leave.'

'I thought you were one of the doom-mongers?' murmured Tom.

'Certainly not! I was merely repeating what's being said at The Raj.'

'Let's not start all that again,' Esmie pleaded.

Mungo said, 'I see no need to panic. Congress and the League will have to see reason and sink their differences. But whatever happens, we shall soldier on at Nicholson's in the best of British traditions. India will need the expertise of the British for years to come. Take tea, for example. We've become a popular school for the sons of tea planters. India will always need them. They're not going to cut off their nose to spite their face.'

He turned to Andrew. 'My wife tells me that you are a war hero.'

Andrew flashed Jeanie a look with his one brilliant blue eye. 'It was her brother John – my good friend – who was the hero, not me.'

'I'm sure you're just being modest,' said Mungo with an indulgent look. 'Perhaps you'd like me to show you around the school – see how things have changed since your day?'

Jeanie's disquiet returned. Why was her husband suggesting such a thing when previously he'd been reluctant to have the Lomaxes visit? Perhaps he was getting carried away by his own enthusiasm for the school.

'You could give a pep talk to the boys about how you turned your life around after a shaky start.'

'Meaning?' Tom asked sharply.

'Well, Andrew's misdemeanours are the stuff of legend here. But if the boys can hear what he's done in the war, then it's a lesson in redemption.'

Tom gave a laugh of derision. 'The misdemeanours were all your predecessor's. Andy's only mistake was standing up to poisonous gossip about me and my wife.'

'Tom.' Esmie put a steadying hand on his arm. 'That's all ancient history.'

'It would seem not,' he snapped. 'And I'll not have my son humiliated in front of–'

'Dad, don't,' Andrew said.

'I have no intention of humiliating anyone,' Mungo said indignantly. 'But I can see that some lessons are never learnt. Whatever the rights and wrongs of the case, Andrew made a savage attack on a fellow pupil and Bishop was right to punish him. I'm sorry you can't see that even now, Captain Lomax.'

Tom stood up; his look strained. 'I'm afraid it's time we left. If we don't get on the road, we won't make it to Gulmarg before nightfall. Thank you for lunch, Jeanie.'

Mungo got to his feet too. 'Well, that's probably for the best. My wife and I must attend the house matches in half an hour.'

'Time for a quick coffee?' Jeanie asked, dismayed at the sudden frostiness between the men. She couldn't help feeling it was Tom's fault for taking umbrage; Mungo had been trying to be conciliatory.

'That's kind,' said Esmie, rising to stand beside her husband, 'but Tom's right, we really should be making tracks.'

Stella gave Jeanie a regretful shrug. 'Come on, Belle. Time to go, sweetheart.'

'Don't want to go,' the girl protested. 'I'm having a picnic with dolly and teddy.'

'Dolly can continue the picnic in the car,' said Stella. 'Come on.'

Belle burst into tears again. Andrew scooped her up. She began screaming for the teddy. Jeanie quickly grabbed it.

'You can take Big Ted with you,' she said, holding out the bear.

'Don't pander to her,' said Tom.

'If it stops that awful racket in the car,' said Hester with a roll of the eyes. 'Help me up, Tom darling.'

'Allow me,' said Mungo, rushing round to her aid.

'Really, I don't mind lending the bear to Belle,' Jeanie said, handing the toy over. 'He can go on an adventure to the mountains, can't he, Belle? And then I'll have an excuse to come and visit you, to get Big Ted back.'

Belle grabbed the teddy and clutched it tightly, her sobs subsiding.

'What do you say, Belle?' Stella prompted.

'Thank you, Auntie Jeanie,' she said with a teary smile. 'I love Big Ted.'

'Good.' Jeanie smiled. 'I know you'll take care of him for me.'

Ten minutes later, the Lomaxes were piling into the car once more. Stella, the last to climb aboard, put a hand on Jeanie's arm.

'I'm sorry if we've spoilt your lunch party,' she murmured. 'Belle's a bit out of sorts. Others too. But it has been lovely seeing you again.'

'You too,' said Jeanie, patting her hand.

'You promise to come and visit us in Gulmarg?'

'Promise.'

Mungo was closing the passenger door, having helped Hester into her seat.

'Do come and stay on my houseboat, Mr Munro,' said the baroness with a wave out of the window. 'You and your beautiful wife. It's just the place for lovers.'

As they waved them away, Mungo said, 'the baroness seems a cheery soul but I don't think much to your new friends.'

Jeanie squirmed. 'I think they're all a bit travel-weary.'

'Lomax Senior was downright rude to both of us,' Mungo retorted. 'I was only trying to extend the olive branch.'

'I know. Thank you for trying. I'm sure they'll be different on their home turf.'

Mungo looked astonished. 'You don't seriously expect me to go and stay with them in Gulmarg?'

'I thought you loved the mountains?'

'I like a bit of fishing with a good friend in camp.'

'Andrew says his father loves to fish and go on shikar.'

Mungo said sharply, 'I would do many things for you, my dearest, but fishing with Tom Lomax is not one of them. He appears to have no moral backbone – I can't imagine how he was ever in the Peshawar Rifles. Please don't ask me to go and stay at his hotel and pretend I have anything in common with the Lomaxes.'

Jeanie decided not to press the matter. 'Well, at least we could take up the baroness's offer of a few days on a houseboat. Doesn't that sound heavenly?'

He gave her an indulgent smile. 'We'll see. It might be just the rest you need in your condition. I'd be happier with that than the thought of you over-exerting yourself in the hills and being at the beck and call of that badly-behaved Lomax child. Her parents could do with exercising a bit of discipline, in my opinion.'

'She wasn't like that at all in Ebbsmouth,' Jeanie defended them. 'I'm sure it was just car sickness.'

'You are far too soft,' said Mungo. 'I won't let the Lomaxes take advantage of your good nature. I'd rather you didn't encourage them to visit again.'

Jeanie swallowed a protest. Given how disastrously the lunch had gone, she doubted that the Lomaxes would be rushing to call again anyway. There was no point arguing about it any further.

Chapter 16

Exhausted, Jeanie fell into bed after the long day. With the house matches and the evening concert, the unsatisfactory lunch party seemed an age ago. The more she thought about it, the more cross she became at Tom's belligerent comments and his lack of civility to Mungo. She remembered how he had been wary of her when they'd first met at Ebbsmouth – or maybe just disinterested – and she couldn't help but recall her mother's gossip about him having left the army in disgrace and abandoned his second wife for Esmie. Perhaps he just wasn't a very nice man, after all.

But that didn't explain the behaviour of the others. Esmie had been tetchy with Hester, Stella had been short-tempered with Belle, while Andrew had been distracted and subdued. What a mistake it had been to invite them. They obviously felt uncomfortable returning to Nicholson's. Maybe it had just been Stella who'd had any appetite for seeing her again. She was the one who had sent the telegram. Yet they hardly knew each other. Perhaps she had put too much store by this new friendship and had blown it out of proportion. If so, it was an indication that she needed to make more effort to establish friends in Murree, where her future with Mungo lay.

'That's a long sigh,' Mungo observed, as he bedded down beside her.

'I'm tired out after today,' she admitted. 'You're right. It's a silly idea to go to Gulmarg. I hardly know the Lomaxes.'

'It's up to you, my dear,' he said. 'But I don't want you getting exhausted.'

'I won't. Perhaps I can see Stella when she's down in Pindi instead.'

'That sounds a better idea.' Mungo kissed the top of her head and reached over to turn off her bedside lamp. 'Now, sleep, dearest.'

***

The malaise Jeanie felt, persisted into the following day. She kept going over the encounter with the Lomaxes and wondering if she could have smoothed things over better. The baroness had been overly dramatic about the state of India and this had seemed to upset Tom. Perhaps they had already been arguing about it previously? Was the country really racing towards independence? And if so, who would be the winners and losers? It was obvious that Stella hadn't wanted to talk about it.

Were the Anglo-Indians like Stella and Rick worried about the future and what their place in a new India might be? Jeanie felt bad that she hadn't paid more attention to the news. She ought to find out more. After all, it would affect them all. If the British handed over power to the Indian political leaders, how many British would stay?

***

Jeanie was glad of the distraction of Matron arriving for tea that afternoon.

'Please, take a seat.' She indicated one of the canvas chairs on the terrace. 'I thought it would be nicer to take tea outdoors. It's such a lovely afternoon and you spend so much time closeted inside. At least, I assume you do. I haven't really seen you. What do I call you? Matron or Miss Lavelle? I don't think I know you well enough to call you Dinah yet. Though you can call me Jeanie if you want.'

'Matron is fine, Mrs Munro.'

Jeanie was acutely aware that she was babbling. Dinah's neatness and quiet composure made her feel garrulous and ungainly. The matron had such slender hands; they lay quite still in her lap. Jeanie fidgeted with her hair, pushing it behind her ears. Dinah's hair was scraped back into a perfect bun. It was the first time Jeanie had seen the woman without her voluminous headdress. Her hair was pale brown and she had small shell-like ears. If it wasn't for her spectacles giving her such a severe look, and her thin colourless lips, she would be quite pretty.

Jeanie ploughed on. 'I thought we could have a good chat – get to know each other – the only two women in School House.' She gave a nervous laugh.

Dinah asked, 'Will the headmaster be joining us?'

'No. He'll have afternoon tea at four.'

She nodded and her hands relaxed back onto her chair arms. Jeanie wondered if the matron was a little in awe of Mungo – or whether she was aware of his disdain towards Anglo-Indians.

Nitin appeared with the tea tray. 'Just leave it there, thank you. I'll serve up.' The servant nodded and left.

Jeanie busied herself pouring the tea. 'Milk and sugar?'

'Black tea, thank you.'

'So, tell me about yourself, Matron. How long have you been at Nicholson's?'

'Since the first year of the war.'

'And before that?'

'I was in Simla.'

'Oh, what was that like? I'd love to visit. I've heard so much about the place.'

'It's very beautiful.' She didn't elaborate.

'And did you work at a school there?'

'No, I was nursing at one of the hospitals.'

'I see. So, what made you decide to become a school matron?'

Dinah took a sip of her tea. 'The war changed things.'

Again, Jeanie waited for the woman to say more. 'I suppose you wanted to be nearer your family in Pindi?'

Dinah nodded.

To fill the silence, Jeanie pressed her to eat the egg sandwiches. She watched in admiration as the matron managed to eat one without dropping a single crumb or piece of egg.

Jeanie made conversation. 'We had friends visiting from Pindi yesterday; The Lomaxes. I believe you know Stella – one of the Dubois family from the Raj Hotel. I wish I'd thought to invite you along to see them.'

'I was working,' Dinah replied. 'And I don't know Stella that well.'

Jeanie scrutinised her. 'I got the impression from Sigmund and Ada Dixon that you were friends with their family. They're related to the Duboises, aren't they?'

Dinah dabbed at her mouth with a napkin, though there was nothing to wipe. 'I know Ada quite well as she's married to my cousin Clive. I like Ada. She's sensible and a good wife and mother.'

'But you don't approve of Stella?' Jeanie asked.

Dinah gave her a direct look; surprise flickered in her brown eyes. 'I didn't say that.'

'No, but your tone implied it.' Jeanie waited.

'I always thought Stella a little selfish,' Dinah admitted.

'In what way?'

'She was engaged to my cousin Monty – Clive's twin brother – during the war.'

Really?' Jeanie was surprised. 'I didn't know that.'

'Well, it didn't last. While Monty was away, fighting for king and country, she was seeing another man behind his back.'

'Andrew?' Jeanie asked.

Dinah gave a huff of disapproval. 'No, another man – an Irishman. Quite the charmer, according to Ada. She was engaged to him too but for some reason broke it off. It was third time lucky with Andrew Lomax.'

Jeanie thought she sounded bitter. 'At least that seems to be a happy marriage,' she countered, 'so it worked out for the best in the end.'

'Yes, Stella was lucky. He took on Belle too,' said Dinah. 'There was always a bit of a mystery surrounding the girl's birth. Esmie and Tom claimed to be the parents but she was obviously Stella's and born out of wedlock. Probably that Irishman's.'

Jeanie was uncomfortable at their gossiping about Stella. For someone who claimed not to know Stella and her family well, Dinah seemed well-informed about them. It reminded her of her own mother's eagerness to pass on tittle-tattle about the Lomaxes.

'These things happened during the war, I suppose,' said Jeanie. 'I'm not going to judge her.'

Dinah pursed her lips.

'What happened to your cousin Monty?' Jeanie asked.

'He got engaged to another of Ada's cousins – Lucy Dixon. They're going to marry this summer, now that Monty's been demobbed.'

'That's lovely! Happy endings all round.' Jeanie smiled.

Dinah's expression was hard to fathom. Perhaps all these tales of love were difficult to bear for a spinster matron. She struck Jeanie as a lonely woman.

Dinah folded her napkin, smoothed down her skirt and stood up. 'Thank you for the tea, Mrs Munro.'

'There's no rush,' said Jeanie. 'I've got nothing until four if you'd like to stay and sit in the garden.'

She gave a tight smile. 'I have jobs to do. Perhaps another time.'

'Of course. Anytime you want. This is your garden too. If you want to come and sit and read a book, please do.'

'Thank you, Mrs Munro.'

'How about we take tea again next Thursday afternoon?' Jeanie suggested, not quite knowing why. They didn't seem to have any rapport.

But Dinah nodded in agreement. 'If you like.'

Jeanie watched her walk away. What a strange, inhibited, rather waspish woman. She didn't warm to her at all but was intrigued to know more about her.

***

The following week, Jeanie received a letter of thanks from Stella.

'... this is part apology as well as part thanks. None of us behaved very well and you'd gone to such trouble to give us a lovely picnic. I feel terrible that we might have spoilt your day and given the wrong impression to your husband. I can only say that Andrew and his parents were a bit spooked by returning to Nicholson's and being overwhelmed again by memories of that unhappy period in their lives. It's not an excuse, just an explanation. Who would have thought that events in childhood could still overshadow life in adulthood?

Also, the baroness was in one of her contrary moods. We love Hester dearly but she sometimes loves to provoke a drama. I think she finds it unsettling to leave her friends at the hotel for her months at Dal Lake, even though she loves it once she's there – and she finds Pindi far too hot in summer.

146

We're easing back into life at Gulmarg – Belle is happy again. It was so kind of you to lend her your bear. You may find it a hard job getting it back as she takes Big Ted with her everywhere! Andrew is doing a large part of getting the hotel ready for the season as his father is not in the best of health and Esmie is making him rest. I think I told you that Tom is prone to depression when he gets fatigued, which is hardly surprising as he's had a lot of sadness in his life. He's worrying about the political situation. Andrew tells him that everything will be fine and that there are a lot of sensible people trying to work out the best for India. But a worrier is a worrier.

I hope none of this will put you off coming to visit us – I know you'd love it here – it's the most beautiful place and I'm grateful every day that I live here with Andrew and Belle and the Lomaxes. So please say you will come during the school holidays.

Your loving friend,

Stella

p.s. Andrew and I might be down in Pindi in June for my cousin Lucy's wedding. Perhaps we could meet up there too?'

Jeanie was heartened by the frank and affectionate letter. Her suspicions that the Lomaxes were unnerved at being at Nicholson's, as well as worried about their future, were true. She sighed. They were unlikely to want to visit her here again, so there would be no point in asking them. If she wanted to be friends with Stella, then she would have to visit Gulmarg or Pindi. But Mungo was unlikely to want to do either. Maybe if she showed him the letter, he would understand that the Lomaxes had been acting out of character.

147

Reading it again, Jeanie was struck by Stella's observation that childhood events could overshadow adult lives. Without her knowing it, her own growing up had been marred by her mother's lost babies and resentment of India – Clara's desperation to have children – or more specifically, to have a son. Jeanie had always known that John was their mother's favourite but perhaps Clara could never fully allow herself to love her daughter because she feared losing her. Life for infants in India was just too fragile and precarious.

It prompted Jeanie to sit down and write an airmail letter to her mother, telling her the good news about the baby and that, come November, Clara would be a grandmother.

' ... Please, _please_ come and visit. October is a good time to sail to India – not too hot – and you'd be here in time for the birth. Or why not fly and get here sooner? I long to see you again, Mother. There are so many things I want to show you and talk about. I love receiving your letters but it would be even better to have you here in person! I'll write again soon with an update on 'baby'.

All my love
Jeanie xx'

She decided not to mention the fraught lunch party with the Lomaxes or Mungo taking offence at their rudeness. She didn't want to give her mother further reason to refuse to meet Stella and Andrew when she came to stay. Somehow, she would engineer for Andrew to take her and Clara to visit the place where John was buried. Rick had encouraged the idea and Jeanie was determined that one day it would happen.

Chapter 17

In the early hours of Thursday morning, Jeanie awoke. She wondered what had disturbed her. Maybe Mungo had got up early but stretching out her hand she felt him there, a warm presence in the bed. Then she felt the shooting pain in her abdomen. Jeanie gasped. It came again. She clutched her stomach.

'What is it?' Mungo was instantly awake.

Jeanie winced. 'Pains ...'

'What sort of pains?'

She shuddered as familiar cramps seized her. She felt the dampness between her thighs. Disbelief turned to panic.

'I think I'm bleeding.'

Mungo switched on the light. 'Bleeding?' He pulled back the covers. 'My God!'

The horror on his face told her everything. He leapt out of bed. 'What do I do? Should I go for Matron? Call the doctor?'

Jeanie swallowed down a sob. She shook her head. 'I don't think there's anything they can ...' Bile rose in her throat as the pain gripped her again. 'Please help me to the bathroom.'

A few minutes later, Jeanie was sitting on the thunderbox, clutching her stomach in distress as menstrual blood trickled into the bowl. Mungo called to her beyond the closed door. 'Can I get you anything?'

Tears stung her eyes at his tender, bewildered words. There would be no baby.

'Perhaps a hot water bottle,' Jeanie said, grimacing at the pain. It made her nauseous.

By the time she emerged from the bathroom, the bed linen had been changed and a fresh nightgown laid out for her with a hot water bottle. Humza must have been summoned. She changed and climbed into bed. The dawn was filtering in between the curtains.

Mungo hovered at the bedside, his hair unruly and face haggard. 'Is it over?' he asked.

Tears welled in her eyes as she nodded. He hesitated and then kissed her forehead. 'I'll leave you to sleep.'

She longed for him to stay with her, lie down and hold her tight. But he went, closing the door quietly behind him.

***

Jeanie spent the morning in bed. With the help of some Aspirin and sleep, she felt less pain when she awoke. Yet the disappointment at no longer being pregnant engulfed her anew. She dissolved into fresh tears. Her mother wouldn't even have received her letter telling her about the baby. She felt foolish for having made such early plans to beg her mother to come out to India – for looking ahead to a November birth – when she hadn't even been checked over by a doctor.

She shouldn't have told Mungo either. Now he was reeling from disappointment. She should have saved him from that. Yet she had been so joyful at the thought of them becoming parents and knew how much he wanted it too. She longed to give him happiness and to make up for having lived apart for years.

Jeanie was glad that she hadn't confided in Stella about being with child. It was only just over a week since the Lomaxes' visit and yet it seemed an age ago. She felt the first twinge of bitterness. How easy it was for some women to fall pregnant; all those unplanned pregnancies and unwanted babies during the war. Then she chided herself. She and Mungo had only been reunited for a couple of months. It was early days. They had plenty of time. This was just a set-back but not the end of the world. So why did it feel like it was?

Jeanie buried her head under the covers, muffling her weeping. What if she was like her mother and couldn't easily have children? She didn't know if she could bear one miscarriage after another. Right then, she longed for her mother. Only she would really understand how she felt. Jeanie hugged her knees and cried. She had never felt so alone.

***

Briefly, at lunchtime, Mungo appeared. 'How are you, my dear?'

'Not great,' Jeanie admitted. She had made an effort to bathe and dress but she had no appetite for the cutlet and vegetables on her plate.

'Try and eat something,' he urged. 'Must keep your strength up.'

Strength for what? Jeanie wondered. The words were meaningless but she realised Mungo was also struggling to come to terms with what had just happened.

He didn't linger. 'I'll see you at tea-time. Will you be all right this afternoon?'

She nodded. He kissed the top of her head and left. She felt bereft.

Later, she wandered into the garden. The mountains of Kashmir were shrouded in cloud, yet the garden was bathed in sunlight and the air was laden with the scent of wallflowers. The mali was planting out one of the borders. Jeanie didn't want to speak to anyone for fear she would burst into tears, so she retreated to the summerhouse.

The bats and balls that Belle and Andrew had been playing with, were in a box by the door. Jeanie's insides knotted at the memory of Belle running across the lawn,

151

chasing a tennis ball, her fair curls lifting in the breeze. Would she ever have a daughter to gladden her heart?

Jeanie curled up in a wicker chair and let the tears roll down her cheeks.

A tap on the glass door startled her. She turned around to see Dinah Lavelle peering in. Her heart sank. What did she want?

'Mrs Munro?'

Jeanie sat up and blew her nose. 'Yes, Matron?'

The woman hesitated. 'I can come back another time.'

Jeanie looked at her, puzzled.

'For afternoon tea,' Dinah prompted. 'Had you forgotten?'

'Oh, goodness! Sorry, yes, I had. Completely slipped my mind.'

'Don't worry.' Dinah hesitated. 'Are you all right, Mrs Munro?'

Jeanie swallowed, the woman's concern making her instantly tearful again. She shook her head. Dinah stepped inside and approached her.

'You're feeling unwell?'

'Yes,' Jeanie said hoarsely.

'You're looking pale,' said the matron. She put a hand to Jeanie's forehead. It felt cool and dry. 'But you don't feel feverish.'

'I'm not,' Jeanie answered. 'I'm … just … upset.'

Dinah sat down in the opposite chair. 'Would it help to talk about it?'

Jeanie shrugged. She tried to speak but found she couldn't. She squeezed her wet handkerchief savagely.

'Take your time,' Dinah encouraged.

The warm summerhouse filled with the scent of lavender; Dinah must be wearing the same eau-de-cologne as her mother. The thought of Clara, unlocked Jeanie's misery.

152

'I was expecting a baby. Last night I lost it. I'm having the most awful cramps and feeling like death.'

Dinah's eyes widened in shock. 'That's awful. I'm so sorry. I didn't know.'

'No one did – apart from my husband. It was very early on. Less than two months, I suppose.'

'Are you bleeding heavily?'

'Fairly. But I do most months.'

Dinah's look was direct. 'Travel can disrupt monthlies. It's not uncommon for them to stop temporarily from some hiatus. And you've had to adapt to a lot of change in a short time.'

Jeanie stared at her. 'What are you saying? That I might not have been expecting at all? That I'm just having a heavy period?'

'It's possible.'

Jeanie reddened and looked away. She whispered, 'How stupid of me. I should have waited …'

'Not stupid,' Dinah said gently. 'Whether you were or not, you've still suffered a shock and a disappointment. You're bound to be feeling seedy. Have you taken any pain relief? I can give you something.'

'I've got Aspirin. It seems to be helping.'

'Let me order up some ginger tea,' Dinah said, getting to her feet. 'That's always very soothing.'

Jeanie allowed Dinah to take control, ordering tea and biscuits, along with another hot water bottle and tucking a rug around her knees. She was soothed by the matron's calm, efficient manner; neither too brisk nor too emotional. They talked about other things; Mary Dane's badly behaved new terrier, a boy who was prone to sleep-walking and Mrs Ord's flirtation with spiritualism.

'Isn't that a bit embarrassing for the chaplain?' Jeanie asked.

'Highly, I would think,' said Dinah with a wry look. 'Reverend Ord has forbidden her to hold seances at home.'

'How do you know all this?' Jeanie was amused.

'Mrs Golightly can't keep a secret. She often helped me out when I first came here – she'd filled in as matron before me and knew the boys well. We've remained friends since.'

Jeanie was intrigued to know that Dinah did have friends in Murree – or at least one confidante. Perhaps the matron wasn't as lonely as she'd suspected.

When Dinah got up to leave, Jeanie said, 'Thank you, Matron. You've been very kind. I feel a lot better having told you. You will keep it to yourself though, won't you?'

Dinah fixed her with one of her severe looks. 'Of course, Mrs Munro. I would never break a confidence.'

Jeanie felt the reserve between them return. Once the matron had gone, Jeanie continued to sit in the summerhouse, dozing. Though she was still upset at what had happened, she was a little comforted by the thought that she might never have been pregnant in the first place. Maybe it had been kindness on Dinah's part to suggest such a thing but it had had the desired effect. Perhaps, in time, she and Dinah could become friends. Fleetingly, she had broken through the woman's reserve and had seen a more caring side – one that the pupils knew and that made her popular with them.

As Jeanie pondered the traumatic day, she realised one thing clearly; her desire for a child was stronger than ever.

Chapter 18

16th May

Jeanie switched on the wireless in Mungo's study just before a quarter to nine in the evening. She felt jumpy with expectation. Mungo was writing a report for some conference he was due to attend in June.

'I don't know why you're getting so het up,' he said. 'You would think it was the king about to speak.'

'It's Lord Pethick-Lawrence,' said Jeanie. 'He's almost as important. He's head of the Cabinet Mission, after all.'

'I know who Pethick-Lawrence is,' Mungo said with slight irritation.

The newspapers had divulged little of what was taking place at the conference in Simla but all the political party leaders had been there and Lord Pethick-Lawrence himself – head of the British government's attempt to bring about a transition to independence – was due to make an announcement at any moment.

'This could be huge,' she persisted. 'A blueprint for how India is going to be run in the future.'

'Even if it is,' Mungo said, not bothering to look up from his papers, 'it could be years before the reins of power are transferred to the Indians.'

'From what I've been reading,' she said, 'I don't think Congress or the League will be prepared to wait that long.'

He glanced up and gave a snort of amusement. 'Why this sudden obsession with politics? I didn't think you were remotely interested.'

Jeanie hesitated. In the past few weeks, she had seized on any diversion to take her mind off the huge disappointment of not being pregnant. She had taken up painting again –

155

using the paints that the Lomaxes had kindly given her on her birthday – and she had become an avid reader of the *Times of India*. But she couldn't say this to Mungo in case he took it as a criticism of their failure to conceive.

'I've been interested since the war, I suppose. Being in the A.T.S really opened my eyes to the wider world. I'd listen to Phyllis arguing with the officers in the mess about voting Labour and how cock-a-hoop she was when Attlee's government was elected. Before that, I never really questioned how things were run and–'

'It's very different out here.' Mungo interrupted. 'India is not Britain and it's naive to think it's in any way similar. I think your Labour-wallahs like Phyllis haven't grasped that. They can't just wash their hands of India and walk away.'

Jeanie smothered a protest. She should have known that Mungo wouldn't like her talking about her time on active service or her army comrades. For some reason it made him defensive. She in no way thought he'd shirked war work – his efforts to keep Nicholson's going through the war had been heroic – but he was prickly about the subject.

Pethick-Lawrence coming on the wireless stopped the conversation. Jeanie leaned in, eager to hear every word. He spoke in a ponderous voice, delivering his proposals – long and detailed – in English only. It went on for over quarter of an hour. Jeanie struggled to take it all in: a federation … in or out of the British Commonwealth … the proposal must either be accepted or rejected in its entirety.

When it was over, she turned to Mungo. 'What did you make of that?'

'Sounds sensible.'

'So,' Jeanie said, 'if I understood it correctly, this federation would mean that central government takes control of things like defence and foreign affairs but the provinces can decide other things for themselves.'

'That's the gist of it,' Mungo agreed. 'And provinces can band together on certain issues.'

'Which means that Muslim states can act together to protect their interests?' Jeanie queried.

'Yes, I think so.' Mungo nodded.

'That's good news then? They can run things how they want within a united India. And Congress gets its Swaraj.'

He gave her a quizzical look. 'You're beginning to sound like a Congress-wallah.'

'You don't have to be a member of Congress to know that swaraj means independence,' she said with a wry smile. 'Oh, Mungo; I think this is very encouraging. The different parties must have agreed to this, or why would Pethick-Lawrence be announcing it? There's been so much talk in the press about civil unrest if the mission fails. Surely this is cause for optimism?'

'Let's hope so.' He sat back and rubbed his eyes.

'You work too hard.' Jeanie stood up and went over to his desk. She squeezed his shoulders and felt him tense. 'Why don't we get an early night?'

'I want to get this finished,' he said, leaning forward to shuffle his papers. 'You go up – I'll join you soon.'

She stifled a sigh of frustration. She had just started another monthly bleed and she knew he was disappointed. They had been making love every other night in an attempt to make her pregnant. The lovemaking was routine and brief – like brushing teeth – as if it was something they had to fit in before going to sleep. Jeanie was not even sure that her husband was enjoying it anymore; it certainly lacked any spontaneity. She knew he wouldn't touch her while she was having her period, yet she longed for him just to hold her in bed and let her fall asleep in his arms. She wanted to rekindle the tenderness that he'd shown her when they'd briefly

157

thought she'd been with child. Now he seemed too distracted by work and his leadership responsibilities.

She was asleep before he came to bed and by the time she awoke in the morning, he was already up and gone.

***

At the staff coffee morning, there was animated chatter about the Simla announcement.

'It's a big concession to the Muslim League,' said Reverend Ord. 'Jinnah's a wily old bird.'

'I disagree,' said Robert Dane. 'Old Pethick-Lawrence said there was to be no sovereign Pakistan – so no autonomous Muslim state.'

'No, but he's offering a federation of Muslim provinces banding together in the spirit of Pakistan,' Ord pointed out.

'Not sure Congress will like that,' said Major Lucker glumly. 'Gandhi's been telling them to read the proposals in their own language before deciding.'

Captain Rae gave a disparaging huff. 'That half-naked fakir! He hates anything English. They should take what's offered and be grateful.'

'We're the ones who should be grateful, Captain,' said Jeanie. 'The Indians have helped us win the war and swaraj is the reward. It is their country, after all.'

The men looked at her warily. Mungo intervened quickly.

'What my wife means, is that the British government's proposals give us hope that things will go smoothly.'

The games master gave a grunt of disbelief. 'There are too many hot-heads out there just waiting to stir up trouble. Those soldiers you're so grateful to, Mrs Munro, are already arming themselves for civil war. And we British could well be caught in the cross-fire. It's the Indian temperament; they can't help themselves. Too volatile.'

'That's nonsense,' Jeanie retorted. 'I've met men who served with Indians during the war and they showed colossal bravery and cool-headedness. My own brother and his fellow officers—'

'My dear,' Mungo cut in. 'We don't need a lecture on how the war went in India. We were here and you weren't.'

Jeanie flushed. 'I didn't mean to lecture.'

Captain Rae smirked. 'And many of your brave Indians deserted to the Japanese to save their skins, Mrs Munro. No loyalty there.'

***

In the days that followed, Jeanie remained tight-lipped about current affairs in front of Mungo and his colleagues. She was still smarting at the way he had belittled her in front of the other men and she found it difficult to be civil to Captain Rae, who lost no opportunity to needle her about the deteriorating situation.

'What do you think of the Attlee government now, Mrs Munro?' he asked disparagingly. 'Still want to sing its praises? It seems old P-L can't get the Indians to agree on anything after all. And in the meantime, the illiterate hordes are out stabbing each other with increasing enthusiasm. Didn't I warn you it would be like this?'

'The mission hasn't failed yet,' she said, struggling to stay calm.

'It's not looking good, I'm afraid,' Reverend Ord interjected. 'And it's not just the Hindus and the Muslims who can't agree. The Sikhs are threatening to take matters into their own hands too.'

Jeanie knew there was truth in what he said. She'd read in the *Times of India* at the outrage of the Sikhs who were accusing the British of trying to 'atom bomb' them and destroy their homeland in the Punjab by putting their fate in the hands of the Muslim League. The Sikhs were a minority – although a large minority – in the mostly Muslim Punjab, but the government plan didn't appear to address their needs at all. She wondered what their Sikh khansama, Dalip, thought of the situation but didn't feel she knew him well enough to ask.

Often, Jeanie turned to painting to distract her uneasy thoughts from the growing crisis. One hot June afternoon Mary Dane appeared with her dog, Butler. Jeanie was in the garden, embarking on yet another watercolour of the Kashmir mountains. Butler tore across the lawn and jumped up at her, barking and knocking over the easel.

'Down, Butler!' Mary shouted ineffectually as Jeanie tried to grab her picture from the dog's jaws. The terrier ran off with the half-finished painting. 'Butler!' Mary went after him.

'Don't worry,' said Jeanie, laughing. 'It's not very good.'

'I'm so sorry,' Mary sighed, giving up on chasing the dog. 'He's such a naughty boy. Robert says I'm far too soft on him. I don't know what I'm going to be like as a mother ...' She stopped abruptly.

Jeanie stared at her and for the first time noticed the swelling beneath her frock.

'You're expecting?' she gasped. Mary blushed under her sunhat and nodded. Jeanie gulped. 'That's wonderful, Mary. I'm so happy for you.'

Mary flopped into the cane chair next to her, pulled off her straw hat and fanned her face. 'I'm over half-way through,' she admitted. 'Not feeling sick now, but I don't seem to have any energy – especially since the hot weather started. Robert says I've got to take it steady – not do as much – but we're just getting to grips with running the boarding house and I can't just put up my feet like some

160

burra-memsahib and order everyone around. Apart from anything else, I'd be bored silly.'

Jeanie thought how different it was for Mary who had a husband who actively encouraged her to help him run Trafalgar House and get to know the boys in their care. Mungo wouldn't let her have anything to do with the boarders in School House. Her duty was to appear at his side at the occasional school lunch or cricket match, and entertain at dinner parties. But the only guests Mungo would invite were other members of staff, so Jeanie's enthusiasm for hosting was dwindling.

'That's why I've come over to ask a favour,' Mary continued. 'It's Robert's idea.'

'Go on,' Jeanie encouraged.

'We were wondering if you would paint the scenery for our house play? Robert wants it to be our show-piece at the end of term. I was going to do it but he suggested I ask you – said he remembers you doing a really good job of it before the war.'

Jeanie smiled. 'That was kind of him to remember. I did the scenery for a school play – and enjoyed it. So yes, I'd love to help out.'

'Oh, that's marvellous!' Mary exclaimed. Then she gave a cautious look. 'Of course, you'll want to ask Mr Munro first, but as long as he's happy about it ...'

Jeanie winced. Was it obvious to everyone that she continually had to defer to her husband before taking a decision? Mary was a gregarious young woman but even she was a little overawed in Mungo's presence. It was probably the difference in their ages but Jeanie knew it was also because Mungo inspired deference and a touch of trepidation in others.

'I'm sure Mungo will be delighted for me to help out,' Jeanie answered. 'He's getting rather tired of me painting

161

just the view from this garden. And I'd like nothing better than to work on a bigger canvas.'

She ordered up lemonade for them both and they moved their seats further into the shade of the trees. While Butler dug up holes in the flowerbeds and sprayed the lawn with soil, Mary chattered animatedly about the play.

'We'll need indoor scenery – French windows and a view to a garden. And maybe you can help me find some props and costumes. Beg, borrow and steal. But only if you want to get that involved.'

'Of course I do,' Jeanie said. 'It'll give me something fun to focus on and take my mind off the gloomy news.'

'What news?' Mary looked at her in concern.

'The political situation,' said Jeanie. 'Looks like the Cabinet Mission is going to fail.'

Mary gave a baffled look. 'What's that got to do with us? It's just Indian politics.'

'It's the future of this country,' Jeanie pointed out. 'So that's our future too.'

Mary shrugged off the suggestion. 'Well, if the worst comes to the worst and they kick the British out, we'll just go home. Our husbands will always find jobs there or in other parts of the Empire.'

The conversation was interrupted by Butler racing back to them, barking and jumping at butterflies. Soon afterwards, Mary left, pulling Butler by his collar. 'I'll see you at Friday's rehearsal – four o'clock,' she called as she went.

Jeanie sat on, pondering Mary's lack of interest in the British situation in India. Did she not feel a part of India or comprehend the centuries of connections between their peoples? But then Mary was new to India and her family did not have the same ties as Jeanie's had. She and John had been born in India and their father had made his career here. John had died defending India from Japanese invasion. And there were other families – like Stella's and Rick's – who went back generations in this country. Their family histories, jobs, homes and sense of belonging were woven into the very fabric of India. If the British withdrew with no settlement in place, would they not be betraying the Anglo-Indians who had served them for generations?

She didn't know if she wanted to stay or go, if or when the British pulled out. India hadn't really felt like home since she was a young girl. She supposed her fate would depend on what Mungo wanted to do and she knew he was keen to make his mark as Nicholson's headmaster.

Jeanie sighed. There was nothing she could do about the mission and its repercussions. Best just to make the most of her life at the school and not look too far ahead. The thought of helping out Robert and Mary with their play, gave her spirits a lift.

Chapter 19

Late June

'Can't I come too?' Jeanie asked, watching Mungo gulp down his afternoon tea. 'I've never had a proper look around Lahore.'

'Dearest,' said Mungo distractedly, standing up. 'I'll be at the conference the whole time. It'll be deadly dull for you.'

'I could amuse myself,' Jeanie replied.

'I'd worry about you on your own – especially when there's talk of more unrest – the cities aren't the safest places to be at the moment.'

Jeanie didn't hide her disappointment. For the past few weeks, she'd been working hard on the Trafalgar House play, partly to please her husband. Mungo had said it was good to see her guiding Mary Dane in the ways of a housemaster's wife and setting a good example to the younger woman. But all the scenery was now completed and the Danes had guests staying with them all week.

'But there's nothing for me to do while you're away. You said yourself, Major Lucker will be in charge.'

'Well, you could be a help to matron if there are any domestic decisions to be made. Keep an eye on the servants – that sort of thing.'

'Matron's going to a wedding in Pindi at the weekend,' Jeanie reminded him. 'The deputy matron from Agincourt House is covering.'

'Jean,' Mungo said a little impatiently, 'we managed six years apart, so I'm sure a woman of your resourcefulness can cope with four days without me.'

She was stung by his bluntness. 'Wouldn't it be a good opportunity for us to be together away from the school?'

Jeanie persisted. 'Even if you're busy during the day, we could have the evenings free.'

She knew from his guarded expression that he understood what she meant; that they needed time alone together to reignite some passion in their marriage. Their hopes of her conceiving had been dashed once again. Since her latest monthly bleed, Mungo had not sought intimacy with her.

He hesitated, struggling with some thought. 'We'll have plenty of time together once the term is over,' he said, kissing the top of her head.

She caught his hand before he could rush off. 'And go away somewhere together?'

'Yes, if that's what you want,' he agreed.

'I was hoping you would want it too,' Jeanie challenged him.

'I do, of course.'

'Then let's take up Hester Cussack's offer to stay on her houseboat.'

For a moment, Mungo looked puzzled as if he had no idea what she was talking about. 'Oh, you mean the old baroness?'

'Yes, with the houseboat on Dal Lake,' said Jeanie. 'Wouldn't that be heavenly? Somewhere to really unwind after a hectic term.'

'It does sound tempting, doesn't it?' he agreed. 'Perhaps you'd better write to her and ask if the offer still stands.'

'I will.' Jeanie smiled.

Then he was disengaging his hand and striding away.

***

Three days later, on the last Thursday in June, Mungo left by car for Lahore. As soon as he'd gone, Jeanie felt at a loose end. The town was filling up with the families of civil servants escaping the heat of the plains and white army tents were sprouting like daisies among the hilltops as their summer camps were established. It looked just the same as the summer before the war, yet Jeanie knew that it wasn't. The Cabinet Mission had failed; Pethick-Lawrence and his colleagues were on the point of returning to Britain empty-handed. The newspapers were reporting that far from there being any consensus on independence, the delegation was leaving without even an interim, provisional government in place.

The earlier optimism reported in the press was giving way to fears that more extreme nationalists on both sides were gaining the upper hand and militias were growing in strength. The doom-mongers were claiming that the British administrators had already lost control in the Provinces. Jeanie couldn't shake off her feeling of apprehension, despite the normal goings-on in the hill station.

That afternoon, Jeanie took tea with Dinah Lavelle. Since her heart-to-heart with the matron two months previously, they had met up fortnightly on Dinah's day off. Their chats were mostly of trivial matters to do with running the house, though the older woman occasionally talked about her brother in Poona and her cousins in Pindi. She smoked a lot and Jeanie shared the occasional illicit cigarette too, while she reminisced about home and the war. Jeanie had tried to draw out Dinah's opinions on the independence negotiations but the matron seemed fatalistic.

'What will be, will be,' she had said. 'I'll hope to stay here at Nicholson's and keep working as long as I can. Isn't that what you want too, to stay at the school?'

'Yes,' Jeanie had said, though she hadn't been entirely sure.

That afternoon, she told Dinah of her disappointment at not going to Lahore. 'I'm in half a mind to turn up and surprise him – do something spontaneous for once.'

Her eyes widened behind her spectacles. 'I don't think Headmaster would be pleased.'

'No, you're probably right.' Jeanie sighed. 'He's not the spontaneous type.'

Dinah offered her a cigarette. For a few moments they both smoked in silence. Then abruptly, the matron asked, 'If it's spontaneity you want, why don't you come to Pindi for the wedding with me?'

Jeanie gaped at her. 'I couldn't possibly. I'm not invited. They don't even know me.'

Dinah gave a rare smile. 'I know you. Come as my guest. Stella Lomax will be there – and Ada. You know the Dixons.'

Jeanie's insides fluttered. Would Rick be there? She glanced away, conscious that she was blushing. 'That's very kind of you but I can't simply gatecrash your cousin's wedding.'

'We don't see it like that in my community,' said Dinah. 'When it comes to celebrations, it's "the more, the merrier".'

Jeanie felt a kick of excitement. 'But where would I stay?'

Dinah said, 'I'm being put up at my aunt's house. I'm afraid that will be chock-a-block. But the reception is at The Raj Hotel. Why don't you book in there?'

'I could ring Jimmy Dubois,' Jeanie said eagerly. Then her doubts returned. 'But Mungo is expecting me to hold the fort here.'

'There's nothing for you to do, Mrs Munro,' Dinah pointed out. 'Deputy Matron is covering for me till Sunday. Major Lucker is in charge of any school matters and Tasker

167

is a very sensible head prefect – the boys won't be any trouble.'

Jeanie reddened at her blunt words. It made her realise how superfluous she was to the running of School House. Mungo knew that, yet he would rather her stay here than go with him.

'I'll come,' she said impulsively. 'Thank you for asking me.'

Chapter 20

The Raj Hotel, Rawalpindi

On the Friday evening, Dinah dropped Jeanie off at The Raj. They'd travelled down together in the matron's Ford car with Dinah explaining the web of cousins, aunties and uncles that Jeanie would meet who were related to either Lucy Dixon or Monty Gibson. Jeanie's head spun as she tried to learn and remember. Dinah had already rung ahead to alert her Gibson cousins that Jeanie would be attending and that Jimmy Dubois was expecting her at the hotel.

'I'll see you tomorrow,' Dinah said, with a wave as she drove off.

Jeanie was greeted by a beaming Jimmy and his young son Charles, who was his father in miniature, with the same round face and thick black hair.

'We have put you in the baroness's room, Mrs Munro,' said Jimmy. 'The hotel is bursting at the seams for Lucy's wedding. But the room is very comfortable – one of our best.'

'I hope the baroness won't mind?' Jeanie felt guilty for imposing when the hotel was so busy.

'Not in the least,' Jimmy assured. 'I rang and got her permission. She's delighted that you are getting to the wedding party.'

'Is Stella here?' she asked.

'Indeed.' Jimmy nodded. 'My sister arrived earlier with Andrew and Belle. They're over at our Auntie Rose's, catching up with the family. She's delighted to hear you are coming.'

Just then, some more guests arrived and young Charles ran forward on sturdy legs to greet them.

169

'I'll find my own way to the room,' Jeanie said, seeing how busy Jimmy was.

'Dinner is served at seven in the dining-room,' the manager said, handing over the key. 'The regulars are looking forward to seeing you. Mr Ansom has requested that you sit at their table.'

'How kind.' Jeanie smiled, infected by the buzz of excitement.

**

Later, after dinner, Jeanie retreated to the resident's sitting-room to play cards with Ansom, Fritwell and Bahadur. They were missing Hester's company but were in lively form. They were full of excitement about the wedding, to which they'd also been invited, although Fritters grumbled about some of the guests.

'Taking over the damned lobby,' he muttered with indignation, 'and sitting at our table. Jimmy had to have a word. Flighty lot from Lucknow.'

Ansom chuckled. 'Still, it's a tonic having you here, Mrs Munro. We haven't been able to play whist or bridge since the baroness left for Kashmir.'

'It's my pleasure,' said Jeanie. 'My husband doesn't like playing cards so I haven't played for months either.'

'Shame he had to attend a boring conference,' said Fritters, 'instead of accompanying you to the wedding.'

'Yes, it is.' Jeanie kept to herself how Mungo would have balked at attending an Anglo-Indian wedding and how he knew nothing about her being in Rawalpindi.

They were just about to start a second game – Bahadur having won the first – when the door flew open and Belle came running in.

'Auntie Jeanie!' she cried, catching sight of her. She threw herself at Jeanie.

'Hello, poppet!' Jeanie hugged her in delighted surprise at the enthusiastic greeting. The girl's eyes were shining and her cheeks were flushed.

'She's a little over-excited,' said Stella, laughing, as she came into the room with Andrew. 'The Dixons have been spoiling her rotten.'

Jeanie stood up and the women kissed cheeks. Andrew shook her hand.

'Auntie Jeanie, will you play with me?' Belle asked, pulling on her arm.

'It's well after bedtime, young lady,' said Stella. 'We just said you could come in and say goodnight.'

'But I want to play!' Belle protested.

Andrew lifted her into his arms. 'There'll be lots of play tomorrow with your cousins.'

'And with me,' Jeanie promised.

She expected the girl to make a fuss but she sank back and snuggled into Andrew's broad shoulder. She nodded and put her thumb in her mouth.

'Night, Auntie Jeanie,' she mumbled.

'Goodnight, sweetheart,' Jeanie said, blowing her a kiss. 'Sweet dreams.'

An hour later, as Jeanie was making ready for bed, there was a knock followed by Stella popping her head round the door.

'Just wanted to say a proper hello; it was all a bit rushed with seeing family and putting Belle to bed. How are you?'

'Fine,' said Jeanie, beckoning Stella in. 'And you? You're looking blooming.'

Stella pulled a face. 'Not feeling it.' She perched on a chair. 'It was touch and go whether we came. That's why I didn't contact you beforehand.'

Jeanie felt a stab of concern. 'Are you ill?'

Stella gave a sheepish smile. 'Not exactly. Unless you call 'morning sickness' an illness.'

Jeanie's heart thumped. 'You're expecting?'

Stella nodded. 'Andy's over the moon. So am I. I just feel sick a lot. But I know it'll pass soon.'

Jeanie leaned towards her and squeezed her hand. 'I'm so pleased for you both. For all of you. Do Andrew's parents know?'

'Yes. Me throwing up after every meal was a bit of a giveaway,' Stella said ruefully.

'How is the Captain?' Jeanie asked. 'You seemed a bit concerned about him in your letter.'

Stella looked reflective. 'He's not in the best of health. Gets very anxious about things. Esmie tries to distract him from the news – encourages him to paint and take regular walks – but he's lacking in energy. He didn't really want Andy to go – hates him being away.'

'Well, I suppose he had to live through all the uncertainty of the war and Andrew being on active service.'

'It's more than that,' Stella confided. 'It all stems from misunderstandings in Andy's childhood when he went to live in Ebbsmouth with his mother and Tom didn't seem him for years. I think he worries that Andy is somehow going to disappear again, even though Andy tries to reassure him he never would.'

'Poor Captain Lomax,' Jeanie said.

'Sorry,' Stella said, 'I didn't mean to worry you. He'll be fine. As long as he has the wonderful Esmie there to look after him and raise his spirits, he'll come to no harm.' Her tone brightened. 'Now, tell me what life has been like in Murree.'

Jeanie described her daily routine and made Stella laugh with anecdotes about the teaching staff. She told her the positive things about helping out with the Trafalgar House play and her growing friendship with Mary Dane, despite her annoyingly disobedient dog who was the bane of their mali's life. She didn't speak of her dissatisfaction at Mungo going off to Lahore without her and their failed attempts to conceive a child.

'Dinah Lavelle is still a bit of an enigma,' Jeanie said. 'She seemed very wary of me to begin with but we've become more friendly. I must say, you could have knocked me down with a feather when she invited me to the family wedding. Maybe she felt sorry for me, twiddling my thumbs at Nicholson's while Mungo's away at this conference.'

'Or maybe she likes your company,' said Stella with a smile.

'Whatever the reason, it was very sweet of her.'

Stella gave a snort of amusement. 'Sweet is not a word I'd use in the same sentence as Dinah.'

Jeanie remembered how the matron had been critical of Stella and accused her of two-timing Monty Gibson. 'So how would you describe her?'

'She was always more reserved than the Gibson tribe or the other Lavelles,' Stella mused. 'Aloof. The type who thought herself better than the rest of us. But maybe that was because she was a bit older and I didn't know her as well. Having said that,' Stella added, tapping the side of her nose. 'There were rumours about her time in Simla.'

'Rumours?'

'She was nursing at a hospital there before the war but her posting came to an abrupt end. No one was told why – not officially. But Ada once got a half-admission from Clive, that his cousin Dinah had got into trouble and had to leave. Something about a liaison with a doctor or a patient; Ada was never entirely sure.'

'I find it hard to imagine Matron doing anything remotely scandalous,' Jeanie said in astonishment.

'"Still waters run deep", as they say,' said Stella. 'If it's true, I'm glad Dinah's found happiness as a school matron. She usually steers clear of family events in Pindi, so I'm doubly pleased that she's come and brought you with her. Everyone deserves a bit of fun in their life.'

Jeanie smiled. 'It seems like the whole world has turned up to celebrate.'

Stella laughed. 'Dear Lucy and Monty have been waiting a long time to be wed; they've been engaged since half-way through the war. It's a huge occasion. And the Raj is usually quiet in June with most people decamping to the hills, so there is room to host a big party.'

'I can't wait,' Jeanie grinned.

As Stella got up, she said, 'Oh, I nearly forgot. There's someone who's looking forward to seeing you again.'

Jeanie raised eyebrows in curiosity.

'Cousin Rick,' said Stella. 'He arrived from Calcutta yesterday.'

'Rick?' Jeanie swallowed, feeling a thud in her chest. 'How nice.'

'He's full of beans. Said to pass on regards. But anyway, you'll see him tomorrow in person.'

As Stella left, Jeanie put her hands to her hot cheeks. The sudden news had taken her by surprise. Then she caught sight of herself in the ornate gilt-framed cheval mirror and saw the gleam in her eyes. Liar. At the back of her mind had been the thought that Rick might well come to his cousin Lucy's wedding, even though he now lived hundreds of miles away in Bengal. Had it swayed her precipitate decision to come to Pindi? Not really. Was she excited at the thought of seeing him again? A little. Was she looking forward to the wedding day? Most definitely.

Chapter 21

St Joseph's Catholic Church was packed with those who had come to see Lucy Dixon and Monty Gibson married. From the excited chatter around her, Jeanie knew that the happy occasion had brought family and friends together from all over India. Even though it was Dinah, a cousin of the groom, who had invited her, Jeanie sat with Stella and the residents of the Raj Hotel on the bride's side of the church.

'Everyone's dressed up to the nines,' Jeanie said to Stella. 'I feel a bit dowdy in this summer frock.'

'You look lovely,' Stella assured. 'Yellow suits you.'

Stella broke off their conversation to wave across at Ada, who was sitting with her husband and their daughter June. Belle started shouting and waving at her cousin, setting them both giggling. Jeanie remembered with a pang how Mungo had quickly struck up a rapport with the Dixon girl. For a brief moment, she wished that he was here with her.

Craning round, Jeanie searched the opposite rows for Dinah but could see no sign of her. She sat back and took in her surroundings. The church was richly adorned with statues and paintings, gleaming gold candlesticks and flickering votive candles. The air smelt sweetly of incense. It was an assault on the senses compared with the Presbyterian churches she was used to at home. Stella was pressing a handkerchief to her nose.

'Are you alright?' Jeanie murmured.

'Smell's making me a bit nauseous,' she admitted.

Jeanie squeezed her knee. 'Let me know if you want to slip out. I'll help keep an eye on Belle.'

Someone tapped her on the shoulder. Turning round, she stifled a gasp.

'Rick!'

'Hello, Jeanie.' He gave her a generous smile. She'd forgotten how it made the skin around his handsome eyes crease. 'How are you?'

She swallowed. 'Very well, thank you. And you?'

'Fighting fit,' he replied, as his parents and brother Sigmund shuffled in beside him. This set off a flurry of handshakes and cheek-kissing with Stella and Andrew.

Rick, Sigmund and their father were immaculately dressed in double-breasted suits with buttonholes of cream rose buds. Stella's Auntie Rose was wearing a lilac-coloured dress with a matching slouch hat. Jeanie wished she'd thought to borrow a hat rather than just pin back her unruly curls with two mother-of-pearl clips.

'Where are Jimmy and the family?' Rose asked. 'They won't get a seat.'

'Still finishing off the decorations at the hotel,' said Stella. 'They'll be here soon.'

Shortly afterwards, the organ struck up the wedding march and everyone stood up for the entrance of the bride. Seeing the radiant and pretty Lucy on the arm of her proud father, Ziggy Dixon, Jeanie felt her throat tighten and eyes smart with tears. It reminded her of walking down the aisle with her own father, trembling with nervous excitement at the sight of Mungo waiting for her, standing stiffly at attention and resolute. He hadn't turned around until she was standing right beside him.

As Lucy and her father passed by, she could see that he was openly crying.

'Uncle Ziggy is so emotional,' Stella whispered in amusement. 'He cries at Bing Crosby songs, so he'll weep buckets today.'

The way Monty was beaming as he watched his bride come towards him, nearly reduced Jeanie to tears too. He was passably handsome, though his nose was crooked and

176

his hair receding. Yet at that moment, he and Lucy looked the most glamorous and in-love couple in the church.

The service was longer than Jeanie expected, with Mass as well as the marriage ceremony, but she was uplifted by it. The service was lavish yet intimate, profound but joyful. And all the while, she was acutely aware of Rick sitting behind her; his melodious voice during the singing and his deep chuckle at some joke that Sigmund made.

Finally, they all began to file out of the church behind the bridal party into the humidity and glare outside. As people milled around, greeting relations from afar, Jeanie lost sight of Rick and his family. She was helping steer the elderly gentlemen from the hotel into Andrew's car, when a woman in a broad-brimmed green hat greeted her.

'There you are!'

Jeanie stared at her in bemusement and then recognition dawned. 'Matron?'

Dinah gave a wry smile. 'I think perhaps for today, you can call me Dinah.'

Jeanie laughed, feeling foolish. 'I didn't recognise you with your hair down. It suits you.'

'Thank you.'

Jeanie thought how Dinah's brown hair softened her features, and the deep red lipstick made her lips look plumper. She'd never seen the woman wear make-up before.

'Can I give you a lift?' Dinah asked.

'Well, yes, thanks. It'll save Andrew having to keep ferrying us back to the hotel.'

She told Stella of Dinah's offer. Stella and Dinah greeted each other with a brushing of cheeks and trivial pleasantries.

'Can I come with you, Auntie Jeanie?' Belle piped up.

Dinah hesitated and then gave a tight smile. 'Of course. Why don't you and your mother come?'

177

The street leading to the hotel was busy with cars trying to park and taxis dropping off guests. Jeanie was impressed with the lavish decorations. The path up to the hotel was lined with jardinières of flowers and the portico was festooned with ribbons. As they entered the lobby, it too was decorated with garlands of ribbon and fresh flowers.

'Ah, my favourite women all together!' Rick greeted them, planting robust kisses on Dinah's cheeks, which made her blush. 'You look like Dorothy Lamour in that hat; it must get heads turning in Murree.'

'It never gets worn in Murree,' Dinah said with a laugh.

Rick tickled Belle. Lifting her up, he kissed her on the nose and then pretended to drop her.

'Again, Uncle Rick!' she giggled.

Putting her down, he said, 'Drinks for the ladies first.' He waylaid one of the waiters who was milling around and distributing tray-loads of drinks. 'This looks like Uncle Charlie's famous summer punch. Am I right, Stella?'

'Yes,' she smiled. 'it's Dad's recipe. Exactly the same as his Christmas punch, just with ice thrown in.'

Rick chuckled as he handed round glasses of the amber drink. 'Watch out, Jeanie. It tastes like nectar but kicks like a Bhutanese pony.'

They all clinked glasses together and laughed. Jeanie watched in astonishment as Dinah, after half a glass of punch, became flirtatious with Rick.

'So where are you hiding your fiancée?' she asked. 'I thought we'd get to meet her.'

Rick gave a rueful smile. 'I'd hoped she'd be here too but she's still in England helping her parents settle into retirement.'

'Oh, dear,' said Dinah. 'She better not leave it too long – or some other woman might snap you up!' She giggled.

Rick gave an embarrassed laugh. 'Pammy's the only one who'll have me.'

'I'm sure that's not true,' Dinah said, her look coquettish. 'Ladies; don't you agree, that Rick is one of the most handsome and fun men in Pindi?'

Jeanie began to blush, not knowing what to say. Stella was quick to answer. 'My cousin doesn't need his head swelling anymore than it is.' She gave Rick a playful nudge. 'Besides, you're asking the wrong women; Jeanie and I are already happily married.'

Dinah's expression stiffened. She swigged down the rest of her drink.

'Let me get you another,' Rick said quickly.

'No, thank you,' Dinah said. 'I must go and congratulate Monty. It's wonderful to see him so happy at last.'

Jeanie watched her weave her way a little unsteadily between the crowd of guests and disappear.

'That was a very barbed remark,' said Stella, rolling her eyes. 'She's never forgiven me for breaking off with Monty – not that we were ever formerly engaged – but she still resents me for some reason.'

Jeanie knew that Dinah was jealous of Stella because of Belle – and marrying Andrew – but she wasn't going to say so. Instead, she said, 'She's not a very happy woman. I think she's just taking the chance to let her hair down for once.'

'That's a very charitable view,' said Rick, 'and I'm sure you're right. Dinah needs to have a bit of fun this weekend – we all do. So, who needs a top-up of Uncle Charlie's dynamite punch?'

***

179

Jeanie had never experienced a wedding reception quite like it. In the packed dining-room, the buzz of chatter and laughter competed with a three-piece band playing popular tunes, as the guests consumed huge amounts of food. An endless stream of meat dishes, fish, pastries, curries and vegetables were brought to the tables, followed by delicious desserts, and the drinks continued to flow.

Jeanie was on a table with Dinah, Ada and her husband Clive, Sigmund and two Gibson cousins from Lucknow who had offended Fritters by sitting in his and Ansom's favourite seats in the lobby. They were amusing company and Jeanie was gladdened to see Dinah laughing at their jokes and joining in animatedly. This was a side of the strait-laced matron that she hadn't seen before. Perhaps this was a glimpse of a more spirited Dinah, the nurse who had purportedly got into trouble in Simla.

After the meal, the tables were cleared and pushed back, and the newly married couple led the grand march around the room, as people clapped and cheered. They cut the cake with an army sword that one of Monty's comrades from the war had provided. Jeanie glanced over at Andrew and wondered if he was thinking back to his army days with her brother. How she wished John could have lived to see such a joyous occasion – to have fallen in love and married – to have shared experiences with her in India.

In the midst of such happiness, Jeanie felt a deep pang of regret for life as it might have been. As they raised their glasses and toasted Lucy and Monty, Jeanie's eyes brimmed with tears. The band struck up again and the dancing began. Jeanie slipped out of the room and made for the quiet of the courtyard to catch her breath and bring her emotions under control.

In the shade of the jacaranda, she closed her eyes and breathed in deeply. She felt calmness return.

'Jeanie?'

Startled, she opened her eyes to see Rick regarding her.

'All a bit overwhelming, is it?' he asked.

She nodded. 'Silly, I know. It's such a happy day …'

'But you're missing having your husband here to share it?'

Jeanie glanced away. She hadn't been thinking of Mungo at all. Quietly, she said, 'I was thinking of my brother John – how much he would have enjoyed this – and how he'll never experience these milestones in life. It's still very hard to believe he's gone.'

'From what you and Andrew have told me about him,' Rick said gently, 'I think he would want you to make the most of being alive – of having come through the war.'

'That's true,' Jeanie admitted, 'and I remember you saying something similar in Ebbsmouth when you were trying to comfort me.'

'I wasn't just saying it to make you feel better,' said Rick, his eyes full of compassion, 'it's what I believe. The best tribute to John is to grab life with both hands and live it to the full.'

Jeanie felt a warm glow of encouragement. 'You're absolutely right. That's just what John would have said. Thank you.' She smiled at him. 'I've so much to be grateful for – I shouldn't dwell on sad things.'

She watched him reach into his jacket pocket and pull out a silver cigarette case. Opening it, he offered it to her.

'I didn't think you smoked?' she said.

'I don't.' He gave a wry smile. 'But I have them on hand for those in need.'

She took one. 'I shouldn't – Mungo doesn't like me smoking – but I got into the habit during the war.'

Rick leaned close as he lit it for her with a matching silver lighter. He smelled of a musky cologne. 'Well, your secret's safe with me.'

She took a long draw of her cigarette and felt herself relax. Yet she was very aware of how close they were standing and how Rick was scrutinising her with his attractive eyes.

'So, tell me about life in Calcutta,' she said, trying to break the atmosphere of intimacy. 'Stella said you were hoping to fly civilian planes.'

Rick nodded. 'I've been flying cargo planes – small scale – in and out of Assam mostly.'

'Sounds interesting.'

'It can be. I like meeting the tea planters I'm supplying. They live in such remote places and they love to entertain anyone who drops in.' He grinned. 'Those chaps know how to throw a party.'

'And life in Calcutta at the moment?'

He shot her a look. 'What do you mean? About Pammy not being with me?'

'I was thinking of the political situation,' she said, 'with the Cabinet Mission failing. I've read about unrest in the cities.'

Rick loosened his tie, his look uncomfortable. 'I can't say it doesn't worry me,' he admitted. 'Things feel a bit tense and there have been stabbings.' He shrugged. 'But it hasn't been a problem in our part of the city.'

'So, you're still encouraging Pamela to come out and join you?'

'Of course,' he said hastily. 'I can't wait. And anyway, it was Pammy who wanted us to live in Calcutta – for the social life.'

Jeanie smiled. 'Then I hope it's not long before she does.'

He looked reflective. 'I'm just worried that her father is trying to discourage her from returning to India – he doesn't approve of me at all – and no doubt he's using the political uncertainty to make her anxious.'

'Has she said so?' Jeanie asked.

'Not in so many words,' he admitted. 'But she doesn't seem in any hurry to book her flights out here. Says her mother is still recuperating and that her father is hopeless on the domestic front. They're just excuses.' He gave a grunt of amusement. 'Although it does seem to be more difficult to find staff in Yorkshire than Calcutta. The Dacres don't appear to be coping without the army of servants they're used to.'

'I can imagine,' Jeanie said wryly. 'And it's hard to get used to it again returning to India. At home I enjoyed doing some of the cooking and the gardening; that sort of thing.'

'And fixing cars?' Rick teased.

'Yes!' Jeanie laughed. 'I hardly get to drive a car, let alone tinker with an engine.'

He fixed her with an intense look. 'Jeanie, are you happy in Murree? Life sounds a bit restrictive to me.'

She flushed. 'It's fine really. I shouldn't complain about the small things.'

'They're not small things. You should be allowed to be the person that you are,' he said. 'Be yourself, Jeanie, not what you think others want you to be.'

She was stung by his remark. She dropped her cigarette and ground it under her shoe. 'Don't worry about me,' she said with a tight smile. 'I'm very happy at Nicholson's.'

'Good,' he said.

Just then, someone clattered into the courtyard. 'There you are, Rick! I've been looking for you. The dancing's started and I–' Dinah stopped abruptly as she caught sight of Jeanie. 'Oh, I didn't see you, Mrs Munro.'

183

'I wish you would call me, Jeanie,' said Jeanie with an exasperated laugh.

'I dream of Jeanie with the light-brown hair,' Rick murmured.

'Light brown?' Dinah looked bemused. 'More black, I'd say.'

'It's from an old song,' said Rick, laughing.

'Oh, really? Well. Anyway,' she said tipsily, 'why are you two hiding under a tree?'

'No one's hiding,' said Jeanie, swiftly stepping past Rick.

Rick said, 'And I love to dance, so show the way, Dinah.' He proffered an arm and, with a gurgle of laughter, she slipped her arm through his.

Chapter 22

The dancing was lively and Jeanie joined in with relish, doing the quick-step with Sigmund, the waltz with Andrew and the military two-step with Rick. It reminded her of the village dances she used to go to with her ack-ack friends. They ended up with a progressive two-step where the women peeled off and passed to the next man. Then the bride went off to change into her going away outfit and shortly afterwards, there was a raucous sending off, as Monty and Lucy drove away, cans rattling from the back of their car. Jeanie stood beside Stella and Andrew, waving.

'I bet that was your doing, Rick,' Stella accused. 'I remember you doing that for Jimmy and Yvonne.'

'It was mainly Sigmund this time,' Rick said with a laugh.

Stella slipped an arm through his. 'Next time it will be you and Pamela driving off together – and Jimmy will enjoy getting his own back.'

'I doubt it,' said Rick.

Stella scrutinised him. 'What do you mean? Don't tell me you're getting cold feet?'

'No,' said Rick, 'but the wedding won't be in Pindi. Pammy wants a big do at Calcutta's Anglican cathedral and a reception at The Grand.'

'Well, we better start saving up now,' said Stella, 'isn't that right, Jeanie?'

Jeanie was startled. 'I don't expect to be invited,' she exclaimed.

'Of course you will,' said Stella with an expansive smile. 'You're one of the family now.'

'Yes,' Rick laughed. 'You've danced the jitterbug with Uncle Ziggy; that definitely makes you family.'

Jeanie felt a wave of affection for them all. 'I can't wait for the next wedding then.' She grinned.

The party began to break up and the Lomaxes coaxed a tired Belle away from a game with the other children. A picnic to the Rawal Falls was arranged for the next day, to which Jeanie was invited.

'It depends on my driver,' she said, glancing at Dinah.

'Course,' Dinah said, throwing her arms wide. 'Love t' go. Drive back t' Murree after'ards.'

Her cousin Clive appeared. 'Come on, Dinah, we'll give you a lift.'

'Super day,' Dinah said, kissing them all with emotion, including Jeanie.

They watched her making her way unsteadily down the path with Clive and Ada.

'Well, she was entertaining,' Andrew said in amusement. 'Not like the matrons I remember from my school days. Your husband is obviously changing things for the better at Nicholson's.'

'I think Mungo would be as astonished as me to see the difference in Miss Lavelle after a few drinks,' Jeanie said.

'Well,' said Rick, 'you said she needed to let her hair down and it's good to see her having some fun.'

'She's going to have a very sore head tomorrow,' Stella commented, 'so I just hope she'll remember what a good time she had.'

**

The next day, Dinah appeared after breakfast. She had her hair pinned back in a neat bun and her face looked wan without make-up.

'Are you ready to go, Mrs Munro?' she asked.

'For the picnic, you mean?' Jeanie queried.

'What picnic?'

'To Rawal Falls,' Jeanie reminded. 'You said there'd be time before setting off for Murree.'

Dinah tried to hide her bafflement. 'Oh, I don't think there is time after all. I'd rather we were back before Headmaster returns from Lahore and I imagine you would too?'

Jeanie got the distinct impression that the matron was now regretting having encouraged her to attend the wedding – not that she'd needed much persuasion. She hid her disappointment.

'No problem at all. We'll leave as soon as you want. I'll just go and fetch my case and say my goodbyes.'

'I'll wait for you by the car. It's parked in the street,' Dinah said.

Jeanie went quickly to the Lomaxes' suite – where she and Mungo had spent their first night after being reunited – to say a hurried goodbye.

Belle protested. 'But you must come, Auntie Jeanie! We're going swimming and everything.'

'Another time, I'd love to, sweetie.'

'That's a shame,' said Stella. 'It's been a lot of fun having you here.'

Jeanie was touched. 'For me too. I can't thank you all enough for making me so welcome.'

'We'll only let you go,' said Andrew, 'if you promise to come and stay with us in Gulmarg during the school holidays.'

'That's a promise then.' Jeanie smiled. On the point of leaving, she said, 'Please say goodbye to Rick for me. Wish him well.'

'Of course, we will,' said Stella.

'I hope it all works out for him and Pamela,' Jeanie added.

'If it's meant to be, then it will,' Stella replied.

187

As she left, Jeanie pondered Stella's words. She knew her friend wasn't terribly enamoured with Rick's fiancée because of the way she was keeping him waiting and her reluctance to join him. But it seemed that Pamela had chosen exactly the wedding she wanted in Calcutta and she hoped for Rick's sake that it would take place soon.

Saying goodbye to Jimmy, his family and the residents at the hotel took longer than Jeanie expected. They waved her off and told her to return whenever she wanted.

Dinah was smoking by the car, which was still parked where she'd left it the day before. She was looking increasingly pallid and bilious.

'You took your time,' Dinah said curtly.

'Sorry for keeping you waiting,' Jeanie said, lifting her case into the car boot. 'I can drive if you'd like a snooze?'

'I'm fine, thank you.' The matron stubbed out her cigarette and climbed into the driver's seat.

They didn't speak for much of the two-hour journey back up to Murree. Gone was the vivacious, tipsy woman who had demonstrated the can-can with her Gibson aunt and danced the tango with Rick. Jeanie felt a wave of anti-climax after the joy and laughter of the previous day. She had never enjoyed a wedding as much – not that she'd been to many – but even her own one had been staid in comparison.

She thought of how Stella and her extended family would be setting off for the scenic falls for another day of entertainment. She would love to have gone swimming and played games with Belle. Privately, she had to admit that part of her disappointment at not going was that Rick would be there and that she wouldn't be able to thank him for his kindness to her under the jacaranda when she had succumbed to the emotion of the day.

Maybe it was just as well. She sensed that seeing him today would still not have been enough. She was beginning to enjoy his company far too much and that was like swimming into dangerous waters. Best to smother any feelings for him now. Guiltily, she realised that she had hardly thought of Mungo since arriving in Pindi. Her annoyance at him refusing to take her to Lahore had evaporated and she was now glad that he hadn't. She wouldn't have missed the Dixon wedding for the world.

Dinah wound down her window so that Jeanie's hair blew around her face but the higher up the mountainside they drove, the fresher and more pleasant the air became. As they neared the hill station, Jeanie tried again to engage her in conversation.

'I think your relations are so much fun, Dinah. It must be wonderful to be part of such a big extended family.'

'Sometimes it is,' she said. 'Other times it can be a bit stifling.'

'Well, they know how to enjoy themselves,' said Jeanie. '*You* know how to enjoy yourself. I'll never forget you doing the can-can with Monty's mother!'

Dinah shot her a look of alarm. 'Please don't tell Headmaster.'

'Why not? I'm sure Mungo would be delighted you had a bit of fun.'

'I don't think he'd approve of me drinking.'

Jeanie huffed. 'What you do in your free time has nothing to do with him.'

'Still,' Dinah was adamant. 'I don't want to set tongues wagging at Nicholson's. I know how people love nothing better than to find something to gossip about.'

'I promise I won't gossip about you,' Jeanie assured her.

'Thank you.'

'Not even the energetic tango you did with Rick.' Jeanie teased.

Dinah snorted. 'Pindi's son-of-fun; that's what we used to call him.' She slid Jeanie a look. 'And I won't tell Headmaster about finding you with him, smoking in the back courtyard.'

Jeanie reddened. 'Nothing improper. We were talking about my brother.'

Silence ensued. A few minutes later, Dinah said, 'I'd be very surprised if he marries that English girl.'

Jeanie's heart skipped a beat. 'Stella said much the same,' Jeanie said. 'Do you think she's not serious?'

'I'm not sure his heart is in it,' said Dinah. 'I think if it was, he would have persuaded her to join him in Calcutta by now.'

'There's not much more he can do, surely? He's secured a job and a place for them to live. What more does she want?'

Dinah shrugged. 'I don't know her. But I do know Rick. He's a Pindi boy. I don't know why he wants to settle in Calcutta.'

'To make Pamela happy,' said Jeanie. 'I hope you're wrong and that she makes him happy too.'

Dinah glanced at her again but said nothing more. That look made Jeanie uncomfortable. It was as if the matron had seen through her words and suspected that Jeanie felt more than concern for Rick.

Chapter 23

Murree

'What do you mean, you've been to Pindi for a wedding?' Mungo's face was a picture of incomprehension and shock.

'As I said; it was a spur of the moment thing. I had nothing to do here all weekend, so I went.'

Jeanie had poured him a whisky and soda, and ordered up a light supper in the sitting-room for the two of them. Mungo took a large gulp of his drink.

'But I'd left you here in charge ...'

'No; you left Major Lucker in charge,' Jeanie pointed out. 'And the Agincourt House matron. They managed just fine.'

'But we don't even know these Pindi people! Whose wedding was it?'

'A cousin of Stella's.'

'I might have known she'd be behind this,' Mungo retorted.

Not wanting to get Dinah into trouble, Jeanie let him believe it had been Stella's idea. 'There were other people there I knew too, apart from the Lomaxes; such as Sigmund and Ada, and the Dixon parents – and their son Rick from Calcutta who I met in Ebbsmouth – and Jimmy Dubois and his family. And the groom was Monty, twin brother to Clive – Ada's husband. They were all so hospitable–'

'That's not the point,' he interrupted. 'You hadn't been invited; it was bad form to go.'

'It was a late invitation,' she said, determined to stay calm, 'and it was all on such a grand scale that one more didn't seem to matter.'

'So, this was the wedding Matron attended?' he asked.

'Yes.' Jeanie hesitated. 'She kindly gave me a lift back.'

'I really don't think you should have imposed,' he blustered.

'She was a revelation.'

'Meaning?'

'Knows how to let her hair down,' said Jeanie. 'It was good to see her enjoying herself – she's always so serious here – or at least she is with me.'

Mungo downed the rest of his whisky, still looking flabbergasted.

'Darling,' said Jeanie, 'sit down and tell me all about your weekend. Did the conference go well?'

He went and replenished his drink; it was unusual for him to have more than one. 'Yes, very well.' Mungo sank into the chair next to hers.

'Tell me about it,' she encouraged.

'There were headmasters from far and wide. Made some useful contacts.'

'Such as?'

'Australian chap – been running a school in Naini Tal – full of ideas.' He sipped his drink and sighed. 'He's thinking of returning to Adelaide though – concerned about the situation here and what the future might bring.'

'That's a shame,' said Jeanie. 'Especially if he's a kindred spirit.'

'Says Australia's the place of the future for chaps like us – progressive, British stock. I told him not to be so pessimistic – plenty mileage for us in India still.'

'I'm glad you said that,' Jeanie said with relief. 'I wouldn't want to go as far as Australia to live. It's hard enough tempting Mother to come out to India. She'd never consider the other side of the world.'

This seemed to annoy him. 'Our future will not be decided on the whim of your mother. Besides, I thought you said she wasn't coming anymore?'

Jeanie flushed. 'She might still come. It depends ...'

From his embarrassed look, she knew they both understood. Clara would only come if there was a Munro baby imminent. It had taken Jeanie several weeks to write and give her mother the disappointing news that she wasn't pregnant. She'd delayed sending the letter in the hopes that they might have conceived the following month.

Mungo slurped down his second drink and stood up. 'I've work to finish off. I'll be in my study.'

'But you haven't had supper,' Jeanie protested.

'I'm not hungry. They fed us too well at the conference. No doubt you're tired after all your gallivanting,' he added sourly. 'So, get an early night.'

Jeanie dined alone. Mungo's frosty tone left her in no doubt that he was cross with her for going to Pindi. But she didn't regret it. She hadn't had so much fun since her carefree nights out with Irene and Phyllis during the war. Not only had she been welcomed but she'd also felt that others had enjoyed her company too. In a few short hours, she'd felt more at home with Stella's relations and friends than she ever had at Nicholson's. Sitting there, on her own, she was engulfed with a wave of loneliness.

Taking herself off to bed early, Jeanie determined she would write again to her mother and urge her to visit; baby or not.

Chapter 24

Early August

For the rest of the summer term, Jeanie directed all her energy into playing the headmaster's wife. She attended cricket and tennis matches, helped give out prizes, drummed up support for the Danes' house play and held an end of term garden party for all the staff and their wives. It was also a farewell party for the Bishops who were finally leaving Murree and retiring to East Sussex.

'I really wouldn't want to stay on now,' Mrs Bishop confided in Jeanie after a couple of sherries. 'Look at the violence that's broken out in Gujarat. It's like a wildfire spreading – goodness knows where will be next.'

Jeanie had also read about the rioting in Ahmedabad and was deeply worried but she didn't want to show her concern publicly. 'It's a long way from the Himalayas,' she replied.

'Sorry, my dear; I don't wish to make you panic. I'm sure the British will keep a lid on things.'

Jeanie changed the subject quickly. 'Tell me about where you're going to be living, Mrs Bishop. Mungo says it's near the sea. I love the seaside – grew up a few miles away from the Berwickshire coast.'

The party was a big success and Mungo was pleased at the finish of his first summer term in charge. Two days later, with trunks packed, excited boys were collected by their parents or taken down to Rawalpindi for onward travel by train.

Jeanie waved them away, her feelings a mix of relief that term was over and sadness that the house would be empty of the clatter and noise of the pupils. Matron was going to spend the three-week holiday in Dehra Dun.

'An old friend from my nursing days lives there,' she told Jeanie on their final afternoon tea together.

'How nice. Stella told me it's an attractive place. She went there for work during the war.'

Jeanie was surprised Dinah had never talked about this nursing friend before but then the matron rarely dropped titbits of information about herself. Since the wedding trip the previous month, Dinah had reverted to her more circumspect self, talking largely about the mundane running of Nicholson's. It had been Jeanie's last opportunity to hear news of the Pindi families.

'Are Lucy and Monty settling into their new home after their honeymoon in Dalhousie?'

'I believe so,' said Dinah. 'She's such a good match for him. She'll make a wonderful, loyal wife.'

Jeanie heard the edge in her voice. Before the matron could make some derogatory comparison to Stella, Jeanie countered, 'And I hope he will be a good, loyal husband and make her happy too.'

'That's not in doubt,' Dinah said, a little sharply.

'You never know what life will throw at you,' Jeanie said. 'Even with the best of intentions, marriages are not perfect all the time.'

Dinah eyed her through a veil of cigarette smoke. 'That sounds to me like you are not altogether happy, Mrs Munro?'

Jeanie looked away and said quickly, 'Oh, take no notice. I'm just tired after a long term. I can't wait for our trip to Dal Lake. And for Mungo, it's going to be the perfect antidote to running a busy school. I can't pretend he hasn't been a bit short-tempered of late. You've probably noticed?'

Dinah stubbed out her cigarette in a small brass ashtray. 'I can't say I have. He's always very considerate – and endlessly patient with the boys.'

Jeanie let out a breath. 'Perhaps it's just with me, then.'

Dinah stood up. 'Thank you for the tea.'

'When will you be back, Matron?'

'Last week in August – for the start of term.'

'Have a lovely, well-deserved holiday,' said Jeanie, smiling. 'I'll miss our tea-time chats.'

Dinah smiled and nodded. The next day, she had departed too.

***

Humza helped supervise the packing for their trip to Srinagar to stay with the baroness. It was complicated by arrangements that Mungo was to travel on from Kashmir to join an old friend on a fishing trip to Mussoorie, so all his sporting gear had to be packed too.

'Let me come with you,' Jeanie pleaded on the eve of them going. 'I've heard it's charming and John spoke of it with great fondness.'

'It's just another hill station like Murree. There's nothing there that you can't find here,' he said.

'That doesn't matter; I just want to be with you.'

'But you won't be,' he said with an exasperated laugh. 'I'll be off from dawn till dusk with Easterhouse. And he's a bit stuffy. Not very comfortable in female company. We've been on these trips every year for over a decade, so I can't let him down.'

Jeanie felt mean-spirited. It was yet another reminder that she had left Mungo for years on end to fill in the summer holidays as best he could without her.

'Don't look so down-in-the-mouth,' he chided. 'We're going to Dal Lake together. Isn't that what you wanted?'

'Yes, very much,' she admitted.

'Good. You can stay on there with the baroness while I go fishing. You're always complaining there's not enough female company for you here.'

***

Jeanie was entranced by the drive to Kashmir. They crossed from the Punjab to the Himalayan principality over the fast-flowing Jhelum River at Kohala Bridge and continued on the winding route through the mountains. Stopping only briefly at Baramulla to picnic, Mungo insisted they press on swiftly to reach Srinagar before nightfall.

As they descended into the Vale of Kashmir, Jeanie gasped in wonderment. 'It's so beautiful!'

The evening light glinted rose gold on the waters of Dal Lake, which perfectly reflected the peaks of the surrounding mountains. Srinagar lay surrounded by a network of waterways, its medieval-looking wooden houses with their intricate carved balconies almost touching each other across narrow lanes.

Reaching the lake, they were met by one of Hester's servants who helped them onto a gondola-style boat and loaded on their luggage. Humza was left to look after the car and Mungo's fishing gear.

Jeanie breathed in the perfumed air and trailed her fingers in the cool water as they were rowed across to Hester's houseboat in the shikara. All around floated giant water lilies and the lake's surface was broken by the slipstreams of other boats, while boatmen called out to each other in the clear air.

Hester was waiting on the deck of the *Queen of the Lake* to greet them.

'This is magical, Baroness!' Jeanie cried, as she kissed the elderly woman.

'I told you it would be!' she answered in delight. 'Dear Mr Munro, welcome on board. You must be exhausted after the long drive. I'll get Amir to draw you a bath before dinner. In the meantime, we'll have cocktails.'

'Sounds wonderful,' Mungo said, smiling and kissing her hand.

'What a charmer you are, Mr Munro,' she simpered.

'Please, you must call me, Mungo,' he insisted.

Soon, they were sipping gin fizzes and looking out on the sunset.

'This really is paradise,' sighed Jeanie. 'No wonder you love coming here.'

'I fell in love with the place when my dear husband brought me here long ago – before the Great War. He was friends with a raja who let us stay. When I was widowed, the kind raja let me continue to use it each summer.' She gave a wry laugh. 'Over the years it's sort of become mine.'

'Very romantic,' said Mungo, toying with his glass. Jeanie knew he hated gin.

'And I hope it will cast its romantic spell over you two love birds,' said Hester with a gurgle of laughter. 'It's where Tom and Esmie declared their love for each other. And Stella and Andrew love this place too.'

Jeanie saw Mungo's smile tighten and wished their hostess hadn't mentioned the Lomaxes. Still, it was just the setting to help them relax and fall in love again. She felt a warm glow from the cocktail and anticipation of the days ahead.

Chapter 25

Dal Lake

That night, in the cosy wood-panelled guest cabin, Jeanie and Mungo made love for the first time in a fortnight. During the final hectic weeks of the term, there had been little time or inclination for intimacy. Mungo would fall into bed exhaustedly, long after Jeanie, and be gone before she woke in the morning.

But after Hester's delicious dinner of roast lamb and treacle pudding, followed by a nightcap of whisky, Mungo was in a mellow mood. They tried to be as quiet as possible, acutely aware that the baroness lay in the adjacent cabin.

'Damn bed creaks,' Mungo hissed.

'Her hearing's not that good,' Jeanie whispered.

'Still ...' He rolled away.

Jeanie lay awake for a long time after Mungo fell asleep, listening to the gentle slap of water against the houseboat and the cry of a night-bird. In the darkness, anxious thoughts returned. What would they do if they couldn't have children? What would *she* do? Until the last few months, she had never questioned her ability to become a mother. The long time apart had only delayed the moment when they would both be parents. Yet it wasn't happening.

What would life be like if the barren months turned into years? Mungo had his job – his vocation – to keep him occupied and satisfied. But how would she fill the endless days, being little more than an accessory to her husband? She shivered, yet it wasn't from cold. It was so different to her old life during the war when she had had work and purpose and comrades, as well as a vision for a post-war world. They had been striving for peace and normality and reunion with loved ones. Things had been simpler; the ultimate goal was to survive the war and live to see both John and Mungo again.

But John had died and Mungo had changed. She struggled to recapture in her mind what their marriage had been like for that pre-war year. He'd been protective and affectionate; perhaps with a tendency to pontificate but she had felt cherished. Now, she seemed to constantly irritate and disappoint him. Perhaps it was the strain of work he was under and of trying to get to grips with his new role as headmaster; it left him with no patience. Yet Matron had said he was always patient with the boys, so maybe it was just with her. He was carrying heavy responsibilities, and she, as his nearest and dearest, was taking the brunt of his tiredness and stress.

Or was it she who had changed? She was no longer the woman he had fallen in love with. When they'd first met at a New Year hunt ball in Berwickshire at the beginning of '38, she'd been attracted by his handsome military bearing, his bashful charm and his maturity. His stories of India and his passion for his job had made him much more interesting than the young men of the district, whose interests went little beyond farming and hunting.

She'd been bored with living at home with her parents and doing bits of voluntary work to fill in her time. John was already in India, forging his army career and his letters were full of enthusiasm for his regimental life in the North-West Frontier. She yearned for some adventure too. So, she'd thrown herself into a whirlwind romance with Mungo and accepted his swift proposal. Her mother had been anxious that they hardly knew each other but her father had given his blessing; Mungo was an upstanding fellow member of the Greentoun masonic lodge. By the time Mungo's furlough had ended, Jeanie and he were married and on their way to India.

How young and naïve that twenty-five-year-old Jeanie seemed now. Although she had vague memories of her very early childhood in India, she hadn't been out of Britain since she was five or six-years-old. She had been a weekly border at a private school near Edinburgh where she had been an average scholar, excelling only on the lacrosse and cricket teams. Nobody had suggested university or a vocational job. She had returned home to be the colonel's daughter until marriage presented itself – and the role of wife and mother.

What had Mungo seen in her? Her youthful enthusiasm to learn from him? A chance to mould a young woman in the duties of a housemaster's wife? Had he come specifically on leave to find a spouse and if so, would anyone of her age and social status have done? Thinking of it now, surely there must have been similar young women among the British in India – all those officers' and civil servants' daughters – without him needing to search his old home town; a place he hadn't visited in over a decade.

No point in puzzling over that now. She was certainly not the same woman; the war and life experience had changed her. Perhaps that was what Mungo couldn't get used to.

Jeanie sighed. If she couldn't have children, what did she want from life? She wished she could talk to someone about it. John might have been the one with which to air such thoughts. Perhaps Stella? The one person that she'd been most frank with recently was Rick. The thought made her uncomfortable. Yet it might be ages before they came across each other again and she certainly shouldn't be sharing such intimate thoughts and doubts with him. She turned restlessly onto her side and tried to force him from her mind. Eventually, the soporific sounds of water lulled her to sleep.

By morning, Jeanie's soul-searching in the depths of night seemed over-dramatic and her fears irrational. They were on holiday in paradise; Mungo was refreshed and eager to sightsee. She felt her optimism returning.

Hester lent them her shikara and told them to visit the Mughal gardens.

'I've ordered you a tiffin basket,' she said, 'so you can picnic over there and have a leisurely look around. I won't expect you back till the cocktail hour.'

As the boatman paddled them over the water, Mungo mused, 'I think the cocktail hour is whenever the baroness wants a drink. What time do you think she means?'

Jeanie shaded her eyes against the glare bouncing off the lake's surface. 'I don't think it matters,' she said contentedly. 'Whenever we want. Isn't it wonderful not being ruled by school bells and timetables for once?'

They spent the morning wandering around the Shalimar Bagh.

'I've never seen a more beautiful garden,' she said, admiring the profusion of flowers and enjoying the shade of avenues of trees.

Mungo was enthusiastic about the water systems that fed the gardens along a network of stone-build channels, pointing out the craftsmanship.

'The old Mughals knew a thing or two about irrigation,' he said. 'Got it from the Persians. They were the masters of finding underground sources of water and using it to make the deserts flourish.'

Jeanie tried to follow what he was telling her about water courses, angles and force, but the sound of the gurgling water and the plash of fountains was mesmerising and she found her mind wandering. What had the picnic to Rawal

Falls been like and had they swum? How was Stella feeling now and had her sickness eased? She felt bad for not having written sooner to ask.

'You're not really listening, are you?' Mungo asked. 'What are you thinking?'

Jeanie gave a guilty start. 'I was ... wondering ... if we could go swimming sometime this week. All this water is so tempting.'

'Hester says you can't swim from the houseboat,' he said, 'it's too dangerous – choked with weeds.'

'But people do swim,' she said. 'Andrew talked about it. There's a diving platform somewhere.'

Mungo grunted. 'Well, if he recommends it, it's probably dangerous too.'

'Darling! I wish you wouldn't talk about him as if he was still a naughty schoolboy. Andrew's a grown man and–'

'A war hero,' Mungo cut in, his tone sarcastic. 'Yes, we've all been made very aware of that.'

'Well, it's true.'

Mungo retorted. 'He was injured in combat like thousands of others and then invalided out of the army before the end of the war, so he didn't see any more active service. If you ask me, he rather hams up his hero status with that eye-patch.'

Jeanie was shocked. 'He nearly died of his injuries.'

'If you say so.'

'Why do you resent him so much? Just because he's not one of Nicholson's star old boys, doesn't mean he deserves your disparagement.'

'I'm not being disparaging,' he replied, 'but I refuse to indulge in this hero-worship of yours. Andrew Lomax was a mediocre and disruptive pupil and now he's living off his father's business, doing what?'

'Being a father for one thing,' Jeanie declared.

He glared at her. 'Some say the girl isn't even his.'

'That's beneath you, to say such a thing,' Jeanie chided. 'Andrew adores Belle – and Stella is expecting their second child.'

Mungo flinched. 'Well, lucky him.'

Immediately, Jeanie wished she hadn't told him. 'Let's not spoil this lovely time together, arguing over the Lomaxes.'

'I'd happily not have to talk about them again,' he muttered.

She tried to coax back his former good mood. 'Shall we find a shaded spot for tiffin?'

'Not here,' he said. 'I'd like to see the Nishat Bagh next.'

'But it's so tranquil here. Why rush away? We could do the other gardens tomorrow.'

'I'm not one for sitting around,' he said.

They walked back to the shikara in silence.

***

'And how was your day out?' Hester asked brightly, welcoming them back.

'Lovely but exhausting,' Jeanie said, with a wry laugh. 'Mungo had us rushing round three of the Mughal gardens. The shikara man must be whacked too.'

'I wanted to compare them all,' Mungo said. 'And we're here to see things not laze around. My wife can do that at home in our garden.'

'Sounds like you both need stiff chota pegs,' Hester said, laughing. 'Gimlets for the ladies and whisky and soda for you, Mungo.'

'Thank you,' he said, with a grateful smile.

They enjoyed another convivial dinner. The baroness knew just how to pitch the conversation between the too trivial and too serious, sharing anecdotes of her early days in India that got Mungo reminiscing about his too.

'Best shikar I ever went on was in the Chamba district near Dalhousie,' he said. 'Even shot a bear on one occasion.'

'My father was stationed at Dalhousie after the Great War,' Jeanie joined in. 'Said the mess dinners there were legendary.'

'Do you remember it too?' Hester asked.

'No. Mother took us home to Scotland about that time. After John was born. She'd had enough of garrison life in Peshawar and with two small children …'

Jeanie broke off, not wanting the subject of children raised again after her earlier argument with Mungo.

'What a pity,' said Hester. 'I think she would have enjoyed Dalhousie a lot more than Peshawar.'

'Yes, you're probably right.'

'Fishing was good there too,' Mungo took up the conversation where he'd left off and proceeded to talk about his favourite sport until the main course was over.

***

The days at the houseboat went quickly. For the first four, they took the shikara to different points of interest around the lake. Jeanie took her swimming costume and on one occasion, insisted that they stop at a pontoon in the middle of the lake from which she could swim. Dipping into the cool water was exhilarating and the panorama of mountains shimmering in the heat, reflecting in the glinting water, was dazzling. She lay on her back, floating, and freeing her mind of worries.

Each evening, the baroness would make a fuss of them, plying them with drinks and rich food. Then at night, after retiring to their room, Mungo would make love to her as quietly as their bed would allow. These were the times that Jeanie felt emotionally close to her husband. In the darkness, he mumbled endearments that he could never say in daylight and gave out soft groans of satisfaction.

She was encouraged that their holiday in Kashmir was having the desired effect of bringing them closer together. Even if they weren't the same people as they had been eight years ago when they'd first met, they could still forge a new relationship – a more equal partnership – that would stand them in good stead for a future together.

Another day, they wandered the old streets of Srinagar. Jeanie was fascinated by the workshops of the craftsmen, making wooden furniture, beating metal into plates and painting intricate patterns onto papier mâché.

'It brings back childhood memories,' she told her husband. 'I suppose of the bazaars in Peshawar.'

Although Mungo was interested in their craftsmanship, he found the city too dirty and pungent and didn't want to linger. 'You can come back with Hester another time – when I'm on my fishing trip,' he advised.

On another day, they explored the area by car, taking a picnic and books to read.

'Why don't you take a run-up to Gulmarg and visit the Lomaxes?' Hester unwittingly suggested.

'Bit too far,' Mungo dismissed the idea.

Jeanie found it frustrating that they were less than a couple of hours drive away from the Raj-in-the-Hills and her friends, but she didn't dare press him about it. It would undo all the progress of the past week. Perhaps she could go there after he left, the following week.

On their second last evening, Jeanie felt familiar cramps in her abdomen. Even before she reached the bathroom, she knew that her 'monthly' had started. She crouched down by the bath tub, hugging her stomach as waves of pain coursed through her, and shed tears of bitter disappointment.

She struggled through dinner, without any appetite.

'You're very quiet, darling,' said Hester. 'Are you feeling unwell?'

'A little,' Jeanie admitted.

'Maybe you've caught a touch of sun,' she suggested.

'Or swallowed too much lake water when swimming,' Mungo teased.

Jeanie went early to bed, listening to the other two chatting on the deck over a nightcap. When Mungo came to bed and reached for her, she broke the news.

He withdrew his hold, sinking onto his back and let out a long sigh. She waited for him to come out with his usual comforting but trite remark that there was 'always next month'; but he didn't. Like her, he must be feeling that if they couldn't conceive in a place like Kashmir, then perhaps they never would.

On his final day, Mungo was subdued. Jeanie suggested they went back to his favourite of the Mughal gardens.

'Got to check on my fishing gear,' he mumbled. 'See if I need … anything else to buy …'

While he was gone, Hester commented, 'He seems a little out of sorts today. Obviously, not enjoying the thought of you two being parted for a couple of weeks.'

Jeanie let her believe it. 'I'm thinking of rustling up another shikara to go for a swim. Do you want to come too?'

Hester laughed. 'Well, not to swim. But I'll bring us a cocktail for afterwards.'

Jeanie enjoyed the morning swimming and sipping gins with Hester. They returned a little tipsy at lunchtime but Mungo was still elsewhere. Jeanie fell asleep and only woke when her husband returned as the light was mellowing over the peaks.

207

That night, Mungo seemed fretful. 'Are you going to be all right here? I'm in two minds whether to drive you back to Murree before I head off for Mussoorie.'

'Why wouldn't I be?'

'Just picking up news. Jinnah and his League are planning some day of action – strike and demonstration.'

'Where?' Jeanie asked, sensing his anxiety. It had been blissful not having any newspapers to read for the past week.

'Calcutta. I know that's hundreds of miles away but still …'

Jeanie's stomach lurched. She thought immediately of Rick and his fiancée. 'Do they think there's going to be trouble?'

He shrugged. 'Both sides are ramping up the rhetoric. It could get ugly.'

Jeanie swallowed down her panic. 'As you say, it's a long way from here. I'll be fine. I really don't want to be kicking my heels around Murree with the school empty.'

What she didn't say was how she had a sudden urge to be with Stella and the Lomaxes – to know what was going on and whether they had news of Rick. Mungo seemed to accept her decision and neither of them mentioned it at dinner.

The next morning, after an early breakfast, Mungo kissed both women on the cheek and bid them farewell. Jeanie waved until the shikara was out of sight. She was unsure what the future held for them both. Perhaps a little time apart would do them both good – to see if they missed each other – and to work out their true feelings.

Chapter 26

Raj-in-the-Hills, Gulmarg, mid-August

Hester encouraged Jeanie to visit the Lomaxes.

'I'll miss your company, darling, but it'll be more fun for you up there and I know how well you and Stella have hit it off.'

'I've loved staying here,' Jeanie said, 'and I doubt Gulmarg can provide better fun than you have. But I would like to see Stella and Andrew – and Belle, of course.'

'Yes, they are the epitome of a happy family,' said Hester.

Jeanie nodded. 'And with Stella expecting again …'

'Is she?' Hester cried.

'Oh, dear; perhaps I shouldn't have said.' Jeanie went pink.

'Well, I can hardly spread any gossip on my houseboat,' said Hester in amusement. 'So don't worry. And it's wonderful news. I'm so pleased for them.' She put a veined hand on Jeanie's knee. 'I hope it will be your turn next, dear girl.'

***

Two days later, having received a message back from Stella that they would be delighted to put her up at the hotel and that Andrew would pick her up in Srinagar, Jeanie left Hester's houseboat. It had been a time of mixed emotions, with moments of real happiness in an idyllic setting, yet with an underlying tension between her and Mungo. The pressure to conceive. The feeling that, at times, they were strangers to each other. But Hester had been a generous and entertaining hostess and Jeanie kissed her goodbye with gratitude and real affection.

Andrew was waiting for her, as arranged, outside Nedous Hotel in the town.

'Hope you don't mind rattling around in the hotel van,' he said apologetically. 'But I had supplies to pick up too.'

'I love a lorry,' she said, smiling. 'Reminds me of my ack-ack days.'

Andrew grinned. 'Jump aboard then, Corporal Munro.'

On the drive up to the alpine resort, they chatted almost non-stop about family and India, the war and the hotels. Andrew reminisced about living in Ebbsmouth with his mother and his school days in Durham.

'But I'll be forever grateful that the war – hellish though it was – brought me back to India. Otherwise, I would never have met your brother or been reconciled with my father and Esmie,' he admitted.

'Why had you been estranged?' Jeanie asked.

Andrew gave out a long sigh. 'A series of misunderstandings. I had been fed some horrible lies at Nicholson's about dad being thrown out of the army for cowardice – and malicious gossip about him and Esmie. I don't want to go into all, but it caused a terrible rift in the family, which my mother rather exploited.'

'I'm sorry to hear that,' Jeanie said gently. 'But you've all made your peace now? You seem a very close family.'

Andrew nodded. 'It took a chance conversation with an Indian soldier to discover how heroic Dad had been in the Great War – he saved one of his men from the firing squad by refusing to have him executed. That's why he was court-martialled – quite the opposite of cowardice.'

'How very courageous of him,' Jeanie gasped. 'He was lucky not to be shot himself.'

210

'He says the regimental doctor intervened on his behalf and had him medically discharged with shell shock,' Andrew explained. 'That's how the rumours spread that he was a coward who couldn't cope with the rigours of war. It's true that he's suffered bouts of depression from his experiences but he's still a war hero in my eyes.'

'Poor man.' Jeanie sympathised.

'He's never cared what other people say about him. But he won't stand for any bad words about his family. That's why he took me away from Nicholson's, because Bishop was taking the other boy's side and wouldn't believe mine.'

'He strikes me as a very loyal man,' said Jeanie, feeling ashamed at her previous doubts about Tom.

Andrew glanced at her and gave a grateful smile. 'He is. He can be stubborn and moody but he's a wonderful man. That's probably the influence of Esmie over the years. She's a remarkable woman. So much better for him than my mother.' He gave a wry laugh. 'My parents were a disaster together.'

'Well, they did one thing right,' Jeanie said. 'They produced a very fine son.'

Andrew laughed. 'I can see that charm runs in the Grant family. That's just the sort of thing John would have said!'

Jeanie warmed to him even more. She found him so easy to talk to; his candour was refreshing and she was grateful that he was taking her into his confidence about deeply personal matters. When was the last time she had had such a frank and deep conversation with Mungo? Perhaps never.

'Tell me some more of your stories of the North-West Frontier and my brother,' Jeanie encouraged.

For the rest of the journey, they reminisced about John, until they arrived in Gulmarg.

***

At a distance, the resort reminded her of pictures she had seen of Swiss mountain villages, with wooden chalets surrounded by meadows. On closer inspection, she could see the trappings of the British at play; a golf course busy with golfers, tennis courts and a grey brick church with a green roof.

Andrew greeted a small wiry man with a pock-marked face, who was waiting for them with a stout pony and two mules.

'Manek; this is Munro Memsahib.' The man bowed in greeting. 'Manek has been my right-hand man since my army days,' he explained. 'Now he's also our chief syce – he's marvellous with the ponies. Do you ride, Jeanie?'

'I'm a colonel's daughter,' she said, with a broad smile, 'of course I ride.' She stroked the white pony. 'You're a wee beauty.'

'That's Peony,' said Andrew. 'You take her.'

After Andrew and Manek had loaded up the supplies onto the other two ponies, they set off uphill through the settlement; Jeanie riding while the men led the laden mules. She couldn't remember the last time she'd ridden – probably pre-war – but it felt as natural as if it had been last week. It brought memories of her father flooding back. She had often gone riding with him when he'd retired back to Greentoun; it was one of the many activities they had enjoyed together. She felt a dull ache again at his loss. How he would have loved this place!

Emerging from a belt of trees, Jeanie halted and caught her breath at the sight. Across a steep meadow lay a charming large villa with a deep veranda, perched above a terraced garden of rockery and lawns. A profusion of flowers spilled over their borders and lined the green-painted veranda. She could glimpse people sitting in cane chairs in

212

the shade. Behind the hotel, the hillside climbed away to further meadows and woods, while in the far distance, mountain peaks, still capped in snow, appeared to float on clouds. Andrew caught up with her.

'What a stunning view!' Jeanie gazed in awe. 'No wonder you're all so reluctant to leave here and come to town.'

Andrew laughed. 'Jungli-Lomaxes; that's what they call us in Pindi these days.'

As they approached the hotel, Jeanie heard Belle squeal. 'They're here! Daddy and Auntie Jeanie are here!'

The girl came rushing down the steps with Stella following close behind. In a light summer dress, she now looked obviously pregnant. Jeanie dismounted while Belle threw herself into Andrew's arms. Again, she was reminded of her younger self. One of her few vivid early memories of India was being picked up and whirled around by her father on his return from duty on the North-West Frontier.

'Welcome!' Stella hugged her.

'Thank you.' Jeanie smiled. 'You look well. Are you feeling better?'

'Much better. No sickness – though I still can't stand the smell of chef's mulligatawny soup.'

'She's eating more than her fair share of his lemon meringue pie, though,' Andrew teased, kissing her on the lips. 'Just as well I was able to buy more sugar in town.'

'Good boy,' Stella said with a grin. She turned back to Jeanie. 'It's a bit of a squash in our annexe so we've given you a room in the hotel. It's not very big, I'm afraid. I used to sleep in it when I came up to help here before the war. It's comfortable enough – but I hope you'll be spending your time with us or outdoors, so it's just somewhere to retreat to if we all get too much for you.'

'Sounds perfect.'

'Let me show Auntie Jeanie, let me show!' Belle cried, seizing Jeanie's hand.

Stella rolled her eyes. 'Don't be bossy.'

But Jeanie was thrilled at the girl's gesture. She squeezed her hand. 'Come on then, Belle; show me the way.'

The girl chattered all the way up the steps and across the veranda, where various hotel guests called out to her. She waved at them but wouldn't be distracted from her duty, pulling Jeanie through the lobby and down a passage.

'In here,' she announced, pushing open the door at the end. 'I've given you one of my dollies to cuddle at night. Mummy says you might be lonely without that man with you.' Belle grabbed something off the pillow of the narrow bed. 'There you are!' She handed over a rather threadbare, floppy rag doll with a faded pink sari and a long black plait. 'I'm still looking after Big Ted because he likes to be with me.'

'I'm sure he does. And thank you,' said Jeanie, 'this looks a very special doll.'

'It was Mummy's when she was a little girl. You can keep it in here but you mustn't take it away 'cause I'd be very sad if you did.'

Jeanie put her arm around Belle and kissed the top of her head. 'I promise I won't.'

***

That evening, Jeanie dined in the Lomaxes' cosy annexe, having helped settle an excited Belle into bed by singing Scottish lullabies that she'd dredged up from distant memory.

Over supper, Stella asked, 'Did your mother teach you those lovely songs?'

'No. When we first came back from India, I had a nanny from the Highlands who used to sing to me and John,' she explained. 'Nanny Mackinnon. I haven't thought about her in years.'

Tom smiled. 'They reminded me of my childhood too. A rite of passage for Scottish children. You have a sweet singing voice, Jeanie.'

She gave a bashful laugh. 'I think that's being a bit generous, but thank you.'

'Not at all.'

As the meal progressed and Andrew regaled them with the story of his trip into Srinagar, Jeanie observed them. Stella looked adoringly at her husband and several times they seemed to share private jokes. Esmie was solicitous and kept offering Jeanie more food, delighted at her healthy appetite. Tom joined in the banter too but he seemed gaunter than she had remembered, his vivid blue eyes slightly sunken. He ate half-heartedly and his hand had a tremor as he raised his glass; the sign of a hard drinker.

She knew, from what Andrew had told her, that he wasn't in the best of health and had battled depression on and off for years. It saddened her to think how his life had been blighted by tragedy and war. Yet, he obviously revelled in the company of his wife and family. It must delight him to think of another grandchild on the way. Jeanie had a renewed pang of loss for her own father who hadn't lived long enough to see his own children mature beyond their early twenties, let alone become a grandfather.

Tom caught her staring at him. He held her look with a mix of compassion and puzzlement, as if he guessed at her thoughts. She blushed and looked away.

The meal over, Jeanie took her leave. 'It's been a lovely meal but I hope you don't mind if I slip off to bed.'

215

'Of course not,' said Esmie. 'Is there anything you want before you go? Hot water bottle? It can cool down here at night.'

Jeanie laughed. 'I'm still adapting to the heat after Scotland. I've yet to feel truly cold in India. And I have Belle's doll to cuddle, remember?'

Stella gave a huff of amusement. 'That awful old thing.'

Esmie said dryly, 'I gave you that doll.'

'Oh, so you did!' Stella laughed and kissed her mother-in-law quickly.

'At least Belle loves it,' Esmie chuckled.

'That we can agree on.' Stella winked. 'So, you're very honoured to be lent it, Jeanie.'

'I'm very aware of that,' Jeanie acknowledged with a smile. She left, feeling grateful to be so easily accepted into the ranks of this family.

***

Jeanie soon settled into a busy routine. She got up early and ate breakfast in the annexe with the Lomaxes, went to the stables to help groom the ponies, took Belle for a walk with Stella, lunched in the hotel, went riding with some of the guests in the afternoon and spent the evening with the Lomaxes. She slept deeply in her small but charming room with its yellow curtains and bedspread decorated with exotic birds.

It looked out onto a small courtyard, beyond which lay a wooden summerhouse that she soon learnt was Tom's studio. She would see him standing outside smoking and gazing up at the mountains and she wondered what thoughts preoccupied him.

One day, towards the end of her first week, clouds descended and the rain came on hard. It was too wet and misty to go riding and the guests settled to playing cards and reading indoors. To give Stella a break from Belle, Tom suggested he take the girl to his studio.

'Can I get the paints out, Granddad?' Belle asked excitedly.

'Of course.' He smiled. 'And perhaps Jeanie would like to come too?'

Belle looked at her expectantly.

'I'd love to,' Jeanie said quickly.

They made a dash through the rain to the summerhouse and fell through the door, shaking water from their hair and shrugging off their jackets. Jeanie looked around at the half-finished canvases propped against two walls. The other side was taken up by a table daubed with old paint splashes and covered in jars of dirty painting water, while underneath, artist's materials spilled out of old crates. In the far corner was a battered armchair made comfortable with cushions, and around it were scattered untidy piles of newspapers and books. No room in her parents' house would ever have been allowed to get so messy; she imagined how Mungo would shudder at the chaos too.

'I'll get the paints, Granddad,' Belle announced, rushing over to a tea chest and leaning in.

Tom caught her before she disappeared head first. 'Let me do that, sweetheart. You can fetch paper from the drawer.'

'Okay.' Belle dashed around the table and hauled on the end drawer. 'It's stuck!'

'Let me help,' said Jeanie. She wrested the drawer open and Belle seized on a pile of scrap paper and then clambered onto a chair.

Tom came over with a box of watercolours and brushes. 'Tie this apron on first,' he ordered. While Jeanie helped with that, Tom filled a jar with clean water from a tap outside the door. Soon Belle was absorbed in her painting. Tom lit up a cigarette and watched.

Jeanie said, 'I've started painting again too – thanks to your kind birthday present.'

Tom looked pleased. 'Wonderful. Have you brought anything to show us?'

Jeanie said wryly, 'They are rather mediocre efforts of the same mountain view from our garden. Nothing to compare with yours.'

'That's nice of you to say so, but I'm sure you're being too modest.'

'No, I wish I could paint like you. Your landscapes are so striking – the ones that are hanging in the hotel. The outlines are simple but you somehow convey the magnificence and stark beauty of the Himalayas. It's something to do with the bold colours you use.'

Tom stubbed out his cigarette and smiled. 'I've had a lot more time than you to practice painting mountains. And I've lived among them for years. You get to know them like friends. But I do like experimenting with colours – using ones that are unexpected, such as yellow for a mountain lake. It's an idea I stole from Dawan Lal in Ebbsmouth. He is a master colourist.'

Jeanie nodded. 'I wish I'd had time to go to his studio and learn from him.'

'I'm sure the next time you're in Scotland, Dawan would be delighted to show you.'

Jeanie glanced around again. 'What are you working on at the moment? There seem to be quite a few works in progress.'

Tom sighed. 'I haven't really got down to anything much since we returned from Ebbsmouth. Don't seem to have the concentration … or energy …'

Belle paused and looked at him in concern. 'Have you got the black monsoon again, Granddad?'

Tom looked startled. He recovered quickly and put a hand on her head. 'No, sweetheart. I'm fine.' He looked at Jeanie a little sheepishly and said quietly, 'It's the phrase the family use when I'm down in the dumps. This girl picks up on everything.'

He leaned over Belle's work and said more brightly, 'Just look at that picture! It's going to be a masterpiece.'

'No, it's going to be Jeanie!' Belle laughed. 'Silly Granddad!'

Jeanie and Tom broke into laughter.

'Would you like to sit?' Tom asked, pointing to the armchair at the far end of the room.

Jeanie didn't really want to – she was happy watching Belle paint – but sensed that he needed to sit. She sank into the comfy chair while he pulled out a stool and sat down beside her. He lit up another cigarette.

'Can I have one too, please?' she asked.

'Goodness! Yes, of course.' He offered her one swiftly. 'I didn't think you smoked.'

'I don't,' she said with a bashful laugh. 'Just don't tell my husband.'

He lit her cigarette for her and they smoked in companionable silence.

'You're welcome to use the studio whenever you want,' Tom said. 'Or take some equipment on one of your rides and paint up on the marg – the light is ever changing – you'll find it inspirational.'

'Thank you, I'd like that.' She felt a sudden wave of contentment. 'It's so comfortable and peaceful in here. I'd be forever snoozing in this chair.'

Tom grinned. 'Don't tell Esmie, but that's what I do most these days.'

She wanted to ask him if he was ill but didn't feel she knew him well enough. Instead, it was Tom who alarmed her by asking, 'Does Mr Munro know that you're staying here?'

'Yes. I wrote to him from Dal Lake before I set off. Why do you ask?'

Tom said, 'I know he doesn't approve of us Lomaxes.'

'That's not true,' Jeanie protested.

'It's fine. We're not much liked in British circles here, but I don't want it to be awkward for you.'

'I'm quite capable of choosing my own friends – I don't need Mungo's permission.'

'I'm glad to hear it. And I was also pleased to hear you went to Lucy Dixon's wedding,' he said. 'But it's a shame your husband couldn't go too.'

'He had a conference in Lahore.' Suddenly, she didn't feel the need to defend Mungo. 'Actually, he wouldn't have come even if he'd been free. He thinks it was bad form of me to go without a proper invitation.'

Tom eyed her. She went on. 'I probably had more fun without him there, if I'm honest. He doesn't like crowds or dancing. Doesn't really like Anglo-Indians.' She finished her cigarette and ground it out in an ashtray balanced on a pile of books. 'I've no idea why I'm telling you this.'

His expression was compassionate. 'I'm probably the last person to give you marriage guidance – God knows, I've been a pretty useless husband – but the one thing I'd say is that it's important to do things together – to have interests in common.'

Jeanie struggled to think of anything that she and Mungo had in common. 'I suppose the school is our big mutual interest,' she replied.

Tom nodded. 'You're lucky. Most couples don't have the chance of that shared common aim. Working well together is important.'

'Like you and Esmie.' Jeanie latched onto the idea. 'You built up the hotel business together. Is that why you're so close?'

Tom's expression softened at the mention of his wife. 'We've come through a lot together. I'd be nothing without Esmie. She's quite simply my anchor – as well as the love of my life.'

Jeanie's eyes stung with sudden emotion. Never in a million years could she imagine Mungo saying that about her – or she him. She swallowed.

'How ... how did you know it would be like that with Esmie? You'd been married before ... Sorry, I've no right to pry.'

Tom didn't seem offended. 'My first wife, Mary, was my childhood sweetheart. But she died in childbirth. My life might have been very different if she'd lived.' His expression was full of sadness. Then he stubbed out his cigarette and cleared his throat. 'My second wife – Andrew's mother – well, that was purely superficial attraction and it didn't last long for either of us.' He glanced over at Belle and his expression grew tender again. 'But I knew as soon as I met her that Esmie was special. I've been in love with her ever since.'

He paused, looking directly at Jeanie. 'I think you're an admirable young woman, Jeanie – my family think so too – so it grieves me if you're not happy. You can take what I say with a pinch of salt, but I know what it's like to be trapped in an unhappy marriage. You don't have to stay in one.'

Jeanie felt a rising panic, as her pulse began to race. She stood up. 'I'm sorry; I've given the wrong impression about Mungo. I'm not unhappy. It's just taking longer to adjust ... with being apart for so long ...'

Tom stood up too. 'I understand. I didn't mean to embarrass you.'

221

Belle turned round. 'Are you finished your boring conversation, Granddad?'

Tom laughed. 'Yes, we have. Show me what you've done.'

She held up her painting. The whole sheet of paper was completely covered in multi-coloured swirls, dots and bold lines.

'That's impressive,' he said. 'Is it still Jeanie?'

Belle frowned and then nodded. 'Yes, it's Jeanie on Peony riding through the woods.'

Jeanie moved quickly to stand by the girl. 'I love it. May I keep it?'

Belle handed it over. 'Yes. Here you are.'

'Thank you.' She kissed her lightly on the head.

'Do you want to paint something now, Auntie Jeanie?'

Jeanie hesitated. 'Why don't we paint something together? I'd like that.'

'Yes,' Belle cried. 'Let's do a picture for Mummy and Daddy.'

Jeanie blinked back sudden tears and busied herself finding a fresh piece of paper. A few minutes later, she glanced over at Tom. He was asleep in the armchair.

Chapter 27

The next day, Jeanie came back from riding to find consternation at the hotel.

'Have you heard the news?' cried Mrs Townsend, a plump civil servant's wife, brandishing a newspaper.

'There's been a massacre!' her companion, Mrs Lawson, said with a shudder.

'What? Where?' Jeanie asked in alarm.

'Calcutta,' said Mrs Townsend. 'Thousands dead.'

'Butchered each other in the streets,' added Mrs Lawson.

'Police did nothing …'

'It's hard to believe …'

'Calcutta?' Jeanie felt as if she'd been thumped in the stomach.

'Day of action turned into three days of blood-letting,' said Mrs Townsend. 'Terrible business. Makes you wonder where will be next.'

'Where will be safe?' gasped Mrs Lawson.

Andrew appeared and they started up their querulous questioning again.

'Please, ladies; you mustn't fret. We're a long way from Calcutta.' He smiled reassuringly. 'Let me order you an early chota peg; with our compliments.'

With a bit of cajoling and reassurance, he managed to calm the residents on the veranda and distracted them with discussing the evening's menu. Jeanie's heart continued to hammer. While Andrew dealt with the guests, she picked up the newspaper and took it indoors to read. She was appalled. Shops and businesses had been ransacked and burned, armed gangs had beaten people to death, bodies were left lying in the streets and trucks were piled high with the dead. Jinnah's

Direct Action Day had turned into a communal bloodbath, the scale of which India had never seen before.

Jeanie felt nauseated. She rushed round to the annexe and found Stella supervising Belle's high-tea. She could tell from Stella's anxious expression that she was well aware of the news.

'Have you heard anything from the Dixons?' Jeanie asked. 'About Rick?'

Stella shook her head. 'We rang the garage a couple of hours ago but they've not heard from him since last week. They're trying to find out more and will let us know.'

Jeanie wanted to talk about it but didn't want to do so in front of Belle. She found relief in reading the girl a story while she ate her tea.

Later, when Belle was in bed and the others were gathered for supper, Tom said, 'I know it might sound callous to say so, but the fighting was between Muslims and Hindus, so it's very unlikely that Rick will have come to any harm.'

'Even so,' Stella fretted, 'he might have got caught up in the violence unintentionally – a bystander – mistaken for Indian.'

Jeanie saw the uncomfortable looks passing between the Lomaxes.

'Do we know if Pamela has joined him yet?' Esmie asked.

Stella shrugged. 'Uncle Toby didn't mention her when I rang. But we didn't talk for long. It sounded a bit chaotic and he was distracted.'

'Of course.' Esmie sympathised.

'This is hardly going to encourage his fiancée to join him,' Tom said bleakly.

'It'll be a test of how serious they are,' said Andrew, leaning across and squeezing Stella's hand.

***

That night, Jeanie found it hard to sleep. She couldn't get the sickening details of the Calcutta massacre out of her mind. She didn't know the city but John had written from there when on leave during the war. It was an ancient and cultured place where the people were proud to be Bengali, whether Hindu or Muslim. From what she'd read, it was a city of progressives and radicals – but not one to succumb to mob rule. Was this a direct consequence of the failed Cabinet Mission, she wondered? Had it emboldened the hardliners on both sides to stoke up division?

Yet, also keeping her sleepless was the underlying anxiety over Rick. Was he safe and unharmed or had he been among the thousands injured or – God forbid – killed?

**

The next day, instead of going riding, Jeanie went to Tom's studio and absorbed herself in experimenting with oil paints. She found the activity calming, her thoughts focused on re-creating a sketch she had previously done of the hotel. She was concentrating so hard that she didn't hear Tom enter the open door until he was standing beside her. When she looked up, he was smiling.

'Good news,' he said. 'The Dixons say Rick is safe and well.'

Jeanie let out a long breath. 'Oh, thank goodness!'

Tom nodded. 'A great relief all round. Stella's a bit emotional so I said I'd come and tell you straight away.'

Jeanie's chin trembled. 'Thank you.' She fought to control a sudden desire to cry.

'He's not only fine but he's in Pindi.'

'Really?' Jeanie's eyes widened in astonishment.

225

'He was flying goods into Walton airport,' Tom explained, 'and knew nothing about the riots until he arrived in Lahore. He knew how worried his family would be about him so he took the train to Pindi.'

Jeanie's heart leapt. 'That's wonderful. I'm so happy for them.'

Tom put a hand on her shoulder. It was a simple, comforting gesture that almost made Jeanie weep. She was feeling bafflingly emotional at such good news. After a moment, Tom withdrew his hand and gestured at her painting. 'I like this. It's coming on nicely.'

Jeanie smiled and managed a croaky, 'Thanks.'

'I'll leave you to it,' he said. At the door, he turned. 'Will you be all right?'

Jeanie nodded.

'Join us later for afternoon tea,' he said. 'Belle is making us a surprise cake with Felix the chef. It's Big Ted's birthday, apparently – although I'm pretty sure he had it two weeks ago.'

'You can never have too much cake,' Jeanie said with a tearful smile.

Chapter 28

Rawalpindi

The minute Rick walked into his parents' apartment, his mother ran at him with a shriek of relief.

'My boy!'

Rick had to hold her up as her legs buckled.

'I'm fine, Ma.' He kissed her forehead and steered her into a chair.

Behind him, his father and Sigmund stood grinning foolishly, having followed him upstairs from the garage.

Rick's father produced a handkerchief for his wife. 'Dash it all, Rose! Didn't I tell you he'd come home safe and sound?'

Sigmund added, 'Rick's the brother with nine lives, remember?'

Rose wiped her tears and gave Rick an emotional smile. 'I'm so happy to see you.' But the next moment she was worrying again. 'I don't see why you have to live so far away. Calcutta is not safe. Why can't you come back to Pindi?'

'Because Pukka-Pamela has decreed she will live in no other city,' Sigmund teased. 'Isn't that right, brother?'

Rick refused to be goaded. 'We've both chosen Calcutta. And she'll be here any day now.'

'Which means she still hasn't arrived in India?' Rose gave a disapproving frown.

'By the end of the month,' he replied. 'She's booking flights very soon. I had a letter from her last week.'

He saw the sceptical look pass between his parents and felt tense. Pamela's continued reluctance to return to India was making him anxious. Was he being a fool? Yet she kept assuring him that she was missing him and longing to be with him. Rick knew that her father was putting every obstacle in her way that he could. No doubt the latest eruption of violence in Calcutta would provide Geoffrey with another excuse to delay Pamela's departure, he thought bleakly. Yet, he put on a brave face so that his parents had one less thing to worry about.

His mother began ordering up food and drink. 'Toby.' She flapped a hand at her husband. 'Go and telephone Ada and tell her that Rick is here. She'll want to come round. She's been ringing five times a day. And Stella has been calling too. They're all very worried in the hills.'

'Stella?' Rick repeated. 'That's kind of her.'

'Yes, most worried,' said Rose. 'All the Lomaxes – and that nice Mrs Munro was asking after you too.'

Rick's heart thumped in his chest. 'Jeanie Munro is in Gulmarg?'

'Yes,' said Rose. 'Toby, go and make those phone calls. Chop-chop.'

His father and brother retreated below to the garage while his mother took charge once more. Rick was distracted. His mother kept firing questions at him but all he could think about was Jeanie being at The Raj-in-the-Hills. Was she there with Mungo or alone? What a perfect place to escape the horrors that had engulfed Calcutta. He could take a few days …

'You aren't listening, are you?' Rose said with a laugh of exasperation. 'It's usually Sigmund with his head in the clouds.'

'Sorry, Ma,' Rick said, throwing an arm around her shoulders. 'I'm all ears now.'

'A letter came for you. We were going to redirect it but there's no need now.'

'Who from?'

Rose gave him a wry smile. 'Contrary to what you might think; I don't steam open my son's dak. Though the postmark was somewhere in the hills.'

'Murree?' Rick asked, a bit too quickly.

'No, not Murree. I think it was Mussoorie. Do you know anyone there?'

Rick shrugged. 'It might be Shuggs Kumar – one of the Indian Air Force chaps. He lives in the hills somewhere.'

Rick hid his disappointment, though he knew he was being ridiculous. Why on earth would Jeanie be writing to him? He really must stop thinking about her – even if Jeanie had been concerned about him. He should start by putting from his mind the wild idea of going up to Gulmarg.

Chapter 29

Raj-in-the-Hills, Gulmarg

Morale in the Lomax household was boosted by the news that Rick had escaped Calcutta's deadly riots. More information of the horrors began to circulate over the next two days of chai-wallahs and rickshaw drivers being dragged onto the street and butchered. Muslim leaders in the city were being blamed for most of the violence, though it was emerging that Hindu gangs had also wreaked revenge.

Jeanie didn't like to talk about it in front of Stella, who seemed particularly anxious these days. Jeanie noticed how her friend would automatically cover her baby bump with protective hands whenever talk turned to the recent turmoil. So, Jeanie took the chance to discuss it with Tom when they retreated to the sanctuary of the studio.

She voiced her fears. 'It all seems so volatile since the British mission failed.'

'Attitudes do seem to be hardening,' Tom agreed, sharing his cigarettes.

Jeanie said, 'I understand there are competing visions of what India should be – Congress wanting a united country and the League wanting some form of autonomy for their followers. But that's politics. This feels like something else.'

'Go on,' Tom encouraged.

'It's as if some people are deliberately stirring up religious differences. That makes it harder to come together. People can get so inflamed about religion.'

Tom regarded her. 'Have you always been interested in politics?'

Jeanie gave a self-conscious laugh. 'Not really. My army friend, Phyllis, opened my eyes to a lot of issues I'd never thought of before. And coming back to India … I felt I should take more notice of what was happening here.' She kept to herself that it was a conversation with Rick at Ebbsmouth that had sparked off her determination to engage more with the current situation.

'What do you think?' Jeanie asked him. 'If India gets self-rule, what would you do – stay here or go back to Ebbsmouth?'

Tom blew out smoke rings as he pondered his answer. 'I can't imagine ever leaving Gulmarg,' he said. 'It's home to me in a way Ebbsmouth hasn't been for years. I enjoyed our trip back to see Tibby and Dawan but I was itching to get back here by the end.' She kept silent, sensing he had more to say. 'All that's most precious is here in India; Esmie and the family. Even Mary …' He tailed off.

Jeanie said gently, 'I understand.'

Tom finished his cigarette and asked, 'What about you, Jeanie? Is there enough to keep you here too?'

Jeanie felt her stomach twist when she thought of Mungo and Nicholson's. She didn't want to think of going back there yet and having to drum up enthusiasm for a new term and a fresh attempt to get pregnant. The idea made her despondent. Yet there were other things in India which made her want to stay.

'Yes,' she said. 'This beautiful place for one.'

Tom gave her a quizzical look. 'But what about …?'

Suddenly they were interrupted by footsteps running up the path and Andrew appearing breathless in the doorway.

'What is it?' Tom asked.

'We've got a visitor.' He grinned.

Jeanie's stomach fluttered. 'Who?' Even as she asked, some intuition told her.

'Rick Dixon's just arrived.'

Chapter 30

That evening, Tom ordered up two bottles of champagne to celebrate Rick's visit and the conversation around the supper table was livelier than it had been in days. Rick regaled them with stories of life in Calcutta that did not touch on the recent troubles. He conjured up a world of bachelor parties, cricket matches and trips to the races.

'It all sounds very male,' Stella teased. 'Does that mean Pamela hasn't joined you yet?'

'She's on her way,' Rick said confidently. 'Or almost. Her last airmail said she'd be buying flights at the end of the month.'

'That's wonderful news,' said Esmie. 'I'm sure you can't wait.'

'Will she still want to come?' Stella asked. 'I mean, to Calcutta?'

Rick looked less sure. 'Well, I don't see why not. This will all blow over.'

Andrew came to his support. 'I'm sure it will. Stella's just a little jumpy these days.'

Rick gave a quizzical look.

'I'm expecting a baby,' Stella said, her smile a little anxious. 'End of November.'

Rick beamed. 'Congratulations Cousin! Your Auntie Rose will be pleased to hear that – though she'll just put more pressure on me and Sigmund to get on and start families.'

Jeanie felt uncomfortable at the turn of the conversation and kept quiet. Soon the cousins were swapping more family news. 'I've seen Lucy and Monty,' said Rick. 'They seem very happy.'

'No doubt they'll be wanting to start a family now too,' said Stella.

Rick hesitated. Stella picked up on it at once. 'Won't they?'

'No doubt,' Rick said, nodding. 'Or they might delay a little while longer.'

'Why?'

'There's been some family discussion, apparently. Auntie Lucinda and Uncle Ziggy think perhaps Monty should look for a career outside the Public Works Department.'

'But he's getting on well there, isn't he?' Andrew asked.

'He's happy enough,' Rick agreed. 'But this latest unrest … well, it's got them all talking again about what they should do in the long term. Stay in Pindi or move away.'

'Move away where?' Stella asked in dismay.

Rick shrugged. 'Britain maybe. Uncle Ziggy mentioned Canada.'

'Canada?' Stella cried. 'Surely they wouldn't? I couldn't bear the thought of them all going so far.'

Rick, seeing how quickly she grew upset at such talk, said, 'I'm sure it won't come to that. You know how Auntie's prone to worrying. Lucy was only going through the motions of considering the suggestion just to keep her mother happy.'

Abruptly, Rick turned to Jeanie. 'Anyhow, I want to hear how the end of term play went at Nicholson's. I scoured the theatre pages in the *Times of India* but couldn't find any reference to the magnificent stage scenery.'

Jeanie gave a snort of laughter. 'We managed to get through three performances without any of the scenery dropping off or the French windows falling over. So, it was a huge success.'

***

The next day, Rick went riding with Jeanie and some other guests.

'I'm not very proficient,' he warned. 'More comfortable behind a wheel than in the saddle.'

But he tackled the activity with his usual enthusiasm and panache. They rode up to the high marg and got a glimpse through the shifting clouds to snow-covered peaks.

'The sight of those mountains never fails to take my breath away,' Rick said. 'It's one of the pleasures of flying to Assam – seeing the Himalayas.'

'My brother loved the mountains too,' said Jeanie. 'He was quite an expert on alpine flowers.'

'I'm certainly no expert on these mountains,' Rick said ruefully. 'But we can all get enjoyment from them, can't we?'

'Yes,' Jeanie agreed. 'That's why I'm always trying to capture them in paint. Captain Tom's been kind enough to let me use his studio.'

'Will you let me have a look at what you're painting?' he asked.

'Maybe when it's finished,' she said, with a self-conscious laugh.

'Better paint quickly then. I can only stay two more days.'

Jeanie tried to hide her disappointment at this news. Another of the guests – a businessman with a shipping agency – broke into the conversation.

'I say; do either of you play tennis? We're looking for a couple to make up a game of doubles.'

'I love tennis,' said Jeanie.

Rick grinned. 'Count me in too.'

***

234

The next two days went swiftly. Jeanie and Rick played tennis with their fellow guests and Rick, finding a new enthusiasm for riding, joined in another trek around the resort's perimeter. She let him see her painting-in-progress and was flattered by his complimentary remarks. But the days were bittersweet; she revelled in his company and yet knew she should not. The more time she spent with him, the more she knew her feelings for him were becoming unmanageable. She longed to be with him but knew she mustn't show how much she cared.

Jeanie tried to convince herself that this was just a fleeting time together that meant nothing – a time of friendship and fun – and a respite from the worrying news of unrest and division in the wider world. Soon they would both be gone from the haven of the Raj-in-the-Hills and picking up their separate lives. What was the harm in a few days holiday?

Stella's surprise suggestion caught Jeanie off-guard.

'You need a lift back to Murree and Rick is going that way too. Why don't you travel together?'

Jeanie had been steeling herself to say goodbye. Would this only prolong the agony?

'I'd be happy to do that,' Rick said at once.

'That's settled then,' said Stella. 'Andy and I were worrying about you travelling back on your own, Jeanie.'

On the final evening, after dining with the Lomaxes, Rick escorted Jeanie back to the hotel.

'Want to take a final stroll around the garden?' Rick suggested as they reached the hotel steps. Jeanie nodded in agreement. They took a path to the left that wound through a rockery and climbed steeply to a lawned area with a bench which overlooked the resort. Here, they sat down. Jeanie breathed in the scented air.

'I love seeing the lights of Gulmarg shining through the trees,' she said. 'I'm going to miss this place. It's been a real haven.'

'Stella's going to miss you too,' said Rick. 'It's been good for her having you here – she misses the wider family in Pindi – and she's the sociable type who needs friends.'

'No doubt she'll come down to Pindi for the birth,' Jeanie said. 'Then she can see everyone. I bet all you Dixons and Duboises know how to celebrate Christmas in style.'

Rick let out a sigh. 'Things could be very different by then.'

Jeanie blushed. 'Of course. You'll be married and–'

'I wasn't meaning that,' Rick interrupted.

'Oh, what then?'

'I didn't want to say anything in front of Stella,' he said, 'because of the way she got upset at the idea of Uncle Ziggy and family leaving.'

'Go on.'

'My sister Ada and her husband Clive have also been talking about it.'

'Leaving Pindi?' Jeanie exclaimed.

'It caused a bit of a row at home when they came round to see me. Clive has relations in Ceylon who are encouraging him to join them. Said there are lots of opportunities for young men like him. My parents were very upset at the idea.'

'I'm sure they were.' Jeanie sympathised.

'It didn't help that Sigmund took Clive's side – said he would jump at the chance if it were him. He thinks Colombo is paved with gold and beautiful girls. That started a whole new argument about whether the family should stick together, sell the business and all go. Poor Ada feels caught in the middle. That's why I didn't say much about the family to Stella. It's all so up in the air; what was the point of making her worry?'

236

Briefly, Jeanie put a hand on his arm. 'I'm so sorry to hear all that. You must be worried too. You don't think your father would really sell his business, do you? He has such a good reputation in Pindi.'

'Dad thinks it's a ridiculous idea. He doesn't want to uproot at his age and start again. But these latest killings in Calcutta have unnerved everyone. It's started off all the anxiety again about what will happen to our people once independence comes.'

'What do you want to do?' she asked.

Rick let go a long breath. 'I thought I knew exactly what I wanted but now I'm not so sure. Seeing my family at loggerheads – it's unsettling. Perhaps a new start somewhere else wouldn't be a bad thing.'

Jeanie felt her chest constrict. She was suddenly desolate at the thought of him leaving and never seeing him again. But that was what might happen – *should* happen – once he was married. Whether Rick lived in Calcutta or Ceylon, he would live his life far from her and she mustn't sway his decision.

'And Pamela?' Jeanie asked gently. 'Surely she should have a say?'

'Yes.' Rick scratched his chin and she sensed his awkwardness. 'She might like the idea of Colombo. She doesn't seem to be jumping at the chance to come back to India, so maybe it would be a compromise.'

Jeanie steeled herself. 'Or maybe you should consider going to England? If that's where she really wants to live – close to her parents. You could be a pilot over there. It shouldn't be the place that's important, as long as you're with the person you love.'

Rick turned to look at her. She saw his eyes glint in the moonlight. 'Is that how you feel about your husband?'

Jeanie's heart thumped. 'Mungo had a job lined up in Ebbsmouth and we were supposed to live with my mother in Greentoun. When he got the headship at Nicholson's I accepted that to be with him I would have to come back to India. So that's what I did.'

Rick held her look. 'That's not what I asked.'

Jeanie's heart drummed. She felt them edging towards a dangerous subject.

'I – I chose Mungo years ago,' she said quietly, 'and made promises that I must keep.'

'You don't strike me as a woman who is still in love with her husband,' he challenged.

Jeanie knew she should refute this at once but something about sitting in the darkness of the flower-scented garden made it too easy to admit her thoughts.

'I can't deny it's been difficult at times – being back in Murree – trying to adapt to living with him again. We've both changed. But that's mostly my fault. What we do both want is a family – so far without success.' She stopped and put her hands to her burning cheeks. 'I don't know why I'm telling you this.' She gave an embarrassed laugh. 'You're far too easy to talk to, Rick.'

He reached and took her hand in his. 'You deserve to be happy. I'm just not sure, from what I've heard, that Mungo is the right man for you.'

She flinched and withdrew her hand. 'You don't know him. You've never even met him.'

'Sorry,' he said quickly. 'I didn't mean to cause offence. All I'm saying is, don't stay with him out of a sense of duty – do it because he's the man you want to spend the rest of your life with – whether you have children or not.'

She felt panic constrict her throat. His words echoed those of Tom's about not staying with someone you don't love. She couldn't leave Mungo; it would break him. The stigma of failure would be more than he could bear – and he didn't deserve it – he'd already had to put up with seven years of gossip about a wife who'd chosen to stay away when she could have returned during the war like other wives and families had.

Jeanie stood up, heart pounding. 'I don't think you're in any position to lecture me about my marriage. Where's your fiancée? Don't you think you should be concentrating on your own marriage plans and future, rather than mine?'

He gaped at her. 'Jeanie, I didn't mean to upset you …'

'I'm not upset. I'm just fed up with people making judgements about me and Mungo.'

He leapt up. 'I'm sorry.'

'I shouldn't be here with you,' she said in agitation. 'I've spent too much time with you. It's not helping. I know it doesn't mean anything to you but –'

He seized her hand again. 'That's where you're wrong. I care about you a lot – too much.' He spoke with urgency. 'That's why I came here, because I heard you were at the hotel alone. I know it was wrong but I couldn't stay away. I know you don't love your husband enough – just like I don't love my fiancée wholeheartedly.'

His words nearly felled her. She had no idea that he felt as strongly as she did. How had she allowed this to happen?

'Please don't say that,' Jeanie said in distress.

'It's true,' he said. 'And I think we both know it.' He brushed his hand against her cheek and touched her hair. 'You're beautiful and full of spirit and I wish we'd met years ago.'

Jeanie's eyes stung with sudden tears. She felt a sob build in her chest. Then he was pulling her into his arms. She succumbed to tears. Rick held her, saying nothing. But being in his strong arms was as blissful as she had imagined; she ached with wanting him. He stroked her hair, yet he didn't

239

try to kiss her. She knew if he did, she would respond and not care for the consequences.

A night bird shrieked overhead and the spell was broken. Jeanie pulled away. She was shaking with emotion and the knowledge of how close she had come to betraying Mungo. Her voice, when she managed to speak, was hoarse.

'We can't do this again, Rick. If we carry on, too many people will get hurt.'

She could hardly bear to look into his eyes. They blazed with the same passion and longing that she felt – but she saw the haunted look of guilt too. He sighed heavily and nodded.

In silence, they made their way back downhill to the hotel. The only word they could summon was a strained 'goodnight' to each other as they went to their separate rooms.

Chapter 31

Barely able to sleep all night long, Jeanie got up early and went round to the annexe. She was comforted by the morning routine, being there while Belle got up and then having breakfast with her and Andrew. These days, Stella was lying in bed longer and the older Lomaxes were having breakfast in bed. Jeanie was also avoiding seeing Rick in the hotel at breakfast time; she couldn't bear the thought of them having to make polite conversation in front of the other guests.

Andrew fixed her with his one good eye and asked, 'will Mr Munro be at home when you get back?'

'I don't think so,' she said, feeling leaden inside. It must be guilt.

'Will you be okay? If you're not ready to go, I could always drive you down to Murree later in the week.'

Jeanie was touched. 'That's very kind but I really should be getting back. There'll be lots to do to get ready for the new term.'

'Of course.' He smiled. 'But promise me, you'll come back whenever you want. We've really enjoyed having you to stay. Haven't we Belle?'

The girl nodded vigorously, her mouth crammed with scrambled egg and toast.

'Thank you.' Jeanie's heart swelled with gratitude. 'You've no idea how much I've loved being with you all in this wonderful place. It's been a wee bit of heaven.'

When Stella and the others emerged, Jeanie kept the goodbyes brief. She repeated her thanks. The words sounded inadequate but she felt suddenly emotional at having to leave them and didn't dare linger.

'You've all been so kind ... I've had a wonderful time ... of course I'll write ... and hope to see you in Pindi when the Gulmarg season is over.' She didn't invite them to stop in Murree on their way through and none of them suggested it either. It saddened her that she couldn't have her friends to stay.

Andrew and Tom accompanied her and Rick down to where he'd left his car below the resort. Manek had already organised the transfer of their cases by mule. The men shook hands and Jeanie kissed Andrew and Tom on the cheek. She climbed into the passenger seat and wound down the window. She waved and called goodbyes until they were out of sight.

Rick stretched his arm out of his window as if he were catching the last of the sweet air in his grasp. They drove on in silence. Jeanie was acutely aware of the awkwardness between them. In her mind, she had gone over the words they had spoken in the dark of the garden, countless times. They had each said things that could never be unsaid. But what did they do now?

Last night, she had said that they must stop, yet glancing at his handsome profile under his thick dark hair, she wanted to break the vow she had made to herself at dawn that she would give him up completely. She felt that on this car journey, their fate would be decided. She waited for him to speak first. The road was twisting and narrow and all his concentration was on driving.

Eventually, he glanced at her. 'You're very quiet. What are you thinking?'

Jeanie's pulse began to race. 'About last night.'

He nodded. 'I'm sorry for putting you in such a difficult situation. I had no right to say all those things about you and Mungo. I must have drunk too much of the Lomaxes' whisky. Please forgive me.'

242

Jeanie's stomach twisted. She turned away to look out of the window in case he saw the tears brimming in her eyes.

'There's nothing to forgive,' she murmured. 'I was equally to blame.'

After a pause, he said, 'You were full of wise words. I've taken them to heart. About Pamela. I need to find out where she really wants to start married life. Maybe I will go to England.'

Jeanie just nodded. The ache in her heart was too painful for her to come up with a coherent reply. They drove on in silence.

After a while, Rick appeared to regain his usual cheerfulness and chatted on about inconsequential things, such as cricket and tales about far-flung family members who had been at the Pindi wedding.

They stopped at Baramulla for a picnic which the Lomaxes had provided. Sitting by a stream near the roadside, Jeanie forced down a sandwich and cup of tea. Then she lay back and closed her eyes, allowing her senses to be calmed by the sound of birdsong and the smell of meadows.

She must have dozed off because when she opened her eyes, Rick had packed away the tiffin basket and was crouched next to her, smoking.

'I didn't think you smoked?' she said, leaning up.

'I don't.' He looked sheepish and handed it to her. Accepting it, she took a long draw. The cigarette paper was moist from his lips. Her hand shook as she handed it back.

Rick extinguished it between his finger and thumb. They gazed at each other. He looked so handsome with his collar open and his hair tousled in the breeze. Gently, he took her hand in his and raised it to his lips, kissing her fingers. Jeanie swallowed. The smile he gave her was full of sadness and longing.

Then he stood up and pulled her to her feet. 'I dream of Jeanie with the light-brown hair,' he said and let go his hold.

***

Jeanie slept for most of the rest of the journey. By the time she awoke, they were crossing the bridge at Kohala, back into the Punjab. She felt strangely numb, drained of the emotion of the previous hours. They hardly spoke for the final pull into Murree, except for her to give instructions about how to get to the school.

As they drove through Nicholson's high wrought-iron gates, she felt as if the place was closing in on her and had to steady her breathing. Rick threw her a look of concern.

'Are you okay?'

She nodded. 'I'm fine.'

'Will Mungo be expecting you?'

'He's not due back until tomorrow or the day after, I think.' She pointed to the archway ahead. 'It's through there and into the quad.'

Her heart began to beat rapidly. Soon she would have to say goodbye to Rick and it would probably be for the last time.

'Can I give you some refreshment before the drive to Pindi?' she asked, suddenly wanting to delay the moment of parting.

She saw his hands tighten on the wheel. 'Thanks, but I think it's best if I just push on. There's still half a tiffin basket of food left.'

'Yes, kind Lomaxes,' she said.

Rick brought the car to a halt in front of the School House steps. 'Big house, Mrs Munro,' he said, with a wry smile.

'Very,' she murmured, thinking how large and empty it would feel after Hester's houseboat and then the busy Raj Hotel.

As they got out of the car and Rick went to fetch her case from the boot, Humza hurried down the steps with Nitin.

'Humza!' Jeanie greeted their bearer in astonishment. 'Have you come ahead of Mungo?'

'Sahib is here also,' he replied. 'Welcome back, Munro-Mem'.' He waved at Nitin to take the case from Rick.

Jeanie's stomach clenched. 'Mungo's here?'

The bearer nodded. She exchanged looks with Rick. As the servants moved off, Rick stepped close.

'Do you want me to stay?'

Just then, Mungo strode out of the house. 'Dearest! You're back at last.'

Jeanie's heart lurched as she stepped quickly away from Rick.

'Yes, hello.' Her mouth was dry.

He reached her and kissed her on the cheek. He turned to Rick. 'And you are?'

'Rick Dixon.' Rick smiled and put out his hand.

Mungo gave the slightest hesitation and then shook it. 'Are you one of the Pindi garage people?'

'Yes.'

Jeanie said swiftly, 'Rick was visiting Gulmarg too and was kind enough to offer me a lift on his way back to Pindi.'

Mungo scrutinised him, then said, 'Well, thank you for delivering my wife safely back to me. You must let me give you some money for the petrol.'

Rick's smile stiffened. 'I wouldn't dream of taking any payment. I was more than happy to drive Jeanie here.'

'Some refreshment then?' Mungo said.

'I've already offered,' said Jeanie, 'but Rick has to get back to Pindi this evening.'

'Ah, then we mustn't keep you, Mr Dixon,' Mungo said with a regretful smile. Jeanie could tell by the way her husband was clenching his jaw that he was displeased.

Rick nodded. 'It was good to meet you, Mr Munro.' He turned to Jeanie. For a moment, they held each other's look. Then he shook her hand. 'Goodbye, Jeanie.'

She squeezed his hand back. Her heart was racing. She wanted to hold onto him and not let go. 'Goodbye,' she said, trying to control her voice. 'And good luck.'

He gave a brief smile and withdrew his hand. Jeanie watched as Rick climbed back into the car, started it up and drove away. She waved. When she turned towards Mungo, he was regarding her.

'Was he the man you met in Ebbsmouth?' he asked.

'Yes. He's a cousin of Stella's.'

'Looks a bit of a spiv.'

Jeanie tensed. 'He's nothing like that. He flew Dakotas during the war.'

Mungo huffed. 'Well, I'm glad he's brought you home.'

They walked towards the house. Jeanie was heavy-hearted. This didn't feel like home anymore.

'I thought you weren't getting back till the weekend?' she said. 'How was the fishing?'

He shrugged. 'Not as good as some years. I decided to come home early. Hoped you'd be here. I've missed you, Jean. I hope you've missed me.'

'Of course.' She swallowed, hating herself for the easy lie.

Walking into the gloom of the darkly-panelled hallway, Jeanie had to stem her rising panic.

Chapter 32

Murree, late September

The term started again and Jeanie attempted to push all thoughts of the summer from her mind by keeping as busy as possible. She offered to help the Danes with another school play, she attended rugby matches and recitals; she took her watercolours and painted scenes around the town. She continued holding coffee mornings for the staff and instigated a music appreciation society for teachers and prefects to which they could bring records to play on Mungo's old wind-up gramophone. Only two staff and half a dozen boys came – she suspected the pupils were more interested in the buffet provided – but it was a weekly distraction from evenings largely spent on her own.

Mungo was always closeted in his study, working till late. When with her, he seemed distracted as if he was no longer doing his job wholeheartedly. Neither did he seem to have any enthusiasm for lovemaking. Since being reunited at the end of August, they had been intimate only twice and her period had come again.

'Is there something wrong?' she asked him one evening. She'd gone to bed first but had stayed awake.

'What do you mean?' He sounded jaded.

'You don't seem yourself,' she said. 'Are you feeling run-down? Perhaps you should see a doctor?'

'I'm fine. Don't fuss.'

'I think you're working too hard,' she persisted. 'And you don't get enough sleep.'

'Good grief! You're not my nursemaid.'

'No, I'm your wife and I'm worried about you.'

He glanced at her; his look softening. 'Well, don't be. I'm perfectly healthy. It's a demanding job that's all.' He sat on the bed, half-undressed and sighed. 'And goodness knows what the future will be.'

'For the school or for us?' Jeanie asked quietly.

He shot her a startled look. 'I was meaning in general – India – all the unrest. And the school too, if the British leave.'

'But you've always said how the school will carry on with Indian pupils – how you want to make it a beacon of education in India–'

'I know what I've said,' he snapped. 'But it won't be the same.'

'Are you having second thoughts about taking on the headship?' Jeanie asked. She expected him to deny it but he didn't.

'Perhaps.' He looked suddenly older and careworn. He met her look. 'But I know I can't do it without you by my side. I need you, Jean.'

She felt as if a weight pressed on her chest at his words. In that moment, she knew that she had to stay loyal to him and her marriage vows – no matter how much her heart yearned for another man. She was bound by a choice she had made years ago.

'You have my support,' she answered, putting a reassuring hand on his arm. 'But you have to be honest with me, Mungo. If you are having doubts you have to share them with me – we must make decisions about our future together from now on.'

He nodded. 'Thank you.'

***

248

After their heart-to-heart, Mungo's mood seemed to improve and he strode around the house with a more confident step. Jeanie wondered if she should confide in her mother about her doubts concerning their future at Nicholson's. Perhaps Clara could make enquiries to see if there was still a position for Mungo at the school in Ebbsmouth. The thought of returning to Scotland and being with her mother was growing in appeal. For all that they weren't as close as Jeanie would have wanted, since her return to India, they had struck up a tender relationship by letter.

Jeanie had no real confidantes in Murree; Mary Dane was too liable to repeat things shared in private and Dinah Lavelle was too deferential. The matron always made her very aware of their unequal social positions. Besides, the matron had been too busy with settling in the new boys to socialise and they had only met up for afternoon tea on one occasion since the start of term. Jeanie had been left with the impression that Dinah had had a falling-out with her friend in Dehra Dun as she hadn't wanted to talk about her holiday.

In early October, returning from painting further up Kashmir Point, Jeanie ran into Dinah in the hallway.

'Hello Matron! Hasn't it been a glorious afternoon?'

'Indeed, Mrs Munro.' She seemed a little flustered. After a moment's hesitation, she held out an envelope. 'I was just collecting the post from the table. Here's one for you.'

Jeanie took it, recognising the handwriting. 'Oh, lovely! It's from Mother. I see you've got post too.'

Dinah slipped the other letter into her pocket. 'Yes, from my brother.'

'I'm going to order up some tea in the garden. Have you time to join me?' Jeanie asked.

Dinah smiled briefly. 'Thank you but I've got the laundry lists to check.'

'Another time then?'

'Yes, another time.'

Jeanie watched her walk swiftly away, her bearing upright and tread light. It was hard to reconcile this reserved woman with the uninhibited wedding guest in Pindi. The woman was a puzzle.

Twenty minutes later, Jeanie was settling into a cane chair on the terrace with a steaming cup of Darjeeling tea and her mother's letter. It wasn't just an aerogramme but a satisfyingly thick envelope. She slit it open and began to read.

Chapter 33

Clara

Peshawar, February 1919

'There's a visitor, Memsahib.' The bearer held out a silver tray. Clara put down her embroidery and took the calling card reluctantly. She didn't encourage callers. Her stomach lurched as she read the name: *Miss Olive Armitage, Peshawar Hospital, British cantonment.*

She held the card and hesitated. What did the woman want with her and why had she come to the house? Clara began to tremble. Just seeing the name brought back terrible memories; the hot, claustrophobic wards and the desolation.

Yet, Armitage was a kindly soul. Clara knew she owed the nurse a very great debt for bringing Jean safely into the world. She looked across at her red-cheeked six-year-old daughter, sitting at a low table by the roaring fire, drawing a colourful picture and humming. Her curly dark hair, pulled into two pigtails, was already escaping its ribbons and she had smudges of crayon on her face and fingers. Ayah was squatting on the floor beside her charge, murmuring encouragement.

Jean looked up and saw Clara watching her. She smiled broadly.

'I'm drawing Daddy on a horse.' She held up the picture.

'Very nice.' Clara stemmed a familiar wave of panic. She was paralysed by competing forces; either to rush and protect her daughter, or seal up her heart from loving her too much.

'Ayah, take Jean to the nursery, please.'

The servant nodded and stood up, holding out a hand to the girl.

Jean's face gaped in disappointment. 'But I haven't finished the picture, Mummy.'

'You can finish it later or take it with you,' Clara said. 'I have a visitor.'

'Can I meet the visitor?' Jean asked, brightening.

'No,' she answered too sharply. 'She hasn't come to see you.'

Ayah cajoled the girl out of the room. Clara felt wretched for her harsh words. She shouldn't take out her unhappiness on the child. She instructed the bearer to arrange tea and biscuits, and to show Miss Armitage in.

***

'There was no need to go to the bother of tea, Mrs Grant,' Olive said, tucking into the biscuits. 'But I do have a very sweet tooth.'

Clara observed her. She looked different in civilian clothes, without the severe starched uniform; plumper and more relaxed in her woollen skirt and jacket. She'd never noticed the thick red hair and the tinge of an accent – Welsh perhaps? Even though Clara was a major's wife – soon to be that of a colonel's – she had felt helplessly in the hands of this woman when in hospital. Now the roles were reversed and the nurse sat there as Clara's social inferior, in one of the grander bungalows in the military cantonment. But what did she want?

'How's baby Grant?' Olive asked.

Clara's heart missed a beat. For a moment her mind was filled with the spectre of her dead babies. Olive had delivered two of them.

'I'd hope to see the girl,' Olive added with a smile.

252

Clara gripped her hands in her lap to stop them shaking. 'Jean is six now. She's … with Ayah.'

'Six, of course. Doesn't the time fly.' The nurse helped herself to another biscuit.

Clara tried to stay calm. 'So, you're still nursing at the hospital here?'

She munched and spoke between mouthfuls. 'I was deployed to Taha on the Frontier for a spell during the war. But I got back to Peshawar a month ago. It's been a terrible time for some, hasn't it? A terrible war. And then this Spanish flu. So many deaths; it's hard to take in. But the Lord giveth and the Lord taketh away.'

Clara had forgotten the nurse's enthusiasm for Biblical homilies. She couldn't hold back her impatience.

'Miss Armitage; what is it that brings you here? Is there something I can do for you?'

The nurse wiped her mouth with a linen napkin and brushed crumbs off her skirt. She sat forward, an eager look in her hazel eyes.

'No, dear Mrs Grant; it's what I can do for you.'

Clara felt palpitations in her chest. The room felt suddenly stuffy with the heat of the blazing fire. 'Oh?'

'No one knows more than I how difficult it's been for you, Mrs Grant – how much you've had to bear – with the babies and that.'

'I'd rather you didn't mention …'

Olive held up her hand. 'Let me explain, Mrs Grant. When I was at Taha I got friendly with this sergeant's wife – such a nice lady – Scotchwoman like you. I helped at her son's birth. Well, it all turned tragic after that. Her husband was killed in action in Waziristan. Then two weeks ago, the army padre wrote and told me that my dear friend had passed away too. He said of a broken heart but I know she suffered badly from bronchitis so I think that's the more likely cause.'

253

Clara swallowed hard. 'That's very sad. And the baby?'

'Orphaned, poor boy. With no one to take care of him. And such a bonny looking baby. He'll be sent to an orphanage in Rawalpindi, most likely. Unless ...'

'Unless?'

'Some kind family takes him in.'

'But has he no family in Scotland?' Clara asked.

'She never talked of any.' Olive's look was fervent. 'But I thought it might be God's way of telling me to find a loving home for the baby. I know how much you long for a son, Mrs Grant – you and the major. Would you be prepared to take him into your loving arms? If so, I could write to the padre and tell him–'

'Stop!' Clara cried. She cast around, fearful of someone overhearing them. 'I can't take him.'

'Why not?' Olive challenged. 'You'd be doing a noble thing – the Lord's duty.'

Clara stood up in agitation. 'Major Grant would never consider adopting another man's son – a boy that wasn't of his blood. It's unthinkable.'

'The baby is red-haired just like Major Grant,' Olive persisted.

'The answer is no! Thank you for coming, Miss Armitage, but I think it's time you left.'

The nurse got up and smoothed down her skirt. 'If you change your mind, you know where to find me.'

'I won't ... I'm sorry ... I can't.'

At the door, Olive lingered and said, 'I know baby Jean brought you comfort, Mrs Grant. But I know how much you really wanted a boy – how you said the major would be disappointed with a girl. Maybe this is God's way of giving you a son – and a brother for Jean.'

As soon as she left, Clara collapsed back into her chair and burst into tears.

Clara could think of nothing else. A red-headed baby boy who had no one to care for him. Did he look like any of her stillborn sons? Could she bear the thought of raising him? Could she bear the thought of *not* raising him? She didn't sleep that night, or the night after. Colin was due back from duty at Landi Kotal in the Khyber Pass any day now. She knew that she would have to make a decision by then.

Colin would dismiss the idea out of hand; might even be offended at the suggestion of taking on another man's son – someone else's flesh and blood – and a sergeant's at that. She knew how much blood ties meant to him; how proud he was of his Grant lineage and that his forebears had served in Scottish regiments for generations.

On the other hand, her husband longed for a son as much as she did. He still held out hope that one day he would father a male heir who would grow up strong and noble and serve in his regiment. Clara knew in her heart that she would never be able to give him that much wanted son; all her boys died before drawing breath. These days, she shied away from intimacy with her husband, fearful of falling pregnant again. She made excuses not to lie with him – citing women's problems – but knew that from time to time she had to allow him conjugal relations.

Clara felt increasingly anxious at the thought of Colin's return and what to do. She loved him and he had turned out to be a surprisingly good father to Jean. In fact, he doted on the girl, affectionately calling her Jeanie and was far more demonstrative with her than she, Clara, was. Perhaps she could persuade him to take on the orphaned boy.

As soon as she began to think about how she might do so, Clara knew that she wanted the baby. She could grow to love to him – especially if he resembled Colin in any way – and he would make their family complete. The more she thought about him, the more desperately she wanted him.

**

Colin, sitting opposite Clara by the fire and nursing a hot toddy, looked at her open-mouthed. He was glassy-eyed and sniffling with a bad cold. She wondered if he was too ill to have taken in her suggestion.

'Adopt an orphan?' He looked baffled. 'Someone we don't even know?'

Clara stayed calm. 'An army child – and a Scot. A boy who needs parents and a loving home, whose father died serving his country on the Frontier.'

'What regiment?' Colin asked.

'I'm not sure, but they've been based at Taha.' Clara went on swiftly. 'They were good God-fearing people and we'd be doing our Christian duty by taking the boy into our home.'

Colin took a slug of his medicinal drink. 'But he would never truly be mine. He couldn't grow up being proud of his Grant heritage because it wouldn't be his. And I would never feel the same about him as I do Jeanie – my own flesh and blood.'

Clara's heart was pounding. 'You would learn to love him over time, I'm sure of it.'

'But everyone would know that he was someone else's son – it would be difficult for me … my reputation … not able to sire my own.'

Clara steeled herself. 'I will never be able to give you a son, Colin. The doctors have recently told me that it's too dangerous for me to carry another child – I could die as well as the baby. So, unless you divorce me for another woman, this boy in Taha is your only chance of having a son.'

He looked dumbfounded. His eyes and nose began to stream. He fumbled for a handkerchief and wiped at his face. 'Clara, my dearest! I'm so sorry. Of course I'd never divorce you – what wild talk is this? Is it true you can never – we can never …?'

Clara felt wretched at the pain she was inflicting. But it was near enough the truth; she knew she could never face another pregnancy. It would either kill her – or to bear another stillborn baby would rob her of her sanity.

'I'm sorry, Colin.'

He blew his nose hard. The look he gave her was desolate. 'This boy. Is there some way we could … well … present him as our own?'

Clara experienced a surge of hope. 'I've been thinking about that. People haven't seen much of me for a while – you know how I like to keep to the house – and I could easily be half-way through … you know.' She licked her dry lips. 'I could take Jean to Rawalpindi for a bit – where we're not known – and we could have the baby delivered to us there. After a few months, you can fetch us and bring us back to Peshawar.'

He looked at her with bloodshot eyes. 'You've thought it all through, haven't you? You really want this child.'

Clara's chin trembled. 'Yes – yes I do. Nurse Armitage said the boy has your colouring. I want a son that can grow up to be like you, Colin.'

At last, he gave her a smile of resignation. 'If that's what you want, my dearest, then that's what we'll do.'

Chapter 34

Rawalpindi, summer 1919

They named him John, after Colin's father, and had him christened in the Scots Kirk on the Mall in the garrison town of Rawalpindi as the spring blossom weighted the trees. Clara adored John from the first time she set eyes on him; a ruddy-cheeked, healthy baby with blue-green eyes and soft auburn hair – darker than Colin's – but enough alike for comparisons to be made.

They set up temporary home in the civil lines so as not to attract the attention of army families who might know her husband. Every few weeks, Colin would travel the ninety miles from Peshawar to visit. He grew as besotted as she was over John and would stride around with the baby tucked into the crook of his strong arm, singing him Scottish songs. Gazing at her handsome moustachioed husband and new son, Clara thought her heart would burst with love and pride.

Despite Jean's initial flurry of questions about the baby's sudden arrival in the home, she was good with her new brother, bringing him toys to play with.

'He's too young for bricks and crayons,' Clara would tell her but the girl would just laugh and carry on showing him how to build towers and try to put crayons in his chubby fist.

'Don't do that!' Clara would scold, snatching at the objects. 'He might put them in his mouth and choke.'

Although Clara had never been so happy since coming to India, she couldn't help feeling increasingly anxious. Fear lay in her belly like a poison; an irrational fear that her children would be taken away from her by sickness or force. She didn't deserve them; she was a fraudulent mother who had tricked her husband into lying about John's parentage.

As the months passed and she ruminated on her deception, Clara grew ever more frightened. Soon she would have to return to Peshawar – a town she thought of as a prison – and carry on the pretence. There would be those who knew her secret; Nurse Armitage and the padre from Taha who had arranged the transfer of the baby, whom Colin told her was now with the garrison at Peshawar. He had sworn him to secrecy but careless comments could still slip out.

As the heat and humidity returned with the hot season, Clara knew that some of the other wives would be migrating to the cooler climes of Mussoorie, Murree or Dalhousie. She would be expected to join them but far from feeling relief at the thought, she had always found that people were even more closely observed and gossiped about than in Peshawar. Despite the punishing heat and dust, some years she had refused to leave the frontier town, much to Colin's bafflement.

More and more, her thoughts turned to Scotland and possible escape. She longed for cool rain, for air that was fresh and salty, and sunshine that didn't shrivel up the grass or sear the eyeballs. India was hot and sticky, full of rancid smells and unpalatable spices, of diseases that could snatch young children away between sunrise and sunset. It was the place where her baby boys had died, and where her husband lived in constant danger of being shot by a tribesman's bullet. It's where her existence had shrunk to hiding behind shuttered windows in the humid dark, struggling to keep cool and not lose her temper with a fractious Jean suffering from prickly heat.

When Colin next visited, Clara confronted him. 'I can't stay here any longer – and I can't face going back to Peshawar. The children can't bear the heat and neither can I.'

'I'll take you up to Murree,' Colin offered. 'I did suggest doing so last month, remember?'

'No, not Murree,' Clara snapped. 'It's just endless social calls. I'm useless at chit-chat and playing card games. I can't even ride.'

'You used to be so sociable when I first met you,' Colin pointed out, reproachfully.

'Yes, in Scotland,' Clara replied. 'But I've lost my appetite for society. India's never felt like home. Please can we go home, Colin?'

He frowned. 'Leave India? But I can't possibly. My duty is here with the regiment. And your duty is with me.'

She knew that what he really meant was that he didn't want her to take the children so far away. She tried to explain.

'I just need a short time away. The climate and the worry of the children's health while they're so young ... I could go back to Scotland for a few months, couldn't I? Let our families meet Jean and John. We could stay with your mother at Rowan House – there's plenty of room there.'

She saw him wavering and felt a wave of tenderness towards him; he was a decent man.

'I suppose, if it's just for a short furlough,' he relented. 'And Mama would greatly enjoy seeing the children. I hadn't thought of that. Selfish of me.'

By the time of his departure back to Peshawar, Colin had set in motion the purchase of tickets back to Britain for Clara and his family.

***

They sailed from Bombay in September; Colin having accompanied them on the long train journey from Rawalpindi. Clara said a tearful goodbye to her husband on deck, suddenly filled with remorse that she was separating him from the children he so transparently adored.

She had never seen him so emotional; openly weeping and hugging them each in turn.

'I'll be back,' she promised. 'I just need time to get my strength and spirit back.'

He nodded, gulping back his tears. It was only at this point that Jean fully understood that her father was not coming with them. She burst into tears and clung to his legs.

'D-don't go, Daddy!' she wailed. 'Don't go!'

He hugged her tightly and said something incoherent about being good for mummy.

'No!' she grew hysterical. 'I want to stay with you! Please Daddy …'

Clara had to prise them apart, wrenching on Jean's arm. The girl howled as Colin almost ran down the gangplank and away from his screaming daughter.

By the time the ship's hooter blasted its departure and the boat began to pull away from the quayside, Clara was shaking and sobbing too. What had she done? She was deserting her husband. Did he have any inkling that nothing would induce her to return to India?

Yet, by the following day, as they steamed across open blue sea, she experienced a profound sense of relief. Up on deck, she could breathe – and be herself. She was Mrs Clara Grant on her way back home. She didn't have to defer to anyone, or speak to anyone.

Only Jean pricked her conscience. 'When will we see Daddy again?'

'Soon.'

'When is soon?'

'Before your next birthday.'

'Where is Ayah?'

'In Pindi.'

261

'Why can't she come with us too?'

'Because she's looking after another family now – and you're a big girl and don't need an ayah.'

'What about Johnny? He's not big.'

Clara felt irritated that the girl had picked up Colin's endearment for her son.

'He's called John. And he doesn't need an ayah – he's got me to look after him.'

Jean paused, her expression clouding. 'I miss Ayah.'

'Well, soon you'll meet your Granny Grant. She'll spoil you just like Ayah used to do.'

She thought that would quieten the girl but minutes later, Jean sighed. 'I miss Daddy. When will we see him again?'

'Oh, Jean! Be quiet.'

Jean's eyes filled with tears. 'Why don't you call me Jeanie, like Daddy does?'

'Stop asking questions.' Clara said, cuddling John on her knee.

Jean turned her attention to the baby. She made exaggerated smiles and cooing noises like she'd heard other adults do. 'I love you, Johnny.' She kissed his cheek. 'When you begin to talk, you can call me Jeanie.'

Although Clara began to relax as the journey progressed and they sailed nearer to home, she was constantly on her guard with her garrulous daughter. One day, she caught her describing in detail to a group of women on deck about John's arrival.

'… and we went to a hotel to get him and he had his own cot like Daddy's army bag and this man gave him to my mummy.'

'You got your baby from a hotel?' one of the women said, winking at the others. 'Well, that's unusual.'

'Yes, he's very special. And he already had hair and sucked his thumb and–'

'Jean! Come here please,' Clara ordered, rushing to grab her daughter's hand. She smiled at the women apologetically. 'Sorry, if she's bothering you.'

'Not at all, dear,' one of them replied. 'She's very good company.'

'Well, it's time for her nap.' She pulled her daughter away.

'But I don't want a nap,' Jean protested.

Out of earshot, Clara rounded on Jean and hissed, 'You must never speak to anyone about fetching the baby from a hotel. Do you hear me?'

Jean fixed her with puzzled, frightened eyes. 'Why Mummy?'

'Because it's none of their business and no one wants to hear your tales about the baby.' Clara gripped the girl's arms, willing her to understand. 'I want you to stay with me and the baby and not go wandering off to talk to strangers.'

She could see Jean was biting her lip trying not to cry. Clara felt a wave of guilt for scolding her. None of this was her fault. She softened her tone.

'Do you think you can do that for me?'

Jean nodded, a tear spilling down her cheek.

Clara swallowed. 'Thank you. You're a good girl, Jean … Jeanie.'

Her daughter's pretty face broke into a teary smile. It warmed Clara's heart and gave her hope. The girl would soon forget the memory of going to the hotel and seeing the baby for the first time. Once they were back in Scotland, her memories of India would begin to fade too. Given time, Jean would forget that there had ever been a time when she didn't have a much-loved younger brother.

Chapter 35

Murree, October 1946

Jeanie sat, stupefied by her mother's letter and the story it had told. Her tea had gone cold. She gripped the flimsy airmail paper in her lap so the sheets wouldn't fly off and take their shocking revelations with them. John was adopted. He had never been her real brother – not in the sense of flesh and blood, as her mother had put it.

Jeanie could recall only fragments of her early childhood in India; heat and shuttered rooms, a kind ayah and her mother scolding her for reasons Jeanie had long forgotten. She remembered her brother being brought home in a christening robe, not from a hotel but a church. They were hazy memories that over the years had become muddled and almost lost, her mother never wanting to talk of an unhappy past.

Had John ever known about his adoption? She remembered how he'd mentioned a nurse in Peshawar that he'd met before the outbreak of war; a woman who had asked to be remembered to their mother. Had she told him of his real parentage? From the way he had talked, Jeanie suspected that he had guessed at some secret. Had Clara ever confessed the truth?

The letter explained a lot; her mother's hatred of India, her crippling anxiety at meeting others and her constant worry over her children's safety. She had lost too many babies there, and to compound her neurosis, she harboured guilt at pretending to be John's real mother. Both her parents had felt the social stigma of admitting to adoption and they had kept up the façade for the rest of her father's life – and John's.

Yet, they had loved him deeply; her mother especially. Clara had been unable to hide how much she adored John.

How did she, Jeanie, feel about it? Jeanie wrestled with her emotions; shock at the discovery, sorrow for her parents having to keep such a secret, anger that it had led to them leaving India and a long separation from her father. She had been nine before her father had taken leave and returned to Scotland. Four-year-old John had screamed at this stranger trying to lift him and kiss him.

Jeanie gazed out across the garden to the Himalayas. The peaks dazzled in the clear late-afternoon light. It didn't matter to her that John had been adopted. They had forged a close bond from the beginning; had shared a love of mountains and riding, swimming and song. Her eyes stung with tears as she remembered how special he had been to her. She couldn't have loved him any more if he had been her blood brother.

She read the final page of the letter again.

'... I'm not telling you all this, Jeanie, just to make my burden lighter. But I worry about you making yourself ill and unhappy at not being able to bear children with Mungo. There is always the choice of adopting a baby. No doubt there are many unwanted or orphaned babies in the wake of the war – just as there were in my day. Believe me when I say, it is possible to love such a child with all your heart. Your father would have said the same too.

Take care, my dearest daughter.

Your loving mother.'

Jeanie's eyes blurred. Maybe this was the way forward for her and Mungo; the thing that would salvage their lukewarm marriage and ease the distress of their monthly failure to conceive. Her spirits lifted at the thought. She placed the letter carefully back its envelope and went in search of her husband.

Chapter 36

Jeanie didn't get the chance of a heart-to-heart with Mungo until days later. He kept putting off any conversation longer than a few brief words on mundane topics to do with the running of the house or the day ahead. She was puzzled by his evasiveness and wondered if he was keeping something from her too. Yet she was longing to talk to him about John's adoption; she was bursting to tell someone about it and make it real.

She thought about confiding in Mary Dane, but she was now heavily pregnant and busy preparing for her first child. Jeanie didn't want to burden her with her concerns or having to admit that she was considering adoption too.

Then shocking news began to spread of another massacre, this time in a place called Noakhali. Hindu temples and homes had been burnt to the ground and people slain. Many were fleeing.

Jeanie and Mungo were having breakfast when she read about it in the newspaper.

'Where is Noakhali?' she asked him, appalled at what she was reading.

'Bengal.'

'How near is it to Calcutta?' she asked in alarm.

'I don't know. Why do you ask?' He gave her a look of suspicion. 'Worried about your pilot friend?'

Jeanie reddened. 'Not just him ... all those poor people ... it's horrific. Is it all getting out of hand?'

Abruptly, he snatched the newspaper from her. 'I don't want you reading the papers anymore. It's too upsetting for you.'

She stared in astonishment at his sudden agitation. He stood up, clutching the newspaper. 'I think it is getting out of hand and it worries me …' He stared beyond her, hesitating, his face clenched.

'Mungo, is there something you're trying to tell me?'

He looked at his watch. 'I'm going to be late. We'll talk later.'

'When?' she challenged. 'Because I have something I wish to discuss with you too, remember?'

'This evening. We'll go for a walk. Then we can talk.'

He left her feeling anxious at what he might be going to say.

***

After supper, they walked down the drive and towards the Mall. The stars were out and the chilly air was scented with woodsmoke. Jeanie linked arms with her husband and felt him tense. Then he patted her arm and allowed her to hang onto him. It felt good just being an anonymous couple, strolling in the dark on a mild autumnal evening.

'We should do this more often,' Jeanie murmured.

'Yes,' Mungo agreed.

They said nothing more until they came to the church. Mungo steered them towards a bench, set back from the street. As they sat down, he said, 'You go first. What is it you've been wanting to tell me?'

Jeanie took a deep breath and began to tell him about her mother's startling letter and the revelation about John's real parentage.

'So, John was never really your brother?' Mungo exclaimed.

'Well, we were never related by blood,' she conceded, 'but that doesn't alter the way I feel – felt – about him.'

'But it must make some difference, knowing what you now do?'

'I suppose, a wee bit. I don't love him any less – but I suppose I was upset with Mother for keeping it from me for so long. I wish she'd been able to tell me in person.'

'I don't think she should have told you at all!'

'Why not?'

'What good has it done? It's just given you something to worry over.'

'But it's not good to have secrets from your loved ones,' said Jeanie. 'It's better to know.'

'I don't agree. It's something Clara should have kept to herself. I don't blame your parents for adopting an orphan boy – but that's their private business and no one else's. I hope John never knew he wasn't a proper Grant.'

Jeanie was dismayed by his reaction. 'But he was a Grant – he was brought up as one.'

'From what I knew of your brother,' said Mungo, 'I think it would have destroyed him to be told the truth – shattered his sense of who he was. Following in the colonel's footsteps into The Borderers was all he ever wanted to do – you told me that yourself.' Mungo shook his head. 'Why on earth would your mother tell you this now?'

Jeanie felt her chest tighten with nervousness. 'To help me … help us.'

He swivelled to look at her. 'What do you mean?'

She kept her voice low, so as not to attract passers-by. 'That we could also consider adoption … if we can't …'

'Adoption?' He frowned.

'Mother wanted me to know that it's possible to love an adopted child every bit as much as one you give birth to – perhaps even more. In Mother's case, she certainly found John easier to love than me.'

Mungo stared at her. 'Have you been writing to your mother about us?' he asked sharply.

Jeanie's heart was thumping. She wanted him to understand. 'I had to tell her that I wasn't with child after writing to say that I was. Since then, she keeps asking. I'm not going to pretend that there aren't problems.'

She heard his intake of breath but carried on. 'And she's right; adoption is something we could consider. I'd certainly be happy to look–'

'No!' he stopped her. 'Don't ask me to take on some other man's child. It's not something I could do.'

'Why not?'

'It's a matter of pedigree. Someone else's baby – well, you'd never really know what traits they might inherit from their real background.'

'We could be careful about choosing,' Jeanie persisted.

'It won't come to that.' Abruptly, he took her hand. 'Jean, we just need more time. It's still early days.'

She was surprised by his gesture; in recent weeks he had been reluctant to touch her. But she had to let him know how she felt.

'It's been nearly nine months of trying,' she said. 'Not to mention the year when we were first married.'

'That's what I want to rekindle, Jean,' he said more urgently. 'That first year of marriage. I want the sweet young Jean that I married.'

'But Mungo …'

'Frankly, what we need is a fresh start together,' he said, not letting her voice her doubt. 'Away from the bad memories and the expectations of other people, watching us and waiting for an announcement.'

Jeanie was alarmed. 'What are you saying?'

Mungo gripped her hand harder. 'Leave Nicholson's. Start again somewhere else where no one knows us.'

She was dumbfounded. This was not what she had been expecting. 'But you love it at Nicholson's.'

'Not anymore. Being headmaster was a mistake. I find it too much. I'd be happier going back to teaching and perhaps a housemaster's role.'

'I didn't realise you were that unhappy in the job,' she said, squeezing his hand in return.

'It was foolish of me to think I could make a difference,' he admitted, 'especially with things becoming so unsafe in India. I no longer see a future here.'

Realisation dawned. 'Are you saying that you don't want to find another position anywhere in this country?'

His expression was tense as he nodded. 'It's time to leave. These latest atrocities have only strengthened my resolve.'

Jeanie grappled with the idea. 'I suppose I wouldn't mind returning to Greentoun. It's what I was expecting at the end of the war. You could enquire about Ebbsmouth again.'

He let go of her hand. 'That's not what I have in mind. When I say a fresh start, I don't mean in Scotland. That would be a backward step – tantamount to admitting failure.'

Her heart began an erratic beating. 'Where then?'

'Australia,' he said firmly.

'What?' Jeanie gasped.

'I've been laying plans,' he admitted. 'I've already corresponded with Sidney Gilmartin about the school in Adelaide. He said they'd welcome an experienced maths teacher with open arms.'

Jeanie felt dizzy at the turn the conversation had taken. 'Adelaide …? Who's Sidney Gilmartin?'

'The chap I told you about – met him at the conference in Lahore.'

Jeanie had a vague recollection of an Australian being mentioned. 'Why haven't you said any of this before?' she exclaimed.

'I had to be sure that I'd be successful first. Wouldn't want to get our hopes up if it came to nothing.'

Jeanie was at a loss for words. 'But ...'

'I know it's a lot to take in at once,' Mungo said, 'but this is the right thing for us both. You're not happy here and neither am I anymore. I'd thought we could leave after the Lent term – before the hot season – but now I think we should go sooner – before Christmas when the school goes on the extended winter holiday. Start 1947 in a new country and a new school. They've said I can begin anytime.'

She was still in shock. 'It's so sudden. I can't believe you haven't told me what was in your mind. When did you decide all this?'

'I've been mulling it over since the conference,' he admitted, 'and kept in touch with Gilmartin. But I made up my mind in the summer holidays ... on the fishing trip ... plenty of time to think.'

She swallowed her annoyance that he had said nothing to her for over two months. 'What about Nicholson's? Surely you'll need to give them more notice to find a new headmaster?'

'That won't be a problem,' he said. 'Major Lucker is itching to take on the job – was disappointed when Bishop recommended me as his successor. If I tell them now; it gives them two months to sort it all out, as well as the long winter break.'

'What about Mother?' Jeanie asked, casting around for reasons not to go. 'India was far enough but Australia is the other side of the world.'

'She was preparing to come and stay with us when she thought you were expecting,' Mungo reminded her. 'I'm sure she'll be just as eager to join you in Adelaide once we start a family.'

'And if we can't?' she challenged.

He gave her a direct look – almost beseeching – and said, 'We must try, Jean. Things can't stay as they are.'

Chapter 37

Jeanie spent the next few days in turmoil, trying to work out if she was prepared to up-sticks yet again and follow Mungo across the world. The news that he had been preparing all this behind her back had shaken her. Yet, he was right in one sense; what would have been the point of raising the matter if the school in Adelaide had turned her husband down? She wasn't even sure where in Australia the town was and had to consult a school atlas.

Being able to pinpoint it on a map, helped it seem more real. But she agonised over whether it was the right step for either of them. Wasn't it just running away from their deeper problems? Was Mungo blaming Nicholson's and India for his disappointment in his wife and his marriage? Going to Adelaide wouldn't change who they were – and Jeanie doubted it would make any difference to their childlessness.

What would it be like being isolated with Mungo in a country where she literally knew no one else? Although she wasn't happy at Nicholson's, at least she had friends in India; Stella and the Lomaxes, Baroness Hester and the Dixons in Rawalpindi. At the core of her reluctance to go, she knew was the certainty that she would never see Rick again. Even though they could never be together – surely, he must be with Pamela by now? – while she, Jeanie, remained in India there would always be the chance of coming across him in Pindi from time to time.

It was a selfish thought and she disliked herself for continuing to harbour feelings for the handsome pilot but she was being truthful to herself. She had sleepless nights and distracted days, agonising over it. Deep down, her conscience was telling her what to do. She knew she must come to terms with the idea of going to Australia, and gradually she did.

Mungo was being far more affectionate towards her than he had been since the early days of her return to Murree. It was as if a huge burden had been lifted from his shoulders to finally admit that their life at Nicholson's was untenable. He was eager to start anew.

Jeanie, wrestling to subjugate her feelings for Rick, came down on the side of duty. She had made promises to Mungo when they married and she had to stick by them. She might have taken her vows as a naïve young woman, never suspecting that her adulation for an older, more mature and self-assured man might wane over time. But she owed it to her husband to try and make their marriage work. He was prepared to do the same for her.

At the end of the month, when a letter of confirmation had come from Deuchar's Academy in Adelaide that Mungo had been accepted onto the staff from January, the announcement of Mungo's resignation from Nicholson's was made public.

Jeanie steeled herself to write to Stella, having put off telling the Lomaxes about her leaving India. Somehow, it would make the move to Australia seem real – and final. They had been so kind to her and to leave India almost felt like a rejection of her friends. She softened the news by promising to try to see her once Stella's baby was born and before Jeanie left.

Jeanie had already written to Clara telling her of their momentous decision to emigrate from India to Australia and warning her that there would be no time to take leave in Scotland beforehand. Since receiving her mother's letter about John's adoption, they had been writing to each other even more frequently than before. Jeanie found relief in being able to put her thoughts down on paper and suspected it was the same for Clara.

In the most recent airmail letter from Scotland, Clara had sounded a word of caution.

'... It is a very big step to take, as you say. Are you absolutely sure it's what you want? I worry about you being so far away, although that is partly my own selfishness. I'm not sure I could ever embark on such a long trip to join you in Australia. But I appreciate you asking me to come and live with you.

What concerns me more, is that you don't seem wholly committed to the idea. I worried less about you starting a new life in India because I knew of your love for the country and that you had friends there. I regret now that I did not make the effort to meet Stella and her family. Again, it was selfish of me. You have sounded the happiest when you were describing your time with the Lomaxes in Gulmarg and the wedding in Pindi. You are perhaps giving up more in India than you realise. Mungo too, as he has lived there for most of his teaching career.

Please reassure me that this isn't a hasty decision that you both might come to regret – and that you are fully behind the move. However, if it really is what you want, then I will support you wholeheartedly, of course.

I thank you again, dear Jeanie, for being so understanding about my confession concerning John's adoption. I worried for days after I sent the letter that I shouldn't have done so, but your letter back was compassionate and generous. Your honesty, that it made no difference to your great regard and love for your brother, has gladdened my heart.

I hesitate to tell you this but, as you are soon to be leaving India, I wanted you to know. I have discovered that Nurse Armitage has retired from Peshawar to Murree. Don't feel obliged to call on her but I am writing to tell her that you might. She knew my circumstances and our family in those early days, and perhaps she can answer some of your questions that I felt unable to, face-to-face, when I had the chance. The decision is yours. Her address is below.

Ever your loving mother.'

Jeanie, having reconciled herself with the move to Adelaide, was unsettled by her mother's words. Had she really sounded lukewarm to the new venture in her letters? She hadn't meant to. And she was also perplexed by this sudden information about the nurse from Peshawar who had delivered her mother's stillborn babies. Had she also delivered her? Jeanie realised that she didn't know. What a strange twist of fate that the retired nurse had ended up in Murree. But why was Clara telling her this now? Before the letter about John's real parentage, her mother had spent years avoiding any mention of her time in Peshawar – even denying that she remembered Nurse Armitage – and yet now, not only had she gone to the trouble of tracking her down but she was encouraging Jeanie to seek her out and ask more about her mother's past.

Jeanie was alarmed that it might mean her mother was ill. Was she reflecting back on her life, wanting to make amends before it was too late? Full of concern, she wrote at once to ask her mother if this was the case.

275

Chapter 38

Murree, November

Mungo stormed into the sitting-room, shaking something in his fist. 'What is the meaning of this?'

Jeanie was startled. She'd been dozing in front of the coal fire and for a puzzled moment, thought she was back at Rowan House with her mother.

'Meaning of what?' she asked.

'This letter!' He hissed.

'Mungo, I don't know what it is–'

'From your lover!'

Her heart lurched. 'Don't be so dramatic. I don't have a lover.'

'Rick-bloody-Dixon,' he seethed, his face puce with anger. 'How long have you been deceiving me?'

Jeanie rose to her feet, feeling dizzy.

'I can see from your guilty look that you know exactly what I'm talking about,' he accused.

Jeanie faced him. 'No, I don't know what you're talking about. Rick and I have never ... you must have got hold of the wrong end of the stick. What letter is this anyway?'

He thrust it at her. Her heart pounded as she took it. The envelope was addressed to her, yet she'd never set eyes on it before. Rick had never written to her – she wouldn't even have known his handwriting. She tried to stop her hands shaking as she attempted to read it. Words swam in front of her eyes.

'*... our last chance ... I've broken off my engagement to Pamela ... I'm planning to leave ... go to Ceylon with Ada and Clive ... a new start ... I can't go without knowing how you feel ... whether you would join me ... unhappily married*

... leaving at the end of the month ... want you to be happy ... your decision ... I'll always love you, my Jeanie of the light-brown hair ...'

Jeanie could hardly breathe. She looked up at Mungo, her face a guilty red. He was livid.

'While I've been planning our future – thinking of how to make you happy – you've been conniving behind my back with this man. How long have you been thinking of deserting me and waltzing off to bloody Ceylon?'

'I-I haven't,' she stuttered. 'There's no plan.'

'So, he's a liar as well as a philanderer?'

'No, some of his family members are considering going to Ceylon – Ada and her husband.'

'Then you did know about this?'

'Not that Rick was thinking of going ...'

'He's broken off his engagement for you, Jean.' Mungo looked at her in contempt. 'You must have led him on.'

Jeanie was suddenly indignant. 'No one led anyone on. I can't deny that I've felt attraction for Rick – but I've never been unfaithful – and I've chosen my life with you. I'm supporting you in this move to Australia about which I was never consulted; so don't say that I've betrayed you.' She glared at him. 'And this was addressed to me. You have no right to open my letters.'

'I've every right,' he said angrily. 'How else would I have learnt about your deception?'

'I haven't deceived you,' Jeanie retorted. She stepped past him and left the room, shaking so violently that she almost tripped and stumbled. She fled to their bedroom.

The servants had already drawn the curtains and lit the fire. The room was stuffy and confining but she had nowhere else to escape to. Sitting on the bed, she tried to still her rapid heartbeat and take calming breaths. What on earth was Rick thinking of writing to her in such a way? He knew that she had chosen to stay with Mungo so why make things difficult for her? She had a surge of anger towards him. He was behaving like the philanderer that Mungo accused him of being; playing with her affections.

He said he'd broken off his engagement to Pamela, but was that even true? Perhaps she had rejected him and this had prompted his attempt to win over another man's wife. Yet, why wouldn't it be true? Rick had already told her that he didn't love Pamela enough. Now he was going to start a new life in Ceylon with his sister and brother-in-law, so was offering her a chance to leave a loveless marriage and go with him.

Jeanie felt leaden inside. How tempting that was! Now, the worst had happened; Mungo knew she had feelings for Rick and was furious with her. Had she already spoilt their attempt at a fresh start in Australia? She sank back on the bed and re-read the letter more carefully.

'My darling Jeanie,

I am back in Pindi at my parents' house and have hesitated whether to write this letter at all, given that our last parting was so final. But I decided it was better to risk a rebuff than to miss our last chance of a future together. I've broken off my engagement to Pamela. She was never keen to return to India and I don't love her enough to live with her in England. It's a relief. Since I've met you, I know I could never be truly happy with any other woman.

I've given up my job in Calcutta but am not staying in Pindi either. I cannot bear the thought of being so near you and yet not able to be with you. I'm planning to leave and go to Ceylon with Ada and Clive – it'll be a new start in a new country that won't remind me every day of you.

But Jeanie, I can't go without knowing how you feel – whether being apart is as hard for you as it is for me – and whether I could dare to hope you might join me. I know you put a brave face on your situation but you can't hide from me that you are unhappily married. I'm leaving at the end of the month. If there is the slightest chance that you would come with me, I would wait longer.

But what I want is not the most important thing; it's your happiness. Above all else, I want you to be happy. It's your decision. If you choose to stay, then I accept that and wish you well. I will never attempt to contact you again - but in my heart I will always love you, my Jeanie of the light-brown hair.

Rick x'

Finally, the tears came; streaming down her face and wetting the counterpane. Skimming it before in a panic under Mungo's hostile gaze, she had not realised how tender and loving a letter it was. His tone was almost apologetic, as if he guessed that she would remain loyal to Mungo. Yet there was a sense of urgency; he needed to let her know what was in his heart but would not stay around to see her live a life with another man. How ironic that he should think of leaving India and starting anew, just at the same time as she and Mungo were.

Perhaps she should tell him about their going to Australia; would it make him reconsider the drastic action of leaving his family home and business in Pindi? If anyone was at the centre of a large, loving group of family and friends, then it was Rick. He was giving up far more than she was in leaving the country of his birth and upbringing. But she knew that she should not contact him – not if she was to remain loyal to Mungo and go through with his Australian plan.

Her heart was torn in two; she loved Rick but could not betray Mungo. How hurt her husband must have been to read such a love letter. He did not deserve it. For that, she was to blame. It must have been too obvious to Rick that she had fallen in love with him – as he had with her – and had left him with a spark of hope that she would abandon her wifely duty to Mungo and run away with him.

What a mess she had made of her life! She felt utterly alone. If only she could talk it over with her mother or a good friend like Stella. Abruptly, she recalled the words of advice that Tom had spoken to her that summer. '*You can take what I say with a pinch of salt, but I know what it's like to be trapped in an unhappy marriage. You don't have to stay in one.*'

Yet Jeanie felt that she should. She had never got over the guilt of leaving Mungo alone for over six-and-a-half-years; she owed him this second chance in Adelaide. Besides, she thought bleakly, Rick would be gone by the end of this month and beyond temptation.

Emotionally bruised, she sat up and began to put the letter back in its envelope. Something caught her eye. The letter was dated in early October; over a month ago. With a lurch of the heart, she realised that he would already have gone. Too late to give him any sort of answer. Perhaps just as well, she told herself harshly. Yet it puzzled her. How had it taken so long to arrive? The postal service between Rawalpindi and Murree was swift and daily.

Had Mungo been holding back the letter for weeks? But his shock was genuine and he was not the kind of man who would brood over her suspected infidelity; his temper would get the better of him. It must have lain somewhere – dropped down the back of the hall table – out of sight. But the servants were scrupulous in keeping the public areas clean. Had one of the house staff had it in their possession for some reason? It didn't make sense. Who else would sort through the post?

Something nagged at the edge of her thoughts. A memory came back to her of Dinah at the dak table – a little furtive – handing over a letter from Clara while slipping another into her pocket. Jeanie had no proof that it was the letter from Rick, except it would have been around that time that it was sent. But why on earth would Matron interfere and withhold Rick's letter, only to produce it at this stage?

***

Mungo appeared late that evening when Jeanie was already in bed.

'I'll sleep in my dressing-room,' he said curtly.

'Mungo, don't do that,' Jeanie said, sitting up. 'Please can we talk about this.'

'There's nothing to be said.' He looked more resigned than angry.

She was contrite. 'I'm sorry for the pain this has caused you. I never meant to hurt you. You should never have seen it.'

'But I have,' he said, his look haggard. 'And now I know that my wife is in love with another man. I suppose it was a matter of time before you fell for someone younger.'

'It's not like that.' Jeanie said.

'What is it like then? He claims to be in love with you. I know his type – typical Anglo-Indian – charming but shallow. No scruples about stealing another man's wife.'

Jeanie wanted to defend Rick but knew that would only rile her husband. She had made her decision.

'He hasn't stolen anyone's wife. I made my promises to you years ago, Mungo, and I'm not going to break them now.'

He regarded her warily. 'So, you're still prepared to come with me to Adelaide?'

'Yes,' she said with more conviction than she felt.

He looked relieved. Sitting down on the bed, he said, 'Thank God. I need you, Jean. I need a wife by my side – I

281

can't do this on my own. Deuchar's Academy are expecting you too.'

He went into his dressing-room but returned minutes later, in his flannel pyjamas.

Jeanie steeled herself to ask, 'How did you come by the letter?'

He shot her a look. 'What does that matter?'

'It was dated over a month ago. Why produce it now?'

He looked uncomfortable. 'It was brought to my attention by a concerned colleague.'

'Matron?' Jeanie asked.

His jaw reddened. 'You don't need to know who.'

She swallowed her indignation. 'I didn't think you'd approve of staff withholding other people's letters.'

Mungo said in irritation, 'In this case it was obviously the right thing to do. She must have had her suspicions. She was being loyal to me, which is more than I can say for you.'

She bit back a reply. There was no point riling him again. But when she opened her bedside drawer to put the letter away, he snapped, 'You're not going to keep it, are you?'

She muttered, 'just being tidy.'

'Put it on the fire,' he ordered.

'Mungo ...'

'If you still love me, show it by burning that bloody letter!'

Jeanie was nauseated. That was the last thing she wanted to do. It was the only true love letter she had ever received – from the man she was prepared to give up – yet she wanted to treasure it. But she knew this was a test from Mungo; if she refused to burn it then he would know that her words of contrition were empty.

Her temples pounded as she climbed out of bed with the letter and went to the fire, which had been banked up for the night. Stifling a sob, Jeanie threw it onto the hot coals. It didn't burn immediately.

Back in bed, Mungo turned to her and said, 'That's the end of it. We'll never speak of this again.'

He turned off his side lamp and lay with his back to her. Jeanie did the same. For a long time, she stared at the small flames flaring around the side of the packed coals and dross. They licked at the letter. Numbly, she watched as Rick's heartfelt words turned slowly to ash.

Chapter 39

For several days, Jeanie tried to put the whole traumatic episode from her mind and get on with preparations to leave. In just over a month, they would be sailing for Australia. The term was busy too and Mungo hardly had a spare minute to spend with her. She knew that it suited them both to keep out of each other's way, while the tense atmosphere between them had a chance to dissipate.

Dinah, she knew, was deliberately avoiding her. They had not met for afternoon tea in weeks but the matron did not come to consult her about domestic issues either. Jeanie could not stem her growing anger at the woman's interference; she wanted answers.

A week after the letter incident, Jeanie marched through the baize door that divided the headmaster's quarters from the boarding house, and searched for Dinah until she found her alone in the linen room.

The matron looked up, momentarily startled and then composed her expression.

'Mrs Munro; can I help you?'

Jeanie came straight to the point. 'Why did you take a letter addressed to me?'

'I don't know what you mean–'

'Don't give me that *holier than thou* expression,' Jeanie said in exasperation. 'You know exactly what I mean. A letter from Rick Dixon to me. I know you took it – I *saw* you take it, for goodness' sake! Why would you do such a thing?'

Dinah pursed her mouth in disapproval. 'I could tell you were losing your head over him. I had to be sure. When I saw the letter from Pindi, I suspected it would be from him – and it was.'

'You had no right to read it!' Jeanie was indignant.

'I was saving you from making a terrible mistake,' she said with a prim look.

'So why show it to my husband? Why didn't you come to me first?'

Dinah hesitated. 'I felt it my duty to alert Headmaster to the danger – the danger of you running off with that man and causing a scandal for poor Mr Munro.'

Jeanie flushed. 'If you thought that, then why take a month before you showed it to him?'

'I – er – didn't want to have to show him,' she said, becoming flustered. 'Naturally, I wanted to avoid such upset. But I had to.'

'Why?' Jeanie demanded.

'Because of the terrible announcement ...'

Jeanie was baffled. 'What announcement?'

'Headmaster's resignation and his leaving to go to Australia,' she said, her voice becoming querulous.

'I know it's been a bit of a shock for the staff,' Jeanie admitted. 'It's been unexpected for me too. But I don't see what any of that has to do with showing my husband Rick's letter.'

Instantly, Dinah's manner changed to open hostility. 'To show him what a disastrous mistake he was making! Going with you to Australia. Make him see what an unfit wife you are – one who has affairs with riff-raff like Rick Dixon.'

Jeanie stared in stupefaction, momentarily speechless. Dinah glared back, her cheeks darkening with anger.

'Dinah,' Jeanie said in confusion, 'I had no idea you disliked me so much.'

'It's not a matter of liking or not liking you,' she said, her tone bitter. 'It's your lack of suitability as the headmaster's wife that counts. I could tell from the beginning you weren't up to the job – always going on about your dead brother and moping about having no friends – and then when I saw the way you carried on with Rick Dixon at the wedding. Well, I knew then that you would cause trouble for Mr Munro. I needed to show him how his devotion to you was misplaced – how you would let him down again in Adelaide – a leopard doesn't change its spots and all that.'

In disbelief, Jeanie said, 'Are you trying to sabotage us going to Australia?'

Dinah was shaking as she answered. 'I'm trying to make him see sense before it's too late!'

Jeanie saw the passion blazing in her dark eyes. All of a sudden, the truth dawned on her. It was a revelation. 'You're in love with my husband, aren't you?'

Dinah's expression was taut. She didn't deny it.

Jeanie stood stunned as Dinah stared back in defiance. Reeling, Jeanie left without another word. She didn't know whether to feel pity or contempt for the unhappy woman.

*

Chapter 40

Jeanie's first reaction to Dinah's revelations was to tell Mungo. She doubted he had any inkling of the woman's love for him. The matron was such a reserved, private woman who kept her emotions so firmly suppressed that no one could have guessed at her true feelings – until now.

She was furious and shaken by Dinah's vitriolic words towards her. Why if she disliked her so much, had she invited her to attend Lucy and Monty's wedding? Had Dinah's disapproval been tinged with pity that Mungo had left his inadequate wife behind while he went to the conference?

Jeanie searched back over the conversations she had had with Dinah and was humiliated to think of what she had confided. Her likely miscarriage which the matron had confidently assured her was most likely a late period. Her grieving for John and her fraught relationship with her mother. Her loneliness. Their discussions of the Lomaxes. She remembered how, several times, she had defended Stella when Dinah had been critical of her friend. No wonder Dinah envied Stella her happy marriage and family; she was a childless spinster in love with a man she could never marry.

Jeanie had to admit that she had probably talked too much about Rick; their first meeting in Ebbsmouth and his encouragement of her to visit John's grave someday; her reminiscences about the Pindi wedding which always centred around Rick. She cringed to think how – on the last afternoon tea with Dinah in September – she had spoken too warmly of Rick's visit to Gulmarg. It must have been obvious to the matron how much time she had spent in Rick's company. While Dinah had observed her and said little, Jeanie must have given away her true feelings. So, had the matron – seeing her first loyalty to be to her revered headmaster – been so very wrong in trying to warn him about the threat that Rick might pose to his marriage?

Jeanie decided there was nothing to be gained by telling Mungo about Dinah's infatuation with him. In a month's time, they would be leaving Murree for good. Why embarrass either of them by revealing the truth? Soon, her anger at the matron began to turn to pity. Dinah would be dreading Mungo's departure; her solitary future without him to admire and work for must seem bleak.

Thinking of Stella, made her realise that she'd heard nothing recently from her friend, except for a brief note acknowledging Jeanie's letter about leaving for Australia in which she didn't try to hide her dismay at the news. The birth of the Lomax baby must be imminent and Jeanie wondered if they were still in Gulmarg. It spurred her on, that afternoon, to ring the hotel at Gulmarg. The line was crackly and it took her a few moments to realise that she was speaking to Manek.

'… not here, Munro-mem',' he explained. 'All gone to Pindi.'

'Has Stella had the baby yet?'

'Not yet, memsahib … not well … tests.'

'Sorry,' Jeanie said, jamming the receiver closer to her ear. 'I didn't hear that. Is Stella unwell? What tests?'

The line was suddenly clearer. 'Captain-sahib is not well. Bad lungs. He has gone to see the doctor in Pindi. All Lomax family in Pindi since last week, Munro-mem'.'

Jeanie's heart thumped with shock. 'How unwell is he, Manek?'

'Captain-sahib say all a big fuss about nothing,' the bearer replied. 'But Lomax memsahibs say he must go to see the doctor.'

Jeanie felt a fraction better at this. She could just imagine Tom getting annoyed at Esmie and Stella fussing over him and making light of their concern. Yet, in the summer, Jeanie had wondered if there was something wrong with Tom's health. She wished now that she had mentioned it to Esmie.

She thanked Manek, rang off and was about to ring the hotel in Rawalpindi when she heard the chaprassy arrive with the post. Jeanie dashed out to check the letters before anyone else could. She didn't trust Dinah not to cause further trouble. There were two addressed to 'Mrs M. Munro'; an aerogramme from her mother and a letter with a local postmark. Irrationally, her heart leapt that it might be another one from Rick and she tore it open. It was a short message.

'Dear Mrs Munro,

Your mother has written to me giving me permission to speak to you. I was the first person to meet you at the beginning of your life, which makes me feel that we've always had a bond. I was your midwife and delivered you into this world!

I hear you are soon to leave Murree so would very much like to meet you before you go. May I invite you to afternoon tea tomorrow, say three o'clock? If this is suitable then send round a chit to confirm.

Yours sincerely

Miss Olive Armitage.'

Without thinking about it further, Jeanie dashed after the chaprassy.

'Please can you wait a minute while I send a reply to this invitation?'

Moments later, she'd scribbled an acceptance on a piece of headed notepaper from the pile on the hall table, and dispatched it with the chaprassy.

***

Jeanie didn't have a chance to ring the Raj Hotel that day. In the afternoon, she accompanied Mungo to an inter-house rugby match, followed by tea in the central dining-hall. In the evening they had the Golightlys and Ords for dinner; the first of a round of farewell dinners that Mungo had insisted that they hold for his circle of friends.

Jeanie found it hard to concentrate on their conversation; she fretted over Tom Lomax's health and whether Stella had gone into labour. She must find a way of seeing them before her departure. Also, she couldn't help ruminating over Dinah's outburst and at the back of her mind was the nagging feeling of loss for Rick.

'My wife's a bit distracted these days,' Mungo said loudly, catching her attention. 'Please forgive her rudeness.'

'That's quite all right,' said Mrs Ord, 'I'm not surprised.' The chaplain's wife smiled at Jeanie. 'You must have a lot on your mind. I was asking if you are very excited about your move to Australia?'

Jeanie went hot with embarrassment. 'I'm sorry … I didn't mean to ignore you. And the move – well – it's a bit daunting.' She caught Mungo's watchful look. 'But exciting too, of course.'

By the time their guests had left, Jeanie decided it was too late to ring the hotel in Rawalpindi. She had a restless night thinking about the Lomaxes but by the morning had convinced herself that Tom was probably right and Esmie was just being extra cautious. They would have gone to Pindi to be in situ for the birth of their grandchild anyway. No doubt Esmie thought it would be a good chance to have Tom checked over while they were there. If he had been seriously ill, surely Stella would have sent a message to say so?

Jeanie decided she would ring the Raj after her visit to Olive Armitage. Then she could make some arrangement for a quick visit to Rawalpindi. She was feeling ridiculously nervous about meeting the retired nurse, though she wasn't quite sure why. Maybe it was because, after all these years of her mother being so averse to talking about her time in Peshawar, she was actively encouraging Jeanie to find out about those far off days.

Jeanie's curiosity was mounting too. She wanted to meet her midwife, not only because she had delivered her at birth, but also because John had met her in Peshawar. The nurse could tell her about that meeting – and also give her more details about John's blood parents. Here would be someone who wouldn't mind talking about John with her; unlike Mungo.

At breakfast, she told Mungo that she would be out in the afternoon, visiting the retired nurse.

'The one who arranged John's adoption?' he asked in surprise. 'She lives in Murree? You never mentioned that.'

'I only recently discovered she was here and I'm keen to meet her.'

He frowned. 'I don't understand this obsession of yours about John being adopted. Surely the woman can't tell you more than you already know?'

'Maybe not,' Jeanie conceded. 'But she's invited me for tea, so where's the harm in it?'

'When will you be back?' he asked.

'Five at the latest, I would imagine. She lives at Pindi Point so I'll drive.'

'I'll get Humza to take you,' Mungo said. 'Don't want you driving around in the dark when the roads are turning icy.'

'I'll be fine.'

'Don't argue.'

This irritated Jeanie more than it should have. When the afternoon came, she set off twenty minutes early to avoid a confrontation with Mungo's bearer, and drove out to Pindi

Point. It was a cold day and the air was sharp but clear. Getting out of the car at the bottom of the path to Celandine Cottage, Jeanie caught her breath at the view. She could see all the way down to the plain below where the roofs of Rawalpindi glinted in the low sun. Her heart skipped a beat. In another life, she might like to have lived there.

Olive Armitage was a stout woman with fading red hair and a cheery smile. Only the age spots on her hands and the deep wrinkles across her brow betrayed her real age – Clara had said she was in her seventies. She looked much younger. She appeared on the path to greet Jeanie.

'I'm sorry I'm early,' Jeanie apologised.

'Don't be. I'm glad. This is the most exciting day I've had all year.'

To Jeanie's astonishment, the nurse came right up to her and took both of her hands in hers. She beamed at her. 'You're just like I thought you'd look. So pretty; just like your mother.'

Jeanie held back sudden tears. 'Thank you, Miss Armitage.'

Inside, the cottage was gloomy and smelt musty but Olive showed her through to a cosier back sitting-room that was warmed by a wood fire. It was starkly furnished with two mismatched armchairs, a gateleg table that was already laid out for tea and a wooden dresser against the far wall with a treadle sewing machine next to it. The walls were bare apart from two framed prints of what looked like Biblical scenes.

Olive bustled to and fro from a small kitchen, filling the teapot with boiling water and cutting up cake. She didn't appear to have a servant. All the while, she threw out questions, wanting to know all about Jeanie's life after she had left India as a six-year-old.

Finally, she sat down in the opposite chair. 'I met your brother John, did you know? In Peshawar before the war – the recent war.'

'Yes, I did,' said Jeanie. 'Funnily enough, he mentioned it when he came to say goodbye to me in Pindi in the summer of '39. I was going home to help my mother look after Dad. It … it was the last time I saw my brother alive.' Her throat watered and she couldn't continue.

Olive leaned over and patted her hand. 'Mrs Grant wrote and told me about his death. I'm sorry. He was a lovely young man, so he was. A fine gentleman.'

Jeanie nodded. She took a sip of the strong milky tea and composed herself. 'I'm so glad that you persuaded my parents to take John into their care. He was the most wonderful younger brother. I think I had a much happier childhood because of him. I always got on with my father but he was largely absent until I was about fifteen – when he retired from the army and came home from India. Sadly, I was never as close to my mother.' Jeanie sighed. 'Strange to say, but we're the closest we've ever been now, even though we're thousands of miles apart. We write several times a week. But when I was growing up, she was never very loving – not in the way she was with John. She seemed to find me hard to love as a child.'

Olive's expression crinkled in concern. 'Poor lamb! You mustn't think that. Mrs Grant loved you very much – I saw that for myself. But she always worried about you – feared that she'd lose you.'

'Because of the other babies she'd lost?' Jeanie asked.

The nurse fixed her with a pitying look in her hazel eyes. 'Ah, the babies – those little angels.' She nodded. 'It began with the babies.'

Chapter 41

Olive

Peshawar, January 1913

It was bitterly cold outside and snow was coming in flurries. Olive decided she would stay overnight in the hospital rather than risk walking back to her digs. She hurried into the maternity ward, which was set apart from the main building in a low hut that in the summer was used as a fever ward. Taking over from her colleague, she was surprised to find the young subaltern's wife, who had been in labour for many hours, had still not produced her baby. It was her first; her husband was away on piquet duty and she was scared.

'It's coming too soon,' she kept fretting.

'It'll be fine,' Olive reassured her. 'It's a good size. You mustn't worry.'

'Will you stay with me till it comes?' Her eyes were huge and fearful.

'Of course, I will.'

As it grew dark, it began to snow harder. Half-way through the night, glancing out of the window, Olive saw drifts banking up against the side of the ward.

It wasn't particularly warm in the labour room but the subaltern's wife was sweating and her brow was hot to the touch. She moaned in pain.

'How much longer?' she whispered. 'I can't bear it.'

Olive bathed her face and neck to try to stop her burning up. 'Not long. And you *can* bear it. God will give you the strength.'

But the labour appeared to have stalled. As well as being a jangle of nerves, the young woman was slim and delicate, and for the first time Olive feared for her. Silently, she began to offer up prayers for mother and baby, while staying outwardly cheerful and encouraging.

'Rest for a little while and we'll try again in an hour. There's nothing to worry about.'

Dawn was breaking when the contractions started again. Much weaker, the young woman hardly had the energy to push. She was exhausted. Olive, also tired out, wondered where her colleague, Lavinia, was; she should already have arrived for the next shift. She wondered if she should send an orderly to call a doctor from the main building to come and help.

Just then, the young woman yelled in agony. Olive went to her aid; cajoling and urging her to breathe and push. 'You can do it. Baby's coming. One last effort!'

Finally, the dark crown of the baby's head was followed swiftly by its small pink, mucous-covered body. Olive deftly cleared its airways and it gave out a querulous cry.

'It's a girl!' Olive announced.

The mother was too exhausted to reply. She lay struggling for breath, utterly spent. Olive set about wiping and swaddling the baby, who gazed at her with unfocussed blue eyes.

Shortly afterwards, the other midwife appeared, snow still clinging to her hair and took over. 'Town's come to a standstill 'cause of the weather.'

Wearily, Olive went to the staff room, lay down on the spare camp bed and fell instantly asleep.

***

Olive awoke hours later, feeling groggy from a deep sleep. Checking her watch, she saw that it was almost time to go on duty again so she hurriedly dressed and helped herself to the scrambled eggs that their cook had provided. It would soon be dark again.

In the corridor outside the room where she'd delivered the subaltern's baby, she found Lavinia coming out looking anxious.

'She's not doing well.'

'Mother or baby?' Olive asked.

'Mother. No strength in her to feed the baby. Hardly saying a word, except to ask when her husband can come.'

Olive took a deep breath and entered the room. It reeked of childbirth. With the help of an orderly, she gave the mother a bed-bath and had the sheets changed, silently cursing her slapdash colleague. The young mother rallied a little, fretting over her baby.

'I can't feed her. Help me.'

Olive showed her how to put the baby to her breast but the infant found it hard to latch on. The mother sank back in defeat. Olive was alarmed; the woman was giving up.

'She's such a bonny baby.' Olive tried to lift her spirits. 'Have you given her a name yet?' she asked.

The mother smiled for the first time – fleeting but tender. 'Amelia; after my husband's mother. He was very fond of her.'

'That'll please him,' Olive said brightly.

'Where is he?' she suddenly asked. 'When can he come?'

'Soon,' Olive assured, though she knew he was likely to be snowbound for days, if he was up in the mountains. 'You need to get your strength back and feed this little one.'

She tried again, this time a little more successfully. After a few minutes, the young woman lay back exhausted but was soon fretting again.

'Can you cut a lock of her hair for me … put it in my locket … please? For my husband.'

'Of course,' Olive said, humouring her. 'But he'll see the real thing in a day or two.'

'Please,' she said.

Olive did as she asked, placing a tiny curl of hair into the pretty gold locket, next to a wedding photograph of her and a handsome man in uniform. The woman thanked her and relaxed with a sigh, clutching the locket.

A short while later, the young mother grew agitated again. 'Amelia mustn't be sent to that man.'

'What man?' Olive asked.

'The ... old colonel. My father-in-law ... He's too strict ... don't let him take her!' She was panting now, her breathing ragged.

'Please don't worry,' Olive said, taking her hand and stroking it. 'No old colonel is going to take your baby.'

The patient clutched at her, though her grasp was weak. 'Promise me!'

'I promise. Now, you mustn't get upset. You need to rest and have strength to feed your daughter.'

Just then, an orderly appeared with a message. Another expectant mother had been admitted.

***

Hours later, having delivered a baby boy, Olive glanced in on the young subaltern's wife but she was sleeping. She went to the nursery and gazed at Amelia's little round face and rosebud mouth; she was perfect. Olive picked her up and the baby's eyes opened. They fixed on her trustingly and her heart skipped a beat. If she had a daughter one day, she'd want her to be just like this one.

'Time for a feed, little lamb,' she crooned.

The room where Amelia's mother lay was dimly lit by a kerosene lamp. As Olive approached the bed, she was aware of an ominous stillness. Quickly, cradling Amelia in one arm, she put out a hand. The woman's skin was cold to the touch. Olive gasped in shock. She felt for a pulse. There was none. The back of her neck was still faintly warm. She must have slipped away in the past few minutes.

Olive sat down, trembling. She cuddled the baby close. 'Oh, my poor lamb!'

She wasn't sure how long she sat there in the quiet gloom – it seemed an age – but was probably just minutes. It was Amelia who galvanised her with a bleating cry. She needed feeding.

Olive stood up. 'Don't worry, little pet,' she whispered. 'God will provide.'

***

Within an hour, Olive had arranged for a wet-nurse to come in from the town to feed Amelia and arranged for the mother's body to be transferred to the morgue. She felt desolate for the newborn and the father who was still unaware of the tragic death of his young wife. At least she would be able to give him the locket and present him with his baby daughter.

Over the next couple of days, while the cantonment was almost cut off by snow, Olive kept watch over Amelia, determined to protect her and keep her alive. Lavinia went out into the cantonment to help deliver babies at home.

After three days, Olive heard that the subaltern's platoon was still snowbound and no message had got through about his wife. Better not to know until he arrived back at barracks, Olive thought, as there was nothing the poor man could do. The final words of Amelia's mother preyed on her mind; the fear that Amelia would be left in the guardianship of her grandfather. Olive determined that she would tell the subaltern when he returned to Peshawar. That evening, another expectant mother was brought to the ward.

***

As soon as Olive knew who it was, she had a feeling of trepidation. This poor woman had lost three babies already – all boys – and Olive had delivered two of them. They had all been premature but perfectly formed. Little Angels. The last time, the mother had been very unwell and Olive had feared they might lose her too. She sent up a silent prayer that this time, both mother and baby would be spared and that finally, they could embark on a family life.

The new patient's face lit up when Olive entered the room.

'I'm glad you're on duty, Nurse Armitage,' she said. 'I don't want any doctors to see me – no men – just you. You understand me – what I've been through.'

'Of course, I do. I'm sure this time – God willing – everything will be fine. So let me check things over.'

As soon as she began to examine the major's wife, Olive knew there was something wrong. It didn't feel right. She listened for a heartbeat. Her alarm grew. She tried to hide her concern.

'And you've been feeling the baby moving today?' she asked as casually as possible.

The major's wife looked at her with anxious eyes. 'Not today.'

'Can you remember when?'

The woman shook her head, her eyes welling with tears.

'My waters,' she whispered. 'I think they broke. I wanted to come in earlier but it was treacherous in the snow, so we waited. Should I have come sooner?'

'No, you've done the right thing coming in now,' Olive assured her.

'I've never got this far before,' she said tearfully. 'Is it going to be all right?'

Olive didn't like to lie. 'We'll do our very best.'

***

In the middle of the night, the major's wife went into labour. It was swift. An hour later, Olive delivered a baby girl. Despite the pregnancy having gone on longer this time, she was no bigger than the tiny boys who had gone before her. There was no cry to gladden the mother's heart after all her pain and effort.

The major's wife let out an agonised wail. Olive wrapped up the silent baby and bundled her into her mother's arms.

'At least look at her and hold her,' Olive encouraged. She still felt guilty for having whisked away her previous dead babies before the mother could see them. But that's what she'd been instructed to do. *Don't want any hysterics*, was the doctor's view.

'I'll leave you for a few minutes,' Olive said gently and slipped out of the room.

Olive entered the nursery and as soon as she saw Amelia, she burst into tears. Life could be so unfair! This girl would grow up never knowing a mother's love – might be sent to an unloving home – and yet the distraught woman who lay next door might never experience the joy of motherhood. How very randomly cruel childbirth could be. Yet the Lord giveth and the Lord taketh away, as her Baptist minister father had often quoted when hardships had to be borne.

Olive picked up Amelia and cradled her tightly, kissing her brow. In a short while, the wet-nurse would be here

300

again. She hesitated for only a moment more and then took the baby from the nursery.

The major's wife was dozing, her dead baby lying in her lap. Olive gently placed Amelia on the bed and lifted up the lifeless bundle. The mother woke. She stared at Olive in confusion.

'What … what are you doing?'

'"The Lord Giveth and the Lord Taketh Away",' said Olive, putting down the dead baby and picking up Amelia. 'This baby has recently lost her mother.'

'How terrible …'

'You could be that mother for her.'

'Me?' The woman looked both alarmed and excited.

'Would it not be a kindness to take on this little one?' Olive asked. 'Give her a loving Christian home.'

'But whose is she? Does she not have a father?'

'A young subaltern who won't be able to look after this child without his wife. He'll probably have to send her home to be brought up far away by his cruel father.'

'How do you know he's cruel?' the woman gasped.

'The subaltern's wife said as much. Pleaded with me not to let the old colonel take the child. Was most insistent.'

The bereaved mother looked in an agony of indecision.

'How can I take another woman's child? It's my own baby I want!' She began to cry again.

This set off Amelia. Olive swiftly pushed the baby into the woman's arms. 'She needs a mother to feed her or she'll not survive either. You could feed her. God works in mysterious ways.'

Gulping back her tears, the major's wife took the baby. She was shaking with fear and emotion. Olive had a momentary panic that she was doing the wrong thing – interfering where she shouldn't – but as soon as she helped Amelia latch onto the woman's breast, her doubts

301

evaporated. It was like a nativity scene; mother and child in blissful harmony.

She was acting in the best interests of both the distraught and grieving mother, and the motherless baby. The subaltern was young and would marry again. His time to be a father would come in due course. What mattered now was to do the best for Amelia.

When the baby had fed, Olive said, 'She should have a new name. What would you like it to be?'

The woman could hardly take her gaze from the baby as she answered. 'I don't know. I've hardly had time … We'd hoped for a boy. What do you think?'

'Something personal to you,' Olive suggested. 'A family name.'

The woman gave the baby a tentative kiss. 'We'll call her Jean; after my mother.'

Olive nodded. 'Jean Grant; that's a pretty name.'

Abruptly, Clara Grant began to weep. 'That poor woman! Sh-she sh-should be nursing this wee one.'

Olive put a comforting hand on her shoulder. 'Sadly, she never will. God has decided otherwise. You are doing the best thing for this child, Mrs Grant; please believe that.'

Swiftly, Olive picked up the dead baby and made for the door. It was best if the major's wife thought no more about the girl that she had given birth to. She would have to report the death, send away the wet-nurse and tell Lavinia that Amelia had sadly succumbed too, after only four days on this earth. At the door, Mrs Grant asked in sudden anxiety, 'The subaltern? He's not with the Borderers, is he?'

Olive shook her head. 'He's with the Peshawar Rifles.'

'W-what's his name?'

'Lomax,' said Olive. 'Thomas Lomax.'

Chapter 42

Murree, November 1946

Jeanie felt as if her heart had stopped.

'W-what are you saying?' she stammered. 'That I'm that baby? That you swapped me at birth?'

Olive nodded. 'You're Captain Lomax's daughter by blood.'

Jeanie began shaking with shock. 'I can't believe my mother would do such a thing!' she cried. 'I call her mother – but according to you, she's not!'

'Of course, she's your mother,' Olive said calmly. 'She's the woman who's nurtured and raised you.'

Jeanie felt sick and bewildered. 'No wonder she found me hard to love – I was never her daughter.'

'She loved you from the minute she first held you. That's what I've been telling you. I saw it with my own eyes.' Olive sat clasping her hands. 'Don't blame your mother; it was entirely my idea. She was in distress about the stillbirth and I took the decision. But I did it for your sake.'

Jeanie stared at the old nurse, confounded. 'You played at being God,' she accused. 'I should have been brought up as a Lomax ...' The idea made her head spin.

'You'd have been a motherless child,' said Olive, 'the most disadvantaged of children. And no doubt, you would have been sent home to be raised by a cruel grandfather or packed off to boarding school at too young an age. Instead, you had a happy childhood with two parents and a brother who adored you. Isn't that so?'

'Yes, but ... poor Captain Lomax ...'

'I know, I thought the same for a while,' Olive said. 'But I followed his career and he soon married again and had a son. Not that the second marriage lasted long. Now he's married for a third time. So perhaps he wouldn't have been the most reliable of fathers.'

Jeanie was filled with sudden rage. 'You have no idea of the damage you caused by giving me away. I know the Lomaxes. For years, Tom Lomax has suffered mentally for the loss of his first wife and baby.'

Olive's look of conviction faltered. 'I'm sorry to hear that. But I know what I did was for the best at the time. For you and for dear Mrs Grant.'

'How can you be so sure?' Jeanie demanded angrily. 'My mother – the one I call mother – has struggled to be the loving one you make her out to be. She must be riddled with guilt.'

'Not guilt,' Olive protested. 'But she did fear that somehow the Lomaxes might hear about it and claim you back – even though I told her I would never breathe a word. Maybe that is why she was not as demonstrative as she wanted to be. But you went to a godly home – and a loving home – I know that much.'

Something suddenly occurred to Jeanie. 'Have you been in touch with my mother all this time?'

'In the early years,' Olive admitted. 'Your mother would write to me to let me know how you and your brother were both getting on. She was so grateful, you see. But then the letters stopped when your father, Colonel Grant, retired to Scotland. He never knew about you not being his. Only recently, did Mrs Grant get in touch again.'

'Why now?' Jeanie asked.

Olive shrugged. 'I suppose because you'd returned to India and she'd begun thinking about the old days again.' The old nurse leaned forward, twisting her hands. 'She wanted you to know the truth before you set sail for

304

Australia. I would never have said anything without your mother's permission.'

Jeanie's head pounded. 'It's too much to take in. I can't believe Mother has lied to me all this time. How do I know that anything you've told me is true? I don't know the first thing about you.'

She saw the hurt on Olive's face. 'I would never lie to you, Mrs Munro. I've always had a great fondness for all the babies I've delivered, but especially for you. I felt a bond with you the moment you came into this world. I'm sorry your blood mother died – I did what I could for her – but death in childbirth was all too common in those days.' She fixed her with a keen expression. 'I read about your marriage to Mr Munro in The Civil and Military Gazette – and of your arrival at Nicholson's. That's why I retired to Murree; to keep close to you in case you should need me.'

Jeanie felt uncomfortable at the woman's words. Was Olive Armitage's interest in her and her family verging on the unhealthy? Suddenly, she found the cottage stifling and the revelations overwhelming. She got up quickly.

'I have to go.' She tried to muster polite words. 'Thank you for the tea, Miss Armitage. I'm not sure I wish to thank you for telling me what you have – it's been a terrible shock – but it was brave of you to do so. My mother should have had the courage to tell me herself. I'm not sure I can ever forgive her for keeping such a secret from me all these years.'

Olive stood too. 'You're wrong, Mrs Munro; she has been very courageous. She knows that you're free now to contact Captain Lomax and tell him the truth, if you so wish. And she risks being cut off from your life if you let anger rule your heart. Please don't blame your mother. The fault is all mine. I gave her little choice.'

Jeanie's eyes stung with tears. She felt both furious and regretful, yet unable to put any of it into words. She hurried into the passageway and grabbed her coat from the coat stand.

'Mrs Munro.' Olive hurried after her, holding out her hand. 'You must take this; it belongs to you.' She pressed a metal object into Jeanie's hand. 'Mrs Grant refused to take it – at the hospital – so I kept it. I always hoped, one day, that I'd be able to give it to you, dear.'

Jeanie peered closer. It was a large gold locket with a tiny diamond on its casing. Her heart thumped as she opened it. On one side was a wedding photo of a young Tom Lomax and a dark-haired woman; on the other, a curl of black hair.

Olive put a hand on her arm. 'Your baby hair,' she said. 'I put it there myself. It was your blood mother's dying wish.'

Jeanie's chest constricted. She had never seen a picture of Mary Lomax before. It was surprisingly clear still; she looked like a slender, younger version of herself. Her voice wavered as she asked, 'When you said I looked just like my mother; you meant Mrs Lomax, didn't you?'

'Yes, dear,' Olive said, her expression sad. For the first time, the nurse looked her age, her face sagging. Perhaps, after all, even this woman of rigid convictions had had moments of guilt and regret for what she'd done.

All at once, Jeanie couldn't maintain her anger. Olive had had only moments to make a decision, and for right or wrong, she had done so, not for any self-gain, but out of compassion for Clara – and pity for Mary's baby.

Jeanie clutched the locket tightly in her fist, emotion flooding her throat. Impulsively, she brushed the old nurse's cheek with a kiss.

'Thank you, Miss Armitage.'

Quickly, she pulled on her coat and hurried from the cottage.

Chapter 43

The cold air froze the tears on Jeanie's cheeks as, numbly, she sat in the car, trying to take in all that she'd been told. It altered everything. Only weeks ago, she had discovered that John wasn't her blood brother but she had still been secure in knowing that she was a Grant. It had often been said that she had her mother's delicate nose and her father's blue eyes. But people saw what they wanted to see. She and John were in no way related and yet they had unknowingly shared a common bond; they were both the children of other parents.

Was John the lucky one in never knowing the truth? He had been happy with his lot, basking in the pride of his father and the love of his mother and sister. But she had the burden of knowing everything; that she had been taken from her real family when only a couple of days old and given to the Grants.

Her stomach churned with anger to think how her mother had kept up the deceit all these years, only to let a stranger tell her. What was she supposed to do with this knowledge? Did her mother want forgiveness? Was this a way of easing her conscience at a distance and not having to be the one to tell her?

Jeanie gripped the steering wheel; her hands were shaking too much to start driving. She closed her eyes and thought of Clara. Miss Armitage had called her courageous for confessing the secret; a secret that she had kept from her own husband for the rest of his life. What must that have been like? Her mother must have been so desperate to have a child that she was prepared to lie – and steal – to keep her. Jeanie knew the power of that longing. Yet would she have gone to such lengths to keep a baby? Probably not.

It struck Jeanie that the difference was that her mother had loved her father so deeply that she had done what she did as much for his sake as her own. And Jeanie's father – the man who had brought her up – had been a loving and giving man, so perhaps Clara's actions had been justified. Jeanie wanted a child with Mungo but not at any cost. She didn't love him enough.

She thought back to the previous Christmas and New Year in Greentoun. No wonder Clara had been so reluctant – fearful – of meeting the Lomaxes. She must have dreaded that somehow Tom would see a likeness in Jeanie to the long-dead Mary, or that too much questioning about Clara's time in Peshawar would reveal a link to Jeanie being born at the same time in the same hospital as her stillborn daughter.

Clara had shunned any contact, which Jeanie had put down to her continuing grief, whereas it was more likely terror of the truth coming out. Or maybe guilt? Was she making sure that Jeanie now knew who her real father was while she still had a chance of telling Captain Tom and being reconciled with her blood family?

For the first time, Jeanie let herself think of Tom as her father. He had seemed a little wary of her when they had met in Ebbsmouth. Could he possibly have been disconcerted by seeing a resemblance to his first wife? But she had quickly warmed to him and in Gulmarg she had felt them growing closer. Not only had he encouraged her painting – a talent she must have got from him – but he'd provided a listening ear and compassionate words of advice. Just like a father would. Jeanie's eyes smarted with fresh tears.

She must get back to Nicholson's and ring the hotel to find out how he was. For all she knew, Tom was seriously ill. She felt a surge of panic. Yet as she started up the car and drove back through the town, Jeanie had doubts about whether to tell him Clara's explosive secret. It might be too much of a shock for Tom to discover that his much-mourned daughter Amelia had been alive and well all these years.

And what would be the consequences for her mother? Had Clara committed a crime by taking Tom's baby? She had at least been guilty of collusion. For all that Jeanie was angry with her mother, she would never want to get her into trouble. She would ring and find out how Tom was – how Stella was too – and make no mention of her family secret. It was not something that could ever be talked about over the telephone anyway.

As she drew up outside School House, Jeanie wondered what she should tell Mungo. He had always admired her father – Colonel Grant – whereas he had not tried to conceal his contempt for Tom Lomax. Perhaps she shouldn't tell him either. Yet she was bursting to share the news with someone – a person who would listen without condemnation and not be judgemental – someone like Rick.

A feeling of regret and loss pressed on her chest as she thought of him. He would be long gone from India now. The thought was a relief but it also caused a jabbing pain to her heart. What would Rick have said? She imagined him smiling with encouragement and saying something about her now having two brothers; Andrew as well as John.

The realisation that Andrew was indeed her brother – or half-brother – was a sudden source of delight. She had warmed to Stella's husband from the start and found herself at ease in his company. It was partly because they shared a bond with each other, having known John; but Jeanie believed it was more than that. Friendship had come swiftly and naturally. Another thought gave Jeanie sudden pleasure; the delightful Belle was her niece.

As she hurried up the steps in the near-dark, Jeanie felt a new lifting of her spirits. Clara had given her a whole new family. Jeanie's heart began to soften towards her mother.

***

All was quiet as she rushed to the cloakroom to put through a call to Rawalpindi. Jimmy answered and swiftly handed over to Andrew. Jeanie's pulse raced to think she was speaking to her brother. She gabbled at him.

'Just wanted to check how Stella was – and your father … Manek said he was unwell.'

She held her breath while he answered.

'It's lovely to hear you, Jeanie.' His voice was deep like Tom's. 'I was going to send you a message but you've beaten me to it. Stella gave birth to our son yesterday.' She could hear the pride in his voice. 'Both are doing well. I'm having a hard job keeping Belle out of the bedroom. She just wants to mother the baby too!'

Jeanie's throat tightened with emotion. 'That's wonderful news! I'm so happy for you. Does he have a name yet?'

'Thomas Charles,' said Andrew. 'After my dad and Stella's father.'

Jeanie stifled a sob. She swallowed hard. 'That's a lovely name.' She cleared her throat. 'And your father?'

There was a hesitation and then Andrew said more sombrely, 'He's a bit tired and breathless. He's been to the hospital for tests. We'll know more in a day or two.'

Jeanie shared his anxiety but tried not to sound overly concerned. 'I bet he's thrilled with his new grandson,' she said.

She heard the emotion catch in Andrew's throat as he replied, 'Overjoyed.'

They chatted for a couple more minutes about the family and he asked her for details of the momentous decision to emigrate to Australia.

'I can't pretend we won't miss you,' he said. 'Stella cried when she got your letter about it – but then she cries easily these days.' Jeanie heard the teasing fondness in his voice. 'We'd hoped you'd be godmother to our baby. Perhaps we could hold the christening before you go?'

Jeanie was overwhelmed. 'Godmother?' she gasped. 'I'd love to … what an honour.' Silently, tears began to stream down her face. 'I'll come down and see you all before we leave, I promise. Please give Stella my love and congratulations … and warm regards to your father and Esmie.'

She rang off before she broke down crying. They wanted her to be godmother to her new nephew, even though to them she was just a friend! She was suffused with warmth and tenderness towards them. Their friendship had meant such a lot to her but she hadn't realised how much they must have valued hers too. Yet the knowledge was bittersweet; she was leaving India just as she was gaining her new family.

Jeanie wiped away her tears and attempted to control the turmoil she felt inside. She must find Mungo and tell him everything. Perhaps they could delay their departure a month or two – or she could join him later.

She glanced in the sitting-room but there was no tea laid out. He knew that she would be out and so wouldn't have bothered with tea on his own. All the pupils played games on a Wednesday afternoon; he might still be out watching rugby. Or working in his study.

Jeanie went through the baize door to the boys' side of the house and knocked on the study door. There was no reply. She had hardly been inside Mungo's study since he first showed her around the house – except to listen to Pethick-Lawrence on the wireless – and didn't like to disturb him when working. But this was important, so she went in just in case he was too absorbed to hear her knocking. The lamp on

311

his large desk was lit, illuminating a pile of jotters waiting to be marked. The fire was dying down. He must have been interrupted and called away from his work.

She was about to withdraw when she heard a sound – almost a sob – and peered around again. There was a crack of light coming from between the bookcases. Puzzled, she walked towards it and saw there was a door ajar in the recess that she hadn't noticed before. She pushed it open and entered what appeared to be a storeroom made into a small makeshift sitting-room.

It took a moment for Jeanie to realise what she was looking at; Dinah sitting on a flowery sofa, hair dishevelled and weeping. Mungo was sitting next to her, his arm around her shoulders.

Jeanie gasped. 'There you are ...'

He looked up, startled. 'Jean!'

'What's wrong?' she asked in concern, seeing Dinah's distress. 'Have you had bad news?'

Mungo stood up; his face flushed. 'Matron's just a little upset ... about us going. I was just comforting ...'

Jeanie had never seen him so flustered. She looked between them in confusion. Dinah had discarded her glasses and was dabbing at tear-swollen eyes. She knew that the matron was not the least troubled that she, Jeanie, was leaving. She'd made it clear that she thought Jeanie didn't deserve to be Mungo's wife. No; it was Mungo's going that she was crying over. But Jeanie hadn't expected to find her husband alone with the matron, and with his arm around her. It was disconcertingly intimate.

In a glance, she realised that there was a further door that must lead into the boys' side of the house and possibly the staff quarters. How had she never realised that this private den existed? Dinah was glaring at her now, resenting her intrusion.

Jeanie was about to apologise for bursting in on her privacy, when something stopped her. She'd had enough of secrets.

'What's going on here?' she demanded.

Mungo attempted to steer her to the door. 'Nothing at all. Don't make a fuss.'

Jeanie resisted. 'Why shouldn't I make a fuss when I find my husband hugging another woman – one that we both know is in love with you?'

'Don't be ridiculous,' he blustered. 'I just heard Lavelle crying and went to her aid.'

She turned to Dinah. 'Is that true? Am I being ridiculous?'

The matron's demeanour changed. She too, stood up, holding herself erect and raising her chin defiantly. 'Tell her, Mungo.'

Jeanie was startled by Dinah's use of his first name.

'There's nothing to tell,' Mungo said sharply. 'Don't make a scene.' He took Jeanie's arm, more firmly this time. 'Come with me and I'll explain. Let's go to the sitting-room and order up some tea.'

She threw off his hold. 'Tell me now.'

There was a glint of triumph in Dinah's eyes as she said, 'I'm more than just Mungo's matron – I'm the love of his life.'

Jeanie was staggered. 'Meaning?' she demanded.

'I'm his mistress.'

Jeanie gaped at her, dumbstruck.

'It's not true!' Mungo protested. 'Our liaison is over.'

'It'll never be over,' Dinah insisted with sudden passion, 'not when we both love each other. You can run away to the other side of the world but you'll never be able to get me out of your head – just as I will never stop thinking about you for a single hour!'

Jeanie felt as if all the breath had been sucked out of her lungs. 'How long have you …?'

Mungo shook his head but Dinah went on. 'Years! Ever since we met in Simla – long before the war and *you*.'

'Stop, Dinah,' Mungo said in agitation.

She ignored him. 'We should have married – would have done if there hadn't been a silly misunderstanding. But it led to Mungo going back to Scotland. Then you came and took the life I should have had.'

'That's enough,' Mungo cried. 'The important thing is that it's over – finished with.' He looked pleadingly at Jeanie. 'You must believe that.'

Somehow, she found her voice. 'When did it stop? Once we were married?'

She saw guilt redden his face. He stuttered. 'Yes, yes, of course it stopped then. But – but – when you were away for so long … during the war …'

'Mungo got me the job here,' Dinah interrupted. 'We took up where we'd left off. Even when you came back–'

'That's enough, Dinah!' Mungo looked mortified.

'We had two blissful weeks together in Mussoorie,' Dinah said, her eyes blazing, 'and that's when he said we had to stop. To try and salvage your sham of a marriage.'

'Don't, Dinah …'

'Mussoorie?' Jeanie was nauseated. 'Your fishing trip?'

'There was no fishing trip,' Dinah said dismissively. 'But why should we feel guilty when you were in Gulmarg with Rick. It's obvious how smitten you were – how you were planning to run away together.'

Jeanie looked at her with contempt. 'There was never any such plan.' She turned on her heels and hurried to the door. She couldn't bear to be with them another minute.

'Jean!' Mungo went after her. 'I know it's a shock but you have to see it from my point of view. I didn't know when I'd

314

ever see you again – you were gone for so long.' He pursued her through the study. 'But I really do want to give our marriage another go. That's why I ended the affair – and arranged the move to Australia – begin afresh – start a family like we've always wanted.'

She fled into the corridor where boys were beginning to troop in with a clatter of muddy boots. Mungo stopped abruptly, calling out, 'Quietly boys! And no running in the corridors. How did you get on, Bains? Webster?'

'Beat Trafalgar eighteen points to six, sir,' Webster cried with a grin.

'Excellent,' said Mungo. 'Who scored?'

While the exchange continued, Jeanie – heart hammering – escaped to the private side of the house.

Chapter 44

That night, not bothering to undress, Jeanie lay under the bed covers, sleepless and emotionally spent. Mungo had taken himself off to his dressing-room to sleep. She thought with disgust how the small chamber was linked by a staircase to his study and therefore providing easy access for both he and Dinah to meet in the secret sitting-room. All this time, she had believed his excuses for sleeping apart – that he was a light-sleeper kept awake by her restlessness and that he needed to rise early for work – when he must have been sneaking off to join his lover.

To think he'd been so indignant at Rick's letter offering her escape from an unhappy marriage. The sheer hypocrisy of it! She had resisted her attraction to Rick – how innocent their hand-holding had been! – while all the time her husband had been having an affair with their matron. She was further astounded by the double-standards of a man who could be so scornful of Anglo-Indians, such as Rick and his family, yet take Dinah as his mistress.

Earlier that evening, he had tried again to assure her. 'I promise you; it's over. I'm serious about wanting to make our marriage a success. Once we get to Adelaide, we can put all this behind us – Dinah and Rick Dixon.'

Jeanie had berated him angrily. 'Don't you dare to pretend that my friendship with Rick is in anyway equivalent to your adultery with Dinah.'

'Well, that letter he wrote to you implied as much,' Mungo had retorted. 'But I blame him not you, Jean. And I don't want to lose you. We have a new future beckoning in Australia.'

'Do you still love her?' Jeanie had asked bluntly.

Mungo had hesitated just a little too long. 'I love you, Jean. I'm giving her up for you. I'm so sorry. Please give me another chance.'

Through the dark hours of the night, Jeanie struggled to make sense of all she had discovered in the past few hours. She was a Lomax not a Grant. Her mother was not the woman she had thought she was. Neither was her husband. This seemingly upright, strictly moral headmaster who had been furious at her liaison with Rick, was an adulterer who had been carrying on his affair right under her nose. Where did that leave them now?

Jeanie had felt so guilty for leaving Mungo on his own for the duration of the war that she had tried hard to make him happy since her return. If he had ended the affair before she'd come back to India, perhaps she could have forgiven him. But it had continued right until August. How many times had Mungo gone from the marital bed, straight to lie with Dinah?

It sullied the memory of their romantic holiday on Dal Lake; the trips to the Mughal gardens and the lovemaking on the houseboat. All the time, he had been plotting his escape to Mussoorie and being with Dinah. She was not sure she could every forgive him for that. How did he expect her to go with him to Australia now?

Yet, perhaps Mungo was right in that respect; Adelaide would be a completely fresh start for them both, away from their past mistakes. In time, they would make new friends and build a home for themselves and a family. If they couldn't conceive a child of their own then they could adopt; she would insist on it ...

***

Jeanie rose early, bathed and dressed in fresh clothes. At breakfast, she found a remorseful Mungo.

'Jean, I can't begin to say how sorry I am. I've had a sleepless night thinking about it.'

'I don't want to talk about last night,' she told him. 'I haven't decided if I'm going to Australia with you or not. I need more time to think things over. But if I do go, then it won't simply be as an appendage to you. I'm no longer prepared to just be a schoolmaster's wife. I intend to live my own life.'

'Dearest!' Mungo began. 'I can assure you—'

'There's something else.' Jeanie cut in. 'I need to go to Pindi to see the Lomaxes. I'm going to take the car and drive down today.'

'I don't think that's a good idea,' he said. 'There could be snow in the next day or two. If you insist on going, I could drive you down at the weekend.'

'No, I'm going today,' she said defiantly.

'What's so important?'

'Stella has had a baby boy.'

'You never told me!'

'That's why I was looking for you yesterday.' She saw him shift uncomfortably. 'But that's not all. Captain Tom is ill and I need to see him.'

'Tom Lomax?' Mungo frowned. 'I'm sorry to hear that but I don't see why it's so necessary to rush off and see him this minute.'

Jeanie took a deep breath. 'I discovered something else yesterday – from Olive Armitage – about my family.'

'The old nurse? What did she have to say?'

Jeanie's pulse began to quicken. She must stay calm and coherent. 'My mother and Mary Lomax gave birth in the same hospital in Peshawar a few days apart. My mother's

318

baby was stillborn. I was Mary Lomax's baby. Armitage gave me to Clara when my real mother died.'

Mungo looked flabbergasted. 'Y-you're not Colonel Grant's daughter?'

Jeanie shook her head. 'I'm Tom Lomax's daughter.'

He was speechless.

'So that's why I have to go to Pindi today,' she said firmly, looking him straight in the eye. 'To see my blood family and break the news.'

Chapter 45

The Raj Hotel, Rawalpindi

On the way down to Rawalpindi, Jeanie's resolve to tell the Lomaxes the truth, wavered. She still found it hard to believe herself. She wasn't sure whether it would be the right thing to put Tom through the agony of knowing he had been cheated out of his daughter for thirty-three years. It would cause untold upset – and Clara would be vilified.

Jeanie gripped the wheel in concentration, taking the hairpin bends cautiously as she drove down the switchback mountain road. She had rung the Raj Hotel to book a room for the night and stopped in the town to buy a small teddy bear for baby Thomas. Her visit was ostensibly to see Stella and congratulate her and Andrew on their new son.

She tried to think of other things but that just led to her dwelling on Mungo's betrayal. Dinah's behaviour towards her began to make more sense though; her guardedness and reluctance to become her friend. Dinah had loved Mungo for years – believed they should have married – so was it any wonder that the matron resented her? What had been the misunderstanding between them that had led to Mungo leaving India and searching out a wife in Scotland? Whatever it was, it had not stopped Mungo enabling Dinah to get the job as matron during the war and resuming their affair.

It still puzzled Jeanie why Dinah had chosen to invite her to Pindi for her cousin's wedding. For a short while, she'd believed they were becoming friends and confidantes. As she drove, it began to dawn on her that Dinah might have had another motivation; to push Rick towards her. The matron knew of Jeanie's liking for Rick and she must have seen at the wedding how the attraction was mutual.

Another thought occurred to Jeanie. How did Rick know she would be at Gulmarg without Mungo in August? She had assumed he must have spoken to Stella but what if it had been Dinah who had told him? Had she encouraged him to go, hinting that all was not well with Jeanie's marriage?

Then there was Rick's letter that Dinah had intercepted – just the ammunition she needed to cause trouble between Mungo and his wife. Perhaps Dinah had delayed revealing it until it became obvious that Mungo was serious about leaving India for Australia and abandoning her.

Jeanie had a flicker of pity for the woman; the man she loved had married another – and every day she had had to watch her lover living the lie of a happy marriage, as well as Dinah having to pay deference to the woman who had taken her place.

Mungo had created an impossible situation for them all by marrying her, Jeanie, when his heart lay elsewhere. That made her both angry and sad. Yet, in the early days, she believed he had loved her – perhaps still loved her – and if the war hadn't intervened and separated them, none of this might have happened.

It was useless to speculate on what might have been. What mattered was what course they took from now on.

***

Rawalpindi was bathed in wintry sunshine, the trees along the Mall still fluttering with the last of their golden leaves. Jeanie's heart lifted at the sight of familiar landmarks – the cricket ground, the Scots Kirk and Flashman's Hotel – as she drove towards The Raj.

321

Parking up, Jeanie saw Belle chasing after her cousin Charles who was peddling a tricycle across the lawn. As soon as the girl spotted her, Belle came tearing up the path to greet her.

'Auntie Jeanie! Auntie Jeanie! I've got a baby brother. He's very wrinkly and cries a lot. Do you want to see him?'

Jeanie swept her up in a hug. How good it felt to hold her again. 'I'd love to. That's why I've come – to see you and baby Thomas.' She whispered in the girl's ear. 'Especially you – but we won't tell the others that.'

Belle giggled and kissed her cheek. 'I love you, Auntie Jeanie.'

Jeanie's eyes smarted. 'I love you too, gorgeous girl.'

Belle wriggled out of her hold and ran off after Charles; the pair disappeared around the side of the hotel in the direction of the Dubois' bungalow.

Inside the hotel, Jimmy hailed her with his customary welcome and sent Sanjeev to fetch her case from the car. As Jimmy showed her up the corridor to her room, she congratulated him on the arrival of his nephew.

He beamed. 'We are all so very glad and happy. My sister is resting at the moment but Andrew will join you shortly.'

'And Captain Tom?' Jeanie asked. 'How is he?'

Jimmy's face fell. 'He is not in the best of health. Between you, me and the gatepost, Mrs Lomax Senior is rather concerned. But let's not be pessimistic. He is a strong man. The captain will bounce back to full health, in a jiffy. You mustn't worry.'

'Is he resting too?'

'Yes. He's in the Curzon Room, so that the baby doesn't disturb. Mrs Lomax wants full rest and recuperation for him. But the news of your visit has gladdened their hearts.'

Jimmy unlocked her room and held open the door. 'The residents are partaking of a glass of sherry in the sitting-

322

room – they find it more convivial than sitting in the lobby on a cold day. The fire is blazing. Please join them. Luncheon will be served in twenty minutes.'

***

Jeanie got a cheerful welcome from the long-time residents, especially Hester Cussack, who clasped her in her frail arms and kissed her cheeks.

'You're looking as lovely as ever,' cried the baroness. 'The cold makes you glow, darling. How is that handsome husband of yours?'

'Busy as usual,' said Jeanie, forcing a smile.

'You know, I really can't forgive him for whisking you off to Australia,' she said with a pout. 'I admit things are looking gloomy here but I'm sure Nicholson's will survive, whatever becomes of India.'

'He has his heart set on a school in Adelaide,' she answered and then quickly changed the subject, asking the baroness about the rest of her summer in Srinagar.

Their conversation was carried on over lunch in the dining-room, until Andrew and Esmie suddenly appeared. Jeanie had to hold tears in check at the warmth of their greetings.

'I'll take you up to see Stella as soon as you've had lunch,' said Andrew, 'and before Belle has her afternoon rest.'

'I can't wait,' Jeanie said, smiling. Turning to Esmie, she asked, 'And then could I pop in to see the captain?'

Esmie and Andrew exchanged looks, then Esmie said, 'he gets very tired in the afternoons and usually sleeps. He'll be better in the evening. You can see him before dinner. He's looking forward to it.'

Jeanie swallowed her concern and nodded. 'Me too.'

323

Impatient for lunch to be over, Jeanie declined coffee in the lounge and went upstairs with Andrew. He talked excitedly about the newborn baby all the way to the owner's flat and she was glad that left no opportunity for him to question her about Mungo or Murree.

They found Stella sitting up in bed, her fair hair cascading around her shoulders. She looked tired but her eyes shone. Jeanie rushed to her and they embraced.

'Clever you!' said Jeanie.

'Thank you.' Stella laughed. 'Say hello to your godson.' She stretched out and touched the cradle at her bedside.

Jeanie peered in. Her chest constricted at the sight of the sleeping infant. 'He's perfect.' Tentatively, she brushed his soft cheek with a finger. Glancing round at Andrew, she said, 'He's got your dark hair.'

'Yes.' He grinned widely. 'Chip off the old block, isn't he?'

Jeanie thought of the dark curl of hair that had been kept in Mary's locket since her own babyhood. The same dark hair. She had an overwhelming sensation to blurt out the truth, right there and then. But she restrained herself. This moment was about Thomas and his parents – not her. She stepped back, shaking.

'Are you okay?' Andrew asked in concern.

'Of course,' she said hoarsely. 'I'm just so happy for you both.'

He swung an arm around her affectionately. 'Thank you.'

Jeanie blinked away a tear. 'Silly me! I've got a wee present for Thomas and forgot to bring it. I'll dash back and get it.'

'Don't go,' Stella said. 'He won't know if he gets it now or later, will he?'

'No, he won't.' They smiled at each other in amusement.

'Would you like to hold him?' she asked.

'Can I?'

Stella nodded. Jeanie hesitated.

'I'm not sure how,' she admitted. 'I've never seen a baby this new before.'

At once, Andrew leaned into the cradle and lifted up his son. 'Put him into the crook of your arm, like this.'

He settled the boy into her hold and when she was comfortable, let go. The infant snuffled and let out a juddering sigh. Jeanie froze. Then when he didn't awake or start to cry, she breathed again. The weight and warmth of him in her arms was comforting. She could feel the gentle rhythm of his breathing.

As her confidence grew, Jeanie stroked his hair, marvelling at its softness.

'Can I sing to him?' she asked.

'Of course!' Stella and Andrew said in unison.

Jeanie sang a Scottish lullaby and then the more boisterous *Bonnie Dundee*.

'I don't know why I chose that one,' she laughed, having finished. 'A bit warlike for this wee man.'

'You have a beautiful singing voice, Jeanie,' said Stella.

Andrew smiled; his look tender. 'I remember John singing that. It was his party piece too.'

Emotion caught in her throat. 'Yes, it was, wasn't it?'

Moments later, Thomas awoke and began to grizzle. She swiftly handed him back to Andrew who passed him dextrously to Stella.

'Time for a feed,' she announced.

'We'll leave you to it,' said Andrew.

As they retreated downstairs, he said, 'I need to go and find Belle – encourage her to have a nap – though she'll probably refuse now that Charles is too old for one.'

On the spur of the moment, Jeanie asked, 'Would you like to go for a walk later – before it's dark?'

325

'Yes, good idea.' He smiled. 'About four o'clock?'
'Perfect.'

Chapter 46

Having not slept the night before, Jeanie fell sound asleep and only woke at four because of the gong sounding for afternoon tea. She hurriedly got ready and dashed downstairs, pulling on her coat. Andrew was waiting on the lobby steps, smoking a cigarette. Seeing her, he stubbed it out.

'Sorry, I fell asleep,' she admitted.

'No apology needed.' He smiled. 'You've had a long drive and then a Raj Hotel lunch; enough to put anyone under.'

'Not just that,' she said, with a sigh. 'A sleepless night last night too.'

As they headed down the path, he asked, 'The move to Australia troubling you?'

She hesitated. 'One of the reasons.'

'Do you want to talk about it?'

'Let's walk first,' she replied.

They set off down Nichol Road and turned into Dalhousie Road. Jeanie breathed in the evening air – milder than Murree's – and laced with the aroma of cooking and fires, drifting from the bazaars. The Mall was busy with horse traffic and motor cars, so Andrew led her across the sports ground towards the cricket pavilion. He began to reminisce about his boyhood at the Raj.

'Stella's family were just as close as if they were my own,' he said. 'Jimmy taught me to play cricket – and her cousin Sigmund and I would be out till after dark whacking a cricket ball at all times of the year. Charlie Dubois – Stella's dad – spoilt me rotten. Even her mother, Myrtle, was soft on me, though she could be scarily severe with Stella and Jimmy.'

'Myrtle?' Jeanie smiled. 'She dotes so completely on Charles and Belle; I can't imagine her being severe at all.'

'That's what grandchildren can do to you, apparently,' Andrew said with a laugh. 'I think Dad and Meemee are going to be just the same with Thomas.'

Suddenly, Jeanie stopped walking, emotion catching in her throat.

'Is – is your father really ill?' she asked.

Andrew faced her, fixing her with his good eye. She saw the tension in his face. Quietly he said, 'The doctors say he has cancer … of the lungs.'

Jeanie was shocked by the news. 'That's terrible. Can they operate?'

He shook his head. She saw him struggling to speak. 'They're talking of giving him radiation treatment … try to delay …'

'Oh Andrew! I'm so sorry.'

She saw his chest heave. 'It's so bloody unfair!' he cried. 'Just when things are finally going right for us all – our family – and now we have Thomas …'

Jeanie put her arms around him and for a moment she just held him as he gulped back angry tears.

'Sorry,' he said, pulling away and wiping his eye on his sleeve. He let out a long breath. 'That's why Meemee was a bit cautious about when you could see Dad. Everyone wants to visit him but he gets exhausted. He's really gone downhill since we got to Pindi. Meemee would rather that only family are with him – but she's very touched that you've come all the way from Murree.' Andrew gave her a sad look. 'So, you mustn't be offended if she decides not to let you see Dad. It'll just depend what sort of day he's having.'

Suddenly, the thought of never being able to see Tom was unbearable to Jeanie. To have discovered that she was his daughter – experienced the trauma of Olive's revelations – to then be denied seeing him again was too much.

Jeanie blurted out, 'But I am family!'

Andrew's look was pitying. 'That's kind of you to say so – and we value your friendship, Jeanie but–'

'He's my father too!' Jeanie grabbed his arm. Andrew stared at her uncomprehendingly. 'I was born Amelia – not Jean – in Peshawar. Mary Lomax was my real mother. At two days old, I was given to the Grants.'

His incredulity changed to dawning realisation. 'You're Amelia,' he gasped. 'My half-sister?'

She nodded.

'But that's not possible. Sh-she's buried in Peshawar. I've seen her grave.'

'Not Amelia's,' Jeanie said. 'The baby in that grave is the stillborn daughter of Clara – the woman I've always known as my mother – still think of her as such, if I'm honest.'

Andrew looked stunned. 'She stole you. How could she …?'

'It was the midwife who made the switch – my mother hardly had a choice – she wasn't thinking straight having just lost her baby – her fourth baby to die. She never told a soul; my father never knew – nor John – and neither did I until yesterday when the old nurse confessed to me what she'd done.'

Andrew was shaking his head. She could see he was struggling to make sense of it – to believe her. Jeanie took out the gold locket.

'The nurse gave me this. It belonged to Mary – my real mother – and it holds my baby hair.'

In the dying light of the orange sunset, Andrew opened the locket and stared at the photograph.

'My father,' he said, his voice husky. He closed the locket and ran a thumb over the small diamond on its casing. 'I've

329

seen this before. There's a portrait of Dad's first wife at The Anchorage; Auntie Tibby kept it. In it, she's wearing this locket.'

He looked at her, his eye glinting with emotion. 'You're my sister.'

'Yes, I am.' Jeanie gave a tearful smile.

Then they were hugging each other tightly and weeping, as the sun turned red between the trees.

Chapter 47

Jeanie was sitting with Stella while Andrew was with his father. They'd decided that Andrew should be the one to break the news about her to Tom, and let Tom decide when, or indeed if, he wanted to see her. It would be a huge shock and Andrew didn't want either Jeanie or Tom getting distraught in the telling. Jeanie was a jangle of nerves, despite Stella being delighted at the news.

'You're my sister-in-law! I couldn't ask for anyone nicer.'

Jeanie waited until Stella had finished feeding Thomas – she could hear his delightful snuffling and sucking beneath Stella's shawl – before unburdening herself about Mungo's infidelity.

'I can't believe Dinah would do such a thing!' Stella cried incredulously. 'How intolerable for you.'

'She said she'd been in love with Mungo since they'd met in Simla years ago,' Jeanie explained. 'Some misunderstanding drove them apart and that's why Mungo returned to Scotland to look for a wife.'

'That doesn't mean he didn't marry you for love,' Stella pointed out.

Jeanie shrugged. 'Maybe.'

'But Dinah?' Stella shook her head in disbelief.

'I remember you telling me there was some scandal about her in Simla,' Jeanie said.

'Yes; something to do with a jealous doctor at the hospital where she nursed. She left under a cloud. Perhaps this doctor didn't want her going off with Mungo. Who knows?'

'Mungo used to go on holiday there before he met me. Perhaps I should have asked more questions.'

'How could you possibly have known?' Stella retorted. 'You mustn't take any of the blame for this.'

331

'Mungo says it's definitely over,' Jeanie said.

'Do you believe him?' Stella asked, rubbing the baby's back.

'Probably. He's desperate to go to Adelaide and start afresh.'

'And is that what you want?'

'I haven't made up my mind. There's been too much to think about …'

'Jeanie, if I told you …' Stella broke off.

'Told me what?'

'No, sorry. You're right. You must take time to consider what to do. It's a big step whatever you decide.'

Just then, Andrew appeared at the door. Jeanie's insides lurched. He looked flushed and upset. But then he smiled and came towards her.

'Dad would like to see you now. I've told him everything.'

'Thank you.' Jeanie leapt up and made for the door.

'Good luck,' Stella called after her.

With heart pummelling, Jeanie went to the Curzon Room and knocked. Esmie opened the door and gave her an encouraging smile. Tom was sitting by the fire. She was shocked to see how thin and frail he was, his face gaunt and sallow.

'Hello Dad,' she said, her voice wavering.

As he struggled out of his seat, Esmie went to help him.

'Don't get up,' Jeanie said quickly.

'I'll stand to greet my daughter!' he said, his voice still strong.

A sob caught in Jeanie's throat as she went to him. He held out his arms and the next moment she was being enfolded in his embrace. She didn't want to let go; and it seemed, neither did he. Then he pulled away so he could look at her, still clutching onto her arms. His sunken cheeks were wet with tears.

'My bonny girl,' he rasped. 'The first time I saw you, you reminded me of Mary ...' He swallowed hard.

Esmie touched Jeanie gently on the shoulder. 'I'll be next door with Stella and Andy if you need anything.'

Jeanie nodded, grateful that she was to be left alone with Tom for a short while. As Esmie went, Tom took Jeanie's hand.

'Come and sit next to me, lassie.'

She saw him wince as he sat down, his breathing laboured. She took the seat that had already been placed next to his.

'Andy says you have the locket,' he said. 'Can I see it? It's not that I doubt you in any way–'

'Of course, you can see it,' Jeanie said, pulling it out of her skirt pocket.

His hands shook as he took it and he gave a small gasp as he opened it up and saw his wedding photo and the baby hair. After a long moment, he closed it again and stared at it in the palm of his hand. The diamond sparkled in the firelight. He tried to speak but was too overcome.

Jeanie said, 'Nurse Armitage took a curl of my hair and put it in the locket. It's the last thing my mother asked her to do.'

Tom nodded. He cleared his throat. 'Did she say anything else?'

Jeanie hesitated. She didn't want to distress him further but neither did she want to keep anything from him.

'The nurse said that she kept asking for you – and when could you come and see her. She must have feared that she wouldn't survive because she also made the nurse promise that I wouldn't be sent home to be brought up by my Lomax grandfather. She got upset at the idea.'

333

Tom let out a long sigh, handing the locket back. 'Poor, dear Mary.'

Jeanie asked, 'May I wear it now?'

'Of course!' he cried. 'It's yours. It would bring me great joy to see it on you.'

She took her time fastening it around her neck, giving him a moment to wipe his nose on a large handkerchief and bring his emotions under control. Then she said, 'Please will you tell me more about my mother – my real mother? I know so little.'

Tom nodded and began to reminisce about Mary being a childhood friend who grew into his first love. He described a sweet, shy girl – an only child of elderly parents – who was unfailingly kind. He talked about their growing up in Ebbsmouth and how everyone expected them to marry, which they duly did.

'But I'm not sure she was ever suited to life in India – especially on the Frontier – and I've always felt guilty about that.' He looked at her, his vivid blue eyes gleaming. 'And of course, I felt doubly guilty about losing Amelia – not being there at the birth. But here you are – like an answer to my prayers – after all these years.'

'You don't seem angry at Armitage or my mother – of Clara,' Jeanie said. 'My first response was fury at what they'd done – of the years of lying.'

Tom stretched out his hand and covered hers. 'I've lived long enough to know that people make decisions in the heat of the moment – often wrong or foolish – but with the best of intentions. I don't want us to waste the time we have together, eaten up with regret about the past.'

'I wish I'd got to know you sooner though,' Jeanie said, a sense of loss weighing her down.

He squeezed her hand. 'But we already have memories together,' he pointed out. 'Ebbsmouth in January and Gulmarg in August – special times.'

'Yes, we have,' she agreed.

'It's a good job that I like you,' said Tom with a teasing smile. 'Imagine the embarrassment if we hadn't got on – to suddenly be landed with each other as father and daughter?'

Jeanie gave a teary laugh. 'Yes, I'm thankful that I'm already very fond of you.'

He chuckled. 'Jeanie, you have no idea how much you have lifted my spirits. And to be able to talk about Mary with you too. I haven't spoken about her in years. It's such a comfort.'

'I'm glad,' she replied, squeezing his hand back. 'I want to stay on at the hotel for a bit – spend time with you – and make up for the lost years. Would you let me do that?'

She saw tears spring into his eyes again. 'I'd like that very much. But what about your plans to leave for Australia?'

'They're on hold,' said Jeanie. 'You come first, Dad.'

He made a strange sound – half-sob, half-cry of joy – and nodded his thanks.

Jeanie stood up, realising he was tiring quickly. She leaned towards him and kissed his cheek. 'Tomorrow, I'll come with a sketch pad and you can give me some tips.'

'Tomorrow then,' he said croakily. 'I'll look forward to it.'

Jeanie left him sitting by the fire, her heart brimming with love for her new-found father.

Chapter 48

That night, Jeanie fell into an exhausted sleep. Waking shortly before dawn, she opened the window and listened to the sounds of the city coming to life, welcoming the sharp cold air on her face and clearing her mind.

Shutting the window, she switched on the table lamp and sat down at the dressing-table to write a letter.

'Dear Mungo,

I have been reunited with my real father who now knows everything about my birth. I cannot describe how joyful and special our reunion was yesterday. Until then, I had been full of bitterness for the wasted years of not knowing the truth – not knowing him. But he is so wise and doesn't dwell on the past, looking only to relish the present.

Distressingly, he is unlikely to enjoy much of a future, as he has advanced lung cancer. That is why I am going to stay on at the Raj – I want to spend as much time with him as he has left.

Which brings me to my next decision. Mungo, I am not going to return to Murree and will make arrangements with the hotel to have your car driven back. I won't be going with you to Adelaide and now wish for a divorce. Either you can admit to adultery with Dinah or we can cite my desertion during the war as the reason. Whatever we decide, it should be done as swiftly as these things can be.

I'm not entirely blaming you for the failure of our marriage, despite the shock of discovering your long-term affair with Dinah. I know we have both changed over the years apart – me perhaps more than you – and we have not made each other happy for a long time.

What I have learnt, in the past few days, is that it's important to be truthful and to live for the day. I hope you find happiness in Australia. If you wish to contact me then write to me at The Raj. But don't try to visit – I won't change my mind.

Fond wishes

Jean.'

She felt a great burden lifting as she sealed and addressed the envelope. She wondered how Mungo would take it. Perhaps he would also feel a sense of relief – if not immediately, then in the weeks and months to come. She pondered over whether Dinah would go with him and realised that the idea did not upset her.

Jeanie dressed quickly and handed over the letter at reception for posting before heading into the dining-room for breakfast. She couldn't wait to spend the morning with her father. She'd sketch him while he told her more about his life – and she would tell him about hers.

Chapter 49

'Jeanie, I'm taking you on a picnic,' Andrew announced the following day. 'Dad's going to have a quiet morning and it's time I had my sister to myself for a few hours.'

Jeanie was delighted. 'Lovely! Where are we going?'

'Out to Taxila – the ancient ruins,' he said. 'Have you ever been?'

'Never,' she admitted, 'though I remember John enthusing about them.'

'Yes.' Andrew smiled. 'So he did.'

'Do you want me to drive?' she asked.

'No, this is my treat. You just sit back and enjoy the view. Jimmy's organising tiffin for us to take.'

Jeanie was touched that he wanted to spend the day with her and swiftly went to get ready. All the Lomaxes had been understanding and non-judgemental about her decision to leave Mungo. None of them pressed her for details and she wasn't sure if Stella had told the others about Mungo's affair with Dinah. She was glad not to have to talk about it. She was doing as Tom did; taking each day as it came and wanting to spend it with the family.

It was a beautiful sunny late November morning with vivid blue skies and clear horizons. The far mountains were etched in detail like one of Tom's oil paintings. Would Tom live long enough to see his beloved Raj-in-the-Hills again? She fervently hoped so.

As they drove out of Rawalpindi and headed north-west into the low, scrub-covered hills around Taxila, they chatted about their lives. Andrew talked of his time in the army on the North-West Frontier with John. He'd nearly died of heat stroke but John had got him to hospital in time. Jeanie reminisced about her army days too; the camaraderie and the laughs they'd had despite the grimness and anxiety of the war.

'I hope one day, we'll be able to meet up again,' she said. 'We were such close friends for those intense few years.'

'Will you go back to Scotland, do you think?' Andrew asked.

'Not immediately,' she said at once. 'I want to stay here and be near your –' She corrected herself. '*Our* dad. But maybe after that … It's too soon to say. So much has happened so quickly.'

'I understand,' he said. 'You must stay with us as long as you wish. Don't feel you have to make any snap decisions. You will always have a home with us whenever you want.'

Jeanie's heart swelled. 'Thank you. You're all being so kind to me. You've no idea how much it means to be part of a family again.'

'Good.' Andrew gave her a warm smile.

***

It took over an hour to drive to Taxila but to Jeanie it seemed they were there in no time; they had been so busy chatting. There were few other visitors and they had the site largely to themselves. Wandering among the extensive ruins of an ancient monastery and gazing up at the remains of a stone Buddhist stupa, Jeanie marvelled at the ancient monuments. Andrew told her that the first civilization to be built here had been nearly three thousand years ago.

'It makes you think how insignificant we are in the great play of things,' mused Jeanie. 'The British rule in India is just a blink of an eye, isn't it?'

'All empires fall eventually,' Andrew agreed.

As they picnicked out of the breeze, sheltered by an intricately carved pillar, they continued the conversation.

'What do you think will happen after Independence?' Jeanie asked. 'Assuming it happens in the next year or two.'

'I think most of the British will go home,' he answered. 'All the administrators – the army – the police. The Indians will have no need for them.'

'And the business people like you and Stella?'

Andrew paused and looked out at the serried ranks of low hills. He sighed. 'I really don't know. Stella's family want to carry on at The Raj – they don't see any reason to bail out like others in their community are doing.'

Jeanie felt a pang at his words; people like Rick and his sister Ada. She hadn't felt able to ask Stella about her cousins yet – not wanting to raise the contentious subject of what the Anglo-Indians should do – but she would choose the right moment.

'But,' said Andrew, 'it will depend what dad and Meemee want to do. It's their hotel. Unless they want to sell, we'll carry on in Pindi. It's different for the one in Gulmarg – that's only leased – we might have to give that one up.'

Jeanie knew how difficult that would be for the family who loved their home in Kashmir. She was sorry for making him sad and changed the subject.

'I have to say, these are the best curry puffs I've tasted since I came back to India.'

'Jimmy and his Sikh chef will be delighted,' said Andrew with a smile. 'You must tell them.'

After the picnic, they visited the museum and then explored more of the ancient site. Andrew appeared distracted and kept looking at his watch.

'Do you want to get home?' Jeanie asked him. 'I don't mind when we leave, just say the word.'

'No,' he said hastily, 'we've plenty of time.'

'I'd like to take another look at the stupa,' she said.

'Good idea,' he said. 'I'll just put the tiffin basket back in the car and then join you.'

Jeanie wandered towards the steps of the stupa and gazed at the stone carvings to either side. The afternoon sun was turning the grey stone lemon-yellow and nearby trees rustled in the breeze. For a moment she had the place completely to herself and she felt a calmness and peace descend. This ancient place which had seen different civilisations come and go, put all her worries and concerns – the past disappointments and failings – into perspective. She was alive and loved; whatever the future brought, she would relish life and make the most of it.

She heard Andrew returning, his footsteps on the path. Turning, she saw him passing a line of trees, the sun dazzling behind him. Jeanie shaded her eyes and squinted. Perhaps it wasn't Andrew.

As the man grew nearer, her heart began to pound. He looked like ... but it couldn't possibly be ...?

'Rick?' she gasped, as he walked towards her, grinning. 'How ...? I thought ...'

'Jeanie!'

He said her name with such tenderness that she began to tremble. She felt emotion pressing down on her chest, making it hard to breathe.

'Stella told me everything,' he said, standing before her. 'Andrew arranged this, so we could meet privately and away from prying family.'

He looked so handsome with his dark hair lifting in the breeze and his tawny eyes full of warmth. Still, she could not take in what she was seeing and hearing.

'But I thought you'd gone to Ceylon?' she said incredulously.

'I was going – it was all planned – but in the end I couldn't.'

341

'Couldn't?' she queried.

'I thought it would help to put hundreds of miles between us,' he admitted, 'but realised that it would make no difference. I would still be yearning for you in Colombo as much as in India.' He gave her a loving smile. 'So I decided to stay in Pindi – it's my home – why give that up too? I'm helping dad in the business. Sigmund went with Ada and Clive instead.'

He stepped closer and took her hands in his. She was shaking uncontrollably.

'Jeanie, I love you. Ever since I saw you walking up the drive at The Anchorage – with your pink cheeks and wild hair – I've been smitten. I thought I'd never be able to be with you – but Stella says you've left Mungo for good. Can I hope–?'

'Yes!' Jeanie cried and threw her arms around him. 'I love you too! I was desolate to think you were far away in Ceylon.'

He squeezed her in a tight embrace. How good it felt to be in his arms at last! Then they were kissing each other eagerly, with all the pent-up longing that both of them felt.

They broke off but Rick kept tight hold of her hand as they went to sit on a low wall.

'Kind, interfering Stella,' Jeanie said with a laugh. 'And Andrew. I saw him keep checking his watch and wondered what was preoccupying him. Where is he?'

'If you don't appear in ten minutes, he'll drive back and leave me to bring you home.' Rick smiled.

She kissed his lips. 'He'll have to return alone then.'

His look turned earnest. 'Stella didn't want to tell you that I was still in Pindi until you'd made up your mind about Mungo. The decision had to be yours.'

'I'm absolutely certain I'm doing the right thing for me as well as Mungo,' she reassured him. 'I've asked him for a divorce.' She paused and then said, 'Did Stella also tell you about his long-term affair with Dinah?'

Rick nodded; his look full of compassion. 'I feel terrible about that, but it makes sense now ...'

'What do you mean? You shouldn't feel bad.'

'Dinah encouraged me – told me how unhappy you were with Mungo and how he didn't love you anymore. That's how I knew you were in Gulmarg – and why I wrote that letter. I had no idea Dinah had intercepted it until Stella told me. I thought you'd made up your mind to stick with the marriage and that's why you didn't answer. I had to accept that, even though it left me desolate.'

Jeanie squeezed his hand. 'It caused an awful row with Mungo. But in a way it might have helped bring things to a head and led to my discovery of their affair. Dinah was growing increasingly desperate at the thought of Mungo going. She manipulated you, knowing that I cared for you.'

'She treated you very badly,' Rick said, his indignation rising. 'Pretending to befriend you – and making me think she had your best interests at heart.'

Jeanie shook her head. 'If anything, I feel sorry for her now. She was in an impossible position and Mungo was having his cake and eating it, so to speak.' She laced her fingers through his. 'Anyway, I don't want to talk about them anymore. They can do what they want. All that matters to me is that I'm here with you – I still can't quite believe it! It's dreamlike.'

Rick raised her hand to his lips and kissed it. 'Jeanie; when you're free of Mungo, will you marry me?'

Jeanie's eyes blurred with happy tears as she smiled. 'Gladly!'

The grin he gave her, lit up his handsome face. 'Then that day can't come soon enough, my darling.'

He pulled her to her feet and sealed their promise to each other with a tender kiss. Then, hand in hand, they made their way out of the Taxila ruins towards the golden light of early sunset. Jeanie's heart was brimming with love for Rick. Neither of them knew what the future would bring – or where it would take them – but they would spend it together, and that was the most joyful thought of all.

Epilogue

Greentoun, Scotland, June 1951

'Rowan House

Dear Phyllis
Thank you for your newsy letter in reply to mine – I can't wait for our reunion next month. What a lot of catching up we have to do! I hope, one day, that we can get our husbands together but, in the meantime, it will be wonderful to see you and the other ack-ack girls. You roll your eyes at Irene being on her second husband already, but remember, so am I!

Rick is the most wonderful man – he's everything that Mungo was not – and he's adapting well to living in Scotland (although he still complains about the icy east winds in winter!) It helps that his parents are living nearby too. I think I told you that Rick and his father have bought a garage business together in Greentoun from a nice man, Lorimer, who was retiring? Anyway, they've already got a good reputation for reliable service.

As for the hotel in Ebbsmouth where we're meeting up for our reunion, you asked about it's unusual name. It's the Lomaxes' old family home (it used to be called The Anchorage) but when Andy and Stella moved here two years ago, they decided to turn it into a hotel and call it The-Raj-in-Ebbsmouth, in honour of the Raj Hotels that Andy's dad used to have in India. It gives a link to their past – for both of them – as Stella's family used to manage the one in Pindi.

I'll tell you more about them when we see each other – there's a lot to explain – and better to do so over a large gin and tonic than in a letter!

See you at The Raj soon,

345

Love from Jeanie x'

***

'Rowan House

Dear John

This is such a hard letter to write, knowing that you'll never read it, but it was Andy who suggested I did so. He knows that after six years I am still grieving for my dear brother. How strange it is that Andy should turn out to be a half-brother of mine – and so by extension, yours. You were not just brothers-in-arms but real brothers of sorts. Is that why you both got on so well from the very beginning of your army life together?

You would rejoice to see how happy he is with Stella and their two children, Belle and Thomas, who are both boisterous and happy children. Luckily, they are very sociable too, as their home in Ebbsmouth is now a hotel and they have to share it with an ever-changing flow of guests and commercial travellers. They adore their eccentric Great-Aunt Tibby (Tom's sister who has lived in the family home all her life) and who keeps a secret supply of toffees just for them. For years, she has lived with a Lahori artist, Dawan Lal, who also indulges the children, letting them run amok in his studio and use his precious supply of paints and paper. Tibby and Dawan quietly got married post-war after causing years of scandal in the village!

There are also two very venerable and ancient residents from The Raj Hotel in Pindi, who, after Independence, chose to come and live in Scotland with the Lomaxes; Mr Ansom and Baroness Hester Cussack. They are both remarkable. Ansom (now in his early nineties) goes sea-bathing most mornings in summertime and the baroness (nobody knows

346

her age but she's probably over a hundred) keeps everyone entertained with wild stories about her India days. If only half are true, she's led a more eventful life than most people I know!

I am truly grateful that I got to know my real father, Tom Lomax, before he died. He was already very ill with lung cancer when the truth came out that I was his long-lost daughter – the baby he thought had died in 1913 along with his first wife, Mary. I was able to spend precious months with him in Pindi – he hung on until the spring of '47 – and was buried in the cemetery in Peshawar beside Mary.

Both he and Esmie (his third wife and the most wonderful of women) had decided he would be laid to rest there. Tom had spent all his happiest days in India and didn't want to leave. Esmie promised to join him there when her time comes.

I'm glad he never lived to witness the horrors of Partition that was particularly brutal for the people of the Punjab. It would have broken his heart, too, to see Kashmir divided and for both his beloved Raj Hotels to be separated by a national border; one in Gulmarg in India and the other in Pindi in Pakistan.

We stayed on in the new Pakistan for a while and were there for the momentous day of Independence in August 1947. It was a rainy day in Rawalpindi but there was much pride and speech-making when the new green flag of Pakistan was raised for the first time. Andy and Stella – along with her brother Jimmy Dubois (their hotel manager in Pindi) – laid on a celebratory tea party for local dignitaries and their families.

I don't wish to dwell on the violence and killings that followed the dividing up of the old India but it was a terrible time for many ordinary people and countless numbers died in the enforced repatriations. Jimmy, bravely, hid his Sikh cook in the boot of his car and drove him to Amritsar. There were stories of Muslims helping their Hindu neighbours to stay safe or escape – and vice versa in India – but there were also horrendous tales of bloodletting.

Over the following year, most of the Anglo-Indians decided to follow the majority of British who had left or were leaving Rawalpindi. A few got postings with the new Pakistan government but most have now emigrated to other parts of the world.

In 1949, the Lomaxes decided to sell up and return to Scotland. Andy sold the hotel at a cut price to Jimmy and his family. Stella is in regular contact with her brother, who has found ways to please his clientele without offending the new Muslim state. His "tea" parties, where beer is served out of tea pots, are very popular with the two military old-timers left from pre-independence days, Fritters and Bahadur.

By the time Andy, Stella and Esmie were preparing to leave Pakistan, my divorce from Mungo came through and Rick and I were finally able to marry. We'd already decided by then to return to Scotland and start a garage business. His parents didn't need much persuasion to join us and seem to have settled well into life in the Scottish borders. Rick's father, Toby, is full of courteous charm with the customers, and his mother, Rose, has struck up an unlikely friendship with our mother, Clara ...'

Jeanie broke off from her letter and stood to ease the aching in her back. She walked to the large bay window and looked out onto the sheltered garden. Her mother – for to her, Clara would always be mother – and Rick's mother were sitting on rugs spread out on the lawn, chatting while feeding titbits of paste sandwiches and apple slices to their grandson.

Jeanie's heart melted to see the eagerness with which her eighteen-month-old son took the food and crammed it into his mouth. He frowned in concentration – he was more serious than Rick – though had inherited his father's thick dark hair and fine features.

Just then, Rick came striding across the garden, calling out to the grandmothers in greeting. In one swift movement he scooped up his son and tickled his tummy, setting off delighted giggles. To see father and son grinning at each other with such adoration, made Jeanie's eyes flood with tears. How much she loved the pair of them!

As Rick turned, with the boy in his arms, he caught sight of Jeanie watching them from the window and blew her a kiss. She could see him telling their son to wave to mummy. He did so with Rick's help and she could see the boy mouthing "mummu".

Blowing a kiss back, she retreated to the desk to quickly finish the letter.

'Rick and I have a son with dark hair and green eyes – a solemn wee boy at times – but with an infectious giggle when he's playing with his father. He's called Johnny, after you. One day, he will learn how kind and brave his Uncle John was. You will never be forgotten in our family.

He is a lucky boy; he has three grannies – Granny Clara, Granny Rose and Granny Esmie – who all spoil him rotten. You would be glad to see how our mother has taken to being a grandparent; it's given her a new lease of life. The Lomaxes have never made her feel bad about covering up the truth of my birth and Mother has begun to forgive herself as well. Through the example of Andrew and Esmie's love and generosity towards my mother, I have learnt to forgive and love her again too. We are reconciled now as mother and daughter.

I know that, you being you, (who never held a grudge against anyone and always saw the best in them) would ask me what became of Mungo. He went to Adelaide and took up a job as maths teacher. I heard from a schoolmaster's wife that I was friendly with at Nicholson's (Mary Dane) that he has become a housemaster and that last year he remarried. Mary was a wee bit scandalised because his second wife was the former Nicholson's school matron, Dinah Lavelle. But that's a whole other story. I was glad to hear that he's found someone to love who loves him back.

I'm supposed to be upstairs resting – Johnny will have a younger brother or sister in September – and I'm already pumped up like a balloon, even though there's still three months to go!

There is only one big regret I have about leaving India, and that is my failure to go on pilgrimage to the cemetery in Burma where you were laid to rest. Rick had hoped to take me there, but we decided it was too hazardous an undertaking when the political situation was so volatile.

Yet, since coming back to Greentoun – and Rowan House especially – I feel your presence here, in a way that I never did immediately after the war. Perhaps it's because we talk about you more – Mother too allows me to reminisce to Rick and his parents about you.

So, dearest John; you will remain in our hearts and memories for the rest of our days – and our children will talk of you too. Maybe, one day, we'll be able to take them back to India – and Pakistan – and show them the places where the Grants, the Lomaxes and the Dixons once lived, and loved and thrived. Until then, be at peace, dear brother.

Your loving big sister,
Jeanie xx'

Jeanie kissed the letter and placed it in an envelope, addressing it to John. She put it inside the leather attaché case with its writing equipment which had been a gift from Tom before he died. *For keeping in touch with your loved ones*, he'd said with a tender expression tinged with sadness.

350

Getting up from the desk, she felt a sudden lightness of spirit, of a farewell undertaken that she had been avoiding for a long time. It was time to concentrate on the living – and the life inside her. Glancing out of the window, she saw Rick rolling on the lawn with Johnny, getting grass stains on his white shirt. Rose was gesticulating but Rick was paying no attention. Jeanie laughed – and instantly felt a kick in her womb from the baby. She placed a hand lovingly – excitedly – on her swelling body and felt another answering jab.

Swiftly, Jeanie left the quiet of the sitting-room and hurried outside to join her family in the sun-filled garden.

~~~

GLOSSARY

Anglo-Indian	mixed race with British paternal lineage
ayah	nurse or nanny
babu	Indian clerk (derogatory by British)
bearer	chief servant, valet
box-wallah	person in trade
burra	big, most important
chai-wallah	tea seller
chaprassy	messenger
chota hazri	breakfast
dak	mail/post
dhobi	washerman
durries	rugs
fakir	holy man living off alms
jungli	from the jungle, wild
khansama	house steward
koi hais	veterans of service in India
mali	gardener
marg	meadow
memsahib	polite form of address for woman
nawab	Muslim man of high status
pukka	good, genuine
puris	puffed breads
sahib	polite form of address for man
shikar	hunting
shikara	open boat on Lake Dal, Kashmir
stupa	dome-shaped Buddhist shrine
swaraj	freedom
syce	groom/stableboy
tonga	light carriage drawn by one horse
topi	sunhat
thunderbox	primitive toilet

ACKNOWLEDGEMENTS

As with the previous two novels in the Raj Hotel Series, I would like to acknowledge the support and help of writer and journalist, Ali Khan. His treasure-trove of a book; *Rawal Pindi: The Raj Years*, has been invaluable.

I'd also like to thank Peter Renshaw for sharing his interesting and amusing tales of life as a young assistant teacher at a school in the Himalayan foothills and his memories of Murree in Pakistan, post-Independence.

Thanks too, to my wise and eagle-eyed editor, Janey Floyd, for her care and attention over the manuscript and to Michael Star for his stunning cover. Lastly, but not least, my gratitude to Graeme for continuing to keep me going with coffee-breaks and meals while I've been deeply immersed in the world of the Raj Hotel.

About the Author

Janet MacLeod Trotter is the author of numerous bestselling and acclaimed novels, including *The Hungry Hills*, which was nominated for the *Sunday Times* Young Writer of the Year Award, *The Tea Planter's Daughter,* which was nominated for the Romantic Novelists' Association Novel of the Year Award, and *In the Far Pashmina Mountains*, which was shortlisted for the RNA Historical Romance of the Year Award. Her novels have been translated into nine different languages. Much informed by her own experiences and fascinated by family links between Scotland and India, MacLeod Trotter travelled in India as a young woman. Find out more about the author and her novels at www.janetmacleodtrotter.com.

Printed in Great Britain
by Amazon

18118259R00207